**Also available from
Victoria Alexander**

The Lady Travelers Guide to Scoundrels and Other Gentlemen

VICTORIA ALEXANDER

THE LADY TRAVELERS GUIDE TO

Larceny
with a
Dashing Stranger

HQN™

HQN™

PLEASE RECYCLE
THIS PRODUCT IS RECYCLABLE

ISBN-13: 978-0-373-80400-9

Recycling programs
for this product may
not exist in your area.

The Lady Travelers Guide to Larceny
with a Dashing Stranger

Copyright © 2017 by Cheryl Griffin

The publisher acknowledges the copyright holder of the
additional work:

The Rise and Fall of Reginald Everheart
Copyright © 2017 by Cheryl Griffin

This edition published by arrangement with Harlequin Books S.A.

For questions and comments about the quality of this book,
please contact us at CustomerService@Harlequin.com.

® and TM are trademarks of Harlequin Enterprises Limited or its
corporate affiliates. Trademarks indicated with ® are registered in the
United States Patent and Trademark Office, the Canadian Intellectual
Property Office and in other countries.

www.HQNBooks.com

Printed in U.S.A.

CONTENTS

THE LADY TRAVELERS GUIDE TO LARCENY WITH A DASHING STRANGER

This book is for Carol Schrader, my favorite Lady Traveler, road-trip accomplice and dear friend. Regardless of mileage—the adventure continues!

CHAPTER ONE

Mid-September, 1889

IT HAD ONCE occurred to Lady Wilhelmina Bascombe that she would no doubt die with a laugh on her lips and a glass of champagne in her hand. Now Willie suspected she would meet her maker with little more than watered wine and an equally weak smile. It was a sad state of affairs for a woman who, alongside her late husband, had not so long ago been considered the cream of society's fast, young, fashionable set. Still, there was nothing to be done about it. One couldn't go backward after all. One could only bravely lift one's chin and charge ahead.

"So you see Aunt Poppy—" Willie adopted her brightest smile "—I have decided that a change of scenery would be ideal. I was thinking the Mediterranean. The south of France perhaps. Or possibly Italy. Or, oh, I don't know, Venice?"

"Venice is not on the Mediterranean, dear," Aunt Poppy, Mrs. Persephone Fitzhew-Wellmore—who was not her aunt at all but rather her godmother—said in a serene manner. "It's on the Adriatic."

"Adriatic, Mediterranean—" Willie waved off the comment "—one vast body of water is as good as another."

"Is it?" Poppy took a sip of her tea and studied Willie with a sharp eye that belied her advanced years.

"I should think so, yes. After all, the idea is to move on with my life." Willie heaved a heartfelt sigh that was rather more sincere than she had expected. "Lay George and the past completely to rest, that sort of thing."

"Something you find difficult to do at home here in England?"

"You understand how these things are, Poppy. Life here is overshadowed by everything George and I shared together. Why, even our friends are constant reminders of what we had. And what I have lost." There was no need to add that she had seen nothing of those friends in the two years since George's untimely death in an absurd boating accident. Oh, certainly they had been most solicitous at first but it did seem their concern—as well as their friendship—vanished the moment George had been laid neatly to rest.

Still, a certain lack of friendly overtures might well be expected as Willie had disappeared from society after George's death, fleeing to Wales and the home of her late grandmother's companion. Dear Lady Plumdale, Margaret, had welcomed her with open and loving arms and Willie had stayed until a few months ago, contemplating her loss and what now lay ahead of her. Which in and of itself was shocking as Willie had never especially contemplated anything. Still, when one has lost a husband in an absurd boating accident a certain amount of contemplation is probably to be expected. What was completely unexpected were the revelations Willie discovered about her life, some of them brought about by an unceasing barrage of correspondence from solicitors and debt collectors.

Willie truly had no idea that she and George had existed primarily on credit in recent years. And really who would have imagined such a thing? After all, he was Viscount Bascombe of the Suffolk Bascombes, an old and venerable family. Willie had thought her husband quite a dashing sort and life with George was never dull. Indeed, it was great fun and filled with adventure and amusement. They never seemed to pause for so much as a moment between house parties given by what then were friends, masked balls and flamboyant dinners, races and hunts and all manner of entertainment. She now wondered if the ultimate purpose of their life of fun and frolic had been the avoidance of more serious matters. And really one does not have to contemplate the grave aspects of life—annoying details like finances and responsibility—if one never pauses in pursuit of a jolly good time. And it had been fun.

After George's death, however, the ongoing party that was their life together had ground to a halt and it was time to pay the piper, as they say. A piper who had apparently not been paid for quite some time. Pity Willie had few funds with which to do that.

"That makes a great deal of sense, dear." Sympathy sounded in the older woman's voice. "Although, haven't you spent much of the time since George's passing away from London, hiding in that charming little village in Wales?"

Poppy knew full well where Willie had been as she was the only one who had continued regular correspondence with her. "I wouldn't call it hiding exactly but, well, yes, although—"

"I should think that would have been long enough to accept the harsh reality that life with George has ended." Poppy patted Willie's hand. "I know it's difficult, dear, but we are Englishwomen and we are made of sterner stuff. We must bravely sally forth into the unknown regardless of what may lie ahead. Why, I remember when

I lost my dear Malcolm. It took some time to accept that my life would never be the same." She heaved a resigned sigh. "I confess I miss him to this day. I daresay you'll continue to miss George, as well."

"Yes, of course," Willie said weakly, and while she would hate to admit it to anyone—let alone Poppy—she didn't miss George so much as she missed the blissful state of ignorance she had apparently inhabited through the ten years of her marriage.

In addition to the discovery of George's—or rather now *her*—financial state, Willie had come to the distressing realization that while she had truly loved George, he was not the grand passion of her life nor was he her soul mate, although they were very much kindred spirits. It was a revelation she suspected she never would have had if he hadn't died. Indeed, she would have gone on for the rest of her days never realizing the man she had married was not her one true love even if he was exciting and adventurous and a great deal of fun. Whether coincidental or deliberate, her life with George had never paused long enough to come to that realization. Willie couldn't help but wonder what might have happened if it had.

"But George is gone and as you said, I do need to bravely forge ahead. Which is precisely why I wish to get away from England."

Poppy nodded. "Although you have no money to do so."

Willie stared. "Why on earth would you say such a thing?"

Poppy raised a knowing brow.

"Even if it's true." Willie sighed and collapsed against the flowered cushions of the overly comfortable sofa that was far and away too large for the parlor in Poppy's modest house on a tree-lined street in Bloomsbury. "How did you know?"

"For one thing, Wilhelmina, your dress is two to three years out of fashion. I have never known you to be clad in anything but the latest styles." While the widow of an explorer, adventurer and lecturer of modest success, Poppy had always had an unexpectedly keen eye for things like fashion and decor, even if she hadn't always had the means to support her taste.

"I have been in mourning, Poppy," Willie said staunchly. "Being a bit behind the dictates of fashion is to be expected."

"Perhaps but do not forget I have known you nearly since the day you came into the world." Poppy cast her a chastising look. "I would not call you vain but even as a young girl you were determined to be fashionably attired."

"Yes, well, some things are not as important as they once were." Although it did rather pain Willie to look into the mirror these days. While still serviceable, the extensive wardrobe she'd had before George's death was starting to appear the tiniest bit sad. Even so, she'd been more than willing to discard the unrelenting black that was the required fate of any new widow. It had never made much sense to Willie that there were strict rules as to how a widow should behave and what she should do. It seemed to her that mourning a lost husband or parent or companion should come from one's heart, not an edict from society. With her fair hair and blue eyes, she looked absurdly good in black but Willie much preferred to choose black rather than have black thrust upon her.

"Beyond that…" Poppy paused to consider her words. "Your husband's creditors apparently had little confidence they would ever see their money."

Willie stared. She wasn't at all certain she wished to hear more. Still, in her recent experience, knowing was far better than not knowing. "Dear Lord, please don't tell me they have bothered you. I've paid them all. Unless I have missed some. Entirely possible, I suppose. But you have no money to speak of."

"Yet at the moment I am more than comfortable."

Heat washed up Willie's face. "I am sorry, Poppy. I didn't mean to—"

"Of course you didn't, dear, and you are quite right. I have no particular fortune—I never have. I am the last person creditors would approach in their efforts to seek repayment. But you know how determined those sorts can be when they wish to get what is owed to them."

"Actually, I'm afraid I don't," Willie said, bemoaning once again her failure to pay the slightest bit of attention to George's finances. But then what woman did know the true state of her husband's financial affairs?

Admittedly, in hindsight, there were subtle hints as to their dwindling resources. Willie had noted the country house was showing signs of disrepair but whenever she had mentioned her concerns, George had said he would arrange to have it taken care of. They would then be off to London or to a party hosted at a friend's estate in Essex or Kent or wherever and upon their return nothing had changed. Willie had suggested on more than one occasion that they sell the terrace house in Mayfair left to her by her grandmother in favor of a larger residence, as it was nearly impossible to entertain properly. George would dismiss the idea by pointing out they were rarely in London and wasn't it far more fun to be a guest at someone else's party than to go to all the bother and expense of hosting their own gathering? She hadn't given his objections a second thought at the time. Now it struck her it wasn't so much the bother as the expense that concerned him.

"No, dear, creditors looking to recoup their losses would never contact me, especially as we are not blood relations. However…"

Willie sucked in a sharp breath. "Father?"

"I'm afraid so." Poppy winced. "He called on me, oh, a good six months ago when you were still in Wales. It did appear to be a strictly social visit although, as I have only seen him a handful of times since your baptism, it did seem rather odd."

"No doubt," Willie said under her breath.

"He wanted to know if I had heard from you and of course I said no." She cast her goddaughter a smug smile. "I had no idea why he wished to know and no intention of offering him any assistance whatsoever."

"Thank you." Willie and her father, the Earl of Hillborough, hadn't spoken in nearly eleven years. On occasion, she missed the father he might have been but not once did she regret the loss of the father he was.

"Any man who disowns his own child simply because she has the temerity to follow her heart and marry the man she loves, even if against his wishes, will get no help from me," Poppy said staunchly. "At the very least, he could have given you your dowry."

"That would have been helpful."

"It was entirely inappropriate of him not to do so. You are his only child after all." Poppy huffed. "Children are a blessing and are not to be squandered simply because they have minds of their own. I know if dear Malcolm and I had been lucky enough to have children, we would never have turned them away because of a difference of opinion."

Willie managed a half-hearted smile. In addition to everything else, all that contemplation in Wales had brought her to the inescapable conclusion that in his objection to her marriage with George, Father might well have been right. Something Willie was determined never to admit aloud. Regardless, her father's rejection made little difference in her life as he had effectively disowned her when she was not born male.

"After a bit of not very subtle probing on his part, your father finally admitted that he wished to contact you to inform you George's creditors had contacted him. He wanted you to know he would not settle the debts of a man he disapproved of." Poppy's lips pressed together in a hard line. "He was quite firm on that point."

"Nor would I ever ask him to." Willie raised her chin, a gesture of defiance that had driven her father mad for as long as she could remember. "I would become a beggar on the streets before I would ask him for anything."

Not that it would come to that. At least not yet. In the few months since returning from her self-imposed exile, Willie had reluctantly sold the country house and had managed to pay off all of George's creditors. She had also discovered most of the jewels given her by her husband were paste, nice enough to look at but essentially worthless. She did hope any jewelry he had no doubt given those women who had been the objects of his fleeting affections through the years was no more valuable than hers.

Willie had long suspected George had not been entirely faithful but in this Willie was something of a coward. She had never confronted him about his dalliances with other women. Upon reflection she wasn't sure why, although there was a vast difference between vague suspicion and certain knowledge. She had on occasion been tempted to stray from her own vows of fidelity but could never quite bring herself to do so. In spite of her many faults—and she was fairly certain that was a very long list—disloyalty and dishonesty were not among them. Still, it was one thing to lie outright and quite another to prevaricate, evade and omit.

"Exactly how bad are your financial circumstances?" Poppy asked.

"Well…" Willie searched for the right words. As much as she needed Poppy's help she did hate to worry the old girl. "They're really not nearly as bad as they were." She drew a deep breath. "I sold the country house—fortunately it was not entailed and so mine to do with as I pleased. And I am now debt-free."

"A difficult step but I must say I am impressed by your decision."

"I did so love that house." Willie couldn't quite hide the mournful note in her voice. From the moment she'd first set eyes on Bascombe Manor, a vaguely whimsical concoction of every popular construction style of the last three hundred years surrounded by grounds that were every bit as capricious as the house itself, she had fallen head over heels. It was a happy, welcoming sort of place and a far cry from her family's country house. Hillborough Hall was an imposing, unyielding fortress of marble and granite. The building proclaimed someone of unrelenting propriety and single-minded determination held sway here and fun would not—would never— be allowed.

"And your house in town?"

"That I have managed to retain, at least for the moment." It was perhaps best not to tell Poppy that the Mayfair house was very nearly stripped of all its contents. Willie had felt obligated to pay the servants at both Bascombe Manor and the London house what was owed to them before she regretfully terminated their employment. Her butler and cook—Majors and his wife, Patsy—had refused to accept their dismissal, declaring she was their family and one did not abandon family when times grew difficult. As much as Willie felt a great deal of affection for them, she did not expect this kind of loyalty. The kind that brought a warm rush to one's heart. Willie and Patsy had wrapped their arms around each other and wept for a few moments. Even Majors—as properly trained as any butler anywhere—had sniffed back something that might well have been a tear. "I would hate to lose that house, as well. I do need somewhere to live."

"Perhaps, Wilhelmina—" Poppy chose her words with care "—now is not the appropriate time for a trip abroad."

"On the contrary, Poppy, this is not merely the appropriate time but it's imperative that I leave as soon as possible."

"Are you in some sort of danger?" Poppy's brows drew together. "Have those beastly creditors threatened you in some way?" Her expression darkened. "I daresay between Lady Blodgett, Mrs. Higginbotham and myself we can probably come up with a name or two of some disreputable types who might be able to—"

"No, no," Willie said quickly. "It's nothing like that. As I said, I have already paid off George's debts and I have enough left to repay a loan and reclaim something of great importance to me. Well, to my future really." Willie paused for a moment to consider her words. She did so hate to make George appear more of a disappointment than he was but it really couldn't be helped. Besides, he was dead and probably would be more amused than annoyed by her revelations. And she did need to look out for herself now. After all, aside from two loyal servants and an elderly relative, she was on her own. "When I began to sell, er, take inventory of the furnishings in the London house—something I admit I should have done years ago—I became aware that a few somewhat valuable objects were missing. A small Ming vase from China, an exquisite snuffbox that reportedly belonged to a queen of France and a painting left to me by Grandmother."

Poppy gasped. "Not the Portinari!"

Willie wrinkled her nose. "I'm afraid so."

"Your grandmother loved that painting."

Poppy and Willie's grandmother Beatrice had gone to school together and had remained fast friends throughout the rest of Grandmother's life, even if their lives had taken entirely different courses. Grandmother had married the Earl of Grantson, who died far too young and never lived to see his only child—Willie's mother—past her third birthday. Poppy, of course, had married Malcolm Fitzhew-Wellmore and had become—according to Grandmother—shockingly independent as her husband was out of the country as often as he was home. As Grandmother had made that pronouncement with what sounded suspiciously like envy, Willie understood that being an independent woman—while not especially accepted by society—was not a particularly bad thing either. Beatrice and Poppy did manage to see one another several times a year. Some of the brightest memories of Willie's childhood were of those meetings between the two old friends.

When Willie's mother died when Willie was barely ten, she was sent off to Miss Bicklesham's Academy for Accomplished Young Ladies. It was to her grandmother's house she returned for holidays and the summer months. Even if her father seemed to have little use for her in those years, Willie had no doubt as to the affections of her grandmother, her godmother and dear Lady Plumdale.

"Do you have any idea what might have happened to it? Was it stolen, do you think?"

"Not exactly." Once again Willie was reluctant to place the blame on George where it belonged. This was her late husband's doing and she wouldn't pause for a moment to point an accusing finger at him if he were still alive. But one did hate to speak ill of the dead even when they deserved it. "According to some correspondence and a note of collateral I discovered in George's study, he used the Portinari to acquire a loan from an Italian gentleman. A conte, I believe, a resident of Venice and apparently a passionate collector of Renaissance art. I have enough left from the sale of the country house to repay the loan as well as the accumulated interest." She drew a deep breath. "What I don't have is the means to get to Venice."

"I see."

"Once I reclaim the painting, I intend to offer it for sale." She shook her head. "I have no other means of support, Poppy."

"You could marry again."

"And I am not the least bit opposed to marrying again."

Although the next time Willie plighted her troth she would be somewhat more discriminating about who she plighted it to. A man of responsibility and maturity would be a welcome change. Not at all the type of man she ever imagined she might want but then she had never been thirty years of age before with few prospects and no financial security. Although finding a man of that nature who was not, as well, extraordinarily dull might prove difficult. Such a man was not the type to marry frivolously. And aside from everything else, Willie wanted a man she could love. Admittedly, it might well be easier to swim to Venice than find the sort of man she wanted.

"I do not, however, have the slightest desire to marry simply because I have no other choice." Her jaw tightened. "That painting is my salvation. As much as I would hate to sell it, proceeds from the sale will support me for several years."

Poppy studied her for a long moment. "Your grandmother would have it no other way."

Relief washed through Willie. "You don't think she'd mind, then?"

"Oh, I think she'd mind a great deal." Poppy paused. "I daresay you're not aware of how she came by the painting but it was given to her by a gentleman she cared for deeply. Who I believe shared her feelings. I don't know all the details—your grandmother could be remarkably discreet when she chose to be—but I do know he was married and nothing could come of their feelings. He gave her the painting as something of parting gift."

"I had no idea," Willie murmured. Indeed, the thought of her very respectable grandmother having a liaison with a married man was somewhat shocking.

"So yes, she would mind but not nearly as much as she would mind your being penniless or having to marry simply to keep body and soul together. She would mind that far more."

"As would I," Willie said wryly then paused. "You wrote me about your Lady Travelers Society, how you and your friends started it and then sold it. But you also said the three of you still play an active role in the society."

"Oh my, yes." Poppy nodded. "Why, we give lectures and produce pamphlets and lead fascinating discussions with our members as well as offer sage advice on the caprices of travel. We are consulting travel advisers." A smug smile curved her lips. "And we are quite good at it."

"I've no doubt of that," Willie said, although she was fairly certain Poppy had never actually traveled to any great extent beyond a few months in Paris as a girl.

"I must tell you, Wilhelmina, that the most wonderful things in life are often those we least expect. We are having a grand time. Who would have imagined at our age?"

"No one deserves to have a grand time more than you," Willie said firmly. "I was hoping, as you and the other ladies are the founders of the society and are still involved in it, that you might assist me in arranging some way to travel to Venice. As inexpensively as possible," she added quickly. There were still one or two antiquities that had been stored in the attic that might fetch enough to pay at least part of her way to Italy. Although she would have no way to return home.

"Oh, I haven't the vaguest idea how to do that, dear. However..." Poppy rose to her feet. "Gwen and Effie might have a thought or two. I have learned through the years that when one of us has no solution to a difficulty, all three of us together come up with the most brilliant ideas." She nodded firmly. "I had planned on meeting both of them at the Lady Travelers Society offices in an hour or so. We shall put this dilemma to them and we will have a means to get you to Venice in no time at all."

"Why, Poppy." Willie grinned. "You sound most efficient."

"I am a woman of business now," the older woman said primly.

"Are you indeed?"

"I am." Poppy nodded. "And it's all perfectly legitimate. Why, I'll have you know, there isn't even a suggestion of fraud or anything the least bit illegal."

Willie stared. "I never would have imagined such a thing."

"Oh well...good." Poppy beamed then her smile dimmed. "Although after the society was purchased by Mr. Forge, Miss Charlotte Granville was put in charge.

She's most efficient, horribly well organized and really rather brilliant. And she's American, as is Mr. Forge, which is endlessly interesting. I've never known an American beyond a casual introduction in passing. Malcolm, however, knew any number of Americans. Quite candid I would say, although with Charlotte one is never sure if she finds you amusing or annoying. It scarcely matters, I suppose. She is usually quite pleasant under even the most trying of circumstances."

"I thought you and your friends ran the society."

"Oh dear, no. At least not anymore. We are simply figureheads. Consultants and wise purveyors of indispensable travel guidance as it were. It would be absurd for us to try to manage an undertaking of this magnitude." Poppy started toward the door. "Why, none of us have the least bit of a head for business."

"You have to admit, Charlotte," Lady Blodgett said with a knowing look. "Having Lady Bascombe escort a flock of Americans and their daughters on a grand tour is nothing short of brilliant."

"I'm not sure *brilliant* is the word I would use," Miss Charlotte Granville said with a tolerant smile. No doubt she had heard any number of brilliant ideas from the septuagenarian trio in the past. "And it is hardly even in the realm of a petit tour as opposed to a grand tour. It includes only Paris, Monte Carlo, a few stops along the way in Italy, including Venice and Rome, in barely a month's time. But it is what they requested."

Poppy and her friends had explained that Willie was eager to travel as she was still trying to cope with the unfortunate loss of her husband. Since Willie had abandoned black some time ago, she wasn't sure Miss Granville was convinced. The older ladies might not have noticed but Willie could see at once that Charlotte Granville was a force to be reckoned with and not someone easily deceived.

"However, I'm afraid the tour will not come together as expected." Miss Granville's brow furrowed in annoyance. "We have already had one mother and daughter withdraw. Oddly enough, it's the very woman who inquired about a private tour in the first place with specific requests as to what it would include. The others are now uncertain as to whether or not they wish to proceed." She cast Willie a sympathetic smile. "I am sorry but I am nearly ready to cancel it altogether."

"Understandable," Willie murmured, trying to ignore the sense of utter defeat that knotted her stomach.

"Oh, that would be a shame," Mrs. Higginbotham said with a heavy sigh. "I daresay you poor, unfortunate Americans rarely get the opportunity to see those sights that are practically in our own back gardens."

"I would suspect the chance to travel in the company of a genuine viscountess is yet another opportunity that rarely comes along for those poor, dear ladies. Pity really." Poppy glanced at Lady Blodgett. "They don't have titles in America, do they?"

"No." Lady Blodgett shook her head in a mournful manner. "Not a one. Unless I'm mistaken. Charlotte?"

"No," Miss Granville said thoughtfully. "We do not have titles."

"One always wants what one doesn't have," Mrs. Higginbotham said in a wise manner. "It's the nature of mankind."

"But particularly the nature of women," Poppy said.

"Are these American mothers and their daughters wealthy?" Lady Blodgett asked brightly.

Miss Granville nodded. "Our services for a private tour such as this do not come lightly."

"But you said there was indecision as to whether or not there would be a tour at all?" Poppy asked.

Again Miss Granville nodded.

"I would think the chance to make the acquaintance of a viscountess, perhaps becoming friends during the length of even a short tour, possibly with an eye toward having her at some point introduce their daughters to an earl or even a duke…" Lady Blodgett shrugged. "Well…"

"And you do know very nearly everyone who is anyone in London society, don't you, dear?" Poppy cast her an encouraging look.

"Not everyone, of course." Willie adopted a confident smile. "But I do have a large circle of friends and acquaintances. I would say that—"

"And have you traveled widely, Lady Bascombe?" Miss Granville interrupted.

"Well, I—" Willie began.

"Goodness, Charlotte," Lady Blodgett said in a chastising manner. "Lady Bascombe's husband's family can trace its heritage back numerous generations. Wilhelmina's father is an earl with a proud and noble heritage and Wilhelmina herself is a graduate of the prestigious Miss Bicklesham's Academy for Accomplished Young Ladies."

"Yes, well, that's very nice but—"

"I assure you, Charlotte, no prominent family in England would allow their offspring to go into the world without first making certain they have the appropriate knowledge of the capitals of Europe," Poppy said in a lofty manner. "The very thought that Lady Bascombe is not more than capable of leading a small group of Americans around those same capitals is patently absurd."

Miss Granville's cheeks flushed. "I do apologize, Lady

Bascombe." Apparently, wealthy Americans weren't the only ones somewhat cowed by British titles. "Of course, you're more than qualified."

"Thank you, Miss Granville." Willie smiled in what she hoped was a confident manner.

"You're right, ladies." Miss Granville nodded at Poppy and the others. "Having Lady Bascombe escort the tour could be just the thing to get those interested to commit once and for all. Indeed, her addition might well be irresistible."

"Although really, Charlotte—" Lady Blodgett leaned toward the American in the manner of one confidant to another "—I'm not sure you wish to use the words *lead* or *guide* or *escort* even if that is what she'll be doing."

Miss Granville's brow rose. "I don't?"

"It just seems to me that if you offered a tour *hosted* by the incomparable Lady Wilhelmina Bascombe it sounds much more like a group of old friends off on a grand holiday." Lady Blodgett smiled knowingly. "Don't you agree, Charlotte?"

The younger woman considered her thoughtfully. "You never fail to amaze me, Lady Blodgett."

"Thank you, dear." The modest note in her voice was belied by the smug twinkle in her eye.

Miss Granville directed her attention to Willie. "We will, of course, provide for your expenses. All your lodgings and transportation. In addition, you will receive a stipend for unexpected costs as well as our standard compensation for the leaders of tour groups."

"Oh, I think it should be somewhat more than standard compensation." Lady Blodgett shook her head. "She is after all *Lady* Bascombe and more than likely the reason this tour will proceed at all."

Miss Granville thought for a moment. "I see your

point. I will see what I can do. Lady Bascombe, in addition to the stipend, you'll receive half of your compensation upon your departure, the other half when you return. If that is acceptable?"

Willie resisted the urge to grin with delight. "It will do."

"We were originally set to depart in three weeks. While there remain arrangements to finalize, I think that is still possible. Can you be ready by then?"

"Well, I—"

"Of course she can," Poppy said.

"Not merely ready but willing and extremely capable, as well," Mrs. Higginbotham added.

"I must say, I am somewhat envious." Lady Blodgett's eyes gleamed with triumph. "My dear departed Charles spoke very highly of Americans. He thought they were an exceptionally interesting lot. And the chance to go off on even a modest tour with Americans, why, it's a venture simply fraught with exciting possibilities. Don't you agree, Lady Bascombe?"

All eyes turned toward Willie—three pairs filled with encouragement, the fourth somewhat more skeptical. For a moment Willie had no idea how to respond. She still wasn't sure exactly what had happened, although her dear, sweet Poppy and her equally innocuous friends had somehow managed to convince the obviously intelligent and competent Miss Granville that Wilhelmina, Lady Bascombe, was more than up to the task of shepherding young Americans and their mothers on a tour of Europe—regardless of whether it was petit or grand. And had, as well, persuaded her to offer financial compensation above what would normally be provided. This in spite of the fact that Poppy knew Willie had never stepped foot off the shores of England. Still, with up-to-

date maps, brochures and travel guides, how difficult
could leading—or rather hosting—a tour be?

It struck Willie that Poppy and her friends, and even
Miss Granville, were placing their faith in her and the
oddest determination not to disappoint them swept
through her. She'd never had any particular responsibilities but it was time she did. She could certainly do this
and do it far better than she—or anyone else—expected.
And wasn't it past time to live up to expectations? To become a trustworthy, reliable adult?

"I do, Lady Blodgett." Willie beamed. "I do indeed."

CHAPTER TWO

Two weeks later...

"GOODNESS, DANTE." ROSALIND, Lady Richfield, heaved a long-suffering sigh. "I have no desire to spend a month in the country, let alone travel Europe. I can't imagine why you think I would wish to do such a thing."

"Come now, Roz." Dante Augustus Montague glared at his sister. "You needn't be so dramatic. It's not as if I'm asking you to go to the far corners of the world. To some uncivilized, untamed region populated with headhunters and cannibals and deadly vipers. I'm talking about Paris and Monte Carlo and Venice and Rome."

"I don't want to go either," her daughter, Harriet, added. At age eighteen, Harriet had just completed her first, and judging by her mother's comments, extremely successful season. She had, as well—at least in her uncle's eyes—become more than a little conceited and most annoying. In many ways, exactly like his sister.

"I understand that, brother dear." Roz's eyes narrowed. "But what you are proposing is not a trip for the purposes of education and refinement and culture. You are planning nothing less than a farce."

"A French farce really," Harriet said with a smug smile. She looked from her mother to her uncle. "A French farce? Because the tour includes Paris?"

"Ah yes, quite." Dante offered a perfunctory smile.

Someone had told Harriet she was a natural wit and she'd considered herself most amusing ever since. Dante suspected the culprit responsible had been trying to curry favor with the lovely young woman. His sister had mentioned their drawing room was as often as not filled with suitors eager to win the hand of Lady Harriet. Roz was both proud and a bit taken aback by the social success of her only daughter.

"It's not at all a farce." Dante resisted the urge to roll his eyes toward the ceiling but that would only serve to irritate his sister. Some five years younger than Roz, even as an adult, Dante never tired of annoying her. Under other circumstances he would find that most enjoyable. Today, however, he needed her help. "Perhaps you don't understand how important this is. Perhaps I should explain it again."

"I believe we are both well aware of how important you think this is," Roz said. "There is no need for you to expound yet again."

"Goodness, Uncle Dante, we're not idiots." Harriet sighed and ticked the points off on her fingers. "One—a valuable painting that belonged to great-grandfather was replaced longer ago than anyone can remember with a copy and no one apparently noticed until you recently did. Two—the records of Montague House make no mention of the substitution of the original—a Portinari I believe—which has led you to suspect it was not legitimately replaced and might even have been stolen. Three—you have discovered through the efforts of an investigator that the original painting was at one time in the possession of the Viscount Bascombe who is unfortunately dead."

"God rest his soul," Roz said firmly.

"God rest his soul," Harriet echoed and continued. "Four—that same investigator learned the painting was used as collateral for a loan between the viscount and some man in Venice. Five—the widowed Lady Bascombe is about to lead a group of American debutants and their mothers on a trip to Italy, among other places, and you believe she intends to reclaim the painting as part of settling her husband's affairs or something like that. And six—you wish for Mother and I to join this tour so that you too may come along because you certainly can't join it by yourself. Is that correct?"

Dante stared. "I had no idea you listened to me."

"We listen to you constantly," Roz said. "It's impossible not to. Ever since you discovered the substitution of the painting—"

"Ever since you took over management of Montague House," Harriet added.

"—you've rarely spoken of anything else. You've become quite dull."

"I have not." Dante scoffed but even to his own ears it did not ring quite true. Still, it couldn't be helped.

His grandfather, the Marquess of Haverstead, had divided his nonentailed assets upon his death, leaving them equally to his three sons. His youngest son—Dante and Roz's father—had proved surprisingly gifted at all matters financial and, through shrewd investments and sound business endeavors, doubled it. Dante had taken after his father in this respect and at the age of thirty-three had amassed a fortune significantly greater than his father's. Which was all well and good but there was more to life than the acquisition of funds—an edict his grandfather had lived his life by.

Dante only vaguely remembered Grandfather as he had passed on when Dante was six years of age but he never forgot the old gentleman explaining the importance of art and beauty, whether they be depicted in painting or marble or by the fine hand of a master craftsman in a pottery urn created thousands of years ago. "Art," he had once told his grandson, "is man's very soul made manifest."

When the marquess died, his will decreed his grand London house become a private museum, open only to scholars and those with a deep appreciation of art and antiquities and willing to purchase a subscription to help defray costs. He left, as well, a trust to maintain his collections. A curator was hired to catalog the late marquess's acquisitions, organize and display the house's contents, and manage membership as well as all the other varied and sundry details an endeavor of this nature required. Through the years there was another director and another—all with various skills in the management of small museums and Montague House took its place among the lesser sights of London.

Unfortunately, the only one of Lord Haverstead's numerous offspring who shared his fascination with fine art or the remnants of antiquity was Dante. He spent much of his boyhood at Montague House studying the works of Renaissance masters or paging through ancient volumes in the well-stocked library or trying to decipher the Greek or Latin inscriptions on the ancient coins and other metalwork kept behind glass doors. The influence of Montague House lingered through Dante's school years and he considered becoming a scholar of art and antiquities until business and finance proved to be a passion every bit as strong and far more challenging.

"I am not the least bit dull," he said staunchly.

Roz and her daughter traded knowing glances.

"I know that look." He glared at his sister. "Go on, say what you're thinking."

"We're not saying that you've become dull *only* because you've thrown yourself into Montague House," Roz began.

"Although you have taken up residence in the flat on the upper floor," Harriet said under her breath.

"It's most convenient." He huffed. "Besides, it's where the facility director has always lived."

With only cursory family notice paid to Montague House, it was inevitable the museum would fall prey to mismanagement. A state of affairs only discovered some two years ago. In spite of the trust, the enterprise was losing money. Hemorrhaging it really, one of the uncles pointed out. Between maintenance of the building and care of the works it housed, it would be insolvent in no time. And then it would either have to become fully open to the public—an idea that made the more conservative members of the family shudder—or it would be closed and Grandfather's life's work dispersed.

Dante's uncle, the current marquess, assembled his brothers and their children to discuss the fate of Montague House. While none of them wished to see their father's, or grandfather's, wishes ignored, they did realize something needed to be done and perhaps trusting someone outside of the family was not wise.

Upon reflection, Dante wasn't certain who had first raised the idea of his taking over supervision of Montague House. After all, he did have an excellent head for management and business enterprises as well as firm appreciation and understanding of the world of art and antiquities. In certain circles he was considered something of an expert. Certainly he could put Montague House back on solid financial footing and establish a respectable reputation in the process. If not, perhaps it was time to donate Grandfather's collections to a more venerable institution and sell the house. Or use it as the residence it was originally intended to be. Several of Dante's cousins expressed interest in that possibility. Obviously the only one who could—or was willing—to save Grandfather's legacy was the only son of his youngest son.

"We are simply pointing out that it seems the oddest sort of coincidence that you took up residence at Montague House at very nearly the same time you were publically rebuffed by Miss Pauling."

"It is indeed a coincidence and I was not publically rebuffed."

"You were according to what I heard." Harriet shrugged. "Everyone said so."

"Gossip rarely has anything to do with truth," Dante said sharply. "And I was not rebuffed as I was not especially interested in Miss Pauling."

Admittedly, he—along with very nearly every other single man in London—had found Juliet Pauling lovely and exciting. One never knew what to expect from her. She was adventurous and daring and exhilarating. He had indeed called on her several times but eventually realized she had her sights set on bigger fish than the untitled grandson of a marquess. Regrettably, she was as calculating as she was charming, as designing as she was delightful. Which was why it took him far too long to realize he was little more than a pawn in her quest for a title, a means to make a better catch jealous. Unfortunately, thanks to the unrelenting gossip of people exactly like his sister, his name had been linked with hers. When her betrothal to the son of a duke was announced, it came as a surprise to nearly everyone in society and to no one more than to Dante. He hadn't thought she was quite so devious as to not give him even a glimmer of warning.

"We shouldn't tease you about this," Roz said in a sincere manner he didn't believe for a moment. "A broken heart is nothing to make fun of."

"It is dreadfully sad though." Harriet heaved the sort of sigh only a romantic young woman could manage. "The love of your life throwing you over for another man even if he was the son of a duke."

"She was not the love of my life. Nor did she break my heart."

"Obviously a mistake on my part." Amusement shone in his sister's eye. "Silly of me to confuse a broken heart with badly bruised pride."

"I'm quite sure I have mentioned this before, any number of times by my count, but neither my heart nor my pride was broken or bruised," Dante said firmly. Only to himself would he acknowledge that a broken heart was a fate he had narrowly averted and there might possibly have been the slightest bruising of his pride. "Furthermore, that was two years ago."

"And in these past two years you have become something of a recluse," Roz said pointedly. "When you're not engaged in the management of your businesses, you have buried yourself in the Herculean task of setting all in order at Montague House. You have completely ignored any kind of social encounter that wasn't required. And those for the most part have been family obligations."

"For the hundredth time, sister dear." Dante struggled to keep his temper in check. It wasn't easy. Roz refused to accept that between Montague House and his business interests, his life was inordinately full. He had no time for frivolity and no interest at the moment in pursuing anything of a romantic nature. "I have a great deal to attend to and other pursuits are simply going to have to wait."

"Pursuits such as finding a wife?"

"Exactly," he snapped. "I have neither the time nor the inclination right now for romantic entanglements."

Still, responding to his sister's obvious efforts to irritate him would not get him anywhere. Nor did it help to know she only had his best interests at heart as did his mother and every other female member of his family. None of them seemed to understand that while he had no particular aversion to marriage, he did not think it was crucial to his life. At least not currently.

He drew a calming breath. "As you know, the family has given me three years to rebuild, or rather build, Montague House's reputation and put the collections in order. I have accomplished a great deal toward that goal. I have recovered a number of objects that had either been lost in the attics, moved to other family properties or disappeared from the house altogether. The latter at no little expense. It has not been easy." He absently paced the room. "The missing Portinari is the center of a triptych, essentially a three-part painting."

"We know what a triptych is, Uncle Dante," Harriet said in the long-suffering manner of the young.

"What you may not know is that Galasso Portinari was a student of Titian and a painter in his workshop. A sixteenth-century biography of Titian says he considered Portinari his greatest student and predicted he would one day surpass even the master's skill. Unfortunately, he died quite young—plague possibly but the details on that are vague. His original work is exceedingly rare. While students of Titian's—including Portinari—often copied his work, there is no record of more than a handful of any other original Portinaris. Therefore ours are exceptionally valuable. These three paintings are the sorts of things that will make a museum's reputation."

"Then why haven't they done so?" A challenge

sounded in Roz's voice. While not as passionate about Grandfather's legacy as her brother, Dante had thought she was somewhat neutral on the question of the fate of Montague House. Although he now recalled there was a gleam of interest in her eyes when the idea of returning the mansion to a private residence had been raised. "It's not as if they have just been acquired. Hadn't they been in the collection long before the house became a museum?"

"Yes, but previous curators apparently didn't understand what they had. For one thing, the paintings weren't displayed properly. They were hanging in the library on three different walls, separated by bookshelves and one barely noticed them. But they were designed to hang together to create one continuous work. When done so, one can see the continuity between the pieces, the story the painter was trying to tell. All of that—as well as the brilliance of the artist himself—is lost when they are not displayed together." Dante shook his head. "I'm not sure even grandfather knew what he had. He had an excellent eye but he tended to buy what appealed to him rather than what might be a good investment. In fact, I'm not sure any of those we've employed to curate the museum understood the potential value of the Portinaris. Indeed, it's only been in recent years that his work has been recognized. Each painting by itself is brilliant but all three together are nothing short of a masterpiece."

Roz frowned. "I don't even remember them."

"They're relatively small—each is a mere twelve by eighteen inches. And, as I said, they were in the library. It's been kept clean, of course, dusted and swept and all, but little additional attention paid to it. As if valuable first editions could take care of themselves." He scoffed.

His sister traded glances with her daughter.

"According to the house records, the first director

started to catalog the contents of the library but then turned his attention to other matters. The second picked up where the first let off but accomplished little." He couldn't keep the hard edge from his voice. The lack of attention paid to the collections in the house by previous management was nothing short of criminal. One did wonder how his uncle's solicitors—charged with arranging for the engagement of the house staff—managed to find such utter incompetents. "None of the subsequent curators did anything at all toward organizing and cataloging the books or anything else in the library."

It never failed to annoy him that in the quarter of a century between his grandfather's death and Dante's assuming directorship of the museum, no one in his family had paid the least bit of attention to what was occurring. There were gaps in the financial statements and other records that not only pointed to mismanagement but outright fraud and perhaps even theft. Much of which he doubted he would ever be able to reconcile. In many ways it was fortunate the Portinaris were overlooked. Otherwise all three of the originals might be missing.

"So what you're trying to say in that long and tedious way you have is that recovering the painting is crucial to Montague House." Roz eyed her brother thoughtfully. "That this is exactly what you need to increase prestige and credibility. Essentially to save Montague House."

"What *we* need," he said firmly.

"I still don't see why we have to flit around Europe." Harriet huffed. "Why don't you just offer to buy the painting once Lady Bascombe has it?"

"Although I daresay to convince her to sell, you will have to do something about your, well, your demeanor," Roz said.

He frowned. "What's wrong with my demeanor?"

"You're curt, you tend to be condescending, especially when you think you're right or you're the most intelligent person in the room, and you are entirely too arrogant." Harriet glanced at her mother.

"Well, yes," Roz agreed. "But it would have been nice to phrase it a bit more tactfully."

Harriet shrugged. "I phrased it exactly the way I've heard you say it." She cast an apologetic look at her uncle. "Sorry, Uncle Dante."

He stared at his sister. "I am not any of those things."

Roz grimaced.

"Am I really?" Admittedly, he might be the tiniest bit patronizing when he knew he was right and possibly more impatient than he should be and there was the distinct possibility that he did have no more than a mere touch of arrogance. "Yes, well, perhaps some of that might not be entirely inaccurate."

"However," Roz said, "you can be quite charming when you set your mind to it. Indeed, although it has been some time, I've watched you charm any number of unsuspecting females."

His brow shot upward. "Unsuspecting?"

"That might not have been the right word," Roz murmured. "But you are a handsome devil, as well, in a quiet sort of way, and I've never seen you look less than perfect. In addition, your wealth is most impressive. You are a catch, Dante. Women are naturally attracted to you. I don't know why you don't take advantage of that."

"I think it's foolish to depend on one's appearance and fortune rather than one's intelligence."

"What's foolish is your not taking advantage of both," Harriet noted under her breath. "And yet it explains so much."

He ignored her. "Regardless, your point is taken. I shall do my best to be as charming as I possibly can."

Harriet snorted.

"As I was saying, I have considered attempting to purchase the Portinari but I will not make an offer until its true ownership is determined." His jaw tightened. "I would prefer not to have to pay for something that rightfully belongs to this family."

Harriet cast him a skeptical look. "And how will you determine ownership?"

"I have collected every record, every invoice, every bit of correspondence I can find—Father and the uncles have helped with that—in an effort to find some statement as to the disposition of the Portinari. I have the original bill of sale for all three paintings and, at the moment, I have nothing to indicate any of them were sold or ownership transferred in any way. I have studied everything myself and I've hired a firm with expertise in such matters to examine all the records as well as investigators searching for more. I cannot confront Lady Bascombe until I have solid evidence regarding ownership. Once I do, I can demand her proof of provenance. But it scarcely matters until she recovers the painting." He paused. "I intend to be present when she does. Now that I know exactly where the painting is, I will not allow it to vanish from sight again."

Roz frowned. "You don't trust her?"

"I don't know her," he said. "But I do know *of* her. Her reputation does not inspire confidence."

Roz's brow furrowed in confusion then her expression cleared. "Oh. You're speaking of Wilhelmina Bascombe?"

"Is there another Lady Bascombe?" Harriet asked.

"I don't think so." Dante studied his sister. "Do you know her?"

"I wouldn't say I know her but I believe we met once in passing although it was some time ago." Roz thought for a moment. "I rather liked her if I recall. You're right though—she and her husband were part of a fast crowd always engaged in some sort of outing or entertainment or activity verging on the edge of outright scandal. There was talk about her husband's indiscretions, as well, although I don't recall ever hearing anything about her. Still, in that particular group... Now that I think about it, I don't believe I've heard anything at all about her since her husband died and that must be at least two years ago."

"Apparently, she was in seclusion until recently." A fact Dante's investigator had included in the dossier he had prepared. He had also uncovered information about Lady Bascombe's finances. It appeared the widow was forced to sell her country house and various other items to settle her husband's debts and had very little left, although Dante assumed she had reserved enough to pay off the loan and take possession of the Portinari. Her financial state also explained why she was leading a tour rather than simply traveling to Venice on her own.

"One can scarcely blame her for wishing to leave the country for a bit," Roz said. "Put the past behind her and reminders of her husband, that sort of thing. Although shepherding a group of Americans sounds rather daunting to me."

"I believe this is in the manner of a favor to an elderly relative who founded some sort of travel society for ladies. It is my understanding that without the presence of Lady Bascombe the tour was in jeopardy of not proceeding at all."

"It's quite kind of her, then, isn't it?" Roz nodded

thoughtfully. "But I suppose it would indeed serve to take her mind off her loss."

"I would imagine. Difficult time for her, I would think. Not at all the time to confront her about the painting," Dante added with an appropriately concerned frown. It was not entirely feigned. The more he'd learned about Lady Bascombe the more she intrigued him. But surely she couldn't be as interesting as she sounded. More likely she shared a great deal in common with Miss Pauling, at least when it came to character. And that was not the least bit interesting. At least not to him.

"Poor woman," Roz murmured.

"Poor woman?" Harriet stared at her mother. "The lady and her husband were obviously engaged in all sorts of improprieties to have been the subject of so much gossip. There is always an element of truth behind any morsel of rumor—that's what you always say."

"Yes," Roz began, "but—"

"Furthermore, one has only oneself to blame when one's husband wanders." Harriet pinned her mother with a firm look. "Don't you say that, as well?"

"I might have said something like that." The oddest look of panic showed in Roz's eyes.

"And haven't you warned me my entire life that dreadful things can happen to those who misbehave, so it is important that one's behavior be exemplary?" Harriet aimed the words at her mother with the directness of an inquisitor questioning a heretic.

"Well, yes, but—"

"It seems to me this is simply the price of fast living," Harriet said in a lofty manner.

"Good Lord, what have I done?" Roz's eyes narrowed. "Regardless of how one chooses to behave, there are few things worse in this life for a woman than losing her husband. Unless one's husband leaves a great deal of money, the finances of a widow are precarious at best. As I said, I don't really know Lady Bascombe but I would suspect if she has remained in seclusion and only recently returned to London—" she glanced at her brother and he nodded "—then she must have cared a great deal for her husband."

"'The wages of sin is death.'" Harriet smirked.

"Only in the bible, dear," Roz snapped. "And while I am pleased that you have obviously listened to every bit of wisdom I have ever imparted, I am hoping you have heard me when I have talked about compassion or sympathy, as well. Especially among fellow women, whether we are acquainted with them or not."

Harriet had the good grace to blush in spite of her defiant attitude. "I suppose."

"Perhaps," Dante said casually, "it might be beneficial for Harriet to make the acquaintance of a new circle of young women. And see a bit of the world in the process."

"Dante." Roz blew a long breath. "I have a great deal to do and no time to go off wandering Europe."

"Besides, Mr. Goodwin promised to call on me." Harriet breathed a dreamy sigh, obviously in the throes of delighted anticipation.

Roz frowned. "Bertram Goodwin?"

"Yes." Harriet dimpled. "He's quite dashing and very clever."

"He's the third son of an earl with no prospects whatsoever and a questionable reputation. And when I say questionable…I am being kind." Roz stared. "And his mother is…well, suffice it to say she is not one of my favorite people. And I like nearly everyone."

"Nonsense, Mother. You're just being stuffy." Harriet sniffed. "Mr. Goodwin's reputation is no worse than most young men of my acquaintance. But he is amusing and handsome and..." Her chin raised in a determined manner. "And I like him. I like him quite a lot. Why, I might even be in love with him."

"You'll be no such thing. He is entirely inappropriate and a very bad influence." Roz's gaze locked with her daughter's. "I will not permit him to call on you."

"Regardless." Harriet crossed her arms over her chest. "I fully intend to see him whenever possible."

Mother and daughter glared at each other. Tension hung in the air and Dante resisted the urge to step back, out of range of whatever might happen next. He'd never witnessed a confrontation between these two before. His gaze shifted from his sister to his niece and back. Regardless of how much he wished to recover the Portinari, was it wise to join a group made up of mothers and daughters? Still, one did what was necessary. He braced himself.

"Did I mention I would be paying for everything? I will take care of all expenses," he said in what he thought was a helpful manner.

"Your father will like that." Roz's gaze never left her daughter's.

"Father will never make me go if I don't want to." Challenge colored Harriet's words.

"My dear child, you are his daughter." A triumphant gleam sparked in Roz's eyes. "I am his wife." Roz adopted a wicked smile he had seen any number of times in their youth when she'd had the upper hand and knew it. "Dante." Her gaze never wavered from her offspring. "When do we leave?"

CHAPTER THREE

One week later...

"...AND THE NEXT THING I knew—" Willie settled in a plush cushioned chair and cast her most pleasant smile at the first members of her group to arrive at the private train car that would take them to Dover "—I was agreeing to do the old dear a favor and accompany a group of mothers and daughters on a tour. Although I will admit I am quite looking forward to it."

"Geneva and I are very excited, my lady." Mrs. Henderson—Marian she had already insisted Willie call her as she was certain they would soon be fast friends—fairly glowed with barely restrained enthusiasm.

The car's furnishings were more conducive to a parlor or an elegant sitting room than a train, with wine-colored velvet drapes trimmed with gold cord at the windows and luxurious sofas and chairs instead of the more typical train seating. Exactly the refinement one expected from a private car. Marian perched on the sofa at the far end of the car although Willie suspected she might bounce off her seat at any moment—as if even the forces of gravity could not contain her energy. Her daughter, Geneva, sitting beside her, had made appropriate murmurings at their introduction then promptly pulled a book out of a valise and buried her nose in it.

"We have never been to Europe before," Marian continued, "and never imagined we would see anything beyond London. Gerald, my husband, is here for business and is constantly occupied with meetings, which is something of a shame as he has seen nothing whatsoever. Geneva and I simply came along because we're from Chicago and we have never traveled at all. And we have always dreamed of seeing London. We had no further expectations beyond that."

She paused and Willie nodded. It was apparent she would not be able to get a word in until Marian's soliloquy had run its course. Perhaps tomorrow...

"But when Mrs. Vanderflute said she had inquired as to the possibility of a trip to Paris and the Riviera and Venice and Rome—not a grand tour exactly but more of a meandering path, I would say—well, it was one of those things that does not come along often. Certainly I would have preferred a more extensive route that included some of the northern climes but it is autumn after all and the weather being what is it, well, it did seem perfectly suitable. We have been in London for months now so thirty days on a whirlwind trip was nearly irresistible. Gerald is so occupied with business that he will scarcely notice our absence at all. And we will return to London with more than enough time to make our voyage home. How could one say no to that?"

Willie stared. "It would be difficult."

"Besides," Marian continued, "I am a firm believer that when unexpected opportunities present themselves one should seize them with both hands. Don't you agree, my lady?"

For a moment, Willie could do little more than stare—her smile frozen awkwardly on her face. Certainly Willie was known for being unreserved and candid but she wasn't sure she'd ever encountered anyone so, well, *open* as Marian Henderson.

"Well, yes," she said at last. "Yes, I do."

"I thought so. Especially since you agreed to accompany our little group at what was very nearly the last minute. I cannot tell you how grateful I am that you did so, my lady. Why, after Mrs. Vanderflute and her daughter had to return home unexpectedly, I thought surely this trip would fall apart. After all, the itinerary was her doing and, as I said, not my first choice. But she did go to the trouble of arranging the tour and I didn't feel it was my place to make changes even after she decided not to come. You understand. But then the Lady Travelers Society contacted us at our hotel—the Savoy. Do you know it, my lady?"

"I'm afraid not. It's new, I believe."

Marian nodded. "It opened in August I think. And did you know, my lady, it's entirely lit by electricity?"

"I had no idea," Willie said faintly, although she had heard the new Savoy was both grand and thoroughly modern.

"I cannot tell you how thrilled Geneva and I were when that lovely woman from the Lady Travelers Society—oh, what was her name, my lady?"

"Miss Granville?"

"Yes, that's the one. When she informed us, if we were still interested, the tour would now be hosted by the honorable Lady Wilhelmina Bascombe." Marian said Willie's name with the sort of reverence one usually reserved for royalty. Or God.

"And I am certain we shall all have a grand time."

Marian frowned. "I did think though that there would be a tour director or something of that sort."

"Nonsense." Willie waved off the comment. "Miss

Granville has organized everything beautifully and I assure you I am quite delighted about the prospect of leading our group of travelers and handling those minor matters that may arise. It shall be great fun and I daresay it won't even be a particular challenge, although I do love a challenge. Besides, a tour director would prove terribly inconvenient, don't you think?"

Marian shook her head in confusion. "Inconvenient?"

"Of course. It would most likely be a man, which would ruin the spirit of independence inherent in this group. Why, we are a merry band of ladies—of mothers and daughters—out to conquer a corner of Europe with our maps and guidebooks in one hand and our parasols in the other. We certainly don't need anyone, let alone a man, to lead the way. Don't you agree?"

"I do." Marian shook her head eagerly. "I really do."

"Excellent." Willie cast her a brilliant smile, rose to her feet, picked up the leather-clad notebook Poppy had given her as a bon voyage present and tried not to look as if she were escaping. "Now, if you will excuse me, I need to return to the train platform and greet the rest of our tour."

"Ah yes, that would be Mrs. Corby and her daughters, my lady. I've met them but I can't say that I know them. Her husband is engaged in business with mine and Mr. Vanderflute. They're from New York if I recall correctly." A slight frown creased her forehead. "The Corby daughters are a bit younger than Geneva, I think. She's almost nineteen and I am hoping this trip gives her the extra bit of polish she needs to find an appropriate husband—"

Willie might have been mistaken but she could have sworn she heard a faint groan from behind Geneva's book.

"—as she is not getting any younger. Surely you see

my point, my lady? Why, I was married at nineteen and I have been happy ever since." Marian threw her daughter a pointed look. Geneva turned a page. Obviously the young woman was used to ignoring her mother. Willie bit back a smile.

"The train is expected to leave in a quarter of an hour so I expect the others to arrive at any minute." Willie turned toward the door.

"Mrs. Corby strikes me as being a quiet sort, my lady," Marian called after her. "Terribly sensible but a bit timid, I suspect."

"Then we shall do our best to make her feel she is among friends," Willie said over her shoulder.

"Excellent. Lady…" Marian hesitated.

Willie reached the door and turned back. "Yes?"

"I hate to sound, well, stupid but I am at a loss. We don't have titles in America, you see, so I have no idea what it is appropriate to call you, your ladyship." Concern touched with embarrassment shone in Marian's eyes. "Is it Lady Wilhelmina or Lady Bascombe?"

Willie studied the other woman. With light brown hair and a charming smile she was quite attractive, although Willie suspected she might have been slimmer in her youth, and no more than ten years older than Willie, if that. This was a woman who, in spite of an air of confidence, obviously wanted to be liked as well as do what was expected and correct.

"For one thing, it's not necessary to refer to me as *my lady* with every breath," Willie said as gently as possible.

Marian's face fell.

"Goodness, Marian, as you said, you are not from England, so you cannot be expected to know all the myriad little details that accompany forms of address here. Why, I myself get confused on occasion. And I am certainly not the least bit insulted, so do not worry yourself about that for a moment."

"Thank you." Marian offered a feeble smile.

"My title is Viscountess Bascombe and I would usually be referred to as Lady Bascombe. However, as we will be spending a great deal of time together and I agree that we will all become good friends—"

Marian brightened.

"—I suggest you call me Willie."

From the look on Marian's face one would have thought the clouds had parted and a shaft of celestial light had shone upon her. Willie wouldn't have been at all surprised if the dulcet sounds of heavenly choirs weren't ringing in Marian's ears at this very moment.

"Thank you, my..." Marian squared her shoulders, a brilliant smile lighting her face. "Willie."

The oddest sort of snort came from Geneva, who never looked up but did turn the page.

Willie smiled and stepped down onto the platform. This might well be more entertaining than she had imagined. And one should always enter into new endeavors with a sense that they will turn out well. She wasn't sure who had told her that but it was excellent advice. Certainly she had no experience at managing a group of travelers, and admittedly she had never actually traveled herself, but it couldn't possibly be all that difficult.

Confidence surged through her. *Efficient* was not a word that had ever been used to describe Lady Wilhelmina Bascombe. Nor was it a description she aspired to. Yet here and now, standing by the car door in the elegant black-and-white-striped traveling dress—updated with a stitch here and tuck there by the ever-so-clever Patsy—and the jaunty hat that had long ago been ordered from Paris, her new notebook in her hand, Willie was the epitome of efficiency. Or at least her idea of efficiency, which would have to do.

That true personification of efficiency—Miss Granville—had hoped to arrange a tea to introduce Willie to her tour but it had proved impossible. Apparently, Americans in London were entirely too busy trying to see everything there was to see. Coordinating the various members of their group proved daunting even to the well-organized and eminently competent Miss Granville. Right now she awaited the rest of their assembly at the main entry of Victoria Station to see to their luggage. She had explained, while she would usually send someone else to take care of that, this tour was both exclusive and expensive and she much preferred to be present. If successful, it could pave the way for more quick, lucrative European trips, directed especially at Americans who never seemed to have as much time to spend as money. Miss Granville had added that given Willie's experience with first-class travel, she expected absolutely nothing to go wrong. As she had said so with a pointed look Willie had blithely tried to ignore, Willie did wonder if perhaps Miss Granville wasn't entirely accepting of the sterling recommendations given by Poppy and her friends. Still, while Willie wasn't at all sure how businesses like the Lady Travelers Society worked, she was fairly certain what the founders of the society wanted they probably received. Regardless of her lack of experience or the fact that she had never been given any true responsibility whatsoever, Willie would not let Poppy and her friends down. She would rise to the occasion and confront any challenge head-on. And hadn't she always loved challenges? Admittedly, she'd never taken on anything like this but it couldn't possibly be all that difficult. Why, women these days traveled all the time.

Willie pulled a list of names typewritten on a sheet of paper from her notebook. These were her charges, the companions she would spend the next few weeks with, the travelers she had to thank for her expense-free trip to Venice. The unsuspecting tourists she fully intended to abandon there. Once she had her painting in hand, she planned to return to London at once. It would not reflect well on Poppy and her friends, and Miss Granville would not be happy, but Willie had no choice. She vowed to do whatever was necessary upon her return to make amends to all concerned.

Willie had made discreet inquiries with a solicitor, Mr. Virgil Hawkings, who was well-known in art circles. He had agreed to act as a mediator between Willie and potential buyers. When she spoke with him again yesterday, he'd said there was a fair amount of interest, adding the offers for the Portinari might be far more than she had imagined and mentioning a figure she had not dared to hope for. Indeed, he was already setting up a discreet private auction to take place next month. She'd protested that she might not have the painting by then but Mr. Hawkings was adamant that in matters of this nature it was best to strike while interest was still high. She absolutely had to be back with the painting by then. Staying with her group through their visit to Rome would put Willie's return in time for the auction in jeopardy. Even someone who had never traveled knew any number of unexpected problems could occur, many of which were detailed in the numerous pamphlets from the Lady Travelers Society she'd read in the past few weeks.

Willie studied the names on her list in an effort to ignore the bit of guilt niggling at her. Guilt was as foreign to her as efficiency. And now that she'd met two members of their party, there really wasn't anything to feel guilty about. Marian Henderson was chatty but did strike Willie as competent enough. She was American after all and while Willie had never known any Americans, they did have a reputation for charging forth into the unknown with unfailing confidence and a stouthearted lack of hesitation. Willie found it admirable. Besides, she would leave all her maps and guidebooks and make certain everyone in their party had the confirmation telegrams for their hotels and train vouchers and everything else they needed. They would be fine. Probably more than fine. Why, it would likely be the grandest of adventures for them. Her departure would simply add to the stories they could tell about their travels. Admittedly, Willie might not come off particularly well in those stories but she really had no choice, even if she was beginning to—

"I beg your pardon," a quiet voice asked, barely loud enough to be heard over the din of the station. "Are you Lady Bascombe?"

Willie looked up and adopted a welcoming smile. "I am."

A short, attractive fair-haired lady about Marian's age stood flanked by two young pretty blonde women. Two identical young women. Miss Granville had said there were three separate family groups on the tour and according to the list of names, these three were either J. Corby and daughters or D. Montague, R. Richfield and daughter. Apparently, Miss Granville thought abbreviations were efficient. In truth, they were confusing.

"I'm Mrs. Corby." The woman returned Willie's smile. "And these are my daughters, Emmaline and Matilda."

"We prefer Emma and Tillie," one of the girls said.

"Emmaline and Matilda are names for old women." The other girl shuddered. "They shall do I suppose when we are in our dotage but right now they don't suit us at all."

"You understand don't you?" the first girl asked. "Surely you remember what it was like to be young and have a horrible name?"

"Not that it probably matters to you now, of course." Innocence sounded in the second girl's voice as if she had no idea she was implying Willie was old. Willie didn't believe her for a moment. "After all, your name is Wilhelmina." Two pairs of identical hazel eyes, both colored with a definite challenge, stared at her. Identical Cheshire cat smiles curved their identical lips.

"I think Wilhelmina is a lovely name." Mrs. Corby cast a scathing look at her daughters. "It's so much better than Jane, which is my name."

"There's nothing wrong with Jane," Willie said firmly. "I think it's a strong and noble name. Why, we have had two queens of England named Jane."

"Yes, well, if I recall correctly neither of them ended particularly well." Mrs. Corby's eyes lit with amusement. "I will try to do better."

Willie laughed. "I've no doubt of it." She turned to the girls. "You're right, you know. While I do not detest Wilhelmina, I much prefer Willie."

"Lady Willie." One of the girls made a face.

"It's Lady Bascombe, Emma," Mrs. Corby said firmly.

"But as we are all to be friends—" she turned to Mrs. Corby "—I do hope you will call me Willie and allow me to call you Jane."

A slow smile spread across Jane's face. "I would like that very much."

"Now then." Willie studied the twins. "You're Emma." She pointed at the one who had called her Lady Willie.

"Which means you—" she aimed her finger at the other twin "—must be Tillie."

"Oh no, I'm afraid you have already—" Emma began but Tillie nudged her with her elbow and glanced at their mother. Jane's eyes narrowed. Emma sighed. "Yes, I'm Emma."

Oh, these two were going to be interesting. Willie inclined her head toward their mother. "How on earth do you tell them apart?"

"There are all sort of tiny differences we've noted through the years. Depending on their moods, Emma's eyes tend more toward brown and Tillie's toward green but the difference is often negligible. Fortunately, as they are now seventeen, they are old enough to set aside the foolish tricks they were so fond of playing when they were children." Jane smiled but shot a warning look at her daughters. "They understand the consequences of such misbehavior are much more significant now."

"Oh, we do," Tillie said quickly. "Although sometimes…"

"Sometimes it's just too much fun." Emma grinned. "And well worth the risk."

Jane bit back a smile. Clearly the twins were a handful and probably always had been. Yet there was obvious affection between mother and daughters. Willie's heart twisted.

"The tiny differences, however, are mostly in terms of mannerism and remarkably easy to miss. The best way to tell my girls apart is physical." Jane nodded at Emma. "Emma cut her hand on a piece of glass when the girls were eight. There is a J-shaped scar at the base of her thumb on her right hand." She shot a glance at the girls. "Show her, dear."

Emma rolled her gaze toward the far off iron-and-glass

ceiling of Victoria Station, peeled off her glove and held out her hand palm up. The scar was small but distinct if one knew what one was looking for.

"How convenient." Willie grinned at Emma. "That will be most helpful."

"You have no idea," Jane said under her breath.

"We are glad to be of assistance," Tillie murmured with a feeble smile.

Willie studied the twins for a moment. She could remember when she was their age as if it were yesterday. She'd thought the entire world was hers for the taking. The future was bright and filled with promise. Rules were silly annoying things designed only to destroy the fun and enjoyment of life itself. And nothing was impossible. Willie saw a great deal of herself in Emma and Tillie. Without question, these girls would challenge her at every step. She wished them the best of luck but, aside from pretending to be each other, Willie doubted there was anything they could try that she hadn't attempted at their age.

Still, it would be easier for all concerned if they were well behaved. The best way to defuse an enemy was to make him an ally.

"I shall make you a deal," Willie said. "I won't tell anyone how to tell the two of you apart if you agree not to use this formidable weapon of yours against me."

"We couldn't anyway." Emma shrugged. "You know how to tell the difference between us now."

"Which means you needn't make any sort of deal with us at all," Tillie said thoughtfully. "And you are only offering to do so because you want to be friends." She exchanged looks with Emma then grinned. "We can agree to that."

Willie wasn't sure she believed that either.

"The girls have also agreed to be on their best behavior." Jane's gaze met one daughter's then the other's in an unspoken message. "They've always wanted to see Paris and Venice and Rome and they are well aware that if they take even one step out of line, the repercussions will be unpleasant and we will be on our way back to London without hesitation."

The twins smiled weakly.

"I can't imagine we'll have any problems at all," Willie said with an air of unexpected confidence. "Now then, Mrs. Henderson and her daughter, Geneva, are inside the car. If you'd like to join them, we have one party yet to arrive."

"I've met Marian Henderson." Jane waved the girls ahead of her. "She's quite…gregarious, I would say."

"She is indeed."

"This should be interesting." Jane nodded and stepped up into the car.

"It should indeed," Willie murmured and returned her gaze to the last names on her list—D. Montague, R. Richfield and daughter. She did hope they would arrive soon. Leaving behind three members of their party on the first day did not bode well for the rest of the trip. She glanced up and scanned the platform.

Americans didn't look particularly different, although she did believe they walked with a certain spring to their step, as if the world truly were their oyster. She spotted a woman coming in her direction, a definite air of determination about her. She was accompanied by two young women, probably her daughters. Willie adopted her most welcoming smile.

The woman gave her no more than cursory glance as she walked by. And wasn't that rude? Even if she wasn't D. Montague or R. Richfield she could have at least acknowledged Willie's presence in that vague, polite manner acceptable for a casual encounter. Goodness, the manners of some people simply—

"Lady Bascombe?" A decidedly English voice said.

Willie turned and smiled. "Yes?"

"Oh good, I was hoping it was you." An attractive dark-haired woman, perhaps a decade older than Willie, smiled expectantly. A young woman stood behind her, also dark haired and quite pretty with a resigned look on her face.

"It most definitely is me." Willie drew her brows together in confusion. "I do apologize but have we met?"

"Once but it was a long time ago and I daresay you probably won't remember as I wouldn't have if I hadn't been reminded."

"Oh well…" Willie shook her head. "I am sorry but you have me at a disadvantage."

"Of course I do, and it's terribly rude of me. I just said you wouldn't remember me and now I'm expecting you to do just that. Obviously it's now my turn to apologize to you." She smiled. "I'm Lady Richfield and this is my daughter, Lady Harriet Blake."

"You're not American?" Willie stared.

"Not to my knowledge."

"I see. I had no idea. I was told the tour was comprised of American ladies and their daughters so I wasn't expecting a fellow countryman." She glanced at her list of names. "Your names are registered simply as R. Richfield and daughter, which I fear is due to the extreme efficiency of Miss Granville of the Lady Travelers Society."

"Ah yes, the American. She met us at the front of the station and arranged for our bags to be taken care of." Lady Bascombe lowered her voice in a confidential manner. "Do you think all Americans are that efficient?"

Willie's thoughts flashed to the ladies already in the train car. "Oh, I doubt it."

"Good." Lady Richfield nodded. "I have never been the least bit efficient and I frankly find myself somewhat suspicious of those women who are."

Willie grinned. "I couldn't agree with you more."

"So…" Lady Richfield glanced around. "Should we be getting on board?"

"Yes, of course. Everyone else has arrived with the exception—" Willie checked her list "—of D. Montague. I thought she was part of your party but she's not with you?"

"D. Montague should be here any moment." A slightly wicked spark shone in Lady Harriet's eyes. "So this tour is for mothers and daughters? Only mothers and daughters?"

"I don't believe it was restricted to mothers and daughters," Willie said slowly, "but it is my understanding that our members are made up only of mothers and daughters. And aside from museums and galleries, the itinerary includes a number of things females tend to enjoy that men merely tolerate—shopping and theater and gardens and the like."

"That's what I thought," Lady Harriet said in an overly sweet manner.

"Harriet, dear girl, why don't you go on and find our seats." A firm note sounded in Lady Richfield's voice. "You'll have to forgive my daughter. She was not especially eager to come on the tour."

"But, Mother, I have changed my mind. I now see how very wrong I was." An innocent smile curved the girl's lips.

Lady Richfield's eyes narrowed. "No more than two

days ago you were moaning about how your life was over if you were forced to leave London."

"Any number of things can change in two days, Mother. I came to the realization that opportunities like this don't often come along. The chance to go to Paris as well as Venice? Why, it would be quite silly of me not to go. Besides, we'll be gone less than a month. Goodness, Mother, my life can't possibly be over because I'm gone a mere month." Lady Harriet cast her mother a chastising look.

Suspicion colored Lady Richfield's eyes. "I believe that was my point."

"And now I agree with you. You should be happy, Mother."

"And yet…" Lady Richfield studied her daughter.

Lady Harriet stepped up into the car and glanced down at them with a satisfied grin. A bit too satisfied. This was another young woman who would bear watching. "I think this is going to be a grand adventure. Truly an experience to remember."

"As do I, Lady Harriet," Willie said with an encouraging nod.

"Oh, do call her Harriet. Use of a title might be awkward with the American girls." Lady Richfield pulled her gaze from the car door. "Do you have daughters, Lady Bascombe?"

"I'm afraid not. Someday perhaps."

"Yes, well, the idea of daughters someday sounds delightful when someday is very far off. But then someday arrives and you're living with this clever, subtly deceitful creature whose greatest joy in life is outwitting you because she thinks you are the enemy of all she wants in life. Oh, and she's certain you're stupid, as well," Lady Richfield added wryly.

Willie grinned. "Surely not."

"Life with a daughter is a challenge." Lady Richfield straightened her shoulders. "Fortunately, I quite enjoy a challenge."

Willie laughed.

Lady Richfield chuckled. "And you must call me Rosalind. After all, we are going to be spending a great deal of time in one another's company."

"Excellent. And I am Wilhelmina but most people call me Willie as Wilhelmina is rather a mouthful." She wrinkled her nose. "And, as I have been told by the younger members of our party, a bit antiquated, as well."

"They are nothing if not painfully blunt," Rosalind observed.

"I remember all too well." Willie frowned and glanced at her list again. "I do wish your D. Montague would appear. Am I to assume she is English, as well?"

"Oh, definitely English."

"I would hate to leave her behind. And while we do have a private car, the train will leave when expected."

"Yes, well..." Rosalind drew a deep breath. "About D. Montague. You should know—"

"That I am quite looking forward to this." A tall, dashing gentleman with dark hair, equally dark eyes and an impressive air of refined elegance about him—no doubt assisted by excellent, quality tailoring—stepped up beside Rosalind. He carried a black leather traveling valise, the kind used for documents by solicitors and men of business. "You must be Lady Bascombe."

Surely she'd met a man with shoulders that delightfully broad before? And certainly she knew any number who had dimples bracketing the corners of their perfectly shaped lips beneath a sharp straight nose that was just a touch Roman. Without thinking, Willie extended her hand. "I am."

He took her hand and gazed into her eyes. The oddest shiver ran through her. "I am delighted to meet you."

She mustered a weak smile. "And you are?"

"Forgive me. Where was my head? Roz?" He directed his words to Rosalind but kept his gaze locked on Willie's. "Do be so kind as to introduce me."

Good Lord. The most unnerving thought flashed through her mind. Was this intriguing specimen of the male gender here to accompany Rosalind? Was this trip to be some sort of romantic liaison on their part? And in front of her daughter? Not to mention the other girls. While Americans were reputed to be less unyielding about any number of things, Willie was fairly certain Jane and Marian would both be shocked by this. As free-spirited as Willie had always considered herself, this she could not allow.

"Yes, of course. Allow me to introduce Mr. Dante Montague." Rosalind cleared her throat. "My brother."

"Your what?" Relief swept through her. Only because she would not have to take the moral high ground—which she wasn't sure anyone would believe—and not because of the wicked sparkle dancing in his eyes. And the way he looked at her as if she were something rather remarkable. Men had looked at her in similar ways before, of course, but it had always been much more lascivious. And she had been married. And it had been a very long time since.

"Her brother." He grinned. "We've been told there's a certain family resemblance."

"When we were children perhaps." Rosalind scoffed. "Fortunately, we have grown out of it."

"And your name is Dante?" For whatever reason she

couldn't seem to pull her gaze from his. Nor did she want to. "As in the nine circles of hell?"

He chuckled. "My mother had a passion for literary names. You're familiar with Dante's *Divine Comedy*, then?"

An endless, fourteenth-century epic poem that was forced down the throats of unsuspecting schoolgirls in the name of *classics* while they did their best to avoid it? The sort of thing a girl might only skim in order to answer the most basic questions about it? She forced a light laugh. "Who isn't?"

"Excellent. I look forward to discussing it with you."

"You can let go of her hand now," Rosalind said pointedly.

Willie pulled her hand from his. "That does sound like fun."

"I expect this tour to be a great deal of fun, as well." Mr. Montague continued to study her as if he couldn't bear to take his eyes away. It was at once flattering and a bit unnerving.

"I'm curious, Mr. Montague."

"Dante, please." There were those dimples again. "We're going to be together every day for the next month after all."

"Regardless, we have only just met. It would be far too improper and not at all the way to begin an adventure like this." Oh Lord. Why couldn't the man have had a name like Horacio or Ebenezer. Why did he have to have the name of an Italian poet?

And where on earth had this voice of propriety of hers come from? Why, she had never been the least bit concerned about rules before. It was no doubt his fault. This man, this *Dante*, might be very, very dangerous. Or he could be a great deal of fun. She wasn't sure she was ready for fun and certainly not for danger. Her previous life had had entirely too much of both—or the illusion of both—and had, in hindsight, been exhausting. Although she would admit there were frequent moments when she missed it.

"Might I ask why you decided to join a tour directed at ladies and their daughters?"

"Well, I—"

"In truth, this whole thing was my brother's idea," Rosalind answered. "He is paying for our entire trip. The dear man."

"It was a gift," Dante said quickly. "And most deserved."

"It was a bribe." Rosalind smirked. "Also most deserved."

"And as I was at loose ends, with nothing pressing to keep me in London at the moment—"

"Alas my dear brother has not yet found himself a wife." Rosalind heaved a long-suffering sigh.

Dante shot her a sharp look then continued. "I thought it might be nice to accompany my dear, dear sister and her charming daughter."

"How very…thoughtful of you." And indeed it did appear quite thoughtful although one couldn't help but wonder at the undercurrents ebbing between brother and sister and exactly what Dante's bribe was for. And wouldn't that be interesting to find out?

"And then when I discovered you were to be one of the travelers, well, how could I possibly pass up the opportunity to make the acquaintance of the legendary Wilhelmina Bascombe."

"How indeed." She forced a light laugh. *Legendary?* What utter rubbish. She did have a certain reputation—at least she used to—but it had been two years since she'd done anything at all let alone anything *legendary*.

"I believe we should probably get on board," Mr. Montague said to his sister then turned to Willie. "Don't you agree, Lady Bascombe?"

"Yes, of course," she murmured.

Dante assisted his sister up the steps. She said something quietly into his ear then glanced back at Willie and smiled. He turned to Willie and took her hand to help her into the car. It wasn't really necessary. But it was quite nice.

"I cannot tell you how delighted I am that I decided to come along," he said in a low voice behind her.

A frisson of something that might have been delight—or worse, anticipation—ran up her spine. She ignored it.

It had been a long time since she'd felt any sort of attraction to a man. Certainly it was not unexpected that she would do so at some point. She had been a widow for two years after all and even at the age of thirty she did not consider herself old. Nor did she have any desire to spend the rest of her life alone.

But Willie had met any number of dashing, charming, handsome men before. George was dashing and handsome and charming. Her next husband was going to be sensible and rational and practical. A man who had more on his mind than the next ball or rout or hunt. At the very least, a man who was aware of his responsibilities and lived up to them. A man who paid his bills.

No, she was finished with men who were impulsive and wanted nothing more than to enjoy everything life had to offer. The next time she married she wanted a bit of moderation.

A man who put entirely too much effort into charming a woman—even if he was nice to his sister—was not to be trusted. Legendary indeed. Besides, a man who had

the name and the charm of an Italian poet and the looks
of a Roman god was the last thing she needed or wanted.
Even if she suspected he might well be irresistible.

CHAPTER FOUR

"WELL?" DANTE SAID in an aside to his sister, his gaze on Lady Bascombe at the far end of the car. She sat at a table studying a large map and papers that no doubt had to do with the tour, looking shockingly efficient. If there was one word that was not in the dossier he had been given on Wilhelmina Bascombe it was *efficient*. "How was that for charming?"

"Quite good, Dante. I scarcely recognized you." Roz directed her words to him but kept her gaze on the ladies' magazine she paged through. "Not the least bit stuffy. One would think you'd been practicing."

He bit back a grin. He hadn't attempted to flirt in longer than he could remember, and he was never especially accomplished at it as he'd always thought it rather silly. But it was somewhat like riding a horse again when one hadn't ridden for some time. And oddly enough, it was surprisingly enjoyable.

The rest of their party was scattered about the spacious car, having divided according to age. Mrs. Corby and Mrs. Henderson had settled near the midsection of the car apparently ascertaining mutual acquaintances although Mrs. Corby didn't seem to be saying nearly as much as Mrs. Henderson. The four girls were seated as far away from their mothers as possible and appeared to have already forged a friendship. Or more likely an alliance against a common enemy.

"Do you intend to marry her?" Roz said coolly.

"What?"

"Do keep your voice down, brother, if you don't wish for everyone to hear."

"Shock will do that to a man," he said sharply but lowered his voice nonetheless. "No, of course I don't intend to marry her. Don't be absurd. We've just met."

"You are protesting entirely too much, Dante." She turned a page. "I was only going to note that the level of your charm might be entirely too, oh, *extreme* if your purpose is anything short of marriage or seduction."

"Good Lord, Roz." He stared. "My purpose is neither seduction nor marriage. My sole purpose is reclaiming the Portinari. And you are the one who told me to be charming."

"I did not suggest you sweep her off her feet."

"I'm not trying to sweep her off her feet." Admittedly, he was making an effort beyond anything he had done in recent years. Nor was it the least bit difficult. He imagined any number of men found flirtation with the lovely Lady Bascombe to be easy if not natural. He'd been intrigued before but in person she was, well, *more* than he had anticipated. There was something about the unexpected look of intelligence in her blue eyes coupled with a delightful smile, a fine figure and an air of utter confidence that belied everything he had learned about the irresponsible, impulsive, madcap Willie Bascombe. It was very nearly irresistible. Not to him, of course. He was not—nor could be ever be—interested in her as anything other than a means to the Portinari. But he could certainly understand why other men might find her compelling.

"No?" Roz turned another page.

"No," he said firmly. "I am trying to do nothing more than forge a friendship with her. A cordial companionship if you will. After all, we have a full two weeks before we reach Venice."

"A lot can happen in two weeks," Roz murmured.

"Indeed it can." He bent his head closer to his sister's. "If Lady Bascombe and I are on firm, affable footing, if we are indeed friends, by the time she retrieves the painting, it will be that much easier to tell her of our claim of ownership. She will be far more willing to listen to reason with a friend she trusts than with an enemy."

"And that is your plan?"

"And an excellent one it is too." Admittedly, it had only just occurred to him when he'd realized he wouldn't at all mind being friends with Lady Bascombe. Anything beyond that was absurd, of course. But friends, yes, friends would be good.

"And to think, I have always thought you were so much more intelligent than I." She set her magazine on her lap, folded her hands on top of it and met his gaze. "That is the most absurd plan I have ever heard. Although I hesitate to use the word *plan* as it sounds more like an ill-conceived disaster in the making."

"Rubbish," he said staunchly. "If she knows me, if she *likes* me, she'll be much more amenable to my position. I've found that to be an excellent business practice. One that rarely fails."

"Now, there's the overly methodical and somewhat stodgy brother that I know and love."

He ignored her. "It makes perfect sense."

"In business perhaps. But when it comes to women, my poor, sweet, deluded brother—"

"She'll understand."

Roz scoffed. "More likely she'll hate you."

"Don't be ridiculous." His gazed strayed back to Lady Bascombe—Willie. He'd never been one for masculine names on women—he considered them inappropriate and absurd. But Willie suited Lady Bascombe, who was at once independent and uniquely feminine. A woman who would surely listen to reason when he presented his claim. Especially if they were on a friendly basis. "She's entirely too intelligent to hate me."

"Ah yes, that will certainly make a difference. A woman's intelligence always comes to the forefront when she discovers a man has deceived her."

"I'm not going to deceive her." Confidence surged through him. It really was an excellent plan. "I am genuinely going to win her friendship."

"This explains so much." Roz cast him a pitying look, set aside her magazine and rose to her feet. "I believe I will make a few friends myself. I suspect I am going to need them. This is going to be a far longer trip than I imagined," she added under her breath and moved to join the other ladies.

In many ways—his sister was right. No time like the present to begin. He stood and casually made his way to Lady Bascombe's table. "Lady Bascombe?"

She looked up. "Yes, Mr. Montague?"

"May I join you?"

She hesitated then smiled. "Of course."

"Are you sure?" He settled in the closest chair. "I hate to interrupt."

"No, that's quite all right. I am simply going over our itinerary and travel documents." She settled back in her seat and looked at him expectantly. "Is there something I can help you with?"

"No, I just…" Perhaps this wasn't going to be as easy as he'd thought after all. He adopted his most winning smile. "I simply thought it would help pass the time until we arrive in Dover to engage in interesting conversation with the loveliest woman here."

"The loveliest?" Her brow rose. "As well as legendary?"

He winced. "A bit too much?"

"A bit." She smiled. "However, like most women I am not immune to flattery. You will quite turn my head with such talk, Mr. Montague."

He chuckled. "I do hope so."

"And if that doesn't work surely your belief that our conversation will be interesting will have much the same effect."

"And yet I was most sincere."

"Very well then." She studied him curiously. "What interesting topic did you wish to discuss?"

"Oh, there are any number of things we could talk about, I suppose." He thought for a moment. "Politics, literature—"

"I'm not certain I'm prepared to discuss the *Divine Comedy* at the moment." She waved at the papers in front of her. "My head is entirely too filled with the assorted and sundry details of transporting this group from one point to the next to dwell on the various types of sin and indulgence portrayed in the *Inferno*. I daresay the details of simply moving a party of nine from one country to another is complicated enough without considering whether any missteps taken in this life will have to be paid for in the next. Surely you understand."

"Completely." He chuckled. "And I would not wish to discuss as substantial a topic as one of the world's great literary efforts in the brief time we have before Dover but we could consider a different work perhaps. I recently read Mr. Haggard's *Cleopatra* and I found it quite enjoyable. Have you read it?"

"Not yet but I do enjoy Mr. Haggard's work. I quite liked *She* and *King Solomon's Mines*."

"Then you like adventure and dashing heroes and sultry heroines?"

"I can't imagine anyone who doesn't, especially with heroes like Allan Quatermain."

"Some might think such stories are rather frivolous."

"And yet some of the most enjoyable moments in life are completely frivolous." She shrugged.

"As well as unexpected."

"I believe *unexpected* is the very definition of adventure."

"Then one can't plan adventure?"

"Goodness, Mr. Montague." Her blue eyes twinkled. "Where would be the fun in that?"

He leaned forward and gazed into her eyes. "You don't think one can set out to seek adventure?"

"Ah, seeking adventure is a far cry from planning it. One can expect for adventure to arise or hope for it but I suspect exactly what form that adventure might take would always be unanticipated."

He grinned. "Agreed."

She laughed.

He settled back in his seat and studied her. "Why did a woman like you agree to host an excursion like this?"

"As you just noted, I like adventure."

"Shepherding a group of women and their daughters on an abbreviated tour to a handful of countries scarcely strikes me as adventure."

"Adventure, Mr. Montague, is where you find it. Who knows what might happen between here and there." She thought for a moment. "We could encounter famous personages—someone like Mr. Haggard himself—on the boat crossing the channel."

"Which might not be an adventure so much as an interesting moment I would say."

"Oh, then you're hoping for grand adventure." Amusement underscored her words. "Well then, instead of a famous author we might encounter a…a princess. Yes, that's good. A princess in disguise fleeing England and marriage to a horrible beast of a man, who might throw herself on your mercy and beg for you to help her. That would certainly constitute adventure."

He laughed. "Now, I think you've gone a bit too far."

"Goodness, Mr. Montague." She sighed. "You are a difficult man to please. First, you think my suggestion of an adventure isn't truly an adventure and then you think my next idea is entirely too much. Let me think." She tapped her forefinger on the table thoughtfully. "You must agree, travel itself is fraught with adventure."

He nodded. "I do."

"Simply setting foot in a place one has never been before is exciting and exhilarating. Even when difficulties arise, there is an element of adventure. Why, any one of the trains we will be taking could break down and we could be stranded. And perhaps forced to survive by our wits alone. Which would be something of a problem but would certainly be an adventure nonetheless. One never knows what is around the next corner."

"Indeed." He nodded. "Still, this tour does seem a bit, oh, tame for you."

"Ah." Her eyes narrowed slightly. "My reputation precedes me, I see. And here I was hoping *legendary* was the worst of it."

"Come now, Lady Bascombe, you can't expect me to entrust my dear sister and niece into the hands of anyone whose background I have not thoroughly checked."

"Then you no doubt know all there is to know about me."

"I doubt if there is anyone who knows all there is to know about you, Lady Bascombe."

"With any luck at all, Mr. Montague." A knowing smile played on her lips.

"But I confess I am still puzzled as to why you agreed to host this tour."

"It's really quite simple," she said smoothly. "One of the founders of the Lady Travelers Society—Mrs. Persephone Fitzhew-Wellmore—is my godmother. This trip was in danger of falling apart and, as American lady travelers are seen as a lucrative prospective clientele, my godmother was quite eager to see it proceed as planned. Apparently, one thing that appeals to Americans is the presence of a fellow traveler with a title."

"True enough." He nodded. It really was an excellent business strategy and quite perceptive given his own business dealings with Americans. There was nothing more impressive to them than a *lady* or *lord* attached to someone's name.

"One thing led to another and here I am." She paused. "As fate would have it, I was planning to travel to Venice in the near future so this was not the least bit inconvenient."

"Still, leading a tour is not the sort of thing that comes to mind for a woman like yourself."

"*Hosting* a tour, Mr. Montague," she said and frowned. "And I do wish you would stop saying that. That 'woman like you' nonsense. I am not a stock character in a drawing room comedy."

"I do apologize. I didn't mean—"

"I would do anything for my godmother. She has been a rock of support for me in recent years. More so than anyone else I can name."

"Fair-weather friends I suspect?"

She heaved a sigh. "Mr. Montague—"

"Why Venice?"

"Why not?"

"Have you ever been to Venice?"

"Goodness, Mr. Montague. Hasn't everyone?"

He chuckled. "You're evading my question. And it was a remarkably innocent question. Not one I would imagine anyone would ignore."

"I'm not ignoring it. I simply find it curious that someone who has had my background thoroughly checked would not know the answer to that. And I think it's my turn in this fascinating conversation of ours to ask you a question."

"My life is an open book."

"No one's life is an open book, Mr. Montague." The slightest hard note edged her words. "We all have secrets. Even those closest to you have secrets. Only a fool thinks they don't."

"Oh." He wasn't quite sure what to say, given he did indeed have a secret of sorts. "Perhaps you're right. Although I can assure you whatever secrets I harbor are minimal and barely worth the effort to keep."

"Your sister said you're financing her trip as a bribe." She propped her elbow on the table, rested her chin in her hand and smiled into his eyes. "What is said bribe for?"

"My sister was just being annoying." He drew his brows together. "Roz takes great joy in annoying me. She is five years my senior and has always delighted in doing whatever she can to set my teeth on edge."

"So it's not a bribe?"

"No," he said firmly. "It's simply in gratitude for a favor. Saying it was a bribe was her convoluted idea of a joke. And not especially amusing either." He shook his head. "One would think as an adult with a grown daughter she would set such childish pursuits aside."

"Some of us never quite grow up." She smiled in a manner that struck him as a touch wistful. It did the oddest things to his stomach. "Have you?"

"Now, that is an interesting question."

"You wished for interesting conversation, Mr. Montague. I can think of no more interesting question. Or answer. Of course, if you prefer not to answer..."

He laughed. "I'm not quite sure why you asked the question."

"Because, Mr. Montague." Her gaze met his. "I have known any number of charming, handsome men with their slightly wicked manners, the suggestion in the tone of their voices that indicates what they are saying goes far beyond their words and the look in their eyes not unlike a connoisseur evaluating his next morsel. I am neither fooled by them, nor am I the least bit interested."

He stared at her. Roz was right—his concerted effort to be charming had perhaps gone further than he intended. Why, she didn't think he was at all the serious, responsible man that he was but rather some kind of rake or rogue or scoundrel. This was not the way to earn her trust. Still, he rather liked it.

He tried and failed to keep a smile from his face. "I shall keep that in mind, Lady Bascombe."

"Furthermore, Mr. Montague—" she met his gaze directly "—most men of that nature are not quite as obvious about it."

"I wasn't..." He chuckled in a wry manner. "I simply thought a woman like...a woman who has had an exciting life would be more inclined to—" he shrugged helplessly "—like a man who was more...*likable* than I usually am."

Her eyes widened and she straightened. "You wanted me to like you?"

He nodded.

"Why?" Suspicion sounded in her voice.

"Because you may well be the most interesting woman I have ever met." Even as he said the words he realized he had indeed been fascinated by her ever since he'd first read the dossier. Regardless, his goal was not to win her affections, simply her friendship. And that was a means to an end, nothing more. "And I hope to be friends."

She sat back in her seat and stared at him. "I'm not sure what to say."

"You must admit this confession of mine is extremely charming."

"Nor am I sure what I believe."

He arched a brow. "You don't trust me?"

"Trust needs to be earned. And I don't know you well enough to trust you."

"Perhaps by the time we reach Venice you will."

"And will I like you, as well?"

"Without question." He grinned and rose to his feet. That would do for now. It was an excellent start. "If you'll excuse me, I shall leave you to your consideration of our journey."

"Thank you." Her gaze returned to the papers on the table. "I am determined to make certain nothing goes awry," she said, and it struck Dante her words were more for herself than for him. Perhaps she was not as confident as she appeared.

"Please feel free to call on me at any time should you need my assistance in any way."

"Your offer is most appreciated but I doubt your assistance will be necessary."

"As you pointed out—one never knows what might

be around the next corner." He paused. Nothing in her dossier had indicated she was a well-seasoned traveler in spite of her current facade of competence, although admittedly that was not the kind of information he had requested. Still, something had struck him a few minutes ago that he had paid no attention. Perhaps the delightful Willie Bascombe was not as she appeared. "One more thing." He leaned forward, braced his hands on the table and gazed into her eyes.

Her eyes widened but she did not shrink from his direct gaze. "And what might that be?"

"The map you are so dutifully studying." He lowered his voice in a confidential manner. "It's upside down."

CHAPTER FIVE

THERE WAS NOTHING like maneuvering nine people through the complexities of claiming luggage upon arrival in Paris at the *salle des bagages* and the subsequent annoying inspection by customs agents to make a woman feel not merely efficient but supremely confident. It was not easy, especially as everyone rudely insisted on speaking in French. Perhaps language barriers were among the reasons why she and George had never traveled beyond England's shores. Although it was more likely attributable to finances. No doubt they would have traveled someday—if only to escape their creditors.

Still, if asked, Willie would have said she did indeed speak French, more or less. Why, she had studied the language for years in school, as did everyone else she knew, and could say *la plume de ma tante* as well as anyone. But apparently when one was actually *in* France, one's French was decidedly more *less* than *more*.

Regardless, with her Baedeker's guide in one hand, her notebook in the other and the wherewithal to hire a small army of porters, Willie had managed to dispatch their group via three separate cabs to the Grand Hotel. Her charges had heeded Miss Granville's advice on limiting the amount of their luggage given the brief length of time they would stay in any one place. They had also forgone the inclusion of ladies' maids in their party, apparently standard guidance from the Lady Travelers Society. It made a great deal of sense in terms of expenditures and practicality. Every hotel they would stay in provided maids for their first-class guests. The Grand Hotel was no exception.

Upon their arrival nearly an hour ago, all the members of their party had been seen to their respective suites with assurances their every need would be met. Willie's admiration of Miss Granville's efficiency reluctantly notched upward. Who would have imagined Willie Bascombe would ever be impressed by efficiency? Apparently, Miss Granville, and her employer, were skilled in making the impossible possible. Willie had been aware, of course, of the Paris Exposition—why, everyone in the world was talking about the massive iron tower symbol of the fair— but she had never considered what that might mean to the availability of hotel rooms in the city. Indeed, she was fairly certain if she were not traveling under the auspices of Mr. Forge's Lady Travelers Society, she would be hard pressed to find any available rooms at all let alone suites in the luxurious Grand Hotel.

They had arrived at an appropriate hour for a civilized dinner but everyone agreed—given that the proper tea service on the train from Calais had been surprisingly good in both quality and quantity—that no more than a light supper was required. Furthermore, they would all much rather spend their first night in Paris viewing the illumination of the Eiffel Tower.

Willie now awaited the others, resisting the urge to tap her foot impatiently on the highly polished floor of the opulent crystal, marble and gilded lobby and trying very hard to look serene and unconcerned instead of annoyed by their tardiness. They did have a schedule to maintain after all. Willie could not remember a point in her life before now when she was not perpetually late but if she could manage to appear promptly—so could everyone else. Apparently, a desire for punctuality went hand in hand with the acceptance of responsibility. Besides, as the idea for viewing the illumination had been embraced with wholehearted American enthusiasm, one did have to wonder where on earth everyone was. If they didn't leave soon, they would miss the initial lighting, which was reportedly quite a spectacular moment.

At the very least, she expected Dante to arrive at the appointed time. It was difficult to continue to think of him as Mr. Montague even if she was not entirely ready to address him aloud by his first name. It would give the man all sorts of ideas she was not prepared to give him. At least not yet. Regardless, she could forgive him even if he decided to forgo the evening altogether. The poor man had had a rough go of it on their crossing of the channel. The faintest tinge of green had continued to color his complexion on the train from Calais and he'd been remarkably quiet, as well. No doubt if one was struck by mal de mer, the rocking motion of a train probably did not ease one's discomfort. It was impossible not to feel sorry for him.

Besides, he deserved a certain measure of lenience. If Dante Montague was truly trying to earn her friendship, he was going about it in a clever way. He could have made more of an issue over the silly problem with the map. And really, how absurd was it that one could get to the age of thirty and never have had to study a map before? At least a map that wasn't in the pages of a dreadfully dull book of geography or used to illustrate the history of some long-ago conflict, and she'd avoided those whenever possible. No, the man had simply pointed out her error, straightened the map and taken his leave, requiring no explanation from her whatsoever. It was rather gallant of him really, especially as she had no explanation that didn't sound completely incompetent.

She spotted him crossing the lobby toward her and adopted a pleasant smile. It wasn't the least bit difficult. After all, he obviously liked her and had admitted he wanted her to like him. It was at once flattering—what woman didn't want a man to put forth some effort to gain her favor—and rather endearing. Still, she was not sure what to make of Dante Montague. She knew nothing about him other than he was good to his sister, which did speak well of him. The fact that he carried a valise implied he was a man of business or the law. Yet his manner was no different than most of the wealthy, spoiled bon vivants in her previous circle of friends. He was a dashing, likable man of some mystery and all the more intriguing for it.

"Lady Bascombe." A broad smile stretched across his face as if he were genuinely pleased to see her, even if they had only parted a mere hour ago. "I cannot believe any woman can manage to look so refreshed after such a short respite."

"How perfectly charming of you to say, Mr. Montague." She returned his smile, surprised to note she was as pleased to see him as he appeared to see her. Obviously the man's campaign was working. "One does try to be swift when one is engaged in travel and hoping to see all there is to see."

One also tries to steal at least a moment in which to regain one's strength. Willie had collapsed on her bed for a quarter hour and then an excellent maid had assisted her with her hair and dress. It had been a long time since she'd had such a busy day. Traveling was far more wearing than she'd expected.

"I doubt that we can possibly see all there is to see in Paris in the four days we've allotted to the city."

"Goodness, no. There is a great deal of interest to see in Paris." Her Baedeker claimed a stay of two to three weeks was barely sufficient to acquire a superficial taste of what Paris had to offer. "But we shall do the best we can with the time we have." Good Lord, she sounded like a governess. She peered around him. "Do you think the others will be joining us soon? I would hate to miss the illumination."

"About that." He gestured at the exit. "We really should be going."

"We cannot leave without the rest of our party. It would be extremely rude and quite unforgivable." What on earth was he thinking? She crossed her arms over her chest. "The group decided going to the illumination was what everyone wished to do tonight. All were in agreement and adamant about it. I must say, it was most democratic."

"The influence of the Americans no doubt."

"It was not my idea nor is it on the schedule. However—" she drew her brows together "—now that it is on the schedule, we should adhere to it."

"What was on the schedule? Before the illumination I mean," he added.

"Nothing." She huffed. "Since it was a long day of travel, it was thought best not to plan anything for tonight."

"Excellent."

"It's not the least bit excellent." It was all she could do to keep from stamping her foot in frustration. It did seem that if the group decided to do something—whether that was taking in a sight or anything else—members of said group should appear when they said they would.

"It's most annoying. Our entire itinerary has been well thought out."

"Still, one might think a certain flexibility—"

"The *schedule*, Mr. Montague, was changed on the trip from Calais due to the wishes of all involved." There was that governess again. Where did she come from? "Your sister and the others agreed that seeing the illumination of Mr. Eiffel's tower would be a grand way to spend the first night of our travels. It was a most passionate discussion, although I believe you might have been napping at the time."

"Probably." He winced. "I do apologize. My last visit to Paris was more than a year ago and I have an awkward tendency to forget how...distressing crossing the channel can be. Sleep usually helps."

"There's nothing to apologize for." She waved off his comment. "One can't help being prone to mal de mer any more than one can help catching a cold in the winter or sneezing at the scent of spring flowers."

"Spring flowers make you sneeze?"

"On occasion," she said absently and glanced at the front desk. "Perhaps I should request a bellman be sent to their rooms to inquire after them. I really don't understand why everyone isn't here yet."

"They aren't here because they aren't coming."

She stared at him. "What do you mean? Why aren't they coming? This was their idea."

"If you will allow me to escort you to a cab—" again he offered his arm "—I will be happy to explain."

"I'm still not sure we should go without them," she said but took his arm nonetheless. "Are you certain they aren't coming?"

"I am." He steered her toward the door. "And they

aren't coming because apparently the original schedule was best."

"Imagine my surprise," she muttered. Very nearly every minute of their trip had been planned by Miss Granville who'd emphasized the importance of abiding by the schedule. She'd said a group of travelers cannot be allowed to wander freely without purpose. It was not the least bit efficient and certainly not the way to see everything said travelers wished to see. The end result of such a trip being dissatisfaction from all participants and the loss of future business. As well as anarchy and the possible end of the world, Willie had suggested. Miss Granville was not amused. "Miss Granville is excellent at schedules."

A well-trained doorman stationed at the entry opened the doors a scant second before them and they stepped out onto the street, another doorman at once hailing a cab.

Willie paused in midstep. Since the earliest days of her childhood, she had considered twilight the most magical part of the day. The fleeting moments when glimpses of fairies could be caught flitting between flowers. It was silly really. She had grown far past such whimsy. Still, that brief interlude between the setting of the sun and the stars filling the sky had always felt special and filled with possibilities. Why, the very air itself was fraught with anticipation and magic.

And she was in Paris. She'd never imagined she would travel to Paris, at least not recently. When she was a girl, of course she had assumed she would someday visit places like Paris and Vienna and Rome. Certainly she'd had any number of friends who'd had grand tours of the capitals of Europe but then they hadn't run off and married dashing handsome rogues at the beginning of their first season. Although one could say George was the very reason why she was here at all. Which was a point in favor of forgiving him but an extremely small point.

Regardless of the circumstances, she was at last in the celebrated capital of France. The center of art and fashion, of ancient edifices and bohemian adventure. The most extraordinary sense of anticipation swept through her and why not? There was much to look forward to. Streetlights were coming on. Carriages would soon be arriving at the Opera House adjoining the hotel. The evening was cool but not unpleasantly so. And there was a shockingly interesting man by her side. Magic was indeed in the air. While she would never have wished George dead, there might well be a great deal to be said in favor of widowhood.

If, of course, one had the finances to support widowhood in the manner to which one was accustomed, no matter how precariously funded that manner had been. She was not after all traveling on her own money at the moment. The Portinari was the means to change that. Or at least give her time to determine what her next step in life should be.

Dante helped her into the cab and gave the driver directions. The man was remarkably fluid in French and Willie caught little more than their destination—Champs de Mars, the promenade that stretched between the Tower and the main buildings of the exposition. The carriage started off.

"If we took another route we could see more of the city," she said without thinking. She had indeed studied her maps.

"However, this is the most direct and most efficient way to the Champs de Mars. I assure you, Lady Bascombe, Paris has changed little since your last visit." He paused. "When were you last here?"

It was a casual offhand question, idle chatter really. He couldn't possibly know this was her first visit. "It always seems forever when one is away from Paris, Mr. Montague. And I disagree. Paris is constantly changing. Even sights that have been here always are new when one hasn't seen them for a while. Why, that's what makes Paris so exciting."

He chuckled. "You have me there."

"Yes, I know." She couldn't help the smug note in her voice, as if she had just made a hard-earned point in an evenly matched game.

Travel documents weren't the only things Willie had studied in the last three weeks. Miss Granville had encouraged her to refresh her memory about the important landmarks of the places they would visit as it had probably been some time since Willie had been to Paris or Monte Carlo or Venice. The American was obviously much more perceptive than she let on. While Willie had assured her it was not necessary, she had nonetheless read and reread all her guidebooks as well as endless Lady Traveler Society pamphlets. After all, Willie was presumed to be a sophisticated, experienced traveler and should know what she was talking about. She had also perused a few articles about the Paris Exposition as they were scheduled to spend an entire day at the world's fair, including an ascension to the top of the Eiffel Tower. It did seem there was a great deal to remember and Willie had never been good at that sort of thing. Studying was to be avoided in school. She was female after all and destined to marry well. Why on earth would she need to know silly facts about things she didn't care about? It had made a great deal of sense at the time. Now, however, she could add it to a growing list of things she would have done differently in the first thirty years of her life.

"Now then, Mr. Montague, please explain," Willie said when they were both settled in their respective seats in the open-top cab. "What did you mean by the original schedule was best?"

"It seems once my sister made herself comfortable in her room, she had no desire to leave. Apparently, Mrs. Henderson and Mrs. Corby agreed. They decided it would be wise to have a quiet meal in their rooms and begin fresh tomorrow."

"I can understand that but your niece as well as Geneva and the twins were quite eager to begin their conquest of Paris." She addressed her words to Dante but couldn't tear her gaze away from the city of Paris rolling by the carriage. It was exactly as she'd seen in pictures but no mere image could do justice to the broad boulevards and iron-accented, pale stone buildings.

"They listened to their mothers." He grinned. "And there might have been bribery involved."

"I see." Relief and freedom washed over her as if a weight had been lifted from her shoulders. Certainly they'd only been traveling for less than a day but it was surprisingly exhausting and she could see where it might possibly be, now and then, a little more difficult than expected. Although, aside from a few minutes when they were transferring from the boat to the train at Calais and Harriet had wandered off, all had gone remarkably well.

"I, however, did not wish to miss the illumination of the tallest structure man has ever built," he said firmly. "We are living in a remarkable age, Lady Bascombe. There is much to be said for progress."

"Indeed there is." She couldn't remember the last time she'd been this excited. It was all she could do to keep from bouncing in her seat. "I suspect it will be most impressive." A fact from one of the articles she'd read conveniently presented itself. "But it's not just lit by electricity, you know."

"No?" His tone was serious but mild amusement shone in his eyes.

She ignored it. "It was entirely beyond the capabilities of, well, anyone to light it completely by means of electricity so most of the lighting is gas." She tried not to smirk with triumph. It wasn't easy.

"Except for the light projectors at the very top of the structure," he said in an offhand manner. "The ones that are colored white, red and blue."

What projectors? Willie couldn't recall anything about colored electric lights. "Oh yes, I was about to mention that."

"It should add an interesting touch to what is already a spectacular accomplishment."

"The tower you mean?"

He nodded. "This year at least it might well be the most recognizable symbol of Paris. I am quite looking forward to seeing it."

"Forgive me for pointing this out, but we've seen it ever since we stepped foot in Paris. One can't help but see it. It looms over the entire city."

"You're right. I simply meant seeing it closer."

"Yes, of course." She summoned a bright smile. "I agree completely. And seeing it illuminated will be that much more impressive."

"But then there are so many well-known sights in Paris." He waved at the passing scenery. If Willie wasn't mistaken, they were currently passing the Place de la Concorde, marked by an Egyptian obelisk in the center. Which meant the Tuileries Garden were on their left. "Which is your favorite, Lady Bascombe?"

"Notre Dame," she said without hesitation. It was the

first thing that popped into her head. In truth, she'd been so busy preparing to take on the role of experienced traveler, she'd paid no attention to those things she would like to see for herself. She couldn't recall if the cathedral was on their schedule or not. Regardless, she would like to see it with her own eyes. And in spite of Miss Granville's dire warnings, schedules could indeed change without mishap or calamity.

"Really?" He studied her curiously. "I wouldn't have thought you to be an enthusiast of gothic architecture. Flying buttresses and gargoyles and the like."

"Come now, Mr. Montague. Who can possibly resist the appeal of a well-executed flying buttress and a terrifying medieval gargoyle?"

"Who indeed?" He grinned. "Still, I assumed you were more progressive in nature. Looking toward the future, new inventions and—"

"It's the story," she blurted then sighed. "About the hunchback."

"Monsieur Hugo's *The Hunchback of Notre-Dame*?"

She nodded. "I read it when I was a girl and to this day I cannot read it without weeping." Even now the oddest lump formed in her throat. "It's the saddest, most wonderful story I've ever read."

"I understand why you think it sad," he said slowly, "and I agree with you. And while it is certainly well written, why do you think it wonderful? There was torture, betrayal, wickedness, persecution of the innocent and evil. I've always thought it was dreadfully dire and gloomy."

"It is that but ultimately it's about love. Undying and endless and true. There is no better story than that."

"No, I suppose not."

"You look surprised, Mr. Montague. Why?"

"I did not expect you to be quite such a—"

"Reader of classic literature?"

"No, I didn't mean—"

"Perhaps you thought I only read novels of adventure or romance?"

"That's not—"

"Those offerings that are considered frivolous and not of serious literary merit?"

"Not at all. I simply meant—"

"I know exactly what you meant, Mr. Montague." Willie wasn't at all sure why she found this so annoying. In truth, she did indeed prefer more *frivolous* reading material. Novels and stories that were, well, fun and enjoyable rather than tedious as she considered so many classic works. "And perhaps we should add a discussion of *The Hunchback*—" which she should probably reread "—to our talk about the *Divine Comedy*—" which she should definitely read "—which I am most looking forward to."

He stared.

"What is it now, Mr. Montague? Did you think a woman *like myself*, a woman you called *legendary*, based on nothing more than rumor and gossip, I might add, would not appreciate things like fine literature? That she wouldn't have a brain in her head? Because I assure you I do."

The cab drew to a halt at the Champs de Mars and he helped her out of the cab.

"Have I stunned you into silence, Mr. Montague?" A distinct touch of remorse stabbed her. Perhaps she was being just the tiniest bit too sensitive. But she'd had to use her mind since George's death and, as she had no one to do it for her, she'd had to come up with a plan for her future survival. And she'd done a decent job of it. Admittedly, no one was more surprised than she to discover she was far more intelligent than anyone, including herself, had ever given her credit for. But then it had never been necessary before.

"My apologies, Lady Bascombe," he said slowly, "if I implied in any way that I thought you were less than brilliant. I assure you, that is not the case. Indeed, the moment we met, I thought to myself, *That is a woman who is as clever as she is lovely.*"

"That's absurd." She scoffed. "I didn't sound the least bit clever when we met."

"And yet I thought you were." He offered his arm. "And I am an excellent judge of character."

She took his arm and sighed. "You're being extraordinarily nice."

"I am extraordinarily nice." He steered her through the crowded plaza. "As you will soon discover."

"Will I?"

He slanted her a distinctly wicked grin. "I intend to see that you do."

"That's sounds vaguely like a challenge. Or a threat."

"It's a promise, Lady Bascombe. I wish to be friends and I intend to do everything I can to make certain you see my finer points no later than Venice."

"I would not be confident of that if I were you."

"Oh, but I am. Confidence goes hand in hand with extraordinarily nice."

"No doubt." Willie glanced around. "I must say, I didn't expect the crowd to be this large." The plaza was packed with people milling and jostling about to get a better view. Although really, as Mr. Eiffel's tower dominated the landscape, one would have to be blind to miss it. "I had thought, since the exposition has been open since spring, people would have had their fill of the illumination."

He chuckled. "I can't imagine anyone ever getting their fill of such a sight. Besides, the exposition isn't scheduled to close until the end of the month."

"But won't they continue to light the tower even after the exposition? It seems to me, I am hearing as much French in the crowd as any other language."

"It's possible, I suppose, but I doubt it. The structures built for world's fairs are never intended to be permanent," he said, guiding her through the crowd. "While the French have been holding fairs like this one every dozen years or so, even here most of these buildings are not built to last. The tower is to be torn down in twenty years." He found a spot where the crush was a bit less and they turned toward the tower.

"It seems like a great deal of effort for a temporary structure."

"But well worth it, I think."

"Perhaps." Her gaze followed the graceful curve of the structure upward until the tower vanished into the deepening twilight. It really was an incredible achievement. It had looked large from a distance but one couldn't get a true feel for its massive size until one was closer. Built of iron, it yet had the delicate look of lace against the setting sun. This triumph of modern engineering was really quite fanciful in its own way. "Rather a pity it can't last forever."

"Few things do." Dante contemplated the structure.

Without warning, the illumination began. Light swept from the four corners of the tower and raced upward, lighting arches and lattice work and climbing toward the heavens. The multiple fountains around the base of the tower erupted in light, as well. The crowd gave a gasp of amazement. Willie clasped her hands together and tried not let her mouth drop open. It was very nearly impossible. She'd never seen anything so spectacular and never imagined she would.

Beside her, Dante blew a long breath. "Well, that is indeed—"

"Magnificent." Willie could barely sigh the word. "And magical. Why, it's positively enchanting."

"Exactly what I was thinking."

Something in Dante's voice caught at her, something delightful and not entirely unexpected. "Are you still speaking of the tower?"

"No, Lady Bascombe, I'm not."

She slanted him a quick glance. "You're staring at me, Mr. Montague. Monsieur Eiffel would be most offended that you are not gazing with rapt interest at his tower."

"Ah, but he hasn't met you." He shook his head. "You're not at all what I expected."

"Preconceived notions are often wrong."

"Apparently." He chuckled. "But I am looking forward to discovering exactly where I was wrong."

"Good luck to you, Mr. Montague," she said in an overly prim manner. Good Lord, the man was flirting with her and she was flirting right back. She hadn't flirted since before George had died and even then flirtation with other men was of no consequence. She'd been married after all. Now...

Why shouldn't she flirt with him if she wished? Why couldn't she do whatever she wanted regarding Mr. Dante Montague? It wasn't as if she had a spotless reputation to maintain, although she'd been exceptionally faithful when George was alive. Now that he was gone, why, widows were allowed a certain amount of discreet freedom. Dante Montague might well be the perfect man to begin her new life of independence with. Besides, she had always been fond of men with dimples.

"You needn't try so hard, Mr. Montague." Willie bit back a smile and kept her gaze on the tower. "It's really not necessary."

"It's not?"

"Not at all." She turned to him and cast him her brightest smile. "I suspect I will like you long before we reach Venice."

CHAPTER SIX

Itinerary.
(Prepared by Miss Charlotte Granville)

Paris.

Day 1. A full day will be spent at the Exposition
Universelle. *Highlights of which will include an
ascension to the top of the Eiffel Tower and the
perusal of the many international exhibits, both
cultural and progressive. The group will spend the
evening in enjoyment of Buffalo Bill's Wild West.*

*Day 2. The morning and afternoon shall be devoted
to appreciation of the extensive collection of mankind's artistic accomplishments at the Louvre Museum. Following a day of artistic enlightenment,
the entire party has been invited to an evening of
music hosted by the American ambassador.*

"WHAT DO YOU think of her?" Dante said to his sister beside him but his gaze remained fixed on Willie. Halfway
down the Louvre's Salon Carré, with a guidebook in one
hand and a voice that carried, she regaled the rest of their
group with details about the paintings covering the walls
and the palace itself. Today, according to her unyielding
schedule, was to be spent at the Louvre.

"Oh, I think she's marvelous, of course, but then I always have," Roz said. "Something about the play of light and perhaps the use of color makes the subject much more palatable. I recall seeing her on my very first trip to Paris. You remember—shortly after Paul and I were married? No, you probably don't. Regardless, I thought she—no—I thought everything here was quite wonderful. Centuries of artistic accomplishment and all that. I did so want Harriet to have the same experience."

Dante's attention snapped to his sister. "What?"

"It's a mother sort of thing. You wouldn't understand." She dismissed him with a curt wave of her hand. "Did you know those girls are calling Harriet *Harry* now?" She shook her head. "I'm not sure if I'm appalled or amused."

"I—"

"Well, of course I knew you would be appalled. Precisely why I have decided not to be. Besides, while I have always thought a female with a man's name to be the tiniest bit shocking, it is, as well, most delightful. It gives a woman a sense of strength and goodness knows, we could all use that. I know you don't agree, Dante, but it is something you should consider. While you do tend to embrace progress in general, you really need to be open to new ideas when it comes to things like this."

"I am—"

"However, to your credit, I have noticed you don't seem quite so stuffy about it when it comes to Lady Bascombe's name."

"Are you deliberately misunderstanding me?" He glared. "I was not talking about—" he gestured at the painting of Salome receiving the head of John the Baptist on a platter on the wall in front of them "—this."

She smiled in an overly sweet manner. "Yes, brother

dear, I know." She moved to the next painting and he
trailed after her.

For once Dante could ignore his sister's determination
to annoy him. After all, she had done him an enormous
favor when she had begged off seeing the illumination
of the Eiffel Tower, allowing him hours in Willie's company without interruption. Not that there was anything
improper in their evening together, which oddly struck
him as something of a shame when they had retired to
their respective rooms. Shocking idea, of course, but
there it was. Even if she was nothing more than his path
to the Portinari, she was still a fascinating creature and
he was a normal man. Those kinds of thoughts were to
be expected.

Yesterday, they had spent most of the day touring the
exposition and joining thousands of other visitors in taking their turn to ascend the tower. In spite of Dante's belief in progress, the elevators that transported them to
the summit shuddered in a most disconcerting way. Still,
it was well worth a few secret moments of terror. Only
slightly more remarkable than the view was the look of
awe in Willie's eyes when she gazed out over the city of
Paris, a view previously reserved only for birds and an-
gels. It was a fanciful thought and, as Dante was not accustomed to fanciful thoughts, he had no idea where it
had come from. Upon their return to earth, most of the
group headed off to see the villages of the world while
Geneva Henderson and Tillie Corby—at least he thought
it was Tillie—accompanied Willie and Dante through
the Gallery of Machines. A remarkable display of progress that could not only be walked through but viewed,
as well, from the perspective of the heavens by moving
overhead walkways. It was indeed an astonishing age
to live in.

Equally astonishing was last evening's visit to Buffalo Bill's Wild West show, in Paris in conjunction with the exposition but located a short carriage ride away near the Bois de Boulogne. Dante hadn't seen the show two years ago when it was in London and frankly had had no desire to see it at the time. Everyone else in London—including the queen herself—had flocked to it. But the Americans in their group, as well as his sister and niece, were eager to attend. And by God, they were right. By the end of the program he was ready to sit a Western saddle and learn how to lasso. Not that he ever would, of course, but it was an intriguing idea. They were all captivated by the trick riding and the Indian attack but most of all by the female sharpshooter, Annie Oakley. The gleam in the eyes of the young women in their company—and more than one of the mothers—declared they too had momentary dreams of Wild West adventure.

"Well?" he said.

"Well what?"

"What do you think of her?"

"I like her. She's very easy to like." Roz leaned over the brass railing to closer study a sadly washed-out work by Reni. "She strikes me as being at once independent and yet a bit lonely. To be expected, I suppose. She hasn't said it directly but I have the distinct impression her friends—or those she considered her friends—haven't been especially welcoming since her husband's death."

He nodded. "I think you're right."

"Which means she very much needs a friend." She glanced at him then returned her attention to the painting. "And how goes your attempt to fill that role?"

"Quite well," he said with a confidence he didn't entirely feel. He was no longer sure his course of action was correct, an uncomfortable realization for a man who rarely saw the need to question his own decisions. Regardless, his campaign did seem to be working. Why, Willie had even begun calling him by his first name. Which was a success of sorts but did put his efforts in an awkward light.

He had always considered himself an honorable sort and nothing he had done thus far was truly dishonorable. Certainly his initial reasons for cultivating her friendship remained and he had always intended that friendship to be genuine. It would be of no benefit otherwise. There was nothing the least bit deceitful about that. A voice in the back of his head—no doubt an overly active conscience—questioned exactly who he was trying to convince. He ignored it.

"If one didn't know better, one would think you were trying to be more than her friend."

"Rubbish."

"Not at all." She shook her head in dismay at his obvious idiocy. "Flirtation, my dear Dante, is not the best course if all you desire is friendship."

"I am and always have been a perfect gentleman, especially where ladies are concerned," he said in a lofty manner.

"Interesting that you choose not to deny it."

He shrugged. "There is nothing to deny."

Especially as his sister was right. He and Willie were engaged in a definite flirtation. He wasn't at all sure how it had happened. Oh, he had certainly flirted with women in the past but even with Juliet, a woman he considered to have a great deal of potential for a wife, his behavior was never less than proper. Of course—as his sister would attest—he could indeed be charming when he chose to be, although he usually considered such efforts rather silly and certainly not worth the time.

In that perhaps he was mistaken.

Flirting with Willie was oddly natural and effortless. He'd never imagined flirtation with a woman who was every bit as intelligent as she was lovely would be both enjoyable and shockingly addictive. Willie Bascombe brought something out in him he never knew existed. Flirtation with her was like a game of chess or a subtle kind of warfare. Engaging and exciting and irresistible. One never knew where the next move would lead. First and foremost, of course, he wanted the Portinari. Beyond that he had no idea what he wanted. For the first time in a long time, if ever, he didn't know what might happen next. At the moment, life struck him as an unexpected adventure. It was a disturbing and strangely delightful thought.

It had struck him, as well, on more than one occasion, how remarkable it would be to kiss her—to drag her into his arms and kiss her quite thoroughly on the top viewing platform of the Eiffel Tower. Or in the shadow of the giant incandescent lamp at the Gallery of Machines. Or behind the corrals at the Wild West show. It was an absurd thought. Not at all anything he would ever do. He was not a man of impulse nor had he ever so much as considered kissing a woman who had not invited a kiss before. That would be extremely improper. Worse, it would complicate his ultimate purpose. He really needed to ignore such thoughts. And yet he could not get the idea out of his head. Even here, amid the artistic genius of the ages, the idea of pushing her back against the wall between a Titian and a Raphael and pressing his lips to hers...

Willie caught their attention and waved to them to join the rest of the group.

Dante drew a steadying breath. "Aren't you going to

give me any advice? You always insist on giving me advice for this sort of thing."

"What sort of thing, Dante?" she asked in an all-too-innocent manner as they started toward the others.

"I don't know," he said sharply.

"Yes, well, that is a bit of a problem. I would never presume to give you advice on something that was as yet undefined."

He snorted. "You've never let that stop you before."

"Perhaps but you've never taken my advice before." She cast him an assessing glance. "Nor have you ever asked for it."

His jaw tightened. "Today, I am asking."

"And today I have no advice to give."

"You always—"

"Very well." She halted in midstep and met his gaze firmly. "You've never been the least bit indecisive about anything. Nor have you ever considered that you might possibly be wrong."

"That's scarcely advice."

"I'm getting to it. You, brother dear, need to decide what is more important to you. The lady or the painting."

"The painting, of course," he said without hesitation.

She studied him for a moment then nodded. "Very well."

He frowned. "What does that mean?"

"It means a great number of things. One of which is that, as I said, I like Lady Bascombe. I like her a great deal, far more than I expected to. And while my daughter and I are a part of your little plot to be with her in Venice when she reclaims her painting—"

"*Our* painting."

"I shall not in any way assist you in your ill-conceived

plan to become her friend. Or whatever else you now have in mind."

He gasped. "I have nothing else in mind."

"You can lie to yourself all you wish, Dante, but you have never been particularly good at lying to me. You are entirely too honest. Which in the past has served you well."

"I am not lying."

"Regardless, it's no longer my concern. I am washing my hands of all of it. From here on, I am only interested in enjoying this trip you have so generously provided. No more, no less." She turned and started toward the rest of the group then swiveled back. "Oh, and you might want to check your letter of credit. According to the schedule, we are to spend the morning tomorrow exploring the shops of Paris. We shall visit Cartier's—I think Paul would very much appreciate a new watch and I wouldn't mind a discreet bauble for myself—Guerlain for perfume and perhaps a new traveling trunk from Louis Vuitton. But the rest of the day is devoted to appointments at the House of Worth, which Miss Granville arranged for all of us. Both Mrs. Henderson and Mrs. Corby plan on ordering entirely new wardrobes for themselves and their daughters. And while neither Harry nor I need new wardrobes, I should hate to let this unexpected opportunity escape. Especially as you are financing everything."

"I did not intend—"

"*Everything*, Dante." She smirked and headed toward the others.

"And her name is Harriet!"

Roz fluttered her fingers at him but didn't so much as glance over her shoulder. His sister was and always had been infuriating. Even when she might possibly be right.

He paused in front of da Vinci's masterpiece, the *Mona*

Lisa, a portrait of Lisa Gherardini—*la Joconde* as she was popularly known. He'd been in Paris any number of times for his own business interests or representing Montague House. And on every trip, he made the time to wander through the halls of the Louvre and always stopped to admire da Vinci's work. Today, he scarcely saw her.

What on earth had happened to him? He was a rational, sensible sort. It made no sense whatsoever that after a mere handful of days in a lady's presence, gazing into the endless blue of her eyes, breathing in the intoxicating faint floral scent she wore, discovering the way a tiny furrow formed between her brows when she was annoyed, hearing her laugh echo through the halls of museums and galleries, he would have such thoughts. Desires if you will. One would think he was besotted with her. If one didn't know better, of course. If one hadn't been somewhat besotted with the wrong woman in the past and hadn't learned one's lesson. And Willie Bascombe was most definitely wrong. Furthermore, she was not why he was here. He had to keep that in mind, although it was becoming more and more difficult.

"You're lagging, Mr. Montague," Willie said, stepping up beside him. "The others have already gone into next gallery."

He glanced at her. "Last night you called me Dante."

"Last night I feared I might be swept away by a frenzy of marauding Americans." Her eyes twinkled with amusement.

"That would be a very great shame."

"Why, Mr. Montague, you do say the most charming things. However…" Resolve set her chin. "We really shouldn't dally."

"On the contrary, Lady Bascombe, the enjoyment of great art cannot be hurried."

"There is a lot to see and we shall scarcely see even a small portion of it. There are more than two thousand works in the picture galleries of the Louvre, which encompass a total length of five furlongs."

He bit back a smile. "According to your Baedekers."

"Page one hundred and eleven." She paused. "It is an excellent guidebook."

"No doubt. But surely you don't need a guidebook for the Louvre? You've been here before, haven't you?"

"I've never had the time," she said in an offhand manner. "Paris is so filled with...with other sights." The slightest touch of panic shone in her eyes.

The oddest thought struck him and he studied her curiously. "You've never been to Paris at all, have you?"

She scoffed. "Everyone has been to Paris."

He raised a skeptical brow.

"No, I haven't." She glared. "There now, are you happy?"

"I'm surprised. I assumed you were an experienced traveler."

"And I thought you had thoroughly checked into my background."

"Apparently, not thoroughly enough." He grinned. "Aside from Paris, have you ever been anywhere on our tour?"

She hesitated then shook her head with a resigned look of surrender.

"That seems to have eluded my inquiries. It was a question I never thought to ask. Quite frankly, it wasn't something I so much as suspected."

"Then I am doing an excellent job." A smug smile curved her lips.

"Well, you do have a schedule."

"Indeed I do. One that needs to be adhered to." A firm note rang in her voice.

"Regardless—" he plucked the guidebook from her hand "—I have been to the Louvre a number of times."

Her brows drew together. "You will give that back to me, won't you?"

"I will but not now."

"The others are already out of sight and we—"

"*We*, you and I, will spend a few minutes considering one of the most famous paintings in the world. The others will do without us." He gestured at *La Joconde*. "You've seen pictures of da Vinci's *Mona Lisa*, of course?"

"Yes, I suppose." She rolled her gaze toward the gallery's coved, painted ceiling with its massive skylight.

"Surely you studied art during your school years?"

"I was not a particularly good student. Things like this, art in general—" she waved at the painting "—were not at all interesting to me."

He stared in disbelief. *This* was the woman who claimed ownership of *his* painting?

"You may close your mouth now, Dante." She huffed. "And you needn't look at me as if I were an uneducated lout. I simply found the subject to be dry and boring. Judging from your shocked expression, I assume you no doubt find it fascinating. You're probably quite knowledgeable about all of this."

"*I* was an excellent student. In fact, I studied the history and theory of art extensively as well as methods to prove authenticity. My family has always been extremely supportive of artistic pursuits. My grandfather was a well-known collector." There was no need to keep this from her and it would be interesting to note her reaction. "Upon his death, he decreed that his collection and his house be opened as a museum. I currently serve as its director."

"Do you?" She considered him thoughtfully. "And I

assumed you were in business of some sort. Or you were perhaps a solicitor."

"Why would you think that?"

"You carried a valise with you on the train. The sort men of business tend to have." She shrugged. "Men who do nothing but rely on their family's position and wealth for support rarely carry anything that sensible."

"While I am indeed engaged in business, my position as head of my grandfather's museum is a temporary one as the museum's future is uncertain at the moment." His tone hardened. "I intend to remedy that."

"London is full of museums. Which one is yours?"

"Montague House."

She shook her head. "I've never heard of it."

"Precisely the problem," he said under his breath and turned his attention back to da Vinci's work. "Now then, tell me what you see when you look at this."

"There really is no time for this sort of nonsense—"

"We are making time."

"I am not interested in a lesson on art." She crossed her arms over her chest. "We have a schedule to maintain and—"

"I have always been a firm believer in schedules, Willie. Indeed, much of my life adheres to a schedule."

"Then you understand."

"Under other circumstances perhaps. However, I am on holiday at the moment and I have left my schedules behind."

"I have not." She glared. "Nor am I the type of person who has ever followed a schedule of any sort."

"Ah, that explains it." He shook his head. "The newly converted are always more dedicated than those who have long followed a doctrine."

"I have not come to believe in the sanctity of schedules for the most part. But I will admit, as you have ferreted out my secret and uncovered the distressing truth about my lack of travel experience, I am clinging to the schedule as if it were salvation and I was the worst sort of sinner." She paused. "Which I'm not, of course. Gossip is never nearly as accurate as one might think. And even a colorful reputation may not be as *legendary* as might be imagined."

And wasn't that interesting? "I assure you, Willie, I am a man who makes up his own mind based on his own observances."

"I don't know why I said any of that." She shook her head. "Obviously I am more concerned about the schedule than even I suspected."

"I shall make you a promise. Indulge me in sharing my love of great art for a few minutes and then I will do whatever is necessary to resume your schedule."

"You are a stubborn man, Mr. Montague."

"In that we are evenly matched, Lady Bascombe." He nodded, tried not to grin with triumph, then clasped his hands behind his back and considered the painting. "Once again, please tell me what you see."

"Very well." She heaved a long-suffering sigh. "I see an old painting, somewhat dark, of a rather plain woman with no eyebrows and a slight smile."

"*That's* what you see?"

She gestured at the work. "That's exactly what I see."

"Do you want to know what I see?"

"Not especially but as I have little choice, tell me, Mr. Montague, what do you see?"

"I see a remarkable work a man poured his heart and his talent into for four long years with his brushes and his paint. I see endless effort, long hours of labor and toil. And flirtation."

"Flirtation?" She looked at the painting then back at him. "I don't see so much as a hint of flirtation."

"How do you think he managed that enigmatic expression?" Dante cast her what he hoped was a mysterious smile of his own then continued. "Da Vinci surrounded her with musicians and singers and clowns, simply to keep her amused and content while he labored."

"It was the least he could do if it was going to take him four years," she murmured.

He ignored her. "I see a face so finely wrought it could be a photograph, lit by a soft, ethereal illumination. I see eyes that bewitch and compel and hold the merest suggestion of laughter. I see hands so lovingly crafted one can almost feel the softness of them. I see the world depicted behind her, her world, a lush landscape of rich vineyards and surging rivers and nature as yet untouched. I see light captured so expertly it seems to glow from the painting itself, as if you could hold your hand in front of it and see the light reflected on your palm. And of course, I see her smile, subtle and secret on lips that she holds barely in check. As if da Vinci caught her in the very moment before she would lose all control and laugh aloud with a laugh that would reach into your very soul."

"Do you really see all that?" Willie stared at him.

He nodded and turned to her. "I do."

She glanced at the painting. "I must say, Dante, the picture you paint with words is every bit as impressive as anything hanging on these walls."

"I am not the first to be moved by this work but I do thank you." He chuckled. "Now, look at the painting again and tell me your thoughts."

"All right." She squared her shoulders as if preparing for battle, braced her hands on the brass railing in front of the painting and studied da Vinci's work.

"Well?" he said at last, failing to keep the eagerness from his voice. "What do you see?"

"Well..." She winced. "I see a darkened portrait of a woman with no eyebrows whose hands are either too small for her head or her head is too large for her hands."

Surely she didn't just say that? "That's what you still see?"

"I thought her dress was nice," she said weakly. "For that period of time, of course."

"All these paintings—" he waved in a grand gesture "—you don't appreciate any of them?"

"I'm certain they're worth a great deal." She cast an assessing gaze around the walls. "They are old after all."

"They are priceless!" How could she not understand this? "And not just in monetary value but in what they do to a man's soul. Just look around you. These magnificent works are the very expression of emotion—of love and hate and passion. Art, Willie, is man's soul made manifest."

Her eyes widened. "Are you saying I have no soul because I do not appreciate art?"

"No, of course not."

"It certainly sounded like that."

"That's not what I said."

"That I am a philistine?" Her voice rose. "An uncultured barbarian?"

"Oh, I absolutely did not say that."

"A creature who is too frivolous to appreciate *man's soul made manifest*?"

"There's no need for sarcasm, Willie." He tried to stop himself but the words seemed to have a life of their own. "Your failure to appreciate these extraordinary works is obviously due to your lack of education and not any deficiency on your part. You just said you didn't pay attention during your school days to lessons about art."

"Because I found it dull," she snapped. "And I had no interest in it."

"What does interest you?" he said in a sharper tone than he had intended.

"I have no idea!" Her defiant gaze locked with his. "But at the moment, I find Paris to be extremely interesting."

"Then I would be honored if you would allow me to help you discover the city."

"I'm certain you can be of great help to all of us in that regard. The schedule—"

"Have dinner with me tonight," he said without thinking.

"We are to attend a musical evening at the American ambassador's residence tonight, a gathering of those Americans attending the exposition, I understand, but we are all invited. It was arranged before we left London."

"Beg off."

"Very well," she said without hesitation. "We can discuss the schedule. Your knowledge of Paris will be most beneficial."

"I look forward to it."

"A late supper, after everyone has gone to the ambassador's."

"You would prefer not to let my sister and the others know we are dining together?"

"Exactly." She huffed. "Goodness, Dante. I am not prepared to answer questions when I don't know the answers myself."

"That makes no sense at all."

"Nonetheless, it will have to do." She glanced down

the gallery. "Now, if you would please return my guide-book, we can find the others."

He handed her the guidebook then offered his arm. "They probably enjoyed a respite from your constant readings from Baedekers."

"I know I did." She took his arm and they made their way toward the next gallery. "You may well be extraordinarily nice, Mr. Montague, but you can also be incredibly annoying."

"Thank you, Lady Bascombe."

They walked on in silence. How could she possibly find all this—Raphael and Titian and Correggio and, God help her, *da Vinci*—dull? For this reason alone he needed to rescue the Portinari.

"If there is some work you think particularly worthy of notice," she began in an offhand manner, "you may feel free to mention it to me."

"Everything in this room in worthy of notice." He glanced at her. "You wouldn't mind?"

"As apparently there has been an enormous lack in my education, I would be most receptive to hearing your thoughts about—" she sighed "—all this."

He chuckled. "It's not a punishment, you know. You might well like it."

"I wouldn't wager on that, Dante." She summoned a weak smile. "But I am not completely opposed to the acquisition of knowledge as long as you refrain from being superior about it."

"I would never—"

"A moment ago you came perilously close to it." She shook her head. "I do not like to be thought a fool. But I am hopefully wiser than I once was and can possibly see where, in certain areas, I could use some improvement."

"Very few," he said gallantly but it was the truth. At

least as far as he could see. Oh, it was disconcerting that something as big a part of his life as the enjoyment of art had no appeal for her whatsoever. Not that it mattered really. He might well never see her again after they resolved the matter of the Portinari. He brushed aside the oddly unsettling thought. "No doubt there are any number of things you enjoy that hold no appeal for me whatsoever. In fact, I understand raiding the shops of Paris is on the schedule for tomorrow."

"That's right, it is." She brightened. "I am quite looking forward to watching your sister and the Americans spend money with rapt abandon."

"And you do not intend to spend with rapt abandon?"

"Oh, I think not on this trip." She slanted him a quick glance. "Do you plan to accompany us?"

"I daresay I can find something else to occupy my day."

"Pity really. If done correctly, with enthusiasm and passion—" she smiled in an entirely wicked manner "—shopping too is an art."

CHAPTER SEVEN

"I HAVE NEVER had dinner with a man in a hotel room before," Willie said lightly, glancing around Dante's suite.

Calling it a mere room was a disservice. The suite was elegantly decorated in muted shades of green and gold. Far larger than her accommodations, it had the added benefit of a parlor separated by a closed door from what was probably a bedroom. Her own suite—which was indeed more of a room—had only a separate sitting area in an alcove. But then he was paying for his lodgings whereas she was not.

"I hope you don't mind." He grimaced. "By the time we returned to the hotel, it was too late to reserve a table anywhere of note, except possibly the hotel dining room. At least according to the front desk."

"So it was the hotel's suggestion we eat in your rooms?"

"Well, yes. They assured me both the meal and the service would be above reproach," he added quickly as if he wanted to dispel any suspicions she might have.

A cloth-covered table sat in the middle of the room set with fine crystal, china and silver illuminated by an ornate candelabra. A waiter stood beside the table, doing his best not to be noticed. It was an elegant setting for a meal. Or whatever else Dante might have in mind. A tiny shiver of excitement ran up her spine.

"We could still try for a spot in the dining room if you prefer."

"Not at all," she said with a pleasant smile. "The privacy and convenience here will serve us well."

Caution flickered in his eyes. "It will?"

"Of course. We are to discuss the schedule for the rest of our stay in Paris. And perhaps the itinerary for the next few weeks, as well. Why, there are maps to peruse and guidebooks to consult. It would be terribly awkward in a restaurant." She widened her eyes. "Unless you had something entirely different in mind?"

"No, no. Not at all." He shook his head somewhat more adamantly than necessary. She bit back a smile. "Although, I will admit, I do intend to take this opportunity to know you better."

"Do you?" She wandered around the perimeter of the room, pausing at the open doors leading to a small balcony. She didn't have a balcony either. Behind her, he said something to the waiter in a low tone. A moment later, she heard the door quietly open and close. It was most discreet.

"You should know, I have never before had a lady join me for dinner in my hotel room. Although I do often take meals in my rooms when I travel."

"Why?"

"Convenience, I suppose. My travel is nearly always for business purposes and my meal time is better spent studying documents or figures and preparing for my next meeting."

"My, that does sound efficient."

"Well, I do usually have a schedule." A grin sounded in his voice.

She stepped onto the balcony. A slight chill was in the air—more refreshing than cold really. To be expected, it was October after all. Stars twinkled overhead and Willie gazed out over the lights of Paris. "I thought you already knew all there was to know about me."

He chuckled. "I believe we have established that my inquiry was sadly lacking. I dare not assume anything more about you but I was hoping you liked champagne."

"Goodness, Dante, who doesn't?" She turned toward him. "Champagne is probably my very favorite beverage."

"Then my information was not entirely incorrect." He crossed the room and handed her a glass. "You look exceptionally lovely tonight."

"Thank you." It was the first time she'd worn an evening dress that wasn't black since George's death. Admittedly, she'd had nowhere to wear such a gown since she'd returned to London and a life sadly devoid of social invitations. The dress was the tiniest bit out of date but it had long been a favorite with its off-the-shoulder sleeves, mauve satin bodice and tiers of lace on the overskirt. She'd always felt quite fetching in it and, regardless of whether it was the latest style or not, it worked its magic again tonight. There was nothing like feeling one looked one's best to give one confidence. "It's terribly improper, you know, to be alone with a man in his room. Even in Paris, I suspect."

Dante returned to the table for his own glass. "We won't be alone for long. The waiter will return with our first course in a few minutes."

The tiniest twinge of regret stabbed her. Best to ignore it. "Admittedly, in the past, propriety has not been of great concern to me. Or did you already know that?"

"The tales of your misbehavior are indeed legendary." The oddest wave of heat washed up her face. What on earth was wrong with her? She couldn't remember the last time a man had made her blush.

"I'm not sure *legendary* is accurate although it is flattering in an odd sort of way." She offered him a wry smile. "I suppose if one is going to have a reputation it should at least be interesting."

"Excellent point." He chuckled. "You regret it, then?"

"That's rather futile really, isn't it? What's done is done. There is no going back. And George and I did have a marvelous time."

"There is something to be said for a marvelous time." He joined her on the balcony.

"Perhaps you should tell me exactly what you did learn in your thorough check of my background." She sipped her wine and savored the fresh taste of it and the sparkling feel on her tongue. There was nothing in the world as wonderful as champagne and this was an excellent vintage. And no doubt quite expensive. She'd never paid the least bit of attention to the cost of anything before George died. She did so miss not having to be conscious of every price and every penny. "I assume you paid some sort of investigator and did not simply rely on rumor and gossip?"

He nodded. "I did."

"As we have already discovered one area in which your information was lacking, there might be others, as well. If so, you might wish to request reimbursement."

He laughed. "I might at that."

"You did say you wanted to know me better." She raised her shoulder in a casual shrug. "How can I possibly reveal anything of interest to you unless I know what you already know?"

"Excellent point." He grinned. "You are insatiably curious, aren't you?"

"Apparently, when it comes to this." She thought for a moment. "I will admit to many faults but I don't believe I am overly curious."

"Then you're the first woman I've met who isn't."

"However—" she pinned him with a firm look "—I will confess nothing else nor will I say anything more about my past until you tell me what you know about me."

"Everything?" He took another sip and studied her over the rim of his glass.

"Down to the most insignificant detail."

"Very well." He thought for a moment. "You married Viscount Bascombe at the start of your first season, eloping with him, I believe."

"In one's youth, one never imagines one day looking back on those actions that seemed so exciting at the time and wondering exactly what one was thinking." While she'd like to believe she wouldn't make the same mistake again if given the chance, she couldn't be at all sure of that. George had been exceptionally charming. "Still, as I said, regret is pointless and we did have a good time of it."

"You and he were quite the couple," Dante said in an altogether too nondescript tone. Why, one couldn't tell if the man was disapproving or envious. "Outrageous more than truly scandalous I would say. Lord and Lady Bascombe were notably present at every soiree, every party, every gathering, at least those that were not considered eminently proper and endlessly stuffy. The events that provided the most fodder for rumor and gossip I would say."

"You would be surprised how very many of those there are." She sipped her champagne. "They really are the most enjoyable kind of party."

"No doubt." He considered her for a moment. "Your friends were similar—young couples with more money than responsibility, sons who had not yet come into in-heritances, the occasional free-spirited widow. There are any number of stories about that circle."

"All true I suspect but probably better in the telling and retelling than in the truth of them. Still, a good story always improves with repetition. Go on."

"There's really little else to say." He shrugged. "You're quite lovely and are known to be a clever wit."

"True." She grinned and took another sip. This was certainly outstanding champagne and it had been a very long time since she'd had champagne at all.

"Your husband died a little over two years ago—my condolences."

"Thank you."

"And you've scarcely been seen in public since then, spending much of that time residing away from London."

"Yes, well, I am a widow." The excuse sounded weak even to her. "Is that it, then?"

"I believe so."

"You should have saved your money. All of that is common knowledge. I would have told you everything myself if you'd asked."

"I shall remember that the next time I need to look into someone's past."

"It doesn't seem at all fair though." She studied him curiously. "Regardless of how you came by your infor-mation, you know far more about me than I do about you. I know hardly anything about you."

"I believe I have already told you that my life is an open book." He propped his hip on the balcony railing and studied her. "What do you want to know?"

"I'm not sure where to begin with a book I haven't so much as heard about—good or bad. And I've heard nothing about you whatsoever. Which makes me think your reputation must be exemplary."

"One doesn't like to brag."

She laughed.

"There really is little to tell. Aside from my various business pursuits—successful pursuits I might add—"

"But one doesn't like to brag."

"—I am currently head of my grandfather's museum. I studied art nearly as eagerly as I did finance." He paused. "I've never explained my life before. It does sound rather boring, doesn't it?"

"Not at all. Or at least not yet. I'm assuming there's more."

He winced. "Not substantially more."

"Oh, surely there must be. Some sort of youthful prank or misadventure? An indiscretion perhaps?"

He shook his head. "Nothing comes to mind."

She thought for a moment. "Have you never jumped in a fountain fully clothed? Or worse—not fully clothed?"

"Not that I can recall."

"And I imagine you would recall that. Well then, have you never raced at high speed through Hyde Park in the midst of the afternoon promenade on horseback or— better yet—a penny-farthing?"

He stared in confusion. "A what?"

"A penny-farthing. Surely you've seen one? A bicycle with a high front wheel? They were quite popular a few years ago."

"Yes, of course." He nodded with obvious relief. What did he think a penny-farthing was? One did wonder what was going on in the man's head. "I have seen them but I have never ridden one through Hyde Park or anywhere else. Nor have I raced through the park on horseback. That would be most—"

"Improper?"

"And dangerous," he said firmly.

"Of course it is, Dante. The risk—be it of gossip or physical harm—is part of the adventure. That's precisely the idea."

"As much as I do hate to disappoint you, I've never done anything improper, I've never been embroiled in any kind of scandal and the most dangerous thing I do is slit the pages of a new book with a paper knife." He paused. "Which has never bothered me at all until this very moment."

"Come now, Dante. Surely that isn't everything? You are both charming and handsome. And wealthy. I can't believe that hasn't landed you in some sort of trouble at some point."

"I do apologize. I'm afraid not."

"Your family, then? No scandalous black sheep wandering about?"

He shook his head. "My sister would never permit it."

"No mad relatives hidden in the attic?"

"Fortunately, no."

"How very interesting." She shook her head. "I had an entirely different impression of you when we first met." Indeed, she'd thought he was very much like every other attractive, irresponsible man she'd ever met.

"And what do you think now?"

"I think no one can possibly be this perfect." She narrowed her eyes and studied him.

"Again my apologies." In spite of his words, his eyes twinkled with laughter. "I would imagine my grandfather might have had a few scandalous moments."

"The collector?"

He nodded. "According to family gossip as well as his private journals, the Marquess of Haverstead was quite a rake in his day. The previous marquess, of course, not my uncle. Although Uncle Richard as well as my father might have had a few misadventures in their younger days."

Something struck a chord of recognition. "Your uncle is the Marquess of Haverstead?"

He nodded.

She stared for a moment then gasped. "I have heard of you! You're the nephew of the Marquess of Haverstead!"

"I believe I just said that."

Now she remembered the story. According to gossip, Juliet Pauling had led some poor man around by the nose in an effort to make a duke's son jealous. The duke's heir was a nasty, arrogant sort with thinning hair and an exceptionally large nose. Of course, he was outrageously wealthy and would be a duke one day, which apparently made up for the lack of hair and abundance of nose. At least to Miss Pauling. They deserved each other. Willie had crossed paths with her on more than one occasion and had rarely met a woman quite as merciless in her ambitions. Woe be it to anyone who stood in her way.

Rumor had it that the man she had treated so callously had been quite taken with her. But then it wouldn't have been as good a story if he hadn't. Regardless, no decent man—especially not this man—deserved to be publically humiliated. And he certainly wouldn't wish to be reminded of it. Nor should he be. She said the first thing that popped into her head. "You naughty man. Not that I would blame you."

"What?" He stared in obvious confusion.

"You very nearly left her at the altar, from what I heard." That wasn't at all what she had heard but she didn't have it in her heart to tell Dante the truth. Better to tell him a version where he didn't look quite so used.

He stared. "Do I strike you as the type of man who would do that?"

"Any man is the type of man who would do that."

"I would never—"

"What you strike me as is the type of man who would be smart enough to realize he was making a terrible mistake before he made it."

"Oh." He thought for a moment. "That's quite kind of you but I'm afraid what you heard is not entirely accurate. We were nowhere near the altar, I never asked for her hand, and *she* broke it off with *me*. Of course, she was newly engaged to someone else at the time so it was perhaps for the best."

"Good Lord, you are painfully honest, aren't you?"

"I do try."

"I would say you have the better of the deal." She raised her glass to him. "Miss Pauling is a, oh, a work of…of poorly executed art shall we say."

"She's quite lovely." It was a half-hearted defense at best.

"One cannot fault her appearance." Willie took another sip. The very fact that he was unwilling to say anything bad about the woman who had treated him so callously was a point in his favor. "You really are extraordinarily nice."

He grinned. "I believe I've mentioned that."

"I was right. I do like you."

"I knew you would."

"And I could certainly use a friend at the moment. I seem to be sorely lacking in friends."

"I find that hard to believe."

"I do too as I had thought I had a great number of friends. Apparently, they were more my husband's friends than mine." She shivered.

"My apologies," he said and straightened. "It's far cooler out here than I thought. We should go in."

"Probably but the view is well worth it." She turned away, stepped to the railing and gazed out over the city. "I never imagined I'd be in Paris at all, let alone in a hotel room with a dashing stranger by my side."

"It is impressive." He moved closer behind her. "But you're cold. We really should go inside."

She turned to face him. He was a scant few inches away. Close enough to lean in and kiss her if he so desired. Did he? "Do you intend to seduce me tonight, Mr. Montague?"

He hesitated for no more than a fraction of a second but it was enough. "No, of course not."

"Are you sure?"

"Of course I'm sure." He frowned. "I would certainly know if I had intended seduction or not."

"Then perhaps I am using the wrong word. Rather than *intend* seduction, did you hope for it?"

"I assure you, Willie—" indignation rang in his voice "—seduction tonight has not so much as crossed my mind."

He was lying; she was fairly certain of it. His indignation was entirely too emphatic.

"I'm not sure if I'm relieved or rather disappointed." She cast him a wicked look and moved back into the room.

He closed the balcony doors. "I must admit I prefer disappointment."

"Why?" She wandered toward the table.

"Surely you know the answer to that. You are an intriguing woman, quite lovely and clever. A man would have to be dead not to be entranced by you."

"And are you entranced?"

"Completely and thoroughly captivated."

"You do have a way with words, Dante." She nodded at the table. "You realize this is a remarkably romantic setting."

"Or simply dinner."

"Have you ever been engaged in seduction before?"

"Not really."

She glanced at him. "But you're not without, oh, experience? When it comes to women?"

"Good Lord, Willie." He chuckled. "I'm not sure exactly what you're trying to find out but I can assure you I have been with women before."

"And yet while you admit you'd rather I be disappointed at your lack of intent to seduce me instead of relieved, you have no desire to seduce me?"

"That's not at all what I said," he said firmly. "I said I did not intend to seduce you tonight."

She set her glass down on the table and met his gaze directly. The oddest sense of anticipation and what might well have been desire welled within her. Her heart beat faster. "When do you intend to seduce me?"

"Willie, I—"

She held up her hand to stop him. "In spite of what your investigator might have reported or what might have been said through gossip and innuendo, I have only ever been seduced once. And that was by my husband on our wedding night."

"I see." He joined her and put his glass next to hers.

"Did you think otherwise?"

His gaze slipped from her eyes to her lips and back. "I'm not sure what to think when it comes to you. Or what to believe. And you continue to surprise me."

"Do I?"

He studied her as if deciding exactly what to say. "I

did not expect you to take the hosting of this tour at all seriously. I expected it to be yet another lark of yours."

"You expected me to be frivolous and concerned only with a good time?"

"Yes, I suppose I did."

"Let me ask you this, then." She chose her words with care. "While seduction was not your intention tonight, has it occurred to you?"

"Should I be honest?"

"Only if the answer is yes."

"Then yes." He drew a deep breath. "The thought has occurred to me. More than once."

"How delightful." Without thinking, she leaned close and brushed her lips across his. "It has occurred to me, as well."

A quiet knock sounded at the door.

"That must be dinner." He stepped away quickly—entirely too quickly—and moved to open the door. Her cheeks flushed with heat. What on earth had gotten into her? She'd never been that forward before. She'd certainly never kissed a man who was not her husband on anything other than the cheek before. Perhaps it was best they were interrupted.

The waiter entered pushing a cart with an assortment of dishes covered in silver domes followed by a second server. A few moments later they were seated.

Fortunately, the excellent meal provided a respite from the awkwardness of her impulsive action. The waiters stayed until they were finished, forcing their conversation to be far less personal than it had been before dinner. Nothing untoward, no moments of innuendo, no suggestive banter. They discussed tomorrow's schedule and their itinerary after Paris. It began as polite conversation but as the evening wore on she found their talk, and the man, more and more interesting.

Dante discussed his love of art and his grandfather's collection. His passion was most impressive. She spoke of her grandmother and Lady Plumdale and her time spent in Wales. He told stories of his family—it was exceptionally large. With both parents still living, his sister, of course, and her family, two uncles and a number of assorted cousins.

And if every now and then her gaze drifted to the dimples at the corners of his mouth and she remembered the heat of his lips against hers, well it was perhaps to be expected. She was not at all opposed to a bit of seduction.

When at last they were finished, the waiters cleared everything away and they were once again alone.

"It's late," she said with a reluctant smile. "I should return to my room."

"Allow me to accompany you."

Or you could ask me to stay. To finish what we had no opportunity to begin. She dashed the thought away. Even if the man had thought of seducing her, he was certainly making no effort now to do so. But then she suspected he was the kind of man who thought seduction was a prelude to marriage and she wasn't at all ready for that.

He stood and helped her with her chair. She rose to her feet and stepped toward the door.

"Tonight was most enjoyable," she said. "Thank you for a lovely evening."

"Willie." He took her hand and raised it to his lips, his gaze locked with hers. "I too had an exceptional time."

"Yes, well…" She stared into his brown eyes and ignored the strangest sensation of something warm and quivering in the pit of her stomach. Something she hadn't felt for a very long time, even before George had died. Something rather wonderful. "I do apologize for my—"

"Don't," he said shortly. "You simply took me unawares. I told you that you have captivated me, Lady Bascombe. It was not merely a clever thing to say."

"But it was delightful." She had the most insane desire to swoon into his arms but, in spite of giving in to her earlier impulse to press her lips to his, she would not do so again. Although she would not resist him either.

"I will confess—"

A sharp, insistent rapping sounded at the door.

"Yes?" Surely the door could be ignored.

"I just wanted to—"

The rapping became more of a pounding, demanding and unrelenting.

"Go on," she urged.

He released her hand with a reluctant sigh. "And that, as they say, is that."

"But—" she stared "—you were about to confess something."

"Apparently, it will have to wait." He cast her a rueful smile and opened the door.

"Goodness, Dante, I didn't think you'd ever answer. I feared you were already asleep." Rosalind swept into the room then pulled up short. Her eyes widened. "Oh, Willie, I didn't expect to find you here."

"I was just about to leave." Willie stepped toward the door.

"We had dinner together," Dante said. "I assure you there was nothing the least bit improper."

"I wouldn't expect there to be." Her gaze shifted from her brother to Willie and back. "And even if there had been, it's not my concern. You are both adults and I'm certain you know the meaning of discretion."

Dante frowned. "Rosalind—"

"I really should go." Willie had no desire to be caught in the middle of a dispute between brother and sister. "Obviously you have something of importance to discuss."

"No, no, stay. You might be of help." Rosalind waved off Willie's comment. "But do shut the door. I wouldn't want anyone to overhear us."

Willie glanced at Dante. He nodded and she closed the door.

"Please sit down, both of you." Rosalind gestured at the available seating. Willie sat on the sofa, Dante took a nearby chair. "I am entirely too overwrought to sit." She paced the room.

"Now then, Roz," Dante began in a long-suffering tone. "Why on earth are you here?"

Rosalind swiveled toward her brother. "I saw him, Dante! He's here!"

Willie looked at Dante who seemed every bit as confused as she. "Who is here?"

"That boy." Rosalind fairly spit the words. "Or rather man. Young man really, I suppose."

Dante stared. "What young man?"

"Do you ever listen to anything I say?" Rosalind glared at her brother.

"Frequently," he snapped, "but I have no idea what you are ranting about now!"

"Come now, Dante." Willie cast a sympathetic smile at Rosalind. "It's apparent she's upset. Give her a moment to explain."

"Thank you, Willie. I knew you would understand." Rosalind sank down on the sofa, folded her hands in her lap and drew a calming breath. "I saw him tonight— Bertram Goodwin. He has followed us."

"Who is Bertram Goodwin?" Willie asked.

"A rather disreputable young man Harriet is quite taken with." Dante's brow furrowed. "Where did you see him?"

"At the American ambassador's party. I daresay every American in Paris was there as well as anyone else here for the exposition. There was an enormous crush. I ran into several people I know from London." She turned to Willie. "I have never been to a musical evening that was anywhere near as large. I heard Sarah Bernhardt and several of the performers from the Wild West show were there but I didn't see them."

"Is it possible you were mistaken?" Willie thought it might be best if this question came from her rather than Dante.

"No, I saw him, I tell you." Rosalind pressed her lips together in a forbidding manner. "Tall, quite handsome and confident, dark hair. Looks exactly like his father, who was every bit as disreputable in his day."

"Did you see him with Harriet?" her brother said thoughtfully.

"No, I did not but…" She shook her head. "In that crowd it was impossible to keep an eye on everyone at all times."

"Think for a moment, Roz." Caution edged Dante's voice. "What would the youngest son of an earl be doing at a party given by the American ambassador in Paris?"

"The Americans are quite a gregarious lot. Apparently, they invite everyone." She narrowed her eyes. "No doubt he snuck in, probably encouraged by my daughter."

It was precisely the kind of thing Willie might have done at Harriet's age. "Have you asked Harriet about this?"

"Yes, and she denied it, of course. She was quite convincing but then she's had a great deal of practice in recent years spinning tales to persuade me of something. I wouldn't be at all surprised if she and Goodwin arranged this between the two of them before we left London. That might well be why she decided this trip was not objectionable after all."

"But you're absolutely positive it was Goodwin?" Dante asked. "You had a good look at him?"

"Of course I did," Rosalind said staunchly then hesitated. "Not as good a look perhaps as I would have liked but... I'm certain... I was certain." She thought for a moment then heaved a frustrated sigh. "I don't know. I suppose, it might be possible that I was mistaken."

"Still, it would be wise to keep an eye out for the young man," Dante said firmly. "If it was him, we should keep a close watch on Harriet, as well."

Willie nodded.

"She won't talk to me about him at all because she knows I disapprove." Rosalind caught her breath and looked at Willie. "Perhaps you could talk to her? Find out if Goodwin really is here and convince her what a dreadful mistake he is?"

"Me?" Willie's voice was barely more than a squeak. "Why on earth would she listen to me?"

"Because you were the same age she is now when you ran off and married a dashing scoundrel. And look at how your life has turned out. Why, you're a lesson to be learned." She ticked Willie's failings off on her fingers. "You're barely accepted in polite society. You have a reputation that is questionable at best. You have no family or friends to speak of. Your husband's extramarital activities were well—"

"Roz," Dante said sharply. "That's enough!"

Willie's stomach lurched as if she had just been kicked.

Not that any of what Rosalind said wasn't true. But she'd never heard it listed like that before. It was quite awful.

Rosalind's face paled, she sucked in a hard breath and clapped her hand over her mouth. "My God, Willie, I am so, so sorry. I didn't mean to say any of that. I am just so concerned. Not that that is an excuse but—"

"No need to say more. Your apology is accepted." Willie forced a shaky smile. "Besides, you said nothing that wasn't true."

"Even so—" Dante glared at his sister "—she shouldn't have said it."

A stricken look remained on Rosalind's face. "Can you possibly ever forgive me?"

"Of course." Willie drew a deep breath. "I would be more than happy to help but unfortunately I don't think your daughter would listen to me. I am of an age now where she would consider me no more trustworthy than you or your brother. We are all part of that conspiracy of adults who know nothing about love and happiness and are determined to ruin their lives. At least that's how I remember it."

"You're right." Rosalind shook her head. "I don't know what to do other than watch everything she does."

"And while I don't have a great many friends at the moment—"

Rosalind winced.

"—I did at her age. As I recall we did tend to tell each other everything," Willie said thoughtfully. "Perhaps there is another way to find out if Mr. Goodwin is really in Paris and, if so, what plans Harriet might have."

"Do you think so?" Rosalind's worried gaze searched Willie's.

Willie nodded. "I do."

"It's more than you deserve," Dante said in a hard tone.

Rosalind blanched. "I know and once again I am sorry. I shall make it up to you, I promise."

"I have already forgotten it." Willie shrugged.

"I left Harriet in our rooms and should probably get back before she escapes." Rosalind stood and headed for the door.

"Perhaps if you didn't refer to it as *escape*," Dante said under his breath.

Rosalind whirled about and glared at her brother. "Perhaps if you had children you would understand. I am only trying to protect her. To do what's best for her and her future."

"You can't fault her for that," Willie said quickly. "Nor should you." Maybe if Willie had had a fierce mother determined to protect her and not a wonderful grandmother who barely knew where Willie was or what she was up to most of the time, or if she'd had a father who cared even a tiny bit, her life might be entirely different. No better or no worse, possibly, but certainly different.

"No, of course not," he said with a tired sigh. "I do understand, Roz, I want to protect her, as well. And I shall do everything possible to help."

"Thank you, Dante." She summoned a weak smile. "I didn't doubt it for a moment." Rosalind bid them goodnight and took her leave.

"I should go, as well." Willie smiled and moved to the door.

"But we were in the middle of something. I had more I wished to say."

"Regardless, you were right."

"I was?"

"Without question. Seduction here, now..." She shook her head. "It would have been a dreadful mistake."

"A dreadful mistake?" he said slowly.

"I am trying to forge a new life." The words came without thought but she knew they were true. "I know myself and my own nature and I doubt that I will ever be perfect. Nor will I ever be held up as a model of propriety. But you heard your sister."

"She shouldn't—"

"But she did and what she said was no doubt what everyone else in the world says about me." She paused to pull her thoughts together. "I have done a great deal of reflection since George's death. About our life together and how I carry on from here. The past cannot be changed but the story of the future—my future—is yet to be written."

"Willie, I—"

"And I don't think the right way to start my future is by falling into the bed of the first man I find quite, quite wonderful." She smiled, leaned close and kissed his cheek. "Good evening, Dante. I shall see myself to my room."

She was out the door and closing it behind her before he could protest. She hurried down the corridor to the lift, not pausing for so much as a second until she was safely in her rooms.

Willie was not the same girl who had run off with George Bascombe at the age of eighteen. Nor was she the same woman who thought nothing of impulsive races through the streets. Or staying up past dawn to toast the sunrise. Or spending money and friendships as if tomorrow would never come.

Apparently, this was tomorrow. It was time to truly accept that her life would never be the same again. Her finances were dismal. Her reputation was questionable and her future was uncertain. Any kind of dalliance with Dante—be it for a night or forever—wasn't fair to either of them. Not now anyway.

There was no question that he was the kind of man who would insist on marriage after a seduction. And no matter how very much the idea of joining him in his bed produced the loveliest fluttering feeling deep inside her, she did not wish to be his obligation. Even if, in many ways, he was exactly what she wanted.

Still, if she wanted a man like Dante Montague, a man who was indeed responsible and sensible and an adult, perhaps she truly needed to be an adult herself.

And wasn't that a depressing thought.

CHAPTER EIGHT

Itinerary.

Paris.

Day 3. Spend the morning enjoying the delights to be found in some of the best shops of Paris. For a complete list of shops, see Lady Bascombe.

In the afternoon, the group will adjourn to the House of Worth where appointments have been arranged for all tour members as per the request made at the time of the original booking.

This evening will be spent at the Paris Opera, indulging in enjoyment of the current performance and the appreciation of one of Europe's finest operatic venues.

WILLIE STUDIED THE MODELS gracefully circling the drawing room and tried to appreciate the fine fabrics, current colors and newest styles displayed by the lovely young women. It was surprisingly difficult. Willie had always adored being clad in the latest fashion and, as much as everything here was exquisite to look at, it wasn't quite as much fun when one didn't have the means to purchase anything. Besides, she couldn't keep from dwelling on Rosalind's all too candid comments last night. Silly really as a visit to the House of Worth was not something one did every day.

The Americans, Jane and Marian, were properly impressed as was Rosalind, but apparently if one was a young lady between seventeen and nineteen years of age, one was entirely too sophisticated to reveal one might possibly be awed by elegance and grandeur. Still, the eyes of even Geneva, Harriet and the twins did widen in appreciation when they were greeted at the door of the House of Worth by welcoming young men formally clad in frock coats and then escorted up a red-carpeted grand staircase. Ferns and palms and an assortment of striking and exotic flowers bordered the stairs and created the most interesting sensation that one was ascending into another world altogether. A world where with the right gown, and enough money, one could emerge like a butterfly from a cocoon. Resplendent and ready to conquer whatever one wished.

Unfortunately, they were informed upon their arrival that the great designer himself would not be present for their appointments. However, they were assured Monsieur Worth would personally oversee the production of their orders. The clothing created here just for them would be waiting at their hotels—or house in the case of Rosalind and Harriet—upon their return to London. With more than a thousand seamstresses in the fashion house's employ, it was not an idle promise.

The girls were in dressing rooms undergoing the necessity of endless measurements. Their mothers had already experienced the mild indignity of a stranger assessing one's good points and bad. Worth's patterns were reputed to be so exact, a final fitting was never necessary. Neither Jane nor Marian spoke more than a smattering of French but they knew enough to understand that

the comments of the French fitters were not particularly
flattering. Still, Marian declared it was worth it and Jane
reluctantly agreed. She was not quite as eager to spend
what would surely be a considerable amount, although
Marian did point out ordering new Paris gowns from one
of the most renowned designers in the world was not an
opportunity either of them could afford to waste.

They'd been offered tea and biscuits in an airy, light-
filled drawing room of impressive proportions while
models dressed in Worth's finest presented one gown
after another. Jane had an excellent eye and Willie was
hard-pressed to disagree with her opinions on any of the
fashions displayed. Marian on the other hand, did tend
to like shockingly vibrant colors and an excess of embel-
lishment. Rosalind offered her opinion on occasion but,
with Harriet safely ensconced in a dressing room, this
was the first time all day she hadn't looked at once cautious and determined. She sat beside Willie, dividing her
attention between the models, sketches of a selection of
Worth's evening clothes and the door to Harriet's dressing room. Jane and Marian discussed the respective merits of gloves and fans and other assorted items displayed
in a glass case across the room.

Oddly enough, it wasn't Rosalind's assessment of Willie's status in society or her reputation or even her ac-
knowledgment of George's infidelities—Willie had come
to terms more or less with those years ago—but rather
Rosalind's all too accurate observation about Willie's
lack of friends that upset her. The fact that the friends
she thought she had all vanished with George's death
still puzzled her. Nor was it at all fair. She hadn't done
anything to warrant their abandonment. She certainly
would have stood by them.

"I really don't understand why I don't have any friends," Willie said to herself.

"Goodness, my dear," Rosalind said beside her. "I do."

Willie's started. "I beg your pardon?"

Rosalind cast her a sympathetic look. "You didn't realize you said that aloud, did you?"

"No, I certainly did not."

"When one's mind is occupied elsewhere it's not at all surprising when one's mouth says things one did not expect."

"Yes, I suppose." Still, Willie would prefer not to discuss it.

"It's my fault, I'm afraid." Rosalind grimaced. "All those dreadful things I said last night. Again, you have my apologies."

"You were overwrought." Willie shrugged off the apology. "And unfortunately, I can't deny any of them."

The other woman studied her closely. "You are far nicer than I anticipated."

"I am nice." Willie huffed. "I have always been nice, at least I have always tried to be quite cordial and pleasant. People have always liked me. I can understand men not wishing to be friends with an unencumbered widow but I did have a great number of female friends when I was in school. Admittedly, we all went our separate ways. But the women I've considered friends since my marriage—they should still be my friends."

Rosalind stared at her as if she had suddenly grown another head. "You don't understand the nature of women at all, do you?"

"Of course I do." Willie scoffed. "I am certainly a woman."

"A very naive one. I never would have guessed." Rosalind shook her head.

"Can one have a questionable reputation and barely be accepted into polite society and yet be naive?"

"Apparently." Rosalind's brow furrowed. "Let me see if I can explain." She thought for a moment. "You, Willie Bascombe, are quite lovely."

"Thank you?"

"I do mean it as a compliment. However, it is, as well, a curse." She thought for a moment. "The men in your circle of friends—"

"Former circle of friends."

Rosalind nodded. "Those men are not well-known for their marital fidelity. While wives may pretend not to notice that sort of thing—"

Willie winced.

"—they are usually aware of it. No woman wants another woman around—particularly one who is unattached—who they may see as a rival. Or a threat."

"Of course." Willie blew a long breath. It was painfully obvious and she certainly should have realized it long before now. "I hadn't considered that. I thought because we were friends—"

"They would trust you."

"I would trust them if our positions were reversed."

Rosalind raised a skeptical brow.

"I would." Although given George's inestimable charm and roaming eye… She sighed. "Perhaps I wouldn't."

"Unless you intend on engaging in the type of freespirited life you had before your husband's death, it might well be time to find new friends."

"Probably. As for my previous manner of living…" Willie shook her head. "Losing a husband, being forced to make decisions about matters you scarcely paid any heed to, indeed matters that were taken care of for you, as well as far more reflection than I have ever engaged in, well, I think it does make you accept that not all your decisions were wise. I will never be stern and eminently proper—I don't wish to be—but I have certainly changed, for the better I hope. I have no desire to go backward in my life."

"As long as you don't lose that spirit of adventure you seem to have." Rosalind smiled. "I think that would be a great shame. We could all use more of that in our lives. I know Dante could."

"Could he?"

"Oh my, yes. Dante has always believed in, oh, following the rules if you will. He never does anything that could truly be considered *wrong* in a moral or legal sense, although he is certainly not perfect. Unfortunately, between Grandfather's museum and his business concerns, he has become entirely too proper and stuffy in recent years."

"He's seems neither overly proper nor stuffy to me."

"Well, he is on holiday. And he is making a concerted effort to be amenable and charming." Rosalind's brow furrowed. "Still, he does seem different. I believe my brother might be enjoying himself, far more than he has in a very long time."

"Perhaps travel agrees with him."

"Oh, he travels frequently. I doubt…" She considered Willie thoughtfully. "Perhaps you're right."

"I believe your brother and I have become, well, friends." Although it did seem they were somewhat more than friends. How much more remained to be seen.

"Good. While he has a fair number of acquaintances, I'm not sure how many true friends he has." Her gaze met Willie's directly. "And I too would very much like to be your friend."

"Out of pity? Even to my own ears I sounded rather pathetic."

Rosalind scoffed. "Of course not. I would never offer friendship simply because I felt sorry for someone."

"Are you sure about being friends?" Willie adopted a lighthearted tone. "Why, what will people say?"

"While I have nearly always acted within the confines of proper behavior, I have never let what people might say decide what I do. I would be honored to be your friend."

"As would I," Jane said, sitting down beside her. Willie hadn't noticed when the other women had joined them. "I am sorry, I didn't mean to overhear. It just seems to me that true friends are those you can count on through thick and thin."

Rosalind nodded. "Exactly."

"I don't really have many friends either, at least not current friends," Jane continued. "My husband has worked very hard for his success—we were not born to wealth. It's only been in the last ten years or so that we've benefited from the fruits of his labor. We now live in a neighborhood we never aspired to among people who have never wanted for anything." She lowered her voice in a confidential manner. "They are not overly friendly. They see us as interlopers."

"Women can be beastly creatures," Marian said firmly and settled in a nearby chair. "Believe me, I know. I've never wanted for money and yet friends, true friends, have always been difficult to come by."

"All this—" Jane waved at the opulent surroundings "—is fairly new to me. And a bit overwhelming."

"I never would have suspected." Marian cast the other woman an encouraging smile then turned to Willie. "And didn't we say at the very beginning that we would all be good friends?"

Willie nodded. "We did."

"I know I can be a bit forward and I do talk entirely too much, which I would try to do something about but it seems there is always something interesting to say. And I'm afraid if I don't say it when it comes to mind, I will probably explode or something equally unpleasant—"

Rosalind choked.

"—but I was most sincere. About being friends, that is." Marian pinned her with a firm look. "I meant it. Did you?"

Did she? "Yes," Willie said slowly, although admittedly at the time she hadn't given it a second thought. Now, however... "Yes, Marian, I believe I did."

"Good." Marian beamed with satisfaction. "Then we will all be good friends. Jane, Willie and—" she turned to Rosalind "—Lady Richfield?"

"You're not going to make us cross swords and vow one for all and all for one, are you?" Suspicion edged Rosalind's voice.

Jane laughed.

Marian's eyes widened. "What a wonderful idea. A true vow of friendship. Sisters across the ocean bound together forever by an oath of companionship and camaraderie. Tied to each other until we breathe our last."

"Dear Lord, Marian. We're promising friendship not marriage. Still, it does have a nice ring to it." She grinned. "And my friends call me Rosalind."

It struck Willie that friendship wasn't simply something one declared out of the blue but rather something that grew. And indeed hadn't they all started becoming friends on the first day of their travels? Willie considered the other women thoughtfully. So this was to be her new circle of friends. She suspected she couldn't have done better.

"As we are now all officially friends," Willie began and glanced at Rosalind, "I think Rosalind has something she could use the help of her friends with."

Rosalind hesitated.

"Five pairs of eyes are better than three," Willie said to her.

"You're right, of course." Rosalind straightened her shoulders. "I have something of a dilemma regarding Harriet."

Willie noted Geneva leaving her dressing room and settling in a nearby chair, the ever-present book already in her hands.

"While you explain, I believe I will have a quick chat with Geneva." Willie stood.

Marian frowned. "Is something wrong?"

"Not at all, I simply thought she might be of help with a question I have."

"And perhaps you could take the opportunity to point out to her there is nothing wrong with new clothes and trying to look your very best." Marian heaved a long-suffering sigh. "And please try to get her nose out of that book. Dear Lord, I don't know where she gets it from. Her father is not especially intellectual. All he ever talks about is business."

"I'll do my best." Willie nodded and crossed the room. She adopted a friendly smile and sat down beside the girl. "What are you reading?"

"A Thousand Miles up the Nile," Geneva said without looking up.

"Is it good?"

"Very." Geneva turned a page.

"What's it about?"

"It's about a trip up the Nile."

"I suspected as much," Willie murmured. She wasn't

sure what to say next. Moving from "a trip up the Nile" to "Do you know what Harriet is up to?" was not easy. "You're enjoying it, then?"

"I am," Geneva said absently. "It was written by a woman—Amelia Edwards—and it's fascinating. She's an Egyptologist."

"That does sound fascinating."

"It is." Geneva heaved a long-suffering sigh and closed the book. "Did my mother send you to talk to me? Perhaps about what a wonderful opportunity it is to be able to order new clothes in Paris and how I should be enjoying the experience rather than reading?"

Willie laughed. "No, she didn't."

"Then what do you want?"

"Nothing in particular," Willie said lightly. "I simply wanted to chat."

Geneva considered her coolly. "My mother is more than willing to chat with you. In fact, there is nothing she enjoys more than chatting. It's rare when anyone else can get a word in. Perhaps you've noticed?"

Willie nodded.

"I imagine the other ladies are willing to chat, as well."

"Yes, I suppose they are." Willie paused. "I did have a question for you."

"What is it?"

"May I be perfectly honest?" Willie wasn't sure perfect honesty was the best course but she had no other idea.

Geneva studied her as if she weren't certain anyone over the age of twenty or so could be trusted. "I would prefer honest, so yes."

"You are the oldest of the girls here and as such, I would like to be able to count on you to, oh, keep an eye on the others."

"You want me to spy on them?" Geneva's eyes narrowed.

"No." Willie scoffed. "Nothing of the sort." Although really, when it came down to it, that's exactly what she was asking. Willie drew a deep breath. "In the spirit of honesty, yes, I suppose I do."

"Thank you for being honest." She considered Willie for a moment. "My father says one should never agree to a bargain until one knows exactly what one will get out of it. What will I get out of helping you?"

"You would derive the satisfaction of knowing you helped prevent someone from doing something dreadfully stupid and ruining her life." Willie cringed to herself at the pompous note in her voice. She sounded so dreadfully *adult*.

"So out of the goodness of my heart, then?"

Willie arched a brow. "Do you need another reason?"

"Probably not but it does seem to me that I am in an excellent negotiating position and it would be stupid to pass it up."

"Your father must be proud."

"He probably would be if I wasn't female."

"That, my dear girl, is an eternal problem." Willie shook her head. "My own father has never forgiven me for not being born male. And I have never forgiven him for that."

"Mine is not that bad," Geneva said quickly. "He simply doesn't expect me to be any more than my mother is." She heaved a deep sigh. "But I want to be…*more*."

Willie wasn't sure this was a wise idea. Still, that had never stopped her before. "What do you want me to do?"

"I want you to try to convince my mother of the benefits of having a daughter who does something with her life other than trying to catch a man."

"What exactly do you want to do?" Willie said cautiously. She wasn't entirely sure she wanted to know.

"I want to follow in the footsteps of Amelia Edwards. I want to travel Egypt. I want to find and study ancient artifacts." The girl's eyes fairly glowed with excitement. "I want to be an Egyptologist."

"I see." It would do no good to point out Geneva's mother was just the first of many people she would need to convince in order to follow her dream. "Why would your mother listen to me?"

Geneva stared in obvious disbelief. "Because you're *Lady* Bascombe. She thinks there is nothing more wonderful in life than to have a title in front of your name. It bestows you with special abilities—at least socially. And there is nothing more important to my mother than society. Mother thinks it's a terrible shame that we don't have titles in America. She would like nothing better than to be Lady Henderson. Believe me, she will listen to you."

"I doubt that she will listen to me about this, about your future."

Geneva started to say something but Willie held up her hand to stop her.

"Regardless, I will take every opportunity that presents itself to point out what a shame it would be not to take advantage of a fine mind like yours. But I can make no promises beyond that." She paused. "Personally, I find it most admirable that you have a hope for your life that is not within the bounds of what is expected of a woman, even I suspect in America."

Geneva stared. "Do you really?"

"I do." She nodded. "I wish I had been as determined at your age as you are. Even now I have no idea what I am going to do with the rest of my life. I've never had a passion I wished to pursue." She leaned closer in a confidential manner. "I fear I've always been somewhat shallow and extremely shortsighted."

"Well." Geneva considered her curiously. "It's probably not too late. You're not terribly old."

"Thank you." Willie laughed then sobered. "I wish I had the kind of courage you have, to want to be something more than anyone thinks you can or should be."

"Thank you but if I were truly courageous, I would pursue my passion regardless of my parents' objections. I'm afraid I will never see the pyramids of Egypt. I am destined to be married off to an appropriate, ambitious young man. A man who is more enamored of my father's position than he is of me."

"I find that hard to believe," Willie said staunchly. Geneva was lovely in an understated sort of way. She was a bit taller than Willie, and the girl's light brown hair suited her delicate features and quiet manner. But the spark of intelligence in her brown eyes when she spoke of exploring the ancient wonders of Egypt lit her face and transformed her into something quite remarkable. "You're not interested in marriage, then?"

"I am not interested in marrying the type of man my parents think is suitable. And believe me, my mother parades those through my life with an unrelenting determination."

"I can imagine," Willie murmured.

"While I may never see the sights of Egypt for myself—" the girl's jaw tightened "—I refuse to marry simply to satisfy my parents and certainly never someone my mother chooses. Although I haven't managed to meet anyone I find appealing. Or even tolerable." She heaved a heartfelt sigh.

"One never knows what the future holds, Geneva. When you least expect it, you might cross paths with a man who is exactly the kind of man you want. A man whose interests and passions match your own. A man who might well be perfect for you. Why, you could be attending the same lecture or be at the same ball or walking down the same street." *Or boarding the same train car.* Where on earth had that come from? Willie ignored it.

"I will remember that." Geneva stared. "I had no idea you were so romantic."

"I blame it on Paris." Willie smiled. And perhaps Dante? "My godmother and her friends are all widows of men who were well-known explorers in their day. I believe that included expeditions to Egypt. The ladies still have some influence at the Explorers Club and at the British Museum, as well, I suspect. When we return to London, if you'd like, I could ask for them to arrange an introduction to an Egyptologist."

Geneva's eyes widened. "Would you?"

Willie nodded. "I would."

"I would be eternally grateful but…" She grimaced. "As much as I would like to help you, I can't. The other girls and I have become friends and I'm afraid I cannot tattle on my friends."

"You're right, of course." Willie shook her head. "I should have known better than to ask. I simply thought, as it is in the best interest—"

"I'm not sure I would go to the opera tonight if I were you," Geneva said abruptly.

"We are all supposed to attend the opera tonight," Willie said slowly. What was the girl trying to say? "It is on the schedule."

"Just a suggestion." Geneva shrugged and opened her book, her attention returning to the page. Willie wasn't sure she'd ever been dismissed quite as efficiently.

So much for enlisting the aid of—not the enemy exactly—more like the opposition. Willie had never given much thought to the relationship between mothers and daughters—at least not at this age. Observing the tug-of-war between her newfound friends and their offspring was nothing short of fascinating. While there was obvious affection on both sides, neither side thought the other was particularly intelligent. And both mothers and daughters believed they knew what was best. Willie barely remembered her own mother but had often wondered what her life would have been like if her mother hadn't died. Seeing the bond between these mothers and daughters, in spite of their differences, twisted Willie's heart with the strangest wave of regret for what she had never known.

Still, there was nothing more foolish, and more pointless, than regrets about things that couldn't be changed. In this, as in so many other things in life, there was no going back.

WHO WOULD HAVE imagined a day devoted to shopping would be quite so exhausting? By the time they returned to their hotel, there wasn't one of their group—regardless of age—who wasn't a bit bedraggled, at least in spirit. Everyone agreed a few hours of rest in their respective rooms would serve them well. After all, they were to attend the opera tonight.

Willie wasn't sure exactly what opera they were to see. The title wasn't listed on the schedule—an obvious failure on Miss Granville's part—although the tickets had already been arranged for. She did hope it wasn't one of those dreadfully dreary ones with heroines dying of horrendous, incurable diseases after being abandoned by the man they loved. Opera wasn't Willie's favorite form of entertainment. She preferred shorter, lighter operettas especially those written by Gilbert and Sullivan. Although her true penchant was for comedic plays. She'd much rather laugh at a play than weep at an opera. Still, the opera was on the schedule so the opera it would be.

The younger members of their party begged off, claiming they hated opera and would much prefer to stay in their rooms with a good book. Which made perfect sense for Geneva but Willie had yet to see Tillie, Emma or Harriet—now called Harry apparently—so much as glance at a book. Still, if their mothers weren't concerned, Willie saw no reason she should be. And yet she was.

She couldn't ignore Geneva's suggestion about not going to the opera. The girl was trying to tell her something without coming right out and betraying her friends. The more Willie thought about it, the more convinced she was that the girls were up to something. Something Dante and their mothers would never approve of. Something that was probably a great deal of fun if you were young and adventurous and had no sense of your own vulnerability. Willie remembered those days as if they were yesterday. This was precisely the sort of thing she would have done. Now, however, she was older and hopefully wiser. And onto them. She didn't believe that nonsense about reading for one moment. Willie had absolutely no intention of leaving the younger members of their party to do as they wished, regardless of what that might be.

Willie sent Dante and the others on ahead to the opera, saying she had a bit of a headache and might join them later. She then settled in a chair in the lobby, half-hidden behind a palm with an excellent view of the lifts and the doors to the street.

She didn't have to wait long. Barely a quarter of an hour after the opera was scheduled to begin, the girls appeared dressed for an evening out. Willie rose, skirted the perimeter of the busy lobby and stepped into view directly in front of the doors just as the girls approached.

Emma and Tillie gasped in surprise. Frustration and annoyance crossed Harriet's face and Geneva adopted an appropriate expression of alarm.

"Good evening, ladies," Willie said pleasantly. "I'm so glad you decided to join us at the opera after all."

"We would have been there sooner," Tillie began, "but we were reading."

"Fortunately," Emma continued, "we are far faster readers than we expected and we finished our books." She beamed with questionable pride.

"Your mothers will be pleased to see you." Willie smiled pleasantly. "And since the opera is scarcely a stone's throw from the hotel, we shall be there in time for the second act. Why, you will scarcely have missed anything at all."

The girls exchanged guarded looks. Oh, this was going to be far more difficult than Willie had imagined.

"I am sorry, Lady Bascombe." Harriet raised her chin in a defiant manner. "But we're not going to the opera, any of us."

"No?" Willie kept a pleasant smile on her face.

"No," Harriet said firmly. "We are going to a new music hall in Montmartre that is supposed to be quite a lot of fun."

"It just opened this month," Geneva said. "It's called the Moulin Rouge and we've heard it's quite exciting."

Tillie nodded. "It has a giant elephant in the garden—"

"But the building looks like a windmill," Emma added. "There's nothing like it in New York."

"It does sound delightful." Willie's gaze met Harriet's who was obviously the leader of this band of rebels. "I'm sure your mothers will enjoy it."

Harriet paled but held her ground. "Mother is at the opera."

"Oh, but the opera is right next door. I suspect your mothers won't mind abandoning the performance for something like this. And I can't imagine anything more enjoyable than a music hall that looks like a windmill with a giant elephant in the garden. Can you?" Willie glanced at the other girls. "Any of you?"

For a moment, it was as if they all held their breaths.

"Upon further consideration," Emma said cautiously, "I'm not certain that I have actually finished my book. I believe there might have been another chapter or so that I may have overlooked."

"And I really should write some letters home," Geneva said.

"No need to mention this to our mothers." Tillie uttered a half-hearted laugh. "It would only upset them."

"That they had missed such a lovely time, that is," Emma added quickly. "We would hate to cause them any distress."

"Are you all cowards?" Harriet glared at the others who refused to meet her gaze.

"So it would appear," Geneva said under her breath.

"Come now, I can't go by myself." A pleading note sounded in Harriet's voice."

"Sorry." Emma shrugged. She and her sister edged toward the lifts. "Maybe another time."

Geneva forced an exaggerated yawn. "And I find I am really exhausted. It just struck me," she added weakly. "Sorry." She nodded at the Americans and they all headed toward the lifts.

"How could you?" Harriet glared.

Willie grabbed her elbow and steered her to a more private alcove.

"I thought you of all people would understand. I know all about you and your reputation."

"Most people do," Willie muttered and released Harriet's arm. "It's never been a secret."

"This is exactly the sort of thing you would have done when you were my age!"

"Pity I didn't have the opportunity to go to Paris when I was your age." She pinned Harriet with a hard look. "Because you're right. This is exactly what I would have done."

"And I think—"

"Which is why I cannot allow you to do it. For goodness' sake, Harriet, you have no idea what might happen at this music hall. It doesn't sound like the type of place your mother or your uncle would approve of and, yes, I realize that is part and parcel of its appeal." Willie struggled to keep her voice level when she would have much preferred to yell at the top of her lungs. What was the girl thinking? "You know better than this. No proper young lady goes anywhere by herself. At night! In Paris!"

"I wasn't—"

"Or in the company of other young ladies. You're not chaperoned. You're not accompanied by anyone. You're not—"

"You're not my mother," Harriet said with a smug smile. "You cannot forbid me to do anything."

"No." Willie chose her words with care. "I am not your mother. But you are part of my group of travelers. What happens to this group is my responsibility and I refuse to shirk it. As long as you remain a part of this tour, that includes you."

"Then I shall leave the tour," Harriet said in a lofty manner.

"That can certainly be arranged." Willie adopted an

offhand tone. "You have money, I assume? Traveling on one's own can be quite costly. Or perhaps you plan to ask your mother to support your independent travel?"

Harriet raised her chin in a defiant manner. "Never!"

"Then your uncle Dante perhaps?"

"I don't need Uncle Dante's money, nor do I need my mother's. Ber—" Harriet's eyes widened and her mouth snapped shut.

"Please go on." And didn't that just confirm Rosalind's suspicions? Apparently, the disreputable Mr. Goodwin was indeed in the vicinity. No doubt awaiting Harriet even now in a garden with an elephant. "You were saying?"

Panic shone in Harriet's eyes.

"About funding your continued travel?"

"He's not interested in you, you know," Harriet said abruptly.

"I beg your pardon?"

"Uncle Dante. He's not interested in you."

"How clever of you, Harriet." Willie clapped her hands together in approval. "To change the subject so thoroughly. I'm very impressed."

Harriet shrugged. "Which does not negate the truth of what I said."

"Your uncle and I have become friends," Willie said slowly. "There is nothing more to it than that."

"Friends?" Her brow rose. There was a wicked gleam in Harriet's eyes. "Do you really think so?"

"Yes, I do."

"Perhaps you will think differently when you know why he—"

"Finished with your book, Harriet?" Dante appeared beside his niece, his tone harder than perhaps necessary, although he no doubt understood the situation at once.

"Of course, Uncle," Harriet said with a polite smile. "I had intended to join you at the opera but now I find I am really quite tired. I'll retire now, if that is acceptable," she added in an overly sweet manner.

"Sleep well, dear." Dante's pleasant tone and smile matched the girl's.

"I didn't see you arrive. How much did you hear?" Willie said quietly. She directed her words at him but her gaze stayed on Harriet and would remain so until the girl was safely in the lift.

"Enough, I suspect." Dante too kept his gaze on his niece. "I arrived just as the other girls were fleeing for their lives."

"As well they should. Goodness, Dante, can you imagine such a thing? Going off to a music hall? By themselves? At night? In Paris?"

Harriet stepped into the lift and the doors closed behind her. Willie breathed a sigh of relief. For tonight at least the girl was safe—whether she wanted to be or not.

"That's where they were going?" He shook his head in obvious disbelief. "Harriet, all of them, should know better."

"One would think." She frowned. "Why didn't you say something sooner?"

"I thought it best not to interfere. Besides—" he grinned "—I was rather enjoying it. You were doing an admirable job with Harriet."

"From what she said, or rather what she stopped herself from saying, I believe your sister was right. About Mr. Goodwin being here. I wouldn't be at all surprised if this outing wasn't a ploy to meet him."

Dante's jaw tightened. "Then we shall have to redouble our efforts to keep an eye on my niece."

"I would hate to see her make a mistake that would affect the rest of her life."

"As you did?" he said mildly.

Willie had never admitted, even to herself, that her marriage to George had been a dreadful mistake. But hadn't she begun to realize that long before George's death? "Harriet has a large and loving family from what you've said. I doubt your family would ever abandon her, regardless of what choices she might make. In that respect Harriet and I are nothing alike.

"But I was Harriet's age when I too fell in love with a dashing, disreputable rake who swept me off my feet. In hindsight, I could say it was a mistake but what I know of life now and what I knew then are two entirely different things." She met his gaze firmly. "For good or ill, the decisions I have made in my life are what have brought me to this point. And they cannot be undone." She paused. "They call her Harry, you know. The other girls that is."

"Yes, I know." He rolled his gaze toward the ceiling. "They are Americans so I suppose such nonsense is to be expected. And you have changed the subject."

"Indeed I have." Regardless of her feelings about George and their life together, it struck her as extremely disloyal to speak poorly of him. He was dead and could never make amends, so what was the point? Admitting to Dante, or to anyone, that her marriage was one of many mistakes she had made didn't change anything. Not her past at least. And she was determined to make as few mistakes as possible in the future. "I have the distinct impression that you don't like calling women by men's names, do you?"

"Not especially. I certainly don't like *Harry*. Willie, however, does seem to suit you."

"So Willie is acceptable whereas Harry is not?"

"So it would seem. Besides, I prefer to have only one woman in my life with a man's name."

Her breath caught. "Am I in your life?"

"I hope so." His gaze met hers.

"I'm not entirely sure how to respond to that," she said slowly.

"Have I caught you off guard?"

"Somewhat."

He grinned. "Then you know how it feels."

"To be caught off guard?" She frowned. "What are you talking about?"

He leaned close and spoke quietly into her ear. "Do you intend to seduce me tonight, Mr. Montague?"

"Oh." Good Lord, she was blushing again.

He straightened and smiled—no—smirked. Why, the man was an arrogant beast. She rather liked that. There was something about putting an arrogant beast in his place that sounded like great fun.

"I believe I shall retire for the evening," she said coolly. "We have a full schedule tomorrow."

"And we wouldn't want to disrupt that." He waved her ahead and they started for the lift.

"No indeed." Did he intend to escort her to her room?

They stepped into the elevator and gave the attendant their floor numbers. Surely he would not be so bold as to accompany her without her permission?

The lift stopped at her floor and the attendant opened the gate then stepped aside to allow her to pass.

"Good evening, Mr. Montague," she said and stepped out of the lift, glancing back at him.

"One moment if you please," Dante said to the attendant then joined her in the corridor. "Allow me to escort you to your rooms."

"My room is right there." She gestured to the second door from the lift.

"Very well then."

She held her breath. Would he suggest joining her in her room?

"Good evening, Lady Bascombe." He tipped his hat, nodded and stepped back into the lift. A moment later, the gate closed. It was most dramatic. One would have thought he had planned it.

Willie really wouldn't have minded if he had asked to come in with her. She stepped into her room, closed the door behind her and turned the lock. It certainly didn't need to lead to anything of significance. Why, only last night she had told him she had no intention of falling into the bed of the first man who happened by. Of course, she had also said that he was wonderful. Quite, quite wonderful. And indeed, she sighed, he really was. Unless she was horribly mistaken, it did seem clear that he felt she was rather wonderful herself.

At once, she realized what Dante had started to confess last night. It was so obvious she couldn't believe she hadn't seen it before. When Dante had looked into her past, he had become, well, taken with her. From the moment they'd first met, he'd gone out of his way to be delightful and charming and eminently likable. Hadn't it struck her then that he was trying entirely too hard? It was a bit unsettling and yet extremely flattering. And exciting. As he really was extraordinarily nice.

When Willie had realized the only way to avoid marrying simply for financial support was to reclaim the Portinari and support herself with the proceeds from its sale, it had made perfect sense. Besides, she had no desire to marry again in the foreseeable future. One day perhaps. But then she hadn't planned to meet anyone who made her heart skip and her stomach flutter. And she had never expected Dante Montague.

Perhaps Poppy was right. Perhaps the most wonderful things in life really were those we least expect.

CHAPTER NINE

Itinerary.

Paris.

Day 4: Our final day in Paris will begin with a morning bus tour of the city.
In the afternoon, we will say farewell with visits to those iconic places that have long been recognized as belonging to Paris and Paris alone. We shall tour the Pantheon, the Musée de Cluny and the Cathedral of Notre Dame as well as other notable sights as time allows.

DANTE NEVER WOULD have imagined it but Lady Wilhelmina Bascombe was merciless. She had taken on her role of tour hostess with a passion that was nothing short of terrifying. It seemed she was determined to fit every possible noteworthy sight of Paris into this last day.

The Americans didn't seem to mind. Indeed, they moved with an enthusiastic speed he never would have expected from the fairer sex. His sister too embraced their unrelenting pace through the City of Light with a resolve he hadn't realized she had. Although he suspected Roz thought the faster they went from place to place, the more difficult it would be for Mr. Goodwin to catch up with them.

A private omnibus complete with a knowledgeable tour guide had been hired for the morning. And while the gentleman attempted to show his clients as much of Paris as possible, at an impressive speed, it was the most relaxing part of the day. Thank God for the heavy traffic. Otherwise, memories of Paris might be nothing more than a never ending blur of tree-lined streets and mansard-roofed buildings.

They stopped for a too quick lunch at a fashionable café at the Palais Royal arcade facing the gardens and fountain. A lovely spot for a brief respite although Willie did find it necessary to point out the solar cannon fired by the sun. Information she gleaned from one of her many guidebooks. Admittedly, the miniature cannon was remarkable as it was set off by the sun precisely at noon and regulated the Palais Royal clocks as well as giving passersby an accurate way to adjust their own watches. Dante's watch was already exact.

Unfortunately, in her zeal to detail the endless history of the area, she inadvertently mentioned that it was home to some of the most elegant shops in Paris. A mention which did not go unnoticed. Even Willie was hard-pressed to ignore the pleas of the determined Americans and the Countess of Richfield and so a delay of one hour was granted. Which would have been quite delightful if it had given him the opportunity to spend that hour alone with Willie. It was obvious at once that even though the two American mothers had been told of Goodwin's presence and had promised Roz they too would keep a close watch on Harriet, the lure of shops not yet pillaged was irresistible to any of them, including his sister. Even Willie succumbed to the temptation of luxury for sale and it was left to him to keep an undistracted watch on his niece.

It was most regrettable. He wanted nothing more than

a private word or hour or day with Willie. Dante wasn't sure what had happened between them last night but there had been a moment of complete and utter awareness. When he had realized he did indeed want Willie in his life. And wanted her there far beyond Venice.

Dante wasn't at all used to being confused, to not knowing his own mind. But at some point, the lady had become more important than the painting. Certainly his desire to reclaim the Portinari had not lessened, the need to restore the work to its rightful place had not dimmed, but something had changed. Shifted if you will. Willie Bascombe had apparently worked her way into—what? His heart perhaps? As much as he wanted the Portinari, he might possibly want her more. Which did complicate everything and could well be a disaster in the making. Still, he needn't worry about it until they reached Venice. For now he would simply enjoy her company. Relish the occasional brush of her hand. Savor those moments when her blue eyes met his in a silent communication meant only for them.

After a brief visit to the Pantheon with its massive dome and Corinthian columns to pay homage to those brilliant literary minds laid to rest there—among them Voltaire, Rousseau and Victor Hugo—they stopped to admire the ornate fountains and the red-tinged Obelisk of Luxor at the Place de la Concorde—even though Willie pointed out they had seen everything from the morning bus tour. And they practically raced through the Musée de Cluny's collection of medieval works. It was a travesty really, not to spend more time in admiration of the tapestries and altar pieces and sculptures in alabaster and marble, but time was limited and Willie had a schedule to adhere to. It was late afternoon by the time they reached Notre Dame, on the Île de la Cité, the island where Paris began.

Even Willie was awed by the immensity and beauty of the gothic sanctuary. The vaulted ceiling rose more than a hundred feet above them, supported by some seventy-five round columns. The carved wood and stone reliefs were illuminated faintly by the filtered light from the stained glass of the magnificent rose windows. One couldn't help but wonder at all those—the kings and emperors and commoners—who had through the centuries been baptized or wed or crowned or mourned here in this sacred place. One could almost feel the spirits and the history in the very air itself. In spite of the number of tourists milling about, there was a sense of serenity and peace that belied the turbulent desecration that marked the cathedral's long history. The girls too seemed subdued by the grandeur and the stillness of Notre Dame.

Once they had adjourned to the grand plaza in front of the cathedral, Willie addressed the group. "Now then, time was allocated for us to ascend to the gallery between the towers on the top of the cathedral. This is our last stop before we need to return to the hotel. I for one would very much like to climb to the top." She glanced at her guidebook. "It's a scant three hundred and seventy-eight steps and the view of Paris is reputed to be the best in the city."

"Unless, of course, one counts the new Eiffel Tower." A subtle challenge sounded in Harriet's voice, not the first today. Apparently, challenging Willie was to be Harriet's new purpose in life, in obvious retaliation for Willie spoiling her plans last night. Dante or—better yet—her mother needed to have a firm talk with the girl. "Surely, as it is so much higher than a mere church, the view is much better. And we've already seen that view."

"It's scarcely a mere church," Willie said. "It's considered one of the most noteworthy cathedrals in all of Europe. Why, it took nearly two hundred years to complete. The towers themselves are…" Willie's brow furrowed.

"Approximately six hundred and forty years old," Dante supplied.

Willie threw him an appreciative look and continued. "This is a view the people of Paris and visitors have enjoyed for hundreds of years. We would be remiss if we did not avail ourselves of the opportunity to see this city as so many have done before us."

"I'm not sure I want to climb three hundred and seventy-eight steps," Tillie said in an aside to her sister. "No matter how mere they are or how grand the view."

"We could go to the morgue," Harriet suggested innocently. He knew that look. He had seen it on her mother. "It's nearby."

"A morgue?" Marian gasped. "I don't think that's at all appropriate."

"It's in my guidebook, Mother," Geneva said. "Apparently, bodies of those unknown persons who have perished in the river or wherever are laid on marble slabs cooled by flowing water. They're on display in the clothes they were found in."

Marian turned a horrified look on her daughter, "And you wish to see this?"

"I don't. I'd much rather climb to the top of the towers. But if the others want to go…" Geneva shrugged.

"I do." Excitement rang in Emma's voice. "I think it sounds…educational."

"I want to see it too," Tillie joined in.

"Perhaps we should vote on where we go next?" Harriet glanced at the other girls. "Rule by democracy and all that."

"You can vote on whatever you want," Roz said. "I for one have no desire to see the dead unknowns of Paris."

"Well then—" Harriet shook her head "—it seems to me the only thing to do is—"

"While climbing the towers is on our schedule, if most of you wish to go elsewhere—" Willie shrugged "—we will miss the view, of course, and the bells…"

"I think the only thing to do is divide and conquer," Dante said quickly. It would be a dreadful shame if Willie didn't see the great bell Emmanuel that was Quasimodo's favorite. "We can meet back here in, oh, say an hour."

"Half an hour," Willie said under her breath. "We do have a schedule to keep."

"I think three-quarters of an hour will probably do. If the girls really want to see the morgue, I'll go with them. The rest of you can climb the towers." Jane glanced at Roz. "If you agree."

Roz cast Jane a grateful smile. "Of course."

"We don't need a chaperone." Harriet glared. "We can go by ourselves."

"Nonsense," Jane said firmly. "I can't think of anything more interesting than seeing the unclaimed dead of Paris. Why, the ladies at the literary society back home will be fascinated." She nodded, hooked her elbow through Harriet's and started off. "Come along, girls. We would hate to keep the dead waiting."

"Good Lord, Mother," Emma said under her breath.

"I know I want to be at the next literary society meeting." Tillie snorted.

The twins followed their mother and Harriet while he and the others entered the north door of the cathedral. They proceeded up a stone spiral staircase, rather dim and somewhat tight to his way of thinking. After a brief climb, they paused in a fair-sized, high-ceilinged chamber then resumed their march up yet another set of spiral stairs. Geneva led the group with Willie right on her heels. Dante was next with Marian and Roz trailing behind. If one had a fear of tight spaces, he would not recommend this venture. It might have been an illusion but it did seem the space grew narrower with every step.

"I don't suppose anyone is counting these steps." Marian's voice drifted up to him. "Surely we're almost to the top. How many more steps are there?"

He couldn't hear Roz's response but it wasn't necessary. He could well imagine what his sister thought of the endless climb upward.

At last sunlight appeared ahead. Geneva fairly bounded into the light followed quickly by Willie although how they still had the energy to do so was beyond him. Dante considered himself fairly fit but this climb was a challenge for anyone. Nonetheless, he reached the narrow terrace that stretched between the towers with no more than a slight breathlessness. Fortunately, there was no one else on the walkway as it was perhaps no deeper than ten feet. Geneva and Willie immediately headed for the belfry in the south tower to see the great bell. Dante decided it was best to wait for his sister and a few minutes later Roz and Marian staggered onto the walkway.

He studied the two women with concern. "Are you all right?"

"Fine." Marian waved off his question. "Thank you for asking." She and Roz leaned on each other and sagged against the railing.

"The dead are looking better and better," Roz muttered.

"But the view." Awe rang in Marian's voice.

It was indeed well worth the climb. The city of Paris stretched out beneath them in an endless panorama. It had been magnificent from the Eiffel Tower but here, on top of the ancient cathedral, one felt as if one was seeing Paris through the eyes of all who had come before.

The Seine wound its way through the city, a giant snake trapped by the more than two dozen arched stone bridges connecting one side of the city to the other. The rooftops and buildings blended in muted shades of stone and slate. One could see all the Île de la Cité and the towers of the great and ageless churches of the city: Saint-Severin and Sainte-Chapelle and the Basilica of Saint Clotilde. Here too was the Arc de Triomphe and the Louvre and Palais de Justice and the broad roof of the classically styled Madeleine. And rising in the distance, above all the time-worn monuments of Paris, the Eiffel Tower stood watch over the city. A graceful iron testament to man's progress, silhouetted against the late-afternoon sky. Willie was right. It was a shame it was not intended to stand forever. And all within view—the old and the new—was framed by the chimera. Grotesque, mythical stone creatures—demons and birds and monsters; some half man, half beast; others truly unidentifiable as to species—glowering out over the city. One could also observe at close quarters the intricately executed stonework of the cathedral itself and the gargoyles, jutting with open mouths from the wall beneath them.

Roz stared at a nearby chimera and shuddered. "No wonder they called it the Dark Ages."

"On the contrary, Roz," Dante corrected, "work on the cathedral began in the twelfth century, the middle ages or the medieval period if you prefer."

"I don't care."

He ignored her. "And while the gargoyles are original and designed to serve as drain spouts to keep the ravages of rain water away from the building, the chimera were added only about twenty years ago as part of a restoration effort."

"How...fascinating," Marian murmured.

Roz's brows drew together. "Is it any wonder that you are not my favorite brother?"

He smiled. "I am your only brother."

"Then my point is made," she said sharply. "Do you know everything about everything?"

"Probably." He chuckled.

"Lord save me from intelligent men," she muttered.

"I myself prefer a man who simply thinks he's intelligent," Marian said casually. "My husband is an excellent example. The man might well be brilliant when it comes to business but in all other aspects of life he is..."

Roz stared at the other woman as if she hadn't decided whether to agree or smack her and Dante took the opportunity to slip away. He refused to miss Willie's reaction to Emmanuelle.

Geneva stepped out of the belfry door just as he reached it.

"Was the bell as impressive as expected, Miss Henderson?" He offered the girl a pleasant smile.

"It was a bell, Mr. Montague." She studied him as if his intelligence was in doubt. "A very big bell but a bell nonetheless."

"What were you expecting?"

"I'm not sure," she said thoughtfully. "More, I suppose. Something to recall a tragic love story that never existed other than in fiction."

"You're speaking of *The Hunchback*?"

She nodded.

"It's one of Lady Bascombe's favorites, as well."

"Yes, she told me. She too seemed rather disappointed."

"It is just a bell," he said gently.

"I know and it's just a story. But…" She met his gaze directly. "Don't you ever want things to be, well, *more* than they really are?"

He considered her for a moment. "Yes, I suppose I do."

"I'm just being silly about this." She shrugged.

"Not at all," he said staunchly. "The mark of great literature is that the story stays with us forever. Indeed, we are so moved by it, it's hard to believe it never truly happened."

"What an interesting way to look at it." She frowned thoughtfully. "You may well be right."

He nodded a bow and bit back a smile. "Thank you, Miss Henderson." He started around her toward the belfry.

"Mr. Montague?"

"Yes?"

"Could I have a word with you?" She glanced at her mother and lowered her voice. "Privately?"

"Of course."

Geneva moved to the farthest point of the gallery away from her mother and Roz and lowered her voice. "May I ask you something? About Lady Bascombe?"

"Certainly."

"Is she…" Geneva struggled to find the right words. "Well, is she disreputable?"

He frowned. "Why would you ask that?"

"Harry says she has a scandalous reputation and her mother never would have agreed to come on this trip with her if you hadn't insisted."

"Harriet said that, did she?"

Geneva nodded.

"Did she say anything else?"

"Not directly." Geneva paused, obviously debating exactly how much she wanted to reveal. "But she did imply you were quite taken with Lady Bascombe. Which she said was to be expected as your heart had been broken—"

"My heart was not broken," he said in a sharper tone than he had intended. But really—this again?

"Oh." Geneva started. "And your pride? Harry said it was crushed."

He heaved a frustrated sigh. No, he couldn't leave this up to his sister. He would have to talk to her villainous offspring himself. "I assure you nothing was either broken or crushed."

"Good." She smiled. "You seem very nice. It would be a shame if you were hurt by some vixen."

"While I do appreciate your concern, you may rest easy knowing I was not hurt, although I will admit that while my pride was not crushed it might have been the tiniest bit bruised. Quite honestly, Geneva, when all was said and done, I counted myself most fortunate." He leaned closer and spoke quietly into her ear. "The vixen was not as nice as she had first appeared."

Geneva giggled.

Dante straightened and smiled. "As for Lady Bascombe, she and her late husband did have a rather interesting reputation as a couple. But I can truthfully say I have never heard anything truly scandalous about Lady Bascombe herself."

Geneva breathed a sigh of relief. "I'm so glad. I think she's wonderful."

He nodded and tried not to grin. "As do I."

Geneva studied him curiously then her eyes widened in realization. "Oh, I see."

"What do you see?" he asked cautiously.

"Nothing." She shook her head and pressed her lips

together as if to keep the words from coming out but her eyes sparked with amusement. "Nothing at all."

"Miss Henderson—"

"If you will excuse me, Mr. Montague, I need to join my mother." She peered around him. "It appears Lady Richfield has made her escape and I'm certain my mother has any number of fascinating observations." She grinned. "We would hate for her to accost some unsuspecting tourist."

"I see your point," he murmured but she had already skirted around him to join her mother.

He glanced around the walkway but didn't spot his sister. Entirely possible she had gone into the belfry to see Emmanuelle. Or to hide. Willie stood by the stone railing on the far side of the walkway staring out over the city. He started toward her then stopped. She gazed in the direction of the Eiffel Tower and shaded her eyes against the sun with her hand. The light caught the errant strands of fair hair that had escaped from her overly pert hat and danced around her face in the faint breeze, turning them to threads of gold. It was as if she were a figurehead on a ship, facing the next voyage, heading to parts unknown.

She appeared deep in thought and he was reluctant to disturb her. Her expression was at once serene and determined. What was she thinking? Was she considering what she would do after she retrieved the Portinari? Or contemplating her next step in life? Or perhaps thinking about him? It was a surprisingly delightful idea.

"You're going to have to tell her the truth, you know." His sister's quiet voice sounded behind him. "About the painting, I mean."

"I knew what you meant." He blew a long breath. "I have already come to that conclusion." He hadn't but as soon as he said the words he knew he had no other choice. He turned to face her. "I'm just waiting for the right moment."

Roz arched a skeptical brow. "We leave for Monaco tonight and are there for four nights, then two nights in Genoa, two in Verona and then we are in Venice. That right moment had best come quickly."

"I know."

Roz hesitated, her gaze searching his. "As much as this is none of my concern—"

"Although that has never stopped you before."

She ignored him. "Honesty is almost always best. You know that as well as I. It's obvious you have feelings for this woman. You may wish to tell her that, as well."

It was pointless to deny it. "And what do you suggest I tell her about first?"

"I would never presume to tell you that, my dear brother." Roz shook her head. "Besides, it seems to me that regardless of what path you choose, you run the distinct risk of losing both the painting and the lady."

His jaw tightened. "I am well aware of that."

"As long as you're aware of it." She studied him curiously. "I have never seen you the least bit indecisive before. It's rather disconcerting. As if the sun rose in the west instead of the east."

"My apologies."

"I truly have no idea what you confess first but I do know it will soon be too late."

"I am not indecisive." He scoffed.

"Good. Then you won't mind this at all." She smiled wickedly and called to the others. "Marian? Geneva?" Her smile was now a decided smirk. "My brother needs to have a few words with Willie so I suggest we start down before them." She waved them toward the stairs.

Dante clenched his teeth. "Rosalind."

"We shall see the two of you when we are back on firm earth and the word *plummet* is not constantly repeating in my head," she said over her shoulder.

"You missed the bells, Dante." Willie stepped up beside him. "They were quite impressive. Pity we have no time to see them now. We really should follow the others. We do have a schedule to keep and a train to catch." She paused. "But your sister said you wished to speak with me?"

"I do." This wasn't the moment he would have picked but his sister had made that decision for him. "There's something I need to tell you."

"A confession?" She grinned.

"Well, yes, you could call it a confession."

"I love confessions." She hooked her arm through his and they started toward the stairs. "But there's really no need for it."

"There isn't?" he said slowly.

"Of course not." She cast him a look that made his breath catch. "I know what you're going to say."

"You do?" How on earth did she know?

"I do." She nodded. "It's what you started to say the other night when Rosalind interrupted us."

"It is?" Bloody hell he couldn't remember exactly what he had started to say but it certainly wasn't about the Portinari.

"And there's no need." She shrugged. "I know."

"You do?" If there's one thing he had learned in business it was not to show his hand too soon.

"Of course I do." They reached the stairs and she turned to him, a brilliant smile on her face. "I have a confession to make, as well."

"Do you?"

"I do." She drew a deep breath. "I suspect I am feeling very much the same way about you."

"Oh?" This was not what he expected.

She raised an eyebrow. "Oh?"

Any thoughts of telling her about the painting flew in the wake of her revelation. "I'm not sure what to say."

"Goodness, Dante." She huffed. "When a woman admits she might well share your feelings, she might *care* for you, rather a lot really, against all good sense mind you, the appropriate response is to do something a bit more—"

Before she could finish, he pulled her into his arms and pressed his lips to hers. For a moment she hesitated then her arms wrapped around him and she met his kiss with her own. Her lips were warm and welcoming beneath his and he pulled her tighter against him. Her scent surrounded him, floral and slightly exotic. It was absurd, ridiculous but she tasted of sunlight and Paris and adventures not yet had. And tomorrow.

Dante had no idea what came over him but for the first time in his life he acted without giving his actions a second thought. Obviously he should try it more often.

At last he raised his head and smiled down at her. "Is that a more appropriate response?"

"Why, yes." There was a delightfully breathless note in her voice. "I believe that was most appropriate. Surprising but…" She smiled up at him. "I have always adored surprises. Good ones anyway."

"I've been wanting to do that from the moment we met at Victoria Station." The moment the words left his lips he realized they were true.

"Kissing in public at Victoria Station? Goodness, Dante, it's named for the queen. She would not look fondly on such an indiscretion. It would have been terribly inappropriate and quite scandalous."

"But worth it I think."

"I daresay I would have felt compelled to slap your face."

"Still." He grinned. "Worth it."

She laughed. "We really should go down now."

"Well, we do have a schedule."

"And if we are to keep it, you should probably release me."

"Probably but I rather like being here, with Paris spread out beneath us, rooftops sparkling in the sun and you in my arms." He brushed his lips across hers then reluctantly released her and again they moved toward the stairs.

"Your sister is wrong, you know." She cast him a wicked smile. "I don't think you're the least bit stuffy or overly proper."

He laughed. "Well, I am on holiday."

"There is that," she said lightly and started down the narrow spiral stairs.

The descent was no easier than the climb and Dante was glad Willie was in front of him. He couldn't stop grinning like a man possessed. Or a man in love.

The thought pulled him up short and he nearly tripped on the steps. Was he in love? He'd never been in love before, not really. He'd had a certain affection for Juliet and had indeed considered marriage as she would have been most appropriate but in spite of the claims of his sister and niece, his heart was not the least bit damaged when she ended it. In truth, he'd felt more relieved than anything aside from a bit of humiliation. This was different.

Still, it was absurd to think this was love. Why, he'd scarcely known her any time at all. Admittedly, with every day spent in Willie's company, he liked her more and more. And certainly she lingered in his thoughts even when he wasn't with her. And, yes, kissing her had been rather remarkable and he would like to do it again and again and…

And the idea of not seeing her, not being with her, not having her in his life twisted something deep inside him. Bloody hell, it did indeed feel like love. And she'd said she might well feel the same. But if he wanted to win her heart, he was going to have to tread carefully.

Dante had never questioned his intelligence or his honesty. One could argue that he hadn't been dishonest with her. He had simply failed to mention his true purpose in accompanying her to Venice. Given his feelings now, that was obviously a mistake. An enormous mistake. But one he could certainly rectify. He would simply have to think of some way to confess everything about her—*his*—painting that wouldn't destroy what might very likely be his—*their*—future. Surely he'd learned something about subtle deceit from Juliet.

Regardless, this was entirely different. His heart hadn't been so much as bent when Juliet broke it off.

If he lost Willie, he was fairly certain it would break.

CHAPTER TEN

Itinerary.

Monaco.

After a night on board the Calais-Mediterranée Express, considered one of the most luxurious trains in all of Europe, we arrive in Monte Carlo early in the evening. By virtue of climate, breathtaking scenery and cosmopolitan nature, the Principality of Monaco is known as the gem of the Riviera.

"WELL, THIS IS IT." Willie waved in a broad gesture at the building in front of them and adopted her brightest smile. "Our home for tonight."

Her band of weary travelers studied the ancient stone building with varying expressions of dismay or disgust.

"But it's so…" Emma stared at the structure. "Old."

"And falling down," Tillie added.

"Everything is old in Europe, dear." Jane too could not take her eyes off the building. "And I'm sure, if it's stood this long, it will stand a few more nights."

"As long as one of us is sure," Rosalind said under her breath.

"Come now, Mother." Harriet huffed. "Surely we're not really going to stay here? In a *convent*?"

"It's only two nights," Dante said in a manner intending to reassure and failing. Even so, it wasn't the first time he'd come to Willie's assistance. It was most endearing of him. "We don't have any other choice."

"It is rather picturesque," Geneva offered.

"Isn't it though?" Willie said brightly and vowed to do something very nice for Geneva in the future. "And quite an unexpected adventure."

"I'm not sure *adventure* is the word I'd use." Rosalind glanced at Marian. "Aren't you going to say anything?"

"Apparently," Marian said slowly, "I am at a loss for words."

Geneva snorted, Jane coughed, Emma giggled and at once the entire group broke into tired laughter. Willie breathed a sigh of relief and mentally ripped up the strongly worded telegraph to the Lady Travelers Society she had composed in her head.

The ever-efficient Miss Charlotte Granville had failed. Admittedly, it couldn't be blamed on her entirely. Or at all probably but it was rather nice to believe there might be a chink in the American's perfect armor. When Willie and her charges had arrived at the elegant Hotel de Paris in Monte Carlo, they had been informed they did not have reservations for tonight but for the day after tomorrow. Even though Willie indignantly waved their telegram of confirmation and flaunted her title, the desk clerk did nothing more than apologize in a snippy manner, inform her there were no rooms available and unfortunately all the hotels in Monte Carlo were filled to capacity. It wasn't until Dante stepped up, once again coming to her aid, and discreetly handed the clerk a number of francs that he said a convent just outside the city took in guests and offered to send a messenger to the mother superior in advance of their arrival. He also said the hotel looked forward to welcoming them the day after tomorrow. Willie was fairly certain he smirked as he said it but if they were indeed to have rooms the day after tomorrow, she thought it wise not to say anything that might annoy the man. Although it was difficult to leave their fate in the hands of a condescending desk clerk.

"It really doesn't look that bad." Willie forced an optimistic note to her voice. The convent was similar in design to any number of large country houses in England she could name. The style of stonework was different and the grounds were not entirely tidy but the structure did look sturdy enough and well kept. One could see a large vegetable garden toward the back of the building. Still, as amenable as the house appeared, Willie couldn't dismiss the odd feeling of guilt the house gave her. Ridiculous, of course. At the moment, her conscience was clear. For the most part.

She probably should have followed her initial impulse to go to each and every hotel in Monte Carlo to make certain there were no rooms available. But Jane and Marian had stopped her and pointed out the futility of such a quest. If there were no rooms, there was nothing to be done about it and they simply had to make the best of a difficult situation. It had taken two carriages for passengers and a third for baggage to reach the convent and really a quiet night of serenity and contemplation was not altogether a bad idea. Willie had a great deal to think about.

She and Dante hadn't had a moment alone since yesterday when he had kissed her on the top of Notre Dame. When her toes had curled and her heart had thudded in her chest. He had taken her breath away and she wanted nothing more than, well, *more*. But apparently when one was thirty years of age and has embraced the necessity of using one's mind as well as accepting responsibility for one's life and one's future, one wasn't quite as willing to ignore offhand comments as one once was. And as much as she couldn't banish his kiss from her thoughts neither could she ignore his comment about being on holiday. His sister had said Dante was usually quite proper and even stuffy. And according to the gossip surrounding the Juliet affair—as Willie now thought of it—he had been portrayed as both unquestionably proper and extremely honorable. While he did indeed seem most honorable, there was nothing the least bit stuffy and not at all proper about the way he took her in his arms. Still, even though he continued to prove he was extraordinarily nice, she couldn't ignore the unpleasant idea that perhaps she was nothing more than a passing amorous adventure to be put aside the moment his feet were back on England's shores. The very thought made her stomach clench. Lady Wilhelmina Bascombe may have a past reputation for impulse and fun and frivolity but she had never been—nor would she ever be—any man's holiday plaything. Not bloody likely.

They had left Paris late in the evening and had spent the night in an elegant sleeping car on the Calais-Méditerranée Express, arriving in Monte Carlo by late afternoon. It was now nearly evening and while Willie assumed the accommodations at the convent would not be comparable to the Hotel de Paris, they would certainly be preferable to nothing at all.

The huge wooden door of the convent creaked open and a trio of women clad in black habits and veils with starched white wimples stepped out of the building. Willie had never been a religious sort and knew nothing about Catholics but there did seem to be a distinctly forbidding air about them. As if they could immediately see every one of her past sins and were taking note of them.

Silly, of course, but it was difficult not to be apprehensive. In that she was not alone. Each of the girls subtly edged backward to stand slightly behind their mothers. One really couldn't blame them. Pity, Willie didn't have a mother here to stand behind.

"Bonjour, bonjour, mes amis!" The tallest nun on the right stepped forward, a welcoming smile on her face. Willie's tension eased. "The Sisters of Perpetual Devotion welcome you to our home. I am Sister Celestine," she said in heavily accented English. She nodded at the woman on the left. "This is Sister Laudine." Sister Laudine offered a sweet smile. "And this is the Reverend Mother, Mother Emmanuelle." The nun in the middle, the smallest of the three, nodded, her smile reserved but pleasant enough. Still, Willie did feel as if she had just been judged and found wanting.

She drew a deep breath and stepped forward. "I cannot tell you how grateful we are. I'm not sure what we would have done if not for your hospitality."

The nuns traded glances.

"I do apologize," Sister Celestine said with obvious reluctance. "My cousin, Ferrand, is the desk clerk at the hotel and he assumed—"

"Ferrand Chirac is an idiot," Reverend Mother said in perfect English with a decidedly Yorkshire accent. She was of an indeterminate age—somewhere between forty and infinity. "He always has been, he always will be."

Sister Celestine nodded reluctantly. "One could say that."

"I just did say that." Reverend Mother rolled her gaze toward the sky as if asking for heavenly guidance. "Which of you is Lady Bascombe?"

"I am—" Willie had no idea how to address the mother superior of a convent "—your holiness."

"That's for the pope, dear," Reverend Mother said. "You may address me as Reverend Mother or Mother Emmanuelle, whichever you prefer."

"Thank you," Willie said weakly and resisted the urge to bob a curtsy.

"Our order was formed centuries ago to assist weary travelers on their way to the Holy Land. Today, we offer rooms primarily to those who can least afford to stay elsewhere." Reverend Mother's lips thinned in disapproval. "Usually those who have lost their money in that wretched casino. Unfortunately, the casino is extremely busy, which means at the moment we have no rooms available."

Willie's heart sank. What on earth were they going to do now? "I see."

"Don't look so downhearted, dear. There is always hope. Perhaps if you prayed a bit more, you would know that," Reverend Mother said pointedly.

Willie nodded. "I shall keep that in mind."

The older woman cast her a skeptical look. Apparently, she knew a sinner, reformed or otherwise, when she saw one. "However, there is a villa a short drive from here owned by an English marquess. A good man who has long been our benefactor. As he is rarely at the villa, he has instructed his staff to offer shelter to English travelers when we have requested assistance. The moment we received that idiot's—" Sister Celestine winced "—message, I dispatched a note to the villa." Reverend Mother smiled a distinctly satisfied smile. "The staff is expecting you."

Audible sighs of relief sounded behind Willie. "Thank you, Reverend Mother."

"We're not all English," Marian said staunchly, moving to Willie's side. "My daughters and I are American as is Mrs. Corby and her daughters."

"Are you?" Reverend Mother studied Marian closely. "It can't be helped, I suppose." She returned her attention to Willie. "I suspect you could all use a bite to eat. While our other guests will be provided sustenance later in the evening, we are about to sit down to our evening meal and we would be most pleased if you would join us."

Behind her, Willie heard one of the girls whisper, "But it's barely five o'clock."

Reverend Mother craned her neck and peered around Willie. "Vespers is at sunset and we retire shortly thereafter as we rise at dawn."

"While we are most grateful for the offer," Dante said with a charming smile, "we would hate to inconvenience you."

"But we really are hungry," another girl murmured.

"I would not have offered if it would be an inconvenience. And it is our duty to assist travelers, even those of means." Reverend Mother paused. "Furthermore, it has been some time since I've had the pleasure of dinner conversation in the king's English. I admit, there are times when I miss it."

"Then by all means, Reverend Mother," Dante said gallantly, "we would be honored to join you and the other sisters."

Dinner was excellent if a bit simple with a chicken and vegetable ragout flavored with wine and herbs accompanied by loaves of crusty bread and prayer. The sisters said very little but the Reverend Mother was eager for conversation from home as she was born Emily Waters, a subject of Her Majesty. She did not explain what path had led her to her current position as the mother superior of a convent in Monaco. Nor did anyone have the courage to ask.

Conversation at their end of the long table was lighthearted. The Reverend Mother did seem to be enjoying it a great deal and found the very idea of a lady travelers society intriguing. Although she pointed out women of God had long traveled the world on their own without having to rely on men at all.

"But you have God to protect you," Harriet said, a distinct challenge in her voice. Rosalind sighed quietly. "Most of us have to depend on men."

"God protects us all, Harriet," Rosalind said through clenched teeth.

"Of course he does, Mother." Harriet huffed. "I didn't mean that he doesn't."

"I know what she meant. God protects our eternal souls. In a strictly practical sense, we have to depend on others to protect our physical selves," Geneva said thoughtfully. "Although I, for one, think women have been coddled for far too long. I don't think we need protection or at least we shouldn't. We deserve to be able to make our way in the world if we wish. To study medicine or the law, to have a say in how our governments are run."

"To vote," Jane murmured.

Marian winced. Geneva ignored her and continued. "I admire the independence of the sisters and of all women who do not depend on a man." Geneva turned to the Reverend Mother. "And doesn't God help those who help themselves?"

"Frequently," Reverend Mother said.

Geneva nodded at Willie. "Lady Bascombe, as an example of the modern, independent woman, don't you agree? Women should be able to depend on themselves if they so wish?"

"Uh, well…" Willie had been far too busy trying to determine her next step in life to give any consideration to the place of women in the world. If she'd learned nothing else since George's death, she had learned there was nothing easy about being dependent on one's self. Still, everything Geneva said made a great deal of sense. "Yes, I suppose, of course."

"That is all well and good as long as our decisions are prudent and wise." Rosalind shot a meaningful look at her daughter. "If we don't do stupid things that will haunt us for the rest of our lives. I'm certain Lady Bascombe agrees with that, as well."

"Without question." When on earth did she become the standard-bearer for independent women as well as the symbol of foolish decisions? She could acknowledge her past mistakes; however, independence was not chosen but rather thrust upon her. At once it struck her that in this, as in so many other things in her life, there was no going back.

"As much as I would like to debate any number of things that have just been said, you are our guests and unfortunately we do not have all night. Still…" A wicked gleam showed in Reverend Mother's eyes. "I should like to tell you another story about poor decisions and women putting their faith in men rather than in God."

Sister Celestine's face bore a look of good-natured resignation. Willie dared not look at the rest of her party but did hope they wore polite and interested expressions, even if they weren't.

"Longer ago than anyone can remember, a thousand years or so, this area was threatened by Saracen invaders. There was another convent not far from here. The men of the area promised the abbess they would come to the convent's aid in an attack if the convent bell was rung. As they were no doubt ancestors of Ferrand Chirac, the abbess had her doubts. So she rang the bell in the dead of night on three different occasions to test the men's resolve."

"What happened?" Emma asked, eyes wide.

"The men came every time they heard the bell and they were rather annoyed about it, as men tend to be when inconvenienced in the middle of the night. But the fourth time the bell rang—" Reverend Mother paused in the manner of an expert storyteller. Willie glanced around the table. Everyone, including the sisters who had no doubt heard the story before, was captivated. "No one came."

"And what happened to the nuns?" Tillie didn't look as if she really wanted to hear the answer.

"They were carried away by the Saracens." Again she paused. "Although one version of the story says their noses were cut off, as well."

Harriet immediately touched her nose as if to make certain it was still where it should be. Willie was hard-pressed not to do the same.

"Forgive me for saying so, Reverend Mother," Dante said thoughtfully, "but I'm afraid I don't quite understand the point of the story."

"The point, Mr. Montague, depends on what you wish it to be." She smiled in a sage manner. "It is that kind of story. Don't you think the very best stories are those that teach more than one lesson?"

He smiled slowly. "I've really never thought about it but I daresay I wouldn't want to debate the question with you."

"How very wise of you, Mr. Montague." She studied him for a moment. "I think this particular story can be a lesson as to the consequences of making ill-considered decisions."

Rosalind directed another pointed glance toward Harriet.

"Whether that decision was to trust the men in the first place or to test them over and over. We are all the end result of the decisions we have made, good and bad." She cast Willie a knowing smile.

Willie smiled back as innocently as she could manage. She had nothing of note on her conscience at the moment although perhaps it wasn't entirely clear. There was the tiny matter of planning to abandon her charges in Venice. Still, she hadn't done it yet, so it really shouldn't count as any sort of misdeed.

"Of course, the most obvious one is about the perils of crying wolf. Those who lie, Mr. Montague—" Reverend Mother met Dante's gaze directly "—are rarely believed when they tell the truth."

"Of course," he murmured, looking the tiniest bit uncomfortable. Willie suspected the Reverend Mother had that effect on everyone regardless of whether they were guilty of anything or not.

"Although I prefer to think of the story as an admonishment to put your faith in God and not man." Reverend Mother cast them a smile that was both saintly and final. This particular discussion was obviously at an end.

A scant half an hour later, following a few more minutes of prayer, Reverend Mother, Sister Celestine and several of the other sisters gathered to see them off.

Dante assisted the others into the waiting carriages and Willie turned to the Reverend Mother. "Thank you again, Mother Emmanuelle, for your hospitality. I'm not sure what we would have done without your help."

"And thank you for yours." Reverend Mother leaned close and spoke softly for Willie's ears alone. "Your Mr. Montague gave us a very generous donation."

"Oh, he's not my Mr. Montague," Willie said quickly. Reverend Mother's brow arched upward.

"Not that that is what you meant, of course." She wrinkled her nose. "That he and I...well...we are not..."

"The others are waiting, Lady Bascombe. We shall pray for your safe travels." The older woman favored her with a serene smile. "My Irish grandmother had a blessing that does seem most appropriate at the moment." Her gaze met Willie's. "May you find what you are seeking wherever you may roam."

"I assure you, Reverend Mother, I know exactly what I am seeking and precisely where to find it."

"Perhaps." Reverend Mother studied her for a long moment. "You know what is said about best laid plans going awry?"

"Your Irish grandmother again?"

"No, dear." The older woman looked at her as if she were an idiot. "Robert Burns." She sighed. "I shall say a prayer for you, as well."

"Thank you, Reverend Mother."

She nodded and turned back to the house. Willie might have been mistaken but she could have sworn she heard the nun add, "I have no doubt you will need it."

CHAPTER ELEVEN

WILLIE COULD HONESTLY SAY she had no real idea of where they were.

The convent was just past the outskirts of Monte Carlo—and probably in France as Monaco was so tiny—but it did seem the carriages took them back the way they had come although they could have been going in circles for all she knew. Even though the drive from the convent was brief, the sun had set by the time the group arrived at the villa. It was difficult to get a good look but it did seem most impressive, appearing as much castle as villa. Built of stone and plaster, it had a whimsical look to it yet was still elegant and quite grand. The building perched on the edge of a cliff and the sounds of the surf could be heard in the distance. Willie wouldn't feel the least bit guilty here.

"Now, this," Harriet said with a satisfied nod, "is indeed an adventure."

The other girls murmured their agreement.

They were greeted by a butler, or rather a majordomo, who introduced himself as Monsieur Pennier, and were given rooms in what he called the guest wing. Willie's was spacious and charming, decorated in shades of blue reminiscent of the sea with a high ceiling, glass doors leading to a balcony and a four-poster bed that fairly screamed decadence and comfort. She fully planned to take complete advantage of it.

There was nothing on their schedule for the evening, although Willie suspected Miss Granville had understood that after more than sixteen hours on a train—no matter how luxurious the train or how tempting the lure of Monte Carlo—no one would be interested in much more than a light meal and an excellent night's sleep. And indeed, Marian, Jane and Rosalind thought exactly that. The girls, however, protested that it would be a great shame to waste their first night in Monaco. Regardless, it was dark and as they did not have a carriage at their disposal perhaps it would be best to wait until tomorrow to discover the charms of the city. In spite of protests from the younger members of the group, they did indeed retire early.

Willie doubted she would sleep a wink given her head was filled with debate over Dante's comments about being on holiday as well as the memory of his kiss. Nonetheless, the sound of the surf in the distance coupled with fresh sea air lulled her to sleep in no time.

Shocking what a good night's sleep could do for a woman. It was late morning when Willie awoke refreshed and ready to face whatever the day might bring, including Dante Montague. She stepped onto her balcony, gazed at the sun sparkling on the blue Mediterranean and the most intriguing thought occurred to her. Two could play at his game. While she was not about to be his holiday fling, why couldn't he be hers? She had been a loyal, faithful wife but she was now a widow and could certainly do precisely as she wished. And if she wanted a bit of discreet fun with a man who wanted her, why shouldn't she have it? It was a remarkably freeing idea. This, as with everything else in her life, was now in her own hands. Perhaps she truly was an independent woman after all.

A maid helped her dress and she soon wandered downstairs. Jane and Marian were on the terrace outside the dining room enjoying a breakfast of pastries, cheese, tea and coffee.

"Are the others up yet?" Willie took the chair at the table between them facing the sea and filled a plate with some of the same delightful offerings she had so enjoyed in Paris.

"My girls were just starting to stir when I came down. In spite of their protests last night, they were apparently just as tired as we were." Jane gestured at the pots on the table. "Do you prefer coffee or tea? Monsieur Pennier said the coffee is the marquess's special blend."

"Well then, coffee by all means."

"I never imagined I'd be staying in a house owned by royalty," Marian said with a grin. "A marquess is one step down from a duke, isn't it?"

"Yes, it is." Willie didn't think it necessary to point out the difference between royalty and nobility. Besides, staying in a royal residence would be a much better story for Marian to tell when she returned home.

"We were just discussing why Mrs. Vanderflute arranged for us to spend nearly as long in Monaco as in Paris." Marian frowned. "There doesn't seem to be a great deal of interest here, aside from the casino." A gleam shone in her eyes. "Unless, of course, the casino *was* the appeal. I don't know her very well but perhaps Mrs. Vanderflute has a fondness for the gaming tables."

"More likely," Jane began, "as the casino attracts not only those poor souls Reverend Mother takes in but the cream of European society, as well, she hoped to find a potential husband for her daughter here. Or at least an introduction."

"What an interesting idea," Marian said thoughtfully. "How clever of Mrs. Vanderflute."

"Although," Jane continued, "after months in London and our hectic, somewhat frantic stay in Paris—" she and Marian both aimed accusing looks at Willie who simply smiled and sipped her coffee "—perhaps she thought we could all use a few relaxing days in a tranquil setting." Her gaze strayed to the view of the sea beyond the terrace. "I have to admit, a few days of serenity has a great deal of appeal. And it is beautiful here."

"It's entirely possible Mrs. Vanderflute understood how exhausting travel can be," Willie said. "One does tend to forget that in the excitement of planning a tour."

And indeed, there was nothing actually scheduled for the length of their stay in the tiny principality. In her written instructions for Willie, Miss Granville had noted the few sights—the palace, gardens and cathedral—but they were certainly not enough to occupy their time. There was, of course, the casino, and while Willie expected they would visit the gambling palace, she doubted her group would wish to spend every minute there. Still, one never knew.

"When Pennier said we had a houseful of female guests, I had no idea they would be so lovely," a male voice sounded behind her.

Jane and Marian glanced toward the stranger then stared in barely hidden admiration.

"Oh my," Marian murmured and sat a little straighter.

"Oh my indeed." Jane patted her hair to assure it was in place. Both women adopted their brightest smiles.

Good Lord. Willie would have expected something like this from the girls or even Marian but Willie did think Jane was a more sensible sort. In that apparently she was wrong.

"Welcome to the Riviera, ladies."

Admittedly, even his voice sounded fetching and

vaguely familiar in that arrogant, confident tone used only by men who were dashing and handsome and well aware of their charms. Willie had no more than mild curiosity about the new arrival and resisted the temptation to twist around in her chair for a look.

A moment later, he stepped into view. Willie glanced at him then she too stared.

"Allow me to introduce myself." The tall, dark-haired, broad-shouldered newcomer took Marian's hand and raised it to his lips, gazing into her eyes in the tried and true manner of every rogue Willie had ever met. "I am—"

"Percival St. James," Willie said with a grin. "Marian, Jane, allow me to introduce a very old friend. This is the Marquess of Brookings."

"A marquess? How delightful." Marian sighed, her hand still in his. "Lovely to meet you, my lordship."

Val—as he preferred to be called by his friends—straightened, stared at Willie for a moment then grinned. "Good Lord, Lady Bascombe, you are the last person I expected to see. What on earth are you doing here?"

"I am on holiday with my dear American friends." Certainly if one looked at it in an extremely narrow manner, one might consider this a matter of employment rather than a lark with friends but there was no need for him to know that. "I might ask you the same thing. Don't tell me you're the marquess who owns this villa?"

"Very well, I won't."

What sort of an answer was that? "Do you?"

"I do not. However, my stepfather does." He glanced at the other ladies. "The Marquess of Westvale."

"Another marquess," Marian said under her breath. "Imagine that."

"My dear, Willie." His lordship took her hands and

pulled her to her feet. "You look wonderful." He gazed into her eyes. "I was so sorry to hear of George's passing."

"Yes, I received your note of condolence."

"I would have come in person but I was in Paris at the time."

"I believe you mentioned that in your note. You have a house there, don't you?" If Willie recalled correctly, his mother was French and he did seem to spend a considerable amount of time in Paris.

"I do." He nodded.

The marquess had been among her circle of friends, or rather former friends, but he had taken his responsibilities surprisingly seriously when he had inherited his title some six or seven years ago and had not been quite as prone to frivolity as he had been in the past. Duty will do that to a man. Odd, that she'd never before realized how admirable that was.

Jane coughed pointedly.

"But you haven't met my friends." Willie pulled her hands from his and gestured at Marian. "This is Mrs. Henderson of Chicago."

Marian beamed. "What a pleasure to meet you, your highness."

Val cast a questioning glance at Willie. She bit back a smile, made a mental note to explain proper address to Marian later and nodded toward Jane. "And Mrs. Corby. Jane is from New York."

Jane held out her hand and Val obediently took it and raised it to his lips. "A pleasure to meet you, my lord."

"I assure you—" again he gazed into Jane's eyes in that well-practiced manner he had. Still, it was most effective "—the pleasure is all mine."

"Jane," Jane squeaked and cleared her throat. Apparently, even the most sensible among them was not immune to a handsome face and charming manner. "We are all friends here, so you must call me Jane."

"And I'm Marian," Marian added.

"Excellent, Jane, Marian." He favored the Americans with a devilish smile and Willie wondered that the women didn't fan their faces from the heat of it. Some things never changed. "I can always use more friends."

Willie retook her seat and Val settled into the vacant chair beside her. "I meant to call on you, to offer my sympathy in person."

"What a lovely thought," Willie said pleasantly. "And yet you didn't."

"By the time I returned to London, you had disappeared," he said, his tone vaguely chastising. "No one seemed to know where you had gone."

"No one made the effort to find out." She shrugged as if it didn't matter.

He frowned. "That's rather thoughtless. Although I must say I'm not surprised."

"Regardless, it's water under the bridge now," she said blithely, surprised to note it really was over and done with.

"Still, I regret I wasn't there." Sincerity sounded in his voice. "Difficult times are when we most need friends. And I have always considered us friends."

She studied him curiously. Val had always been friendly enough and wildly flirtatious toward her but in the manner of good fun rather than expecting anything to come of it. Of all the people she had expected to remain her friend after George's death, she would not have put Percival St. James at the top of the list. It was rather nice to realize that in that she was apparently wrong. "Thank you, Val."

"I find nothing more attractive than a man who admits when he's wrong," Jane said to Marian.

Val cast her a grateful look. "Lady Bascombe once gave me a piece of profound advice I have never forgotten."

"Did I?" That certainly didn't sound like her.

"I could use a bit of profound advice." Marian fluttered her lashes. "Won't you share with us?" She glanced at Willie. "Unless Willie minds, of course."

"Not at all." At least she hoped she didn't mind but, as Willie had absolutely no idea what he was talking about, she braced herself.

"It was at a party if I recall correctly. She said—" he turned to Willie and met her gaze directly "—it's pointless to mourn those things we can do nothing about. Those things that were not perhaps meant to be. Far wiser to move on."

"My, that is profound." Willie couldn't remember ever having said such a thing. Still, it was at a party and one says so many things at parties although they were rarely profound. If Val believed she had said it, well, why on earth should she correct him? Besides, she could have said it and it was quite delightful to be thought of as profound.

"Have you?" The serious look in his eyes belied the light tone in his voice. "Moved on that is."

Without warning, Dante popped into her mind. She smiled. "Why, yes, Val, I believe I have."

"A new arrival I see." Rosalind sailed onto the terrace. "You look familiar. Have we met?"

Val stood at once. "I'm not sure so obviously we have not."

Rosalind's brow arched upward. "Because you would

never have forgotten meeting a woman as charming and delightful as myself?"

"Exactly." He grinned.

"Rosalind," Willie began, "allow me to introduce an old friend of mine, the Marquess—"

"Of Brookings." Rosalind's eyes narrowed thoughtfully. "Percival St. James. Your mother was French. Your father, the previous marquess, charming man by the way, married Celia Saunders, a delightful woman who is now married to the Marquess of Westvale."

"This is his villa," Marian said helpfully.

Rosalind continued without pause. "You have a grand house in London, another in Paris and an estate in the country—I forget exactly where."

Jane snorted in disbelief.

"Your stepbrother is heir to the Earl of Danby and recently married a woman no one knows much about although she seems respectable enough." Rosalind drew her brows together. "Related to Lady Heloise Snuggs, I believe, who also recently married. You, however, have yet to wed. Your fortune is substantial, your heritage excellent, your reputation is not quite as scandalous as it once was—"

"It's not?" Val adopted a shocked look Willie didn't believe for a moment. "Are you certain?"

"Quite." A smile tugged at the corners of Rosalind's mouth.

Val shook his head mournfully. "I shall have to do something about that."

Willie choked back a laugh.

"So, my lord, do tell me." Rosalind pinned him with a firm look. "Why aren't you married?"

He considered her cautiously. "Who are you?"

Rosalind extended her hand. "Rosalind, Countess of Richfield."

"That explains it, then." He grinned and took her hand.

"Does it?" Jane said under her breath.

"Apparently." Marian considered Rosalind with renewed respect.

"Lady Richfield is well-known for knowing everything about everyone," Val said.

"How charming of you to say. It's a gift." Rosalind shrugged but appeared pleased.

"And I believe we have met although how I could have forgotten—"

"One meets so many people." She waved off his comment. "We only met in passing so you are forgiven."

"I am eternally grateful." Amusement shone in his eyes.

"But you haven't answered my question." Rosalind sank into Val's chair. "Why aren't you married?"

His eyes narrowed. "Did my mother send you here?"

"Lady Westvale?"

He nodded.

"No." Rosalind shook her head. "Although I daresay she'd like the answer to that, as well."

"Yes, but she is my mother and considers it her duty whereas you…" He paused as if struck by a thought. Caution edged his words. "You have a daughter, don't you, Lady Richfield?"

"Indeed I do," Rosalind said with an innocent smile. "She's quite lovely."

"I have a daughter too," Marian blurted. "And she's very clever."

"I have two daughters and they're both smart and pretty," Jane said quickly then frowned. "Neither of whom are old enough for…" She shook her head as if to clear it. "I have no idea why I said that."

"You said it, my dear Jane," Val said with a smile, "because good mothers want only what's best for their daughters. Best, in this instance, means a good match." He grinned. "And I am eminently eligible."

"And I apologize." Rosalind sighed. "I don't know what came over me. Under other circumstances, your reputation alone would be enough to discourage any thoughts I might have about a match. You're more the lesser of two evils at the moment but really not at all suitable. A bit older than I would prefer, as well."

"Thank you, Lady Richfield." Val swept an overly dramatic bow. "Then my reputation has served me well, although I'm not sure I like being the *lesser* of two evils." He grinned, pulled a nearby chair to the table, then sat down next to Willie. "How long will you be staying at the villa?"

"Only tonight. We have rooms at the Hotel de Paris for the remainder of our stay, two more nights." Willie raised a shoulder in a casual shrug. "There was a problem with our reservations."

"Your problem is to my benefit." Val met Willie's gaze firmly. "I am delighted to see you again."

Willie smiled. "It has been a long time."

"Entirely too long." He leaned toward her. "I meant what I said about calling on you. Would that be acceptable?"

Aside from the surf in the distance, one could have heard a pin drop. Willie didn't dare look but she was fairly certain Rosalind, Jane and Marian were absorbing this conversation with bated breath. Was this the sort of idle flirtation Val had always been so accomplished at? Was he indeed only concerned with friendship? Or was he interested in more? A few weeks ago the answer to that would have been most intriguing. But a few weeks ago she not had met Dante Montague. Now everything was, well, different.

She caught a movement out of the corner of her eye and adopted her brightest smile. "Of course, Val. That would be lovely."

"Ahem."

"Good morning, Dante," Rosalind said in a cheery manner and waved her brother to the table. "Do you know Lord Brookings?"

"I don't believe we've met." Dante's gaze flickered between Willie and Val. "I'm Lady Richfield's brother."

Val reluctantly drew his gaze from Willie's and rose to his feet. "Montague, isn't it?"

"Dante Montague." He nodded.

"I've heard your name mentioned before." Val considered him thoughtfully. "You were the one who was…" He winced. "Bad bit of business that."

Willie held her breath.

"What is he talking about?" Marian said softly to Rosalind.

"Good Lord, Marian." Rosalind huffed, her voice quiet. "If I am going to have to tell you every morsel of old gossip that might arise, we are going to have to get up much earlier." She paused. "I'll tell you later."

"I assure you, the accounts of the situation were not entirely accurate," Dante said coolly. "Furthermore, it was exceptionally awkward and somewhat humiliating, which is why I prefer not to discuss it."

"No doubt." Val shook his head. "One never likes to be reminded of one's mistakes. Believe me, I know."

"And have you made many mistakes, my lord?" Dante's

tone was pleasant enough but there was a distinct challenge in his voice.

"Too many to count, Mr. Montague." Val chuckled. "But the ones I truly regret were mistakes not of commission—" he glanced at Willie "—but of omission."

"And isn't that interesting?" Rosalind murmured.

"I'm sure we all make mistakes," Jane offered helpfully.

"Acknowledging one's mistakes is the first step toward ensuring they are not repeated." Dante pulled up a chair to sit on Willie's other side.

"Excellent point." Val retook his seat. "I know I, for one, try not to make the same mistakes again."

"Although not making them in the first place is the best course." Dante shrugged.

Willie's head swiveled from one man to the other. She had the oddest sensation of being caught between two opposing forces.

"Still, none of us is perfect," Val continued. "It is the very nature of man to err occasionally. We all have lapses in judgment brought about by circumstances or events or—" he grinned "—a pretty face."

Dante's jaw clenched. Why on earth was he taking Val's comments as a personal affront? It was more likely Val was speaking of his own errors in judgment and not Dante's. Goodness, Val had certainly made enough of them, especially when it came to women.

"Lord Brookings was just telling us about a bit of profound advice Willie once gave him," Jane said in an obvious effort to change the subject.

"I'm not the least bit surprised." Dante smiled at Willie. "I've found many of Lady Bascombe's comments to be quite profound."

"Have you?" Willie raised a skeptical brow. If one was

going to be considered profound, it would be nice to be aware of exactly what one said. "What, may I ask, are you talking about?"

"About the futility of regrets." Dante met her gaze directly. "About the past and not being able to undo what one has done."

"I'm not sure it's especially profound." Willie shrugged. "More eminently practical, I would say."

"Practical and beautiful." Val chuckled and Willie turned her attention to him. "And wise. It's an irresistible combination."

Willie laughed. "Now I'm wise, as well?"

"I recognized your intelligence the first moment we met," Dante said firmly. "I could see it in your lovely blue eyes."

"Oh, I have long thought she was quite clever," Val said. "But I do think her eyes are as much green as blue."

"You're mistaken." Dante smiled politely. "They are most definitely blue."

"I have been told on occasion, they may be a bit green," Willie murmured. This was absurd. What were these two doing?

"No one argues over the color of my eyes," Marian murmured to Jane.

"As we have nothing scheduled," Rosalind said abruptly, "what shall we do today?"

Willie cast her a grateful glance.

"I have a splendid idea." Val beamed. "I come here regularly so I suspect I know Monaco as well as anyone. I would be delighted to show you around. Weather here is exceptional and there is nothing quite as enjoyable as spending an afternoon walking around town enjoying the sunshine and the views. This is one of the most scenic spots on the coast."

"How very kind of you to offer. I think it's a brilliant idea." Willie glanced at the others.

"As do I," Jane said. "Shall we say an hour from now? That will give the girls time to dress."

"Oh, this will be fun." Marian nodded. "I know the girls will enjoy it."

"An hour, then." Rosalind stood, and everyone else followed suit.

"If you will excuse us, gentlemen." Willie smiled at the two men and hoped leaving them alone was not a bad idea. Jane and Marian started for their rooms, Willie a step behind.

"A moment, Willie." Val stepped close and spoke quietly for her ears alone. "Just out of idle curiosity, who are the *girls*?"

"I thought you understood. The ladies didn't mention their daughters simply to make idle conversation. They have all brought their daughters." Willie resisted the impulse to smirk.

He grimaced. "And there are how many?"

"Four." She choked back a laugh at the stricken look on his face.

"And they all have mothers who would like nothing better than to bring home a marquess." He sighed.

"You're the one who mentioned how eligible you are. But take heart, Val." She grinned. "Jane's daughters are too young for you and Rosalind has already said you would not suit for hers. So only Marian's daughter is left."

"I'm not worried about the daughter." Val's brow furrowed. "But I didn't like the determined look in her mother's eyes."

"Courage, Val." Willie laughed and headed for her room.

Behind her, Rosalind had paused for a word with her brother. "He who hesitates, dear."

Willie couldn't hear Dante's response and wasn't at all sure what it meant.

An hour later they set off to discover the charms of Monte Carlo. Her guidebooks were right—there wasn't a great deal to see. But the setting was magnificent, the picturesque town wedged between the sea and the mountains. Many of the buildings perched on cliffs overlooking the sea. Val led them through the twisting streets of the oldest part of the principality and it struck Willie as remarkably clean. The town itself swept upward from the sea, climbing the mountains with every street higher in elevation than the next. Broad terraces bordered the streets and provided walkways and stunning vistas. They strolled in constantly shifting groups of two or three, pausing here and there to admire the view or appreciate the foliage or listen to some obscure—and often silly—fact that Val had in seemingly endless supply. They walked by the casino, a grand building more resembling a royal palace than a temple to the gods of chance and decided to all try their luck once they had settled in at the hotel. The gardens too were remarkable. Willie had never seen a palm growing outside of a conservatory and here palms and lemon trees and other exotic plants grew unfettered by glass ceilings. She gave a silent note of gratitude to Mrs. Vanderflute for arranging for them to stay in what was surely as close as man could get to paradise.

Not that all of them appreciated the display of nature's bounty as much as they did the company of a dashing gentleman. The girls hung on Val's every word and took turns hanging on his elbow, as well. He was quite chivalrous about it and really wonderfully charming, paying no more attention to one girl over the others. He encouraged the twins to tell him about New York and asked what they had most enjoyed in Paris and London. He and Harriet spoke of mutual acquaintances and while he might not have noticed, the girl did seem distracted, constantly scanning those passing by. Willie did hope she wasn't looking for Mr. Goodwin. Surely the young man had returned to England by now. In spite of Val's best intentions, he did spend far more time chatting with Geneva about the Egyptian artifacts at the British museum than with the other girls. Marian obviously noticed given the satisfied smile on her face.

The only one not appearing to enjoy it all was Dante, whose expression looked more annoyed than apprecia-tive. Although he too summoned a measure of gallantry and chatted with the girls as they wandered the streets.

"He's jealous, you know," Rosalind said, dropping back to walk by Willie's side.

"Who?" Willie stared at the other woman.

"My brother, of course." Rosalind frowned. "Surely you noticed that nonsense on the terrace?"

"Don't be silly." Willie scoffed. "That was nothing more than…"

Rosalind cast her a knowing smile.

"Well, isn't that interesting," Willie murmured. Surely a man who felt the pangs of jealousy wanted more than a temporary liaison. "Very interesting."

"I thought so." Rosalind smirked.

"Then you don't think this is just some sort of holiday flirtation for him?"

"Dante?" Rosalind scoffed. "I would wager my hus-band's entire fortune in the casino against that. Besides, a man is rarely jealous if he doesn't have certain feel-ings for a woman." She smiled in a knowing manner and changed the subject.

Still, the idea lingered in Willie's head. Although one

would think a man who was experiencing jealousy, a man who had *certain feelings*, a man who had very nearly confessed those feelings would make more of an effort to be with her. Why, he'd scarcely spoken to her all day and had made no attempt to be alone with her. One would have thought a passionate kiss overlooking the rooftops of Paris would have led to something more.

By midafternoon Harriett declared she was in dire need of refreshment and Dante volunteered to accompany the girls, who promised to bring back drinks for the rest of them. Marian, Rosalind and Jane all settled on one of the benches conveniently placed along the Avenue—the best promenade in Monte Carlo according to Val—overlooking the sea. Willie braced her hands on the stone balustrade protecting pedestrians from tumbling down the cliff to the rocks below and gazed out on the blue Mediterranean. She'd always loved the sea and treasured those rare trips to Brighton she and George had taken, usually in the company of friends. She didn't miss them, those fair-weather friends, but it was hard not to miss the carefree life she'd once had. Even if she was now fairly certain she would have grown out of it someday. One did have to grow up sometime. Sadly, she didn't really miss George either. It was distressing but there you had it. Certainly it had been two years since his death. Still, one would have thought…

"You look exceptionally lovely this afternoon."

She didn't need to look at him to know Val was wearing his most charming smile. "Did you mean it?"

"Indeed I did. I did say *exceptionally* after all. I never use *exceptionally* unless it's warranted."

"No." She blew a long breath and turned toward him. "I meant what you said about our being friends."

"Absolutely." Sincerity shone in his eyes.

"Then why are you being so incredibly flirtatious?"

He gasped. "I am not."

"You most certainly are." She shook her head. "You have never flirted like this with me before."

"On the contrary, I have flirted with you every time we've met."

"This is different."

"I might be putting more effort into it now."

"Why?"

"Come now, Willie. It's obvious. As you were married, there was nothing that could come of flirtation then."

She studied him closely. "I don't believe that has stopped you with other women."

"I tell you, Willie, there are times when my reputation is a curse." He paused. "Although I am proud of it."

"Good Lord, Val."

"Very well." His expression sobered. "It was my observation that underneath that devil-may-care attitude, you are an honorable woman and not at all the type to betray her marriage vows." He chose his words with care. "I admire that—I always have. Some men do not deserve that kind of loyalty."

He was talking about George now.

"But now." He grinned in a wicked manner. "You are a widow."

"And you are still incorrigible."

"Thank you," he said, feigning a modest smile. "I was serious about calling on you."

"I'm not sure that's a good idea."

"Why not?" His eyes narrowed. "Is there someone else?"

She hesitated. "I'm not sure about that either."

He considered her closely. "It's Montague, isn't it?"

She wasn't quite ready to admit it to anyone, wasn't entirely sure she had admitted it to herself.

"Very well then." He took her hand and raised it to his lips. "Even though you have broken my heart, I shall not let it stand in the way of friendship. And I shall do all I can to lend my assistance."

"Dare I ask what you mean by that?"

"Absolutely not." He chuckled.

Exactly what form Val's assistance would take was soon more than apparent. While he continued to charm the girls and the other ladies, he paid Willie particular attention. On the return to the villa, throughout an excellent dinner and well into an evening of games meant to familiarize them with those played at the casino, he was rarely far from her side.

Dante grew more and more—not forbidding exactly—but stiff. Stuffy. Horribly formal. He scarcely said anything to her that wasn't necessary and perfectly polite.

By the time she retired, Willie had come to two realizations. First—a man who truly wanted a woman, who had *feelings* for a woman, really needed to make some effort in that regard and not expect her to simply fall into his arms. Nor should he act like a spoiled child. It was not at all attractive.

And second—Val was right. Regardless of George's indiscretions, she had never been unfaithful. Now it seemed the type of wife who remained true even to a husband who didn't deserve it was not the kind of widow who had holiday flings. No matter how wonderful the man. Or how thoughts of him were constantly on her mind. Or how independent she was.

Or how she suspected he might well be the love of her life.

CHAPTER TWELVE

"IT DOES NOT serve your cause to appear quite so grim," Roz said in an overly casual manner, as if her words were of no particular importance. Which always meant they were.

Dante took a sip of champagne, his gaze on one of the couples swirling around the crowded dance floor in the grand ballroom at the Hotel de Paris. Willie was breathtaking in a pale gold gown that complemented her hair and was entirely too revealing in the front and too low in the back, with gathered sleeves low on her shoulders that left her arms bare except for her gloves. She was dancing with Brookings. Again. "Appearances, my dear sister, are often deceiving."

"*My dear sister?* My, you are in a foul mood."

He glanced at her. Her gaze too was fixed on the dancers or rather on one dancer in particular. Harriet had been partnered with one eager gentleman after another from very nearly the second they'd stepped into the ballroom. Apparently, a popular daughter was as much a curse as a blessing. And while they had no indication that Goodwin was in the vicinity, Roz refused to let the girl out of her sight.

"My mood is fine, thank you. I simply don't know why we're here in the first place." He noted the petulant tone of his voice but he didn't care. Petulant suited him.

"We're here because Lord Brookings was kind enough to procure us all invitations."

"I would dispute the word *kind*." At that moment, Brookings must have said something amusing and Willie laughed. Dante's stomach twisted. "More self-serving I would say."

"Don't be absurd."

He ignored her. "He said it was a small gathering of friends." In truth, the ballroom was filled to overflowing. "This is scarcely a small gathering."

"Yet another reason to dislike him."

"I don't know him well enough to dislike him."

And yet he did. Quite a lot really. Dante had thought once they'd left the villa, they'd leave Brookings behind, as well. But every time he turned around, the blasted man was right there by Willie's side. Right after they'd checked in yesterday, he'd appeared with an invitation for a sail on the yacht of an acquaintance. Dante had declined—he had no desire to spend more time on the water than necessary—but the rest of their party was delighted. Last night Brookings accompanied them to the casino and seemed to take it upon himself to make certain Willie had an enjoyable evening. And indeed, she did appear to be having a good time of it. At least she had laughed a great deal. Far more than Dante deemed necessary.

Even today Brookings had joined them for lunch and when Dante had spotted Willie on the hotel terrace studying her guidebooks and had started toward her, Brookings was there before him. And tonight, Brookings had danced entirely too many dances with her. Not that it mattered. Not that Dante cared. Admittedly, he had thought himself in love with her but upon further consideration, he might have been mistaken. He wanted the Portinari, nothing more.

"You could ask her to dance, you know."

Dante's jaw tightened. "I will not play this game again, Roz."

She looked at him with surprise. "What game?"

"I will not be played for a fool by a woman again."

Roz stared. "What are you talking about?"

"I know the signs. I have been through this before." He sipped his wine and wished it was something stronger. "If that's the kind of man she wants, I will not allow her to use me to make him come up to snuff."

"That's what you've been thinking?"

"I think it's obvious."

"Good Lord." She snorted back a laugh. "You are an idiot."

"Thank you for your sisterly support," he snapped.

"Dante." She heaved a long-suffering sigh. "I find it hard to believe you cannot see what is right in front of your face."

"I have seen more than enough."

"Willie is not using you to ensnare him. Quite the opposite really, which you would realize if you weren't so busy being stuffy and self-righteous."

"I am neither stuffy nor self-righteous and what do you mean—just the opposite?"

Roz rolled her gaze toward the elaborately carved and painted ceiling. "I mean, *my dear brother*, that if you hadn't been keeping your distance, you might have noticed Willie has done absolutely nothing to encourage Lord Brookings. He is an unrepentant flirt but I do believe his interest in her is genuine friendship. Hard to believe such a thing can happen between a man and a woman but there you have it."

"You still haven't explained what just the opposite means."

"Goodness, Dante, Willie Bascombe is not the type of woman who plays silly games with the hearts of men. Frankly, I don't believe she knows how. She is not Juliet Pauling and she is not trying to use you to make him jealous. Not that you are cooperating the tiniest bit in that."

"Not bloody likely," he muttered.

"Nor do I think she is trying to make you jealous by using him."

He scoffed. "Not that she could."

She cast him a pitying look. "And yet you are jealous."

"Hardly."

"As I said, while she has not encouraged him, Brookings is a man with a mind of his own. I suspect he thinks he is helping her by making you jealous."

"I already told you, I am not—"

"Of course you are. Any fool can see it." She paused. "Except perhaps Willie, who is too busy wondering why you have been cold and remote and not at all pleasant toward her. Why you seemed quite taken with her one day and scarcely spoke to her the next."

"Rubbish. I have been unfailingly polite." Admittedly, every time Brookings made a move toward Willie, Dante took a step back in both manner and proximity. He couldn't seem to help himself.

"You have been an ass."

"Regardless, I refuse to play these sorts of games," he said coolly. "I simply want the Portinari and that will be that."

"You poor, stupid man." Sympathy sounded in his sister's voice. "Somewhere in your quest to become her friend you have fallen in love with the woman."

His jaw clenched. It was pointless to deny it. He had thought exactly the same thing.

"I saw you kiss her," she said reluctantly. "At Notre Dame. I dropped my glove on the top step and returned for it. I couldn't help but see the two of you."

"It was a mere kiss, Roz. Nothing more than that."

She scoffed. "It was far more than a mere kiss."

"You watched?"

"No, of course not. Well, not for long anyway. It was completely inadvertent on my part and hardly more than a glimpse. But it was most impressive." She shook her head. "I had no idea my stuffy, proper brother could be so—"

"That's enough, Roz."

"That was not the kind of kiss a man like you gives a woman he does not love. Nor does a woman kiss a man in return the way she did without sharing his feelings."

"You gathered that from a glimpse?"

"It was more than enough."

"Rubbish. As I said, it was only a kiss. Do not make it into more than it was." Even as he said the words, he knew it was a lie and suspected his sister knew, as well. She'd always been annoyingly intuitive about such things. And as much as he had tried to tell himself in the last few days that he was mistaken about his feelings, that he didn't love Willie, that too was a lie.

"You needn't deny how you feel." Roz shrugged. "I saw it coming from almost the first moment you met. And we have all noticed, with the exception of Willie herself perhaps. Even the girls have mentioned it. Dante." She paused and placed her hand on his sleeve. "I have never seen you so, well, happy as you have been since you met her. There is a joy about you that has been missing for a long time. I feared that nastiness with Miss Pauling, your dedication to your business and the museum, and your tendency toward propriety and following rules and doing what was expected had snuffed that out in you. She has brought it back."

His sister was right. Willie was not at all the kind of woman he ever thought he wanted. Her reputation was not above reproach, her education was questionable, her family connections minimal. But she was amusing and clever, determined and reluctantly independent. And she made him feel as if life itself was an adventure. The woman had worked her way into his heart and it would never be the same again. "While I am not saying you're right," he said slowly, "what would you suggest I do?"

"You're asking for my advice? Again?"

"Apparently." He summoned a wry smile.

"Very well." She thought for a moment. "First, stop acting like a spoiled child. If you want her, go after her. Pursue her as you would a new acquisition for the museum or a coveted business arrangement. Or in the manner in which you tried to gain her friendship. That seemed to be working quite nicely."

"What if she doesn't share my feelings?" He met his sister's gaze. "What am I to do then?"

"Quite honestly, I don't know." She shook her head. "But I do know, dear brother, if you do nothing you may well lose a chance—perhaps your only chance—at true happiness."

"You could be entirely wrong, you know."

"Good Lord, Dante. We are here in one of the premier gambling centers of the world. Allow some of that to rub off on you. Take a chance. Try your luck. Can you feel any worse than you do now?"

"Probably."

"Nonsense." She scanned the dancers. "This dance

is nearly over and I know for a fact Lord Brookings is to dance with Harriet next. Which means Willie is free to dance with you. I suggest you take advantage of the opportunity."

"Very well." He adjusted his cuffs.

"And for goodness' sake, do try to be pleasant and charming." She met his gaze firmly. "Try to be the man you were in Paris. The man who kissed her on the top of a cathedral."

He raised a brow. "More advice, Roz?"

"And excellent advice it is too." She nodded at the dance floor. The music had ended and couples were dispersing. "Now go, before you lose your opportunity and someone else claims this dance."

He started toward Willie.

"You're quite welcome," Roz called after him.

A minute later he met Willie and Brookings coming off the dance floor.

"Lady Bascombe," he began in a manner far more formal than he wished. "May I have the honor of the next dance?"

A slight frown creased her forehead. "I'm not sure I wish to dance another dance at the moment."

"Don't be absurd—of course you do," Brookings said firmly. "You are in for a treat, Mr. Montague. Lady Bascombe is an accomplished dancer."

"Yes, I've noticed."

"Have you?" Willie's tone was cool.

"I should have asked before now. However, if you would prefer not to—"

"Nonsense. She was just saying how long it had been since she'd danced and how very much she missed it," Brookings said with a confident smile. "And I have the next dance with a lovely young woman whose mother does not see me as a suitable match. Exactly the kind I prefer." He grinned at Willie. "I'm confident I leave you in excellent hands, my dear." He nodded at Dante and took his leave.

"Shall we?" Dante said and Willie stepped into his arms.

A sedate waltz began and they danced together with an ease that belied the tension between them. In spite of the pleasure of having her again in his arms, his doubts overshadowed his sister's words. He had no idea what to say or where to start and was shocked to realize he was afraid to say anything at all. Rationally, he suspected Roz was right about Willie and Brookings. But his feelings were an entirely different matter. He'd been horribly humiliated by a woman once. He would not let it happen again.

She drew a deep breath and stared up at him. "Are you angry with me? Have I done something to offend you?"

"No." He paused. "And my apologies if I have given you that impression."

"I don't see what other impression I could have."

"Again, I am sorry."

He led her through a complicated turn and she followed his lead flawlessly.

"Are we to dance the entire dance without saying another word to each other?" Willie asked at last.

"I'm not sure what to say."

"I find that hard to believe." She heaved a resigned sigh. "Very well then." She adopted a brilliant smile. "I find the weather here to be delightful. So warm and sunny and quite unlike England at this time of year."

"Well, we are on a southern coast."

"There is that." She sighed and a moment later tried again. "It's a lovely evening, don't you think?"

"The others seem to be enjoying it. My sister has run into a few people she knows."

"It was quite thoughtful of Lord Brookings to secure us invitations."

He scoffed.

"You don't think it was thoughtful of him?" Her words were measured.

A tiny voice of reason in the back of his head—a voice that hadn't said a word in recent days—warned him to tread carefully. He ignored it. "I think Lord Brookings's motives are suspect."

Her eyes widened. "What on earth do you mean by that?"

"I don't like the way he is always fawning over you," he said in a lofty manner.

"Lord Brookings?" Disbelief rang in her voice.

"Is there someone else fawning over you?"

"You certainly haven't," she said sharply. "And he has not been not been *fawning* over me. Val is an old and dear friend."

He snorted.

"Clever answer, Mr. Montague. Why use words when you can simply grunt in disdain. And why do you care who fawns over me?"

"You know why I care," he said through clenched teeth.

"On the contrary, I don't believe I do. I thought I did. I thought were we both quite clear as to our…feelings in Paris. Now…"

"Now the dashing Lord Brookings is here and you have bigger fish to fry." He regretted the words the moment they were out of his mouth.

"I beg your pardon." She stared. "Do you really think that?"

"I don't know what to think." He knew better than to continue but he couldn't seem to stop himself. "Ever since we've been in Monte Carlo, you have shown little interest in being in anyone else's company."

"That not the least bit true." Her voice rose. "What is true is that you have made absolutely no effort to be in mine."

"I had no desire to be used by yet another woman!"

"And you think that's what I'm doing?" Fire sparked in her eyes. "How dare you!"

"I have been down this path before. I recognize it when I see it."

"You see absolutely nothing!"

There were any number of things he could say, any number he should say, but anger and betrayal and humiliation and all those other feelings Juliet had provoked rushed through him even as that tiny voice—now sounding suspiciously like his sister's—pointed out Willie Bascombe was not Juliet Pauling.

The music drew to a close before he could summon a response. At once Willie moved out of his arms and stepped back as if she couldn't wait to put distance between them.

"We leave for Italy in the morning." Her voice quivered with anger. "Good evening, Mr. Montague." With that she nodded and made her way out of the ballroom.

For a moment he could only stare after her. What on earth had just happened? What had he done? Regret lodged in his throat. How could he have said any of that to her? He turned and stalked off the floor barely noticing Marian and Jane approach.

"That did not go well, did it, Mr. Montague?" Jane pinned him with a hard look.

Marian shook her head. "We expected better from you."

"I have no idea what you're talking about," he said evenly.

"Come now." Jane gave him the same kind of look his sister had. Pity mixed with disbelief. "We watched the two of you."

"We were hoping you would do something about the terrible way you've been acting." Marian studied him as if he were a disappointing child. "Silly of us but we did assume that would take the form of an apology or an explanation or something of that nature. But given the looks on your faces, you did not come up to our expectations."

"Forgive me, ladies, for pointing this out," he said in a hard tone, "but this is none of your concern."

"Willie is our friend." Marian raised her chin. "Which makes this our concern."

Jane glared. "We will not stand idly by and watch you break her heart."

There was no point in arguing with them. It was obvious this was a fight he could not win. Especially since they were right.

"What did you do?" Jane demanded.

"I may have said some things that were, well, not what I intended to say." He blew a long breath.

"Then your sister is right." Marian flicked a disgusted gaze over him. "You are an idiot."

"No one knows that better than I." He rubbed his hand over his forehead.

"Let me ask you one thing." Jane considered him closely. "Do you have feelings for her?"

"Do you love her?" Marian said bluntly.

Dante's gaze shifted between the women. Apparently, not only were they Willie's friends but they had, as well, taken on the role of older sisters. His.

"Yes." He threw up his hands in surrender. "Yes, I do.

I admit it. And I further admit I was wrong. About everything." Why wasn't it as clear to him a few moments ago as it seemed to be now? Perhaps his sister and the Americans were right. Maybe he really was an idiot. "I will apologize to her. I'll do so first thing in the morning. I'll tell her what a fool I've been. I'll beg her forgiveness. Even grovel if I must."

The ladies traded glances.

"That will not do." Jane shook her head. "Morning will be too late."

"The more she thinks about what you said, the worse it will be for you. The last thing you want is for her to retire with the vile things you said on her mind." Marian arched a brow. "And judging from the way she left, I assume they were vile?"

He winced. "I'm afraid so."

Marian huffed. "Then you need to go after her."

He hesitated.

"Go." Jane waved toward the door.

"Very well." He turned to go then turned back. "Thank you both for your help."

"Now!" Jane snapped.

Dante headed for the grand lobby and the lifts. Willie was probably back in her room by now. He had no idea exactly what he was going to say to her. He would apologize, of course, and beg her forgiveness. He would indeed grovel and do whatever else was necessary, which probably included explaining why he had acted as he had. He'd thought he had put that business with Juliet behind him. He hadn't been in love with her after all. But apparently, aside from damaging his pride and holding him up to public ridicule, she had destroyed his ability to trust. At least when it came to women.

He hadn't been the least bit fair to Willie. He should

have known better. Roz had pointed out that Willie wasn't Juliet and he knew that. Logically and rationally and indeed until Brookings's arrival he wouldn't have thought she was. Willie was a woman he could trust. With his life. With his heart. But would she be willing to trust him? After everything he had said?

Dante reached her door and summoned his courage. He'd never been one to jump to conclusions and rarely made errors in judgment of any kind. He couldn't remember the last time he'd had to admit he was wrong. But apparently love played havoc not only with one's heart but one's head, as well. He'd never been in this situation before, never played for stakes this high, and was under no illusion it would be easy. But it was the price one paid for utter and complete stupidity. And a small price to pay to keep Willie in his life. For now and forever.

He drew a deep breath, braced himself and knocked.

CHAPTER THIRTEEN

How could she have been such a fool? To have thought for so much as a moment that she might be in love with that beast of a man! That arrogant, smug, infuriating swine!

Willie paced the width of her spacious room, arms folded across her chest, eyes burning unshed tears. Although she suspected she would weep uncontrollably at any moment. Her grandmother had said proper English women were made of sterner stuff than to cry without just cause—usually death. Willie had cried when her mother died, when her grandmother died and, of course, when George had died. She'd cried when she'd realized her father would never particularly care for her—which did feel very much like death—and she had shed a few tears when she'd discovered she was very nearly penniless. Although those were tears more of anger and outrage and betrayal than heartache. The moment she stopped pacing—the moment she stopped moving—she feared anger and outrage in potent combination with the horrible ache around her heart would rip through her and once she shed the first tear she might never be able to stop.

How could he have thought such a thing of her? Admittedly, they hadn't known each other for long but surely it was long enough for him to know what kind of person she was. She certainly knew what kind of person he was. Or at least she'd thought she had known.

A knock sounded at the door and she considered whether or not to ignore it. She had no desire to talk to anyone at the moment. Especially anyone who might have observed her argument with Dante. Fortunately, no one could have heard them over the music and as furious as each of them was, they had somehow managed to keep fairly polite expressions on their faces. Even so, her new friends had proved surprisingly observant and perceptive.

The knock sounded again harder. Obviously whoever it was was not going to accept being ignored. Fine!

She strode to the door and flung it open. "What—"

Dante stood, hand raised to knock again, apprehension mixed with regret on his face.

"What do you want?"

"Nothing more than a few minutes," he said in a conciliatory manner. "I thought we should talk. Or rather I should talk."

"I think you've said quite enough! Go away!"

"I owe you an apology." He shook his head. "Please, I just want to talk."

"Well, I have no desire to talk. Not to you. Not now. Not ever." She slammed the door, turned on her heel and stalked across the room.

There was nothing more satisfying than slamming a door in a man's face. Not that she had ever done so before but it did seem to carry a great deal of gratification. Perhaps as much as slapping a man's face, which she had never done either but she should have. Right there on the dance floor in front of his sister and the Americans and Val and a room full of strangers.

How dare he think a simple apology would negate the terrible things he had said. Although he hadn't actually apologized. She hadn't given him the chance. Nor did he deserve the chance. Still, it might be interesting to hear what he could possibly say in his defense. Perhaps she should have given him a moment after all.

And weren't there things she wished to say, as well? Things she deserved to say. After all, she was the wounded party here. Why should she deprive herself of the opportunity to tell him exactly what she wished? And what better time than right now when it was all fresh in her mind. Without another thought, Willie flung her door open, slammed it behind her then marched down the hall to his door and knocked sharply. It was his turn to listen to what she had to say.

The door opened and Dante stared at her in surprise, his expression at once hopeful and uneasy. "Willie?"

"Were you expecting someone else?"

"I wasn't expecting you," he said slowly. He had taken off his coat, his collar was loose, his tie missing and his waistcoat was partially unbuttoned. Was there anything more wickedly exciting than a handsome man in disheveled formal attire?

She forced the thought from her mind and nodded. "You were right. We should talk."

Dante continued to stare. What was wrong with the man? He acted as if he'd been struck speechless by her presence.

"May I come in or shall we talk here in the hallway?" She huffed. "What on earth is the matter with you?"

"Nothing." He shook his head as if to clear it. "Please, come in." He stepped aside and waved her into the room.

She swept past him and stopped short in the middle of the room. Good Lord. This was a perfectly appointed parlor decorated in soothing shades of cream and pale blue with a sofa and chairs facing a fireplace and a desk with his open valise sitting on it. Her room was charming enough but he had a suite. A door next to the desk probably led to a bedroom. "Why is it your rooms are always so much larger than mine?"

"I don't know. But I am sorry," he added quickly.

"This—" she gestured at their surroundings "—is not what you have to be sorry about."

"I am aware of that. And you have my apologies for that too. I am so sorry for what I said and what I thought." He hesitated. "You should know I had no intention of leaving your room until we had a chance to speak."

She shrugged. "And yet you did."

"I debated whether to pound on your door until you let me in."

"And yet you didn't."

"You told me to go." He ran his hand through his hair. "I did not want to make things worse. So I left."

"Rather cowardly of you, don't you think?"

"You told me to go," he said again.

"You didn't protest."

"You slammed the door in my face."

"Indeed I did," she said in a smug manner. "It was the very least you deserved."

"You're right. I deserve far worse. I am terribly sorry, Willie."

She crossed her arms over her chest. "You said that already."

"I don't think I can say it enough."

"No, you can't. Is that all?"

"Actually, there's a great deal more." He drew a deep breath. "I should—"

"Not so fast, Mr. Montague." She was here in his far-better-than-he-deserved room to give him a piece of her mind, not to let him have his say. "I have a few things I wish to say first."

"By all means," he said cautiously. "Go on."

"I intend to. First—what were you thinking? Or were you thinking at all?"

"I'm not sure I—"

"No!" She thrust out her hand to stop him. "I don't want to hear it."

"Then you should refrain from asking me questions."

"It was rhetorical," she snapped.

"Actually, I don't believe it was. A rhetorical question is one to which an answer is really not expected. It's used to make a point, so rhetorical would be..." His voice trailed off, no doubt at the look in her eye.

"I am in no mood for a lesson in vocabulary."

"Of course not. But you were wrong and I thought you might wish to know. But probably not," he finished weakly. "Please continue."

"I will!" Even so, she wasn't entirely sure where to begin. She considered his crimes for a moment. "First of all, Lord Brookings is my friend. He is an unapologetic flirt and a great deal of fun but he is my friend. Nothing more, nothing less."

"I really think—"

"I strongly suggest, Mr. Montague, that you keep whatever thoughts you may have to yourself for the moment."

"I simply—"

She aimed a pointed finger at him and he stopped mid-sentence. "Much better. As I was saying, Lord Brookings is nothing more than a friend. And, as my circle of friends is sadly diminished, I cannot afford to lose one. Nor do I wish to. Furthermore—" she paused "—he did indicate to me that he would be interested in something more between us and I informed him that was not something I would be amenable to."

Dante started to respond but she stabbed her finger at him again and his mouth snapped shut.

"Second, I would never use one man to encourage the affection of another. And even if I were inclined to do such a thing, knowing your past experience, I would never employ you in such a manner. The fact that you thought—even for a moment—that I am the kind of person who would so callously do something of that nature is both insulting and horribly unkind." She glared at him. "You hurt me deeply, Dante."

Genuine remorse shone in his eyes. She'd never seen a man look quite so helpless before. It was rather endearing. And almost enough to make her relent and forgive him. Almost but not quite.

"Now, I will concede that perhaps, in the back of his mind, Lord Brookings might have thought his overly enthusiastic flirtation could benefit me by making you a bit more forthcoming with your feelings. And I will further admit, I might not have been completely unaware of his efforts but I assure you it was neither my idea nor was I complicit in it. If anything, you, by your stuffy, remote, standoffish attitude, only served to encourage his attentions."

He took a step toward her.

"Not one more step, Mr. Montague," she said in a hard tone. "I am not finished yet." She drew a deep breath. "You led me to believe you harbored a certain affection for me. I confess, I was—at that time—feeling much the same about you. And you kissed me. Quite thoroughly, I might add. I have been kissed before, of course. But I have never—" she swallowed hard "—been quite as affected by a kiss. One could argue it was nothing more than a mere kiss and yet to me it felt like a great deal more. Which is why your behavior toward me these past few days has been so hurtful. It does seem to me that a man who has feelings for a woman would make some sort of attempt to win her heart." She met his gaze coolly. "You have made no attempt whatsoever."

He winced.

"Which leads me to wonder if something you said at Notre Dame might be noteworthy."

He had the distinct look of a fox run to ground, not certain in which direction lay escape and in which certain doom. Although she did have to give him credit for keeping his mouth shut.

"You said you were on holiday. Is this, whatever it is between you and me, nothing more than a holiday affair? Something with no more meaning than a souvenir? Or is it something…more? Significant if you will. Important. Because I assure you, I am not the kind of woman to have amorous adventures. I never have been and apparently it is not in my nature."

Again, he looked as if he wasn't sure which way to go.

"Well? What's it to be?"

"Did you want an answer?" he said carefully.

"Of course I want an answer." She rolled her gaze toward the ceiling.

"I have no desire for a holiday liaison." He chose his words with care, his gaze locked on hers. "I'm not a temporary sort of man. I—"

"That's enough for now. However, it was an excellent answer. But I have more I wish to say." In fact, she wasn't nearly as angry at him as she had been only a few minutes ago. Perhaps the simple act of saying everything she had to say without interruption defused her ire. She would have to remember that. It did seem she was more rational now, no thanks to him. Willie clasped her hands together in front of her. "I have been giving this a great deal of thought—"

The corners of his mouth twitched as if he found that amusing. Blasted man probably realized she was not as furious as she had been.

"—in the time since I left the ballroom and I believe it all comes down to trust. Trust, Dante, is paramount between a man and a woman. I trusted my husband, in spite of all sorts of indications that I shouldn't. I shouldn't have trusted that he was managing our affairs correctly and Lord knows there was plenty of evidence that I failed to pay any attention to. Nor should I have trusted him with my heart. I will not make that sort of mistake again. I am older and hopefully wiser. In spite of the way you make me feel, a way that quite frankly destroys any semblance of coherent thought—"

Again the corners of his lips twitched.

"I warn you, Dante," she snapped, "if you so much as smile, I will slap your face and never forgive you!"

At once his expression became an exaggerated scowl that was every bit as annoying.

"As I was saying, I do believe, in my heart, that you are most trustworthy. The only remaining question is can you trust me?"

He nodded.

"Go on." She huffed. "You may say whatever else you want to say now."

"Very well." He thought for a moment although surely she'd given him ample time to determine what he wished to say. "First of all, you have my most sincere and ardent apology. I am truly sorry, Willie. The things I said were neither accurate nor were they fair. And I should have— I do—know better."

"Then why did you say them?"

"I'm not entirely sure. No, that's not true." He blew a long breath. "You're right about trust being all important. I was not in love with Miss Pauling but I now see that I did, well, trust her. I had no reason not to. It never so much as crossed my mind that she would use me in the manner in which she did." He paused to choose his words. "These last few days, but tonight especially, everything I had felt at the time came crashing back to me."

Her breath caught. "You said you weren't in love with her."

"Make no mistake, it wasn't heartbreak, although I suppose when one feels deceived and dishonored and humiliated it's no doubt akin to heartbreak. But I suppose I really don't know."

"Because you weren't in love with her?" Why did this seem so important?

"Because I've never been in love with anyone." His gaze met hers. "Until now."

"If you think I will forgive you simply because you now imply that you love me, you should think again." She turned away and moved to the window, gazing out at the night and the stars vanishing into the black of the sea. His view was probably better than hers too. "You kissed me and then you treated me in a nasty, self-righteous manner. Why on earth should I forgive you?"

"You shouldn't," he said simply.

"I don't intend to."

"At least not yet."

"Never." It was a lie and she suspected he knew it as well as she. Good Lord, she was almost ready to forgive him now. Or perhaps she already had.

She heard him cross the room a moment before he rested his hands on the top of her arms, just below her sleeves. Heat rushed through her from his touch. No man should be allowed to have hands quite that warm.

"What are you doing?"

"I have more to say."

"And you feel it's necessary to say whatever it is you still wish to say with your hands on my arms?"

"Yes," he said softly and kissed the curve where her neck met her shoulder.

She sucked in a sharp breath. He had no way of knowing how delightful that was. "Go on, then."

"I will," he murmured against her skin. Delicious tremors washed though her.

"No." She cleared her throat. "I meant say what you want to say."

"Very well." His lips continued their sensual assault on her neck and shoulders and without thinking she tilted her head to the side. "I was indeed jealous. Every time I saw Brookings with you, my heart twisted in my chest. And tonight, seeing you in his arms…"

"You've had every bit as much opportunity as he to be with me." Her voice had the most annoying breathless quality to it. But then it was remarkably hard to breathe at all.

"I know. I was a fool." His hands on her arms tightened slightly and his mouth moved to the nape of her neck. In spite of her determination not to fall prey to his unexpectedly irresistible caresses, a tiny moan escaped her lips and her head dropped forward. "And I was afraid."

He shifted his attention to the other side of her neck and her shoulder. She'd never realized how shockingly sensitive that particular junction of neck and shoulder really was. George had never paid any attention to it but then George had never needed to seduce her either. She was his wife after all.

"Afraid?" She swallowed hard.

"Yes." His lips whispered against her and it was all she could do to concentrate on his words. "Afraid that this dashing, handsome friend of yours who has known you far longer than I have…"

She angled her head to allow him better access to her neck and sighed deeply. "And yet there is much to be said for dashing strangers."

He paused and she felt his smile against her skin. "Afraid that now that he had again appeared in your life, your feelings of friendship for him might deepen."

"I do consider him a very good friend but you, Mr. Montague…" Desire pooled deep inside her. Good Lord, she hadn't felt like this in a very long time. "You have stolen my heart."

"Have I?"

"It's nothing short of larceny, plain and simple."

"Is it?"

"You're a thief, Mr. Montague."

"Apparently, a terrible character flaw I was unaware of."

"I have never been kissed on the back of my neck by a thief before." She could barely get out the words. What was he doing to her?

"There is much to be said for larceny."

"Or on my shoulders."

He chuckled and obediently switched his attention.

"Now do you intend to seduce me?"

"My dear Willie." He chuckled softly. "I believe I already am."

How delightful. Still, a dozen conflicting emotions warred within her. Hadn't she already decided that as a widow she could do as she pleased? And if she wanted to be with this man, in a carnal sense, there was no reason why she shouldn't. But hadn't she also realized it was not in her nature to indiscriminately fall into some man's bed? Not some man, she corrected herself, this man.

"I have always intended to seduce you."

With every caress her resolve weakened.

"And then I plan to marry you."

She sighed, a long, leisurely release of breath. "I was afraid of that."

"But not surprised?"

"It's the kind of man you are."

"Rather dull."

Rather wonderful.

"I hadn't planned on marriage quite yet." She paused. It was pointless to deny her feelings or desires or that she wanted nothing more than to be with him for the rest of her days. "But I hadn't planned on you either."

"Then we have a great deal in common." He turned her to face him, pulling her into his embrace. Her hands slipped around his neck. "You were the last thing I had planned on."

His lips met hers in a kiss tender and restrained, as if he was holding himself in check. A kiss of exploration in a manner both tentative and determined. He tasted vaguely of champagne, delightful and intoxicating. His kiss deepened and his tongue dueled with hers. Anticipation tightened within her and she clung to him and drank of him and lost herself in the joining of his mouth with hers. And wanted more.

Her body pressed against his and she could feel his arousal through the layers of clothes between them. An incessant ache throbbed deep within her. He drew his lips from hers and rained kisses on the corners of her mouth and the line of her jaw. Her head fell back and he kissed her throat and neck. His mouth dropped lower and his tongue traced the line of her bodice along her breasts.

"Dante." She could barely catch her breath. He raised his head. "I believe we have entirely too many clothes on."

He nodded. "I was thinking exactly the same thing." He scooped her into his arms and carried her toward the bedroom, nudging the door open with his foot.

"Good." She stepped out of his arms and turned her back to him. "If you would be so good as to unfasten my bodice."

"How?" Frustration rang in his voice.

"There are tiny fasteners in the seam in the middle. They're supposed to be unnoticeable."

"And they are," he muttered. "Wait." A moment later, the bodice loosened and dropped to the floor. She untied the tapes of her skirt and it slithered to join the bodice.

She turned to face him, clad now only in her corset, chemise and drawers. He had discarded his shirt and waistcoat and his trousers were loose around his hips. His shoulders were as broad as she had suspected, his chest finely chiseled with a smattering of dark hair that drifted down his abdomen to disappear beneath his waistband.

"Much better, I think." Her heart beat faster. Dear Lord, she wanted his man. Desire swelled within her and impatience. He laid her on the bed and she grabbed him and pulled him down with her. And all restraint between them shattered.

His lips, her hands were everywhere at once in a frenzy of taste and touch. Within moments, her undergarments and his trousers had vanished and they lay naked in each other's arms. She explored him with her hands, and her mouth. Tasted the curve of his throat and ran her fingers down the hard muscles of his chest and along the flat of his stomach and lower until her hand curled around his erection. He moaned against her neck then grabbed her hands and shifted, holding her hands stretched above her head in one of his. He toyed with her and worshipped her with his mouth and his fingers and the heat of his body inflamed hers.

He took her nipple into his mouth and sucked and teased until she moaned and writhed beneath his touch. His hand dropped lower over her stomach and lower still and her legs opened to him of their own accord. He shifted his attention to her other breast, teasing with his teeth and his tongue. His hand slipped between her legs and brushed against that core of her desire that had been without the touch of a man for far too long. Pure sensation shot through her. She cried out and her back arched upward. His fingers slid over her, wet with her own need, and she wondered if he could feel her throbbing against his touch. If he could sense that gathering of tension that spread outward from his caress. Dear Lord, she was already so very close to that exquisite explosion of release. Without warning he stopped and let go of her hands.

Not now!

"Dante!" She could barely squeak out the word. "What—"

"I want more, Willie." He shifted to lie between her legs, pulling them over his shoulders. He glanced up at her. "I want to taste you. I want to feel you shatter against my mouth."

She stared at him.

The first touch of his tongue nearly undid her. She twisted the bedclothes in both hands and arched upward to meet his mouth. Any semblance of rational thought— of any thought at all—vanished in the wake of his as-

sault. His tongue toyed with her in long slow strokes of
sheer bliss. He nibbled and sucked in an ever-increasing
rhythm until she thrashed against him. He held her tight
in an unrelenting onslaught of utter delight. It was not
more than a moment or perhaps an entire lifetime but
without warning release shuddered though her in waves
of unrelenting pleasure.

"Good God, Dante." She stared up at the ceiling and
tried to catch her breath.

"What?"

She propped herself up on her elbows and stared down
at him. "You're not the least bit stuffy."

He grinned in an unrepentant manner.

"Remind me to tell your sister."

"There is much my sister doesn't know."

"And much we don't need to tell her." She laughed and
lay back down, urging him upward with her legs. As delightful as that was, it wasn't enough. "I do hope…" She
reached between them and caressed his erection, large
and hard and quite lovely. She ran her fingers lightly up
and down his nicely impressive length and desire again
pooled within her.

His eyes closed and he moaned. "Yes?"

"Well, it just seems…" It shouldn't be at all awkward
to tell a man whose appendage you had in your hand that
you would really like to, well, you would really like more.
"I do hope we are, well…"

"Oh God." He nuzzled the side of her neck. "Indeed we
are," he murmured then settled between her legs, moving her hand away with his and guiding himself into her.

He moved with a deliberate, measured pace and indeed, she was rather tight. It had been a very long time.
But she was as well slick with desire and he slid into her
with a slow, smooth movement. Her body welcomed him

and she wondered that she didn't swoon with the sheer joy of it. He rocked against her with an ever-increasing rhythm and she met his thrusts with her own until she didn't know where he began and she left off. Until they moved as one in tandem with each other, joined in an eternal struggle, locked in an endless dance. And her release came again—stronger and harder as if every part of her was enhanced in this unimaginable eruption of pure pleasure and sheer ecstasy. She screamed out his name and vaguely heard him groan and felt him shudder hard against her.

They collapsed exhausted in a tangle of arms and legs and blissful exhaustion. For endless moments they lay wrapped around each other, his heart beating against hers, her breath coming easier. She had the oddest desire to giggle.

"I have never had an argument with a lady before." Dante chuckled. "It's quite stimulating."

"We shall have to remember that." She grinned.

He laughed. They shifted position until she lay enfolded in his arms. She had no desire to move and could easily stay like this for hours. Someday perhaps.

Willie reluctantly sat up and gazed down at him. "I should return to my room."

"Why?"

"Well, yours is much nicer but—" she sighed "—I would hate for anyone to discover this."

"You're concerned about scandal?"

"I'm concerned about setting a proper example for the girls," she said in an overly prim manner given she was naked. And delightfully satisfied.

He propped himself up on his elbows and grinned. "The legendary Lady Bascombe is concerned about propriety?"

"Obviously you have been a bad influence on me." She sniffed.

"Good." He drew her into his arms. "As you've been an especially bad influence on me, as well."

"Apparently, Mr. Montague." She raised her lips to his and pressed closer against him. "There is much to be said for bad influences."

"Indeed, Lady Bascombe." He grabbed her and rolled over until she lay beneath him. "It might be the wisest course to, oh, embrace that bad influence."

"Whatever did you have in mind, Mr. Montague?" It was a silly question. Evidence of his intention was fairly obvious. My, the man certainly had excellent stamina.

Dante proceeded to show her exactly what he had in mind. And continued to show her until her blood pounded in her ears, faster and harder. Until she rocked against him and urged him on. Until at last she gasped for breath and once again ripples of sheer pleasure cascaded through her. Until she felt Dante's own tremors of relief sweep through his body and he groaned and held her tighter.

Willie giggled with the absolute delight of it and Dante chuckled, his head buried against her neck. She savored the feeling of his body entwined with hers, the exhausted delight of utter satisfaction.

And yet the pounding didn't cease.

CHAPTER FOURTEEN

"Good God." Dante groaned then raised his head and frowned. "Do you hear something?"

Her senses cleared. Blast it all. "I think there's someone at the door."

"Of course there is," he muttered. He rose off the bed, grabbed a dressing gown from the wardrobe and quickly wrapped it around himself. Rather a shame as he had an exceptionally nice backside. The man really was surprisingly fit.

He closed the door behind him and she heard a woman's worried voice. Willie debated whether she should join them but it seemed best to stay where she was. She preferred to keep what had just occurred private. Dante would tell her who had interrupted them soon enough. Besides, she certainly couldn't appear wrapped in nothing more substantial than a coverlet and she couldn't put her gown back on without a little help.

Willie stretched in a lovely lazy manner, savoring the silken feel of the sheets against her naked skin. Dear Lord, she really could stay forever in his bed, in his arms, as his lover and his wife. She wasn't opposed to marriage. She simply had no desire to marry for financial necessity. The possibility of marriage for love hadn't so much as crossed her mind. Now it was not at all a bad idea. Indeed, it was rather brilliant.

Was there any good reason why she shouldn't marry

him? He was responsible and sensible and everything she'd decided she wanted in her next husband. Everything George—God rest his tarnished soul—hadn't been. And Dante was, as well, amusing and generous and kind. Her life would not be outrageous with Dante as it had been with George but Dante was full of surprises and there wasn't a doubt in her mind it would be exciting and nothing short of remarkable. Her heart fluttered.

Dear Lord, she was indeed in love with him.

Marriage to Dante would also mean her financial difficulties would be over. She was fairly certain he had a respectable fortune but if he didn't—she smiled—it really didn't matter. She had her painting to sell. Even better—she could give it to Dante as a wedding gift. He would love it and probably knew all there was to know about the artist. She should tell him about the painting before they reached Venice.

The oddest sense of regret stabbed her at the idea of being dependent upon someone else again. This wasn't at all how she thought her life would be. But Dante was a man she could put her faith in. A man she could trust. Who would have imagined her journey to claim her future would lead to the man she would love for the rest of her days? Apparently, the most wonderful things in life really were those least expected.

The door opened and Dante stepped into the room, their clothes slung over his arm. "She's gone."

"Who was it?" Willie struggled to sit up, clutching the sheet to her chest.

"My sister." He blew a long breath and dropped the clothes on the bed. "Harriet has disappeared."

"What? How?"

"One of the twins said she slipped off into the gardens, apparently to meet someone."

Willie gasped. "Goodwin?"

"We don't know." He ran his hand through his hair. "I wouldn't say this to Roz but I hope so."

Willie's stomach lurched. There were all sorts of dreadful things that could happen to a lovely young woman alone in a foreign country.

"I'm going to look for her." He discarded his dressing gown and pulled on his trousers. "Roz went back to their rooms on the chance that Harriet had returned there to gather her belongings."

"To run off with Goodwin?"

He nodded. "If Harriet isn't there, Roz will meet me in the ballroom."

"I'll go with you." Willie slipped out of bed, snatched up her chemise and pulled it on over her head.

"I think it would be best if you didn't. Frankly, it will take entirely too long for you to dress."

"You're probably right." She shimmied into her drawers. "I certainly can't go wandering around in a total state of dishabille." She grabbed her skirt and stepped into it. "I'll dispense with my corset but if you could help fasten my bodice, I can manage everything else on my own. I really don't want to call for a maid."

He chuckled. "That could be awkward."

"At the very least." She turned her back to him and held her hair up off her neck. She would have to do something about her hair before she left, as well. He fumbled with the fastenings for what seemed like forever but was probably no more than a minute or two.

"It's not nearly as much fun helping you put clothes on as it was taking them off," he muttered.

"Yet something else we have in common."

"Done." A note of satisfaction sounded in his voice and he kissed the back of her neck.

She turned around. "I warn you, Mr. Montague, if you do that again, I will not let you leave."

"I was hoping we'd have the whole night together."

Willie leaned forward and brushed her lips across his. "We'll have other nights together. But until then…"

"Yes?"

"I have grown out of flaunting my sins in public." She straightened his necktie. He was not the sort of man to go out improperly dressed. Indeed, she'd never seen him anything less than perfectly attired. "I would much prefer we keep this between us for now."

"You may count on it."

He nodded and turned to leave then turned back, pulled her into his arms and pressed his lips to hers in a kiss filled with magic and promise and love. When at last he released her, she was hard-pressed to catch her breath. "Marry me, Willie."

"Is that a proposal?"

"Why, yes, I believe it is."

"I know you think the proper thing to do after, well, this—" she waved at the disheveled bed "—is to offer marriage—"

"Might I point out that I mentioned marriage before—" he waved at the bed "—this."

"It was in anticipation but it scarcely matters. The point I am trying to make is that you're under no obligation to marry me. Nor do I expect you to." She held her breath. As much as she wanted him, and wanting him included marriage, she didn't want him to feel he had no choice.

"I know that but I do have to marry you."

"Why?"

"Because I would be a fool not to. And regardless of

what my sister may think, I am not an idiot." He grinned. "And because I love you."

"Well then…" She shook her head. "I'm afraid I shall have to say no."

"No?" He stared.

"I want a proper proposal," she said in a lofty manner. "Something romantic. Not an offhand offer on your way out the door to rescue your niece."

He chuckled. "That can be arranged." He hesitated as if about to draw her into his arms again.

As delightful as the idea was, Willie waved toward the door. "Now go. Harriet and Rosalind need you."

"We will talk later," he said firmly.

"The last time you said we needed to talk—" She glanced pointedly at the bed.

"There is much to be said for stimulating conversation." He cast her a wicked grin and left the bedroom.

"Dante." She hurried after him. "Please let me know when you find Harriet."

"Of course." He nodded and hurried out the door.

She did hate to see him leave but it couldn't be helped. His sister and his niece needed him and he was not the type of man to shirk his responsibilities. He really was quite wonderful.

With any luck Dante would find Harriet, and Goodwin, as well, before they had the opportunity to do something foolish. Running off and marrying came to mind. Willie knew better than most the consequences of one impetuous, romantic decision involving a dashing young man who swept you off your feet.

But even her concern about Harriet couldn't dampen her own sense of, well, happiness. She couldn't recall the last time she had known this kind of utter joy.

She returned to the bedroom and managed to pull her

petticoat on under her skirt then gathered up her corset and other undergarments she hadn't had time to put back on. She folded a towel around everything on the off chance she met anyone on her return to her room. It probably wasn't necessary. Her room was right down the hall and it was late enough that she doubted she would encounter anyone from their party. Still, they had left the ball early and who knew how long it went on.

Willie collected her shoes then returned to the parlor, placing her towel-wrapped bundle on the desk. Although her evening slippers were not new, she hadn't worn them for a long time and they were a bit snug. She sat down and wedged her foot into one shoe then the other, wincing a little in the process. Still, they were all she had brought with her for evening and they would have to do. Besides, they were bronze-colored silk and quite fetching. She stood and grabbed the bundle, knocking over Dante's valise in the process. Papers and files scattered over the desk and floor. She sighed. *Perfect.*

Willie picked up the assorted files and individual papers, glancing casually at the neatly typewritten labels. He really was a man of business. She smiled. Imagine, the *legendary* Lady Bascombe married to a man of business. She stacked everything together then proceeded to gather those items strewn across the desk. One of the files had spilled its contents and she collected the papers she assumed belonged to it, hoping she put everything back where it belonged. She glanced at the label on the file— *Lady Wilhelmina Bascombe*—and smiled. Goodness, she couldn't seem to stop smiling. Life was really rather wonderful. The file was certainly no surprise. Dante had said he had thoroughly checked into her background even though what he had told her he'd found was not at all significant. Nor should it be. Her life with George had been fodder for gossip and therefore relatively public.

Willie sank back into the chair and opened the dossier. Her name was on it after all. Whoever had prepared this for Dante had indeed been thorough. There was a page noting her attendance at Miss Bicklesham's, another concerning her family background with references to her father, Lady Plumdale and Poppy. The next described her life with George in rather startling detail, although there really wasn't anything here that was not public knowledge. Still, it was awkward to read about one's past misbehaviors. It was clear why Dante had called her *legendary*. She turned to the next page, curious about what else might be here as it did appear her entire life had been laid out at this point. This was some kind of report or letter that didn't seem to have anything to do with her. Perhaps she had put the wrong paper in the file. The report dealt with a painting that had gone missing from his museum years ago. The missing painting was a Portinari. What an odd coincidence... A horrible feeling of dread settled in the pit of her stomach.

Something, some voice of self-preservation told her to stop reading right now. Her future, her happiness might depend on it. But she'd lived with one man in blissful ignorance—she would not do so again. Her hand holding the paper trembled slightly but she continued to read.

The report said the missing Portinari had been in the possession of Lord and Lady Bascombe but had been used as collateral for a loan and was now in the hands of a collector in Venice. It went on to say Lady Bascombe was to lead a group of American mothers and daughters to Venice, no doubt with an eye toward reclaiming the painting. The writer further suggested the wisdom of being present when Lady Bascombe once more had the painting in her possession so as not to lose track of it again and speculated she intended the painting's eventual sale. It was all here: the current state of her finances, the debts George had left her with, her sale of the country house, her dismissal of most of her staff—everything.

An odd sort of numbness descended over her, a dark miasma stifling her emotions. She stood, added the file to the stack of papers and slipped everything neatly into the valise. Some part of her mind not stunned by shock urged her to hurry. To return to her room before the import of all she had read ripped her to shreds. She calmly collected her bundle of undergarments, left Dante's suite and strode briskly down the corridor to her room, grateful she did not run across anyone on her way. She wasn't sure she could form a coherent sentence at the moment and didn't have the fortitude to try. With every ounce of strength she possessed, she struggled to maintain an air of unruffled composure although it did seem the distance back to her accommodations was endless.

Willie finally reached her room, stepped inside and closed the door carefully behind her. She rested her back against the door, allowed the bundle to drop and slowly slid down the door to the floor, her knees no longer willing to support her. For a moment or forever she stared unseeing at the room in front of her.

Maybe she was wrong? Maybe she had misunderstood? It was as much a prayer as a question.

Not bloody likely. It was all there. Every bit of it in startling detail. Dante had deceived her from the beginning. Even with what she'd read, it was hard to believe. Or perhaps she just didn't want to believe it. Didn't want to believe that the man she thought she knew was nothing more than a ruse. But it was impossible to deny. He'd joined her tour only so that he could be there when she recovered the Portinari. He'd been charming and endearing and excruciatingly *nice*! And she'd fallen for him head over heels. How could she have been so stupid? So blind?

He'd said he loved her. He'd said he wanted to marry her. Without warning the truth struck her. Of course he wanted to marry her. Once they were wed, everything she had would be his. Her house, what few possessions she still owned and more to the point—her painting!

Was this what betrayal felt like? Dark and heavy and all encompassing? And the kind of pain she never imagined one could endure. As if her heart were being torn apart inside her.

Her immediate impulse was to confront him as soon as possible. Tell him to his face how vile and despicable he was. How she would despise him until the day she died. And beyond if possible. How she would destroy the Portinari before she would ever let him get his hands on it.

She felt a drop on her hand and glanced down. Good Lord, it was a tear. She was crying! She dashed the tears away from her face. The blasted man had made her cry. Well, she refused to waste another tear on him. He wasn't dead after all.

The anger she'd felt toward him earlier tonight was but a pittance compared to this…this rage! Given his past, his response to Val's attentions was somewhat understandable. And admittedly it all might have been the tiniest bit her fault even if she hadn't really given it much attention at the time. That was a mistake on her part.

But this? This was deliberate and calculating and very, very clever. And unforgivable.

She had been furious about his ridiculous behavior but that anger was hot and fierce and had burned out fairly quickly. Now the ire that gripped her was cold and calm and hard. And unrelenting.

Odd how the tables had turned. She had feared that he would not be able to trust her. On the contrary, it was she who should not have trusted him.

She could never forgive him for this deception. This betrayal. He'd worked his way into her affections with cunning and treachery and she'd been taken in by his lies. And she'd fallen in love with the blasted man!

He really had stolen her heart with chicanery and duplicity and dishonesty. What a cad he was. And what a fool she was. The *Inferno*'s nine circles of hell would look like a stroll in Hyde Park on a pleasant afternoon before she was through with him.

He was a liar and a thief. And this act of larceny would not go unpunished.

CHAPTER FIFTEEN

"DARE I ASK what you think you are doing?" Dante's curt tone shattered the relative stillness of the night.

The couple on the stone bench in the casino gardens sprang apart, the man immediately rising to his feet. "I beg your pardon."

The light from a distant lamppost was dim but bright enough for Dante to see his mistake immediately.

"My apologies." He grimaced. "I mistook you for someone else." He paused. "But perhaps this is not the best place for whatever it is you are doing." He nodded, turned on his heel and continued down the walk.

Damnation—where was his blasted niece? Dante had left Roz in the capable hands of the other ladies near the ballroom entry with instructions to wait for him there. The last thing he needed was to lose his sister as well as her daughter. Certainly a possibility if Harriet had been abducted by unknown persons either for financial gain or other nefarious reasons. They were on a coast after all and it would be remarkably easy to spirit a lovely young woman away to God knows where.

The ballroom was every bit as crowded as it had been earlier. Understandable as it wasn't much past midnight. Even so, a great deal had happened since he had left earlier in the evening. A great deal had changed. His life would never be the same.

It would be nothing more than sheer luck if he found

Harriet. Of course, luck did seem to be with him tonight. In spite of his childish behavior in recent days, the most remarkable woman in the world would soon be his wife. After a proper proposal, accompanied by the perfect ring—Roz would help him select one—and an extremely short engagement, Willie would be his. He ignored the absurd desire to grin like an idiot. That was entirely inappropriate given the circumstances. Nothing was more important than finding his niece at the moment.

If indeed luck was with him, then Harriet had neither been kidnapped nor was she running off with her determined suitor but was simply engaged in a clandestine meeting. He hoped his niece was far too clever to elope with the young man but he wouldn't want to gamble on the intelligence of a girl in love. Still, he would wager that Harriet was the kind of young woman who would want a grand wedding with everyone who was anyone in attendance rather than the scandal that would accompany an unexpected union.

Fortunately, Dante had walked the garden paths frequently since their arrival in an effort to remove himself from the constant specter of Willie with Brookings. What an idiot Dante had been. Worse, he had wasted a great deal of time. Why, he could have been enjoying the fresh air and ocean breezes with Willie on his arm rather than stalking these paths alone.

"Well, that was embarrassing, Uncle Dante." Harriet's voice sounded behind him. He turned to find her perched on a bench, a handsome young man standing by her side. "I fully expected the man to punch you at any moment."

Relief washed through Dante. "And whose fault is that?"

"Mother's," Harriet said with a shrug.

"Your mother is beside herself." Dante's gaze shifted between Harriet and her companion. "And you are?"

"I am sorry, sir." The young man stepped forward. "Allow me to introduce myself. My name is Bertram Goodwin."

"Ah yes, Mr. Goodwin." Dante narrowed his eyes. "You've been following us, haven't you?"

"I'm not sure *following* is the right word, sir." He shook his head. "That would be rather unnerving."

"For those being followed you mean," Dante said.

"Well, yes." Goodwin nodded. "I can't imagine the follower would be the least bit uncomfortable whereas the person being followed might be somewhat uneasy. Unless, of course, they were unaware of being followed, which would make the question moot, don't you think? One can't be concerned about something one doesn't know."

Dante stared. He was not about to start a philosophical debate with anyone at this hour. Either this young man was exceptionally brilliant or completely scattered. Regardless, he did seem to have turned the direction of the conversation.

"Accompanying is more accurate," Harriet cut in, "albeit at a distance. At my invitation."

"Your invitation?"

"Well, yes. I had no desire to leave him behind." Harriet cast the young man a brilliant smile. "I should have been more circumspect tonight but I did think Mother wouldn't notice my absence for a while." She sighed. "We'd scarcely exchanged more than a few words when you appeared and it was obvious Mother had sent you to find me. We saw you come into the gardens and thought it would be fun to follow you for a bit."

Goodwin shifted from foot to foot.

"Well, I thought it would be fun. But we weren't the least bit good at it although you never noticed us." Harriet smiled in a smug manner.

"Sorry, sir," Goodwin said under his breath but he didn't look at all sorry.

His sister had this all wrong. Goodwin wasn't the bad influence here. If anything Harriet and Goodwin were two of a kind. Dante's gaze shifted between the young people. "And why, Mr. Goodwin, did you think it wise to follow Harriet—"

"Accompany," Harriet interjected.

Dante ignored her. "Well?"

"Because…" Sheer panic shone in Goodwin's eyes. He glanced at Harriet. She nodded and the young man squared his shoulders. "Because she's beautiful and delightful and magnificent and I don't want to live a moment without her."

Harriet smirked in satisfaction. Good Lord. The girl was leading this poor boy around by his nose. And Goodwin was too smitten to notice or care.

"And your intentions?"

"I intend to marry her, sir," Goodwin said staunchly.

"But not yet," Harriet added quickly. "If I marry without permission before the age of twenty-five, I won't get my dowry. It's a nasty threat and Mother is holding it over my head. Can you imagine such a thing, Uncle Dante?"

"It makes perfect sense to me." Apparently, Roz knew her daughter well.

"You didn't think we were going to run off tonight, did you? I would never be silly enough to elope and become the subject of gossip and scandal." She sniffed. "I have no intention of becoming another Lady Bascombe."

"Oh?"

There must have been something in the tone of his voice.

"Not that she isn't rather respectable now, of course," Harriet said quickly. "And Mother does like her. One couldn't get a better recommendation than Mother's approval."

"You would be wise to remember that, Harriett." Dante turned his attention to Goodwin. "Do you intend to continue accompanying us?"

"Of course he does," Harriet said firmly.

Goodwin straightened. "Yes, sir."

"I see." He thought for a moment. "And where are you staying?"

"I had friends in Paris so I stayed with them." Goodwin chose his words carefully. "Here, I, um, well—"

"Bertie really doesn't have any money for hotels," Harriet blurted. "Poor dear."

"I've been sleeping on the beach, sir," Goodwin said reluctantly. "And using the facilities at the casino. But I do have enough for train fare."

"Don't you think it might be wiser to use that money to fund your way home?"

"Absolutely not, sir." Bertie shot an adoring look at Harriet. "I would follow Harriet anywhere and I would do so forever."

Harriet beamed.

"Forever is a very long time, Mr. Goodwin." Dante studied him closely. "How old are you?"

"I passed twenty-one on my last birthday, sir."

Dante considered the couple for a moment. There were only two ways to resolve this. Dante could insist Bertie return home or at least stop accompanying them and threaten to have him arrested if he didn't. Roz would like that but it could, as well, provoke Harriet and, in spite of her claims, she might decide to elope with him after all. There was nothing more appealing than forbidden love. Or Dante could accept Bertie at his word.

"Very well then, Mr. Goodwin," Dante said firmly. "If you are determined to continue your accompaniment, you shall do it where I can keep an eye on you." He glanced at Harriet. "On both of you."

Harriet's brow furrowed. "What do you mean?"

"I mean—" Roz wasn't going to like this one bit "—Mr. Goodwin is now an official member of our party. Bertie." Dante adopted his most pleasant expression. "From now on, you will share my rooms. And I am going to be right by your side every minute. Unless you have some objection?"

Poor, dear Bertie swallowed hard. "Not at all, sir."

"Thank you, Uncle Dante." Harriet beamed. "I think it's a brilliant idea." A wicked light shone in the girl's eyes. "I can't wait to tell Mother."

"You did what?" Roz stared at him as if he had lost his mind.

"Consider it for a moment, Roz. You'll see it makes perfect sense."

Dante had left Bertie in his new accommodations, sent a bellboy to find Roz as well as deliver a note to Willie telling her Harriet was safe, and then escorted Harriet to her rooms. She and her mother had a suite similar to Dante's and he had waited for his sister in the parlor.

"It makes no sense whatsoever. It's like saying to the fox 'Here is the henhouse. Please come in. Do you see anything you like?'"

"Excellent analogy but you're wrong. People always want what they aren't supposed to have. If we welcome this young man, he will become far less attractive. Besides, if he travels with us, we'll be better able to keep watch on them both."

"You do have a point." Roz glanced at the bedroom door. No doubt Harriet had her ear pressed against it on the other side.

"Unless you have a better idea."

"I have a number of better ideas." She huffed. "Unfortunately, they are all either legally or morally unacceptable."

"Then we shall definitely avoid them."

"But they would be most satisfying." She sighed then eyed him skeptically. "You do realize having Mr. Goodwin in your keeping might make your quest for forgiveness a bit more difficult."

"Oh, Willie has already forgiven me," he said smugly.

"Thank you for confirming my suspicions. While I do appreciate your effort at discretion you should know a man who is awakened in the night does not look the same as one who has not been to sleep. The—" she waved absently at his hair "—dishevelment is decidedly different. In addition, your clothes and hers were strewn about the parlor."

He smoothed his hair. "I assumed you wouldn't approve."

"Why? Because it's terribly improper, immoral and scandalous?"

"All right," he said slowly.

"Apparently, you have not noticed but I stopped being horribly narrow-minded about that sort of thing years ago. Mind you, I do not approve of infidelity or flagrant immorality but I have come to accept that even the best of us are fallible." She paused. "Not me, of course, but most people."

"So you approve?"

"Of your activities tonight? Good Lord, no." She shrugged. "But apparently I don't entirely disapprove either as I don't disapprove of Willie."

"Excellent." He grinned.

"So do you now plan to marry her?"

"I do. As soon as I propose properly." He chuckled. "She's insisting on that and I suspect she wants a proper wedding, as well."

"Good. It does seem that all has worked out as it should, then. You end up with both Willie and the Portinari. Once she marries you, the painting is yours and you can return it to the museum where it belongs."

Bloody hell! He stared at his sister.

"You have told her about the painting, haven't you?" Roz said slowly.

"I intended to."

Roz stared. "You can't possibly be this obtuse."

"Apparently, I can," he snapped. "What am I going to do now?"

"I don't know but you had better think of something." She huffed. "Something brilliant. Anything less will simply not do."

"Yes, well, brilliant is a problem, isn't it?" Without thinking he paced the room. He'd been faced with other dilemmas before. Tricky complicated messes that required clever ideas and superb negotiation to unravel and resolve. "I could pretend to know nothing about the painting and be quite shocked when she reclaims it."

"And assert it's just a startling coincidence when she discovers it's the centerpiece of a trio of paintings and the museum you oversee—*your grandfather's collection*—a collection you know like the back of your hand, has the matching works? Oh yes, that is brilliant."

"Do you have a better idea? And frankly, Roz, I don't care if it's immoral or illegal."

"Good Lord, you are desperate."

"You've noticed that, have you?" He blew a long breath and shook his head. "I can't lose her, Roz."

"I warned you, if you didn't tell her the truth you risked losing her and the painting."

"Apparently, you were right."

"You should have listened to me."

"Yes, well, I didn't." He heaved a frustrated sigh. "I tried to tell her, I really did. But the perfect moment never presented itself."

"Although I daresay there were any number of imperfect moments."

"Perhaps but something like this needs to be handled carefully."

"Perfect is no longer a possibility." She shook her head. "You are—"

"An idiot," he snapped. "Yes, I know." A tiny ray of hope, a light in the darkness flickered and he grabbed on to it. "But she's in love with me, Roz. She'll forgive me."

"And once again you have made my point."

"I'll think of something."

"There is only one possible way to salvage this and even that is questionable." She met his gaze directly. "You have to tell her everything."

"Yes, I know."

"And you have to tell her at once."

"I realize that."

"I daresay, at this point, she will not take your revelations well. When we reach Venice it will be too late." A warning sounded in her voice. "It might already be too late."

"I know that, as well."

"You have four days until we arrive in Venice."

"I am aware of our itinerary."

"It's not enough to know everything about the mess you've made, now you have to step up and do something to fix it. If that is even possible." She shook her head. "You are like a runaway carriage about to plunge over a cliff. If you do nothing to stop it..." She cast him a sympathetic look. "I would hate to see your heart truly broken, Dante, but I fear it will be unless you tread very carefully."

"I intend to."

"You will have no one to blame but yourself."

"For God's sake, Roz!" Did she have to be so bloody superior all the time? "I understand all the ramifications here. Everything that might happen, everything I stand to lose!"

Roz stared in surprise, obviously taken aback by his words. In spite of his successes in life, she still considered him her senseless little brother. "Well, as long as you know..."

"Believe me, I do!" Telling Willie everything now, after she'd shared his bed, after he'd declared his love and his intention to marry her would have to be handled carefully. He needed the right moment and the right words. Anything less would spell disaster. He shook his head. "What I don't know is how I'm going to stop that damn carriage from plummeting over that blasted cliff."

And taking him along with it.

CHAPTER SIXTEEN

Itinerary.

Genoa and Verona.

Today we leave picturesque Monaco behind and begin our journey through Italy, winding our way along the coast to spend two nights each in both Genoa and Verona. After arrival in Genoa, we shall stroll the streets of the ancient seaport and begin our exploration of the home of the Discoverer of America. A full day in Genoa will allow us to enjoy its sun-drenched slopes, scenic beauty and evidence of its fabled history.

Then it's on to Verona, the setting for what many consider to be one of Shakespeare's finest tales. Here we will experience the faded influence of the Roman Empire and the splendor that was the Italian Renaissance.

"I WAS WONDERING, WILLIE…" Marian sat down at the table Willie had commandeered for herself at the far end of the lounge car.

Their party had taken up most of the seating in the car reserved for first-class passengers, much to the annoyance of the occasional traveler who wandered through the car looking, no doubt, for a bit of peace. But with four young women, all talking at nearly the same time and all vying for the attention of a handsome young man, the newest member of their group, an assortment of four other women, including two Americans, and a vile despicable creature, peace was not to be found. At least not here.

Willie looked up from her guidebook and adopted a pleasant tone. "Yes?"

"Actually, we were both wondering..." Jane settled in another seat.

Willie's gaze slid from one American to the other. "Do I want to know what you were wondering or are we all better off keeping our questions to ourselves?"

The ladies exchanged cautious glances.

Jane drew a deep breath. "No, we don't think we are. Better off that is."

"Although I suppose it depends on exactly what you have to say," Marian said.

"Very well." It wasn't hard to guess what had aroused Jane's and Marian's curiosity. As much as Willie tried to act as if nothing at all had happened by throwing herself into the role of tour leader, by being as efficient and informative and pleasant as possible, and by avoiding any private moments with Dante, even she was aware she wasn't quite managing it.

It had been easy to ignore Dante all morning. She'd been busy seeing that her charges were ready to head onward to Italy. They had left Monaco around noon then changed trains for the five-hour trip to Genoa. There was no place to escape on a train but Willie simply made certain she was never alone with him. Not that there wasn't a great deal she wished to say to him but she wanted, as well, to be calm and serene when she did so. Wanted her words to be well planned. Perfect. Better not to say anything at all for now. She feared the moment she said so much as a single word, everything would come pouring forth in an unending display of anger and heartache, exactly what she would prefer to avoid. And once she started, she might never be able to stop. Besides, she did wish to see just how far he would take his charade. Still, restraint wasn't easy. Her fury hadn't abated during the long hours of the night. Nor had her pain.

Willie closed her *Murray's Handbook for Travellers on the Riviera*, folded her hands on top of the book and forced a pleasant smile. "What were you wondering?"

"We want to know if you and Mr. Montague have, well, made up," Marian said.

"Judging from your mood today we suspect you haven't." Jane sighed, no doubt at the stupidity of men in general and Dante in particular. "We thought he was going to apologize last night."

Marian nodded. "We urged him—"

"We insisted."

"—that he do so." Marian shook her head. "He looked so miserable."

"And you did not look substantially better," Jane added.

Willie drew her brows together in confusion. "What are you talking about?"

"We're talking about Mr. Montague's dreadful behavior in recent days, of course," Jane said. "And how last night it looked very much like the two of you had words while you were dancing."

"So we told him to apologize at once." Marian shook her head in disbelief. "He wanted to wait until today but we said that was not a wise idea." She eyed Willie thoughtfully. "Apparently, he did not heed our advice."

"Well?" Jane asked.

"Well what?" Willie arched a brow.

"Are you going to confirm our suspicions?" Jane's eyes narrowed. "Because I warn you, Willie, our imaginations are probably far more creative than what has actually transpired."

"One could say whatever has *transpired* between Mr. Montague and me is no one's concern but ours."

"One could certainly say that," Marian began, "however, when one has friends who are worried, one might feel the need alleviate their anxiety."

"I assure you there is nothing to worry about," Willie said with a surprising show of serenity. "I am quite fine and in an excellent mood."

"Yes, that's what we thought." Marian glanced at Jane who nodded. "Although you are being horribly efficient in your best travel hostess manner."

"There's nothing wrong with efficient. I daresay Miss Granville would heartily approve of my efforts to be competent and capable."

"For goodness' sake, Willie." Marian huffed. "We didn't want to travel with the efficient Miss Granville, we wished to tour with the spirited Lady Bascombe."

"You what?" Willie stared.

"You thought we weren't aware of your past reputation?" Jane scoffed. "How silly of you—of course we were. But after our lengthy stay in England, we had no desire to spend a month traveling with someone unquestionably proper and boring." Jane smiled. "We wanted you."

"Miss Granville took it upon herself to make us both aware of your background before we left London." Marian leaned forward in a confidential manner. "But it did seem to us that far more was made of the incidents she related than should have been which we blame on the relative stuffiness of English society."

"On the contrary, the blame is entirely mine," Willie

said firmly. "Why, I'll have you know, I was impetuous and daring and on occasion even shocking. And while I'm not particularly proud of it, I'm not ashamed of it either. I had a great deal of fun. I daresay I would have been considered quite madcap even in America." Good Lord. Obviously being around Val—a man who was unrepentantly proud of his reputation—had had a horrible influence on her. "Although I have changed a lot since my younger days." She shrugged. "The revelations that accompany widowhood tend to do that, I believe. At least they did for me. I hope you haven't been disappointed if I have not been as outrageous as you had hoped."

"Not at all." Jane waved off the comment. "We really didn't want outrageous as much as we wanted someone who wasn't, oh, stuffy. You've suited us well and we've become friends, which is so much better than we could have imagined."

"And because we have come to know you, it's easy to see that today you are not your usual lighthearted self," Marian added.

"Nonsense. I am exactly as I always am."

"Oh, I don't think so." Jane stood and picked up Willie's guide from the table. She flipped it open and cleared her throat. "On our right," she said in a poor imitation of an English accent as she gestured to the right-hand windows, "we have the Ligurian Sea, lovely on the surface but deceitful and treacherous beneath the waves."

Willie snorted back a laugh. "I do not sound like that."

"And on our left—" Marian rose to her feet and waved at the left-hand windows "—we are passing the charming village of Andora, where one can just make out the ruins of a castle said to be haunted by a papal nuncio who was murdered here some centuries ago. The victim of lies and betrayal."

"Your accent is no better than Jane's."

Jane ignored her. "On the right side, our view of the beautiful Ligurian continues, the sea crashing against the rocky coast with a vengeance known only by those who have been cruelly mistreated and deceived."

"While here on our left, the small village of Alassio, named for the daughter of an emperor who fled here with her lover, who no doubt treated her quite badly in a devious and vile manner as men are prone to do." Marian raised a brow. "Do you see a recurring theme here?"

Willie wrinkled her nose. "Possibly."

Jane sat back and tossed the guidebook onto the table. "You haven't said two words to Mr. Montague all day and those few you have have been nothing more than polite and rather cold."

Marian plopped back into her seat. "There's been none of that flirtatious banter we all so enjoy watching. No sidelong glances, no longing looks."

Willie scoffed. "I have never looked longingly at him."

"Perhaps not but he has looked longingly at you." Jane paused. "He still does."

"It scarcely matters what he does or doesn't do," Willie said staunchly. "I want nothing more to do with him."

"Really?" Jane studied her closely then chose her words with care. "This has nothing to do with his jealousy of Lord Brookings, does it? One doesn't use words like *treachery* or *betrayal* or *lies* when it comes to that sort of behavior. No, Mr. Montague has done something else, hasn't he?"

"I don't wish to discuss it."

"Come now, Willie," Marian said, "you can tell us."

"No, Marian." Jane laid her hand on Marian's arm but her gaze stayed on Willie. "It appears this is far more serious than we had thought. If Willie doesn't want to talk about it, we shouldn't persist. But, Willie." Her gaze met Willie's directly. "If you change your mind, we are always willing to listen." She smiled. "And offer sage advice if needed."

"It's what friends do and we are your friends." Marian nodded. "No matter what, we will always be on your side."

"That is good to know." Her spirits lifted. A man had deceived her and toyed with her affections and, yes, broken her heart, but she had friends. Real friends. Women who were concerned about her, who would stand by her regardless of what might happen. Affection for these women washed through her.

"Now then." Jane's eyes sparkled with amusement. "What charming, picturesque village fraught with treachery and deceit perpetrated by wicked, heartless men will we be passing next?"

COULD ONE ASK for better friends than Jane and Marian? The ladies took it upon themselves to keep Willie from any and all inadvertent, private encounters with Dante, closing ranks around her with the precision of a military exercise. From the moment they arrived in Genoa, the Americans were by her side. And that, together with her schedule, would maintain Willie at least for now.

Willie wasn't at all sure what she had expected, she had studied her guidebooks after all, but Genoa was a bustling seaport with more than a hundred thousand residents. Not as sizable as London by any means but far larger than the rustic village she had expected. Immediately after checking in to the Hotel Continental, the group agreed to a stroll before dinner. Jane had especially wanted to see the monument to Columbus with its marble statue of the explorer together with a female figure representing America and seated figures portraying Geography, Discretion, Steadfastness and Religion on the four corners of the huge square pediment. It was most impressive even if Geneva had felt compelled to point out it was likely Columbus was not actually born in Genoa and, furthermore, the city had turned down his request to fund his voyages; therefore the shrine was the height of irony. Still, it was an imposing monument.

Rosalind decided Bertie would be fully Dante's responsibility. Which meant Dante was also saddled with the girls, all of whom seemed to find the handsome Mr. Goodwin quite dashing, much to Harriet's annoyance. Young Bertie, with his brown hair and blue eyes, was indeed charming even if a bit inexperienced. One could almost see the young man's head swell with every passing moment and every adoring glance from the girls. Apparently, the admiration of not one but four lovely young women stoked the boy's confidence, as well. He was not nearly as intimidated by Dante as he had been last night—at least according to Harriet's account of the story. If Willie had been inclined to give Dante credit for anything, and she wasn't, she might have admired his cleverness at including Bertie in their group. After all, she doubted Harriet had spent any significant time in the young man's company and now that he was part of their tour, they would be around each other constantly. There was nothing that bred contempt quite as quickly as proximity unless, of course, it was deception, betrayal and treachery.

After a pleasant evening and a fine dinner, everyone retired to their respective rooms. Willie noted a moment of gratitude to young Mr. Goodwin. If not for his presence in Dante's rooms, the beast would no doubt have knocked on her door late in the night. She had no desire to have it out with him in the corridor of a hotel in the ancestral home of the discoverer of America. Tomorrow perhaps she would be calm enough to confront him. It was obvious today the man was completely confused by her refusal to so much as meet his gaze. Good. The very least he deserved was confusion.

Their full day in Genoa was bright and sunny, with balmy ocean breezes. The city was a fascinating mix of old and new. Ancient winding streets, so narrow one could almost touch the immensely high, brightly colored buildings on either side, climbed upward from the sea to the mountains in the oldest parts of the city. While few of the palaces from the days when Genoa ruled the sea were open for public viewing, one could easily see into the courtyards with their ornate columns and arches, marble arcades and grand stairways. They spent far more time than Willie would have liked in the Palazzo Rosso, a glorious Renaissance palace that now housed the most extensive collection of paintings in the city. Dante enjoyed it and lectured the others on the importance of one artist or another. The man should have been a professor.

The extent to which the past pervaded was all encompassing. And really quite fascinating. Who would have thought she would grow to like history? But one could almost hear the footsteps of those who had come before. The crusaders and explorers, admirals and princes.

A shrine to a saint or the virgin was on every corner. One wondered if that meant there were too many sinners or not enough. There were nearly as many churches or cathedrals—each and every one of them with something of historic or artistic merit. The earliest cathedral was said to occupy the site of a temple of Diana and included columns from the temple itself. It was a wonder some irate divinity didn't smite them all.

And towering in the southern skies over the harbor the great lighthouse rose nearly four hundred feet into the sky. A suggestion that they climb to the top was met with a distinct lack of enthusiasm.

It was late afternoon when they arrived at the Cathedral of San Lorenzo, a massive structure that had been built and rebuilt and altered for the past six hundred years. The facade was constructed of black-and-white marble so as to give the building a striped effect. Had it not been so imposing, Willie would have considered it rather whimsical in appearance. Still, in spite of the works of art and relics to be found within its walls, she reminded the others —as she had done every time they entered a church—that this was a place of worship and they should be restrained and respectful. Suitably subdued, they filed into the cathedral and immediately scattered. Willie noted Dante following Harriet and Bertie, who were probably just excited to see one of the many frescoes by Renaissance masters and not merely eager to escape the ever-watchful eyes of Harriet's family. They would keep his attention for a while.

It was indeed a remarkable building. Dante would surely appreciate the cathedral's frescoes and sculptures. Art here was part of the very character of the structure. Willie craned her neck to study the fresco in the vaulted ceiling of the choir. As much as she was not particularly interested in anything of an artistic nature, the paintings depicting the martyrdom of San Lorenzo were mesmerizing. Even from this distance, the life-size figures were finely detailed and quite extraordinary. She could see how, possibly, someone might be fascinated by works like this as well as by the men who created them.

"Might we talk for a moment?" Dante asked in a hushed voice beside her.

Blast it all. She'd been so busy staring at the fresco, she hadn't heard him approach. "We're in a church, Mr. Montague, a place of worship. This is neither the time nor the place."

"Yes, of course but—"

"And I am deep in the appreciation of art, Mr. Montague. Art!" Her voice was louder than she had intended, and she drew a calming breath, then directed her attention to him. "Surely you understand art? How one can be taken with a painting?"

"Yes, I do. I didn't expect that you…"

She narrowed her eyes. "That I what?"

"Well, you did say you were not especially fond of art."

"I wasn't." She shrugged. "Now I am."

"I find that hard to believe," he said slowly.

"Believe what you want. But we are in Italy, the heart of the Renaissance. Some of the most magnificent works of civilized man were created during that period." Thank God she continued to study her guidebooks. She sounded shockingly well-versed. "The painting above is the work of Lazzaro Tavarone, considered late Renaissance. He was a native of Genoa, although he also painted in Spain."

Dante stared.

"Close your mouth, Mr. Montague. That look is not at all becoming." She turned to leave but he grabbed her arm.

"Are you angry with me?"

"Why?" Her jaw tightened. "What have you done?"

"Nothing." His voice rang with confused innocence. It would have been most effective had she not known the truth. "If this is about the other night—"

"It's not." She cast a pointed look at his hand on her arm and he released her.

"Because I thought it was remarkable. I thought—" his gaze searched hers "—it was a beginning."

"You were wrong," she said sharply, ignoring the awful hurt that stabbed through her as she said the words.

"If this is about Bertie—"

"It's not." Panic warred with anger within her. Another few moments and she would lose all control and tell him what she thought of him. Tell him how much he had devastated her. And she would do so at the top of her lungs right here surrounded by sacred relics and the ghosts of saints and martyrs. And would no doubt immediately be struck by a thunderbolt from the heavens and eventual eternal damnation. "If you will excuse me."

"At least tell me what I have done." The plaintive note in his voice nearly pulled her up short but she didn't so much as hesitate in her march down the aisle to the front of the church. The significance was not lost on her.

"Willie." He was right behind her.

She whirled to face him. "I can't believe a man of your intelligence cannot ascertain that for himself!"

"Lady Bascombe." Geneva appeared beside them, righteous indignation in her eyes and apparently oblivious to what she'd interrupted. Willie could have kissed her.

She summoned a measure of calm. "What is it, Geneva?"

"Did you know they have the ashes of Saint John the Baptist here?"

Willie nodded. It was in one of her guidebooks.

"They have a special chapel and that's where the ashes are. But—" Geneva paused for dramatic effect "—women are not allowed inside. Can you imagine such a thing?"

"It's probably some sort of superstition," Dante offered.

"No, it's retribution." The girl fairly quivered with

outrage. "Because a woman—Salome—demanded John the Baptist's head."

"I suppose that's the price to be paid—" Willie's narrowed gaze shifted to Dante "—for betrayal and treachery."

"But it's not fair that we all have to pay." Geneva huffed. "I have certainly never demanded some man's head on a platter."

"And let us hope you never need to, although one can certainly understand the temptation." Willie shot a chilling look at Dante then took Geneva's elbow and steered her toward the front of the church.

Geneva leaned close and spoke softly. "You're still angry at him, aren't you?"

"Whatever gave you that idea?" Willie said lightly. "Did your mother say something?"

"Mother didn't have to. It's obvious you're angry. The other girls have been talking about it. And it's just as obvious that he has no idea why."

Willie glanced at her. "You really aren't upset about not being able to go into the chapel, are you?"

"Oh, I think it's unconscionable. It is nearly the twentieth century after all." Geneva shrugged. "But as it looked to me that you were about to smack Mr. Montague at any minute, I thought it best to provide a distraction and initiate a rescue."

Willie choked back a laugh. "You are a clever girl."

Geneva grinned.

"You don't think he knows what he's done?"

"Lady Bascombe, I have two older brothers. I have seen that look on the face of a man before." She hesitated. "I really don't think it's fair, you know."

"Not being allowed into the chapel?" Willie asked in an effort to steer Geneva in another direction. "I'm afraid there is nothing we can do about it."

"Not that, although it isn't fair, but Mr. Montague not knowing why you're mad at him."

"Probably not." Willie's jaw tightened. "But he prides himself on his intelligence. Let him figure it out." The question was—when would he manage to do so? Regardless, she intended to be prepared when he finally confessed all. Forewarned was certainly forearmed in this case. Indeed, at the moment, it did seem she had all the cards.

Now she had to determine exactly how she wished to play them.

THIS TRICK OF getting nine—now ten—people from place to place was proving easier and easier. Perhaps Willie would indeed continue escorting travelers for the Lady Travelers Society. There were worse ways to spend one's life than traveling the world. Certainly Willie's Italian was little better than her French—she would have to work on that—but Geneva and the twins spoke it rather well. The train trip to Verona was uneventful and surprisingly calm, although there were undercurrents ebbing throughout the entire party.

Harriet was not happy with Bertie, who did seem most apologetic even if he did not desist flirting with the other girls entirely. At some point Willie might want to warn Harriet that men who were overly flirtatious in their youth rarely abandoned that tendency in later life. Although one probably couldn't blame the boy. The twins showered him with endless attention and Geneva was an excellent conversationalist and extremely engaging when the discussion was a matter of intellectual interest. Bertie was far smarter than he had first appeared, and it was hard not to see that he and Geneva seemed to have more in common than he and Harriet did. Which might or might not have been noticed by Harriet but was certainly noted by both Marian and Rosalind—to one's dismay and the other's delight. As much as Marian longed for a prestigious match for her daughter, the youngest son of an earl with no prospect of a title was not what she had in mind, although Willie would wager she would have overlooked that discrepancy if the boy was heir to a tidy fortune.

Rosalind was not the least bit pleased with Dante for inviting the young man to join their party and did not waver in her surveillance of her daughter. Dante acted as if nothing whatsoever had happened between him and Willie, which suited Willie, although whenever her gaze accidently strayed in his direction, he was inevitably studying her. She refused to acknowledge him. He could simmer in his own confusion—and hopefully guilt—for all she cared.

Willie and the others continued to marvel at the lack of rhyme or reason for the curious itinerary planned by the absent Mrs. Vanderflute. But there was no disputing Verona was all Willie had ever imagined an ageless Italian town to be with its brick and stucco, red-roofed buildings and cobblestone streets. Like Genoa, Verona was a mix of the ages but here the influence of ancient Rome was still apparent and blended with the glory days of the Renaissance when Verona was under control of Venice. There were certainly charming villages and evidence of ancient Rome's reach in her own country but Willie had never paid much attention. It was simply part of the fabric of Britain. But the Americans were captivated and their enthusiasm was contagious. Willie did wish she had paid more attention to her studies in school but history in a book had been dry and deadly. Here it was alive.

Even the twins were impressed when they arrived at

the Grand Hotel de Londres, a palace built nearly four hundred years ago. Tillie announced that Mozart had once stayed here according to her guidebook. Tillie had only begun looking at a guidebook in recent days. Willie's guide noted there had been any number of auspicious events at the hotel, including the coronations of kings and signing of treaties. She was finding her books more and more interesting. Even in one's hotel room, one had the oddest sense of everyone who had come before. Besides, immersing oneself in history in a place like this was an excellent way to keep one's mind occupied and off despicable cads.

The group settled into their accommodations then gathered to begin their exploration of the city. But it wasn't just the evidence of the Roman past or the faded grandeur of the Renaissance palaces that permeated the atmosphere here. There was an annoying sense of romance in the air, which could be laid firmly at the feet of one of England's native sons.

"Verona." Harriet sighed as they strolled down the street. She cast a pointed look at Bertie. "The home of Romeo and Juliet. Isn't it perfect?"

The other girls murmured their agreement.

"Romeo was a Montague too," Emma said, with a flirtatious smile at Dante. She'd been dividing her attention between Bertie and Dante since they'd arrived in Italy. Of course, Dante had looked well turned out in his formal attire on their last night in Monte Carlo. Quite dashing really. One couldn't blame the girl for developing a crush on an older man. Willie knew any number of couples whose age differences were far greater than Emma and Dante's. It was most annoying. To his credit, Dante did his best not to encourage her. In that alone he might have had a streak of decency.

"Do remember, ladies," Jane said, "they were fictional."

"And they did not end well," Rosalind added in a grim manner, aiming a pointed look first at her daughter and then at Bertie.

"I'm not so sure about Juliet being fictional," Tillie said, reading from her guidebook. "It says right here that the tomb of Juliet...oh."

Emma peered over her sister's shoulder. "It says the author won't mention the tomb of Juliet as it is a dreadful fraud." She frowned. "But he also says the real tomb was destroyed long ago." She looked at her mother. "That makes no sense if indeed Juliet wasn't real."

"It's not our country, dear," Jane murmured.

Surely Willie had not been nearly as susceptible to romantic nonsense about star-crossed lovers at their age? Although it was very nearly at the age the girls were now that she had made the foolish decision to run off and marry George so perhaps her memories weren't entirely accurate. And she had thought herself in love.

Still, if one was going to lose one's heart in an affair that would not end well, perhaps there was not a more beautiful place than Verona in which to do it. Fortunately, as Willie's heart had already been shattered, she would not succumb to the temptation of romance that shimmered in the very air around them, although that was absurd. She was no doubt mistaken. Still, it did seem the ancient city conspired to remind her of Dante should she for a moment put him out of her mind.

They weren't ten minutes from the hotel when they happened upon a piazza with a larger-than-life statue of Dante Alighieri. It was in these grand houses that he had apparently taken refuge after being banished from Florence. The figure carved in marble was of a fine-looking scholarly man. Everyone thought it most amusing although Dante did seem somewhat smug at encountering a statue of the poet he was named after. Perhaps he had failed to notice the pigeons roosting on the head of that particular Dante.

Admittedly, he might have the tiniest reason to be smug. He was certainly in his element. Dante was as well versed in architecture as he was in art and one couldn't take two steps here without tripping over a painting or sculpture by names Willie couldn't pronounce that all tended to sound the same. The man never failed to turn an answer into a lecture and didn't hesitate to flaunt his knowledge whenever possible. As much as she hated to admit it, his explanations were fascinating and while she pretended not to listen, she did. Odd how much more interesting and engaging he sounded now than when they first met. She was truly enjoying the frescoes and marble reliefs, intricately painted domed ceilings of the religious and public buildings, and the oddly compelling church-like spires of Verona's ornate tombs. Although, by their second day in Verona, she would rather see anything as long as it wasn't yet another Madonna-and-child painting. Perhaps her unbending adherence to their schedule was at least partially to blame for her growing impatience. Marian had grumbled about the relentless pace and the diabolical itinerary while Jane had mentioned that Willie herself was beginning to be a bit cranky.

Well, who would have imagined such a thing? Just because that vile loathsome creature had apparently decided that if she wasn't going to talk to him then he wasn't going to attempt to talk to her. Not that she had any desire to talk to him at the moment. But he claimed to be a man in love. Hah! A man truly in love would certainly not give up this easily. It had only been four days after all. Not unless his declaration of love was a lie too. The knife that had lodged in her heart when she'd learned his true purpose twisted. Hard.

After a long day of ornate churches, ancient monuments and fourteenth-century palaces turned museums, Willie steered her weary group to the ancient Roman arena, said to rival the Colosseum in Rome. Oh, it was in some disrepair, much of the outer wall had crumbled, but all in all it was in adequate shape for something built nearly two thousand years ago. At least the vendors who had set up their wares in the shelter of the arcade around the perimeter of the building seemed confident in the integrity of the structure. And apparently it was still used for theatrical performances, as well. The sound projection was said to be as good as any contemporary theater.

Willie was not alone in being somewhat ill-tempered at this point. Harriet had been sniping at Bertie all day, culminating in a spat just before they entered the arena, much to Rosalind's barely concealed glee.

They meandered into the arena and for a moment, Willie could have sworn she heard the cheers of audiences long dead and gone to dust, although it was more likely the groans of her band of tired travelers. Harriet and the other girls immediately climbed the steps to the first tier of seats and collapsed. Jane, Rosalind and Marian declared their intention not to climb so much as a single step that wasn't necessary and instead wandered aimlessly around the interior of the arena, idly examining the ancient structure. Dante and Bertie stood some distance away, engaged in earnest conversation probably about Bertie's quarrel with Harriet given the way the young man kept looking at her. Willie did hope the poor boy wasn't asking Dante for advice.

After a minute or two, Bertie approached the girls

sitting some five feet above him, Dante lingering a few steps behind.

Bertie cleared his throat. "'But, soft, what light through yonder window breaks? It is the east, and Juliet is the sun. Arise, fair sun, and kill the envious moon, who is already sick and pale with grief.'"

The girls exchanged suspicious glances.

"What do you want?" Harriet snapped.

"I am making a—" Bertie glanced at Dante who nodded "—a grand romantic gesture in the city where star-crossed lovers pledged their eternal love."

"He does know they died, doesn't he?" Geneva said to the twins.

"I wouldn't wager on it." Tillie scoffed.

"But he is terribly dashing," Emma said with a sigh.

Bertie glanced at Dante, who nodded. Obviously he was giving the boy the benefit of his questionable wisdom regarding women. Oh, this should be good.

Bertie began again. "'She speaks. O, speak again, bright angel for thou art as glorious to this night, being o'er my head as is a winged messenger of heaven.'"

"That's not the next line," Tillie said under her breath to her sister.

Emma shrugged.

Harriet stood, stepped to the edge of the wall and crossed her arms over her chest. "Go on."

"'Unto the white upturned wondering eyes of...of...'" Bertie cast a helpless look at Dante.

"'Of mortals that fall back to gaze on him,'" Dante said in a stage whisper.

Bertie tried again. "'Of mortals that fall back to gaze on him and...and...'"

"What do you think you're doing?" Rosalind approached her brother with all the fury of a hen protecting her chick. "This has nothing to do with you and I would suggest you stay out of it!"

"I am trying to help the only other male in sight," Dante said sharply. "And I don't care if you like it or not. There comes a time, sister dear, that men have to stand together or we shall all surely perish under the weight of an elegantly shod female foot!"

"And well deserved I might add! You are scarcely one to give advice." She nodded pointedly at Willie. "Might I suggest you resolve your own problems before you try to solve anyone else's!"

He stared at her then nodded. "You're absolutely right." Dante turned to Willie. "Lady Bascombe, if I might have a word?"

For a long moment Willie stared at him. Why not have it out with him here and now? Hadn't she been considering exactly what she wanted to say for the past four days? Even so, she wasn't at all sure she was ready. She didn't want to reflect later on what she should have said now. This was her one opportunity to salvage a tiny bit of her dignity. Still, there would never be a perfect time. Besides, she was tired of wondering what he would say to her. What possible justification he could have for his deceit.

Once again the cheers of the absent crowd rang in her ears.

"Why, Mr. Montague." She cast him a brilliant smile. "I would be delighted."

CHAPTER SEVENTEEN

WILLIE'S SMILE WAS ENOUGH to strike fear into even the most courageous heart but Dante had had quite enough.

"All right, what have I done?" Dante said sharply. "You can't throw a man in prison without a trial. Without a chance to defend himself. I demand to know what no doubt minor, insignificant infraction I have committed."

"Minor, insignificant infraction?" Her brow rose.

"Yes!" he snapped. "Because if it was something of importance I would surely be aware of it. I am not an idiot!"

She scoffed.

He ignored her. "I have gone over every word, every nuance, every, well, *everything* and for the life of me I cannot figure out why we have gone from anticipating a future together to the icy disdain you have directed toward me since we left Monaco."

"Do you really wish to discuss this here?" Willie said coolly and nodded toward the others. "In front of everyone?"

"You haven't given me the tiniest opportunity to speak to you privately. You have avoided me as if I were ridden with plague."

She shrugged.

"As for *everyone*, they would all have to be deaf and blind not to already be aware that you are clearly furious with me for some unknown reason." He adopted a high-pitched tone. "And on this side of the train is a village that appears quite charming but in truth is a den of deceit and betrayal, a hotbed of men who know nothing save lies and treachery."

Her brow furrowed. "I don't sound like that."

Someone murmured, "She does a bit."

"Very well." Her jaw tightened and anger flamed in her eyes. Whatever she thought he had done was obviously substantial. "But I would prefer not to have an audience, if you don't mind."

"What do you think he did?" one of the Americans asked.

"No one knows."

"I'd wager it was awful."

"I see your point," Dante muttered.

She glared. "When we return to the hotel—"

"No, now." He had put this off too long already. It was driving him insane. He'd been racking his brains trying to determine what he might have done. He was in love with the blasted woman after all and she was acting as if he were the worst sort of scoundrel.

"As you wish." She glanced around and indicated an arched arena opening far enough away to eliminate the chance of being overheard. "There?"

"Fine."

She nodded, adjusted her parasol and strode briskly toward the opening—he followed a step behind.

Good. He really didn't want the others to hear more than was necessary. Who knew what he and Willie might say. He most definitely wanted to avoid the girls and Bertie learning about their night together. It was not at all appropriate. For that matter, he didn't especially want their mothers to know either. It was bad enough that Roz knew. He'd much prefer to start his life with Willie without any specter of scandal or impropriety. Surely they could work out whatever it was he had done. How bad could it be if he was unaware of it? It was probably nothing more than a misunderstanding. He would apologize, profusely, even grovel if necessary, and that would be that. They could move on from here. Why, she might be back in his bed tonight. Of course, he would have to banish Bertie and that would take a bit of arranging. Or Dante could come to her room. Better yet—why couldn't they marry right here in Italy? Certainly he had suspected she wanted a proper wedding but surely the romance of Verona carried an irresistible appeal. Yes, indeed he would do what was necessary to make amends for whatever minor infraction he had committed. And once that was resolved, he would tell her about the Portinari. But that was a hurdle he didn't want to jump over at the moment. One awkward dilemma at a time.

She stopped and turned to him, her expression calm and serene and cold.

"Please, Willie." He stepped closer. "Whatever I have done, I am truly sorry. Just tell me my misdeed and I will move heaven and earth to make it right."

She studied him for a long moment. He held his breath.

"I saw the dossier you have on me."

Bloody hell. His stomach lurched.

"You went through my things?" he said without thinking then immediately realized his mistake.

Her eyes narrowed.

"Not that you aren't perfectly welcome to do so, of course," he added quickly. "My life is an open book."

"An open book? Hardly. It's a book of secrets filled with lies and deceit."

"That's not the least bit fair or accurate." He drew his brows together. "I've lived my entire life with propriety and honor."

"As opposed to my life?"

"I didn't say that but I am not the one who invaded your privacy." It was not the wisest thing to say but it was the first thing that came to mind and it did seem an important point.

"The transgression here is not the invasion of your privacy, which I did not do." Her jaw clenched. "I inadvertently knocked over your valise and discovered the dossier when I was putting everything back."

"An accident, then. I can certainly forgive that."

"Oh, I am fortunate." She drew a calming breath. "You said you loved me."

"I do."

"You asked me to marry you."

"I did," he said staunchly.

"Of course you did." She huffed. "If I marry you, you acquire my painting. It's an easy solution for you."

"I daresay there won't be anything the least bit easy about marriage to you. If I want easy, I could have my pick of any number of willing females." His jaw tightened. "But I don't want them, I want you. And acquiring the painting didn't even occur to me when I asked you to marry me." He paused. "Although I will admit it would be convenient."

"Convenient?" Her voice rose. "I assure you, I intend to be anything but convenient."

"I didn't mean—"

She thrust out her hand to stop him. "This is not exactly what I had intended to say. I have given a great deal of thought about what I would tell you when we finally had it out."

"Then please, go on." His tone softened. "I deserve to hear everything you wish to say. I made an enormous mistake by not being completely forthright with you and

I do apologize. But I never lied to you," he added quickly. "I simply didn't tell you why I was accompanying you."

"A lie of omission, then?"

"One could call it that," he said weakly.

For a long moment she stared at him then shook her head. "Upon further consideration, at this point, I don't believe I'll say anything at all."

He stared. "Surely there's more you wish to say. You have to say something."

"Actually, I don't," she said in a lofty manner. "I never wish to say anything to you again. Ever. Until I breathe my last." She turned and started back toward the others.

"You've said that before."

"It bears repeating."

A panicked voice in the back of his head warned if he let her walk away now, he might never get her back.

"I want my painting."

She froze.

"Despite what's happened between the two of us, that painting rightfully belongs to my family."

She turned on her heel and glared at him. "That painting is mine. It was left to me by my grandmother."

"Regardless, the fact remains that the Portinari was originally purchased, along with the companion works, by my grandfather." He could well understand her anger at his not telling her about the painting before now. That was justified and there was no getting around it. But the ownership of the work was another matter altogether. "I have no idea how your grandmother came by the painting but—"

She gasped. "Are you implying she stole it?"

"I did not say that." Although the moment she said it had come to her from her grandmother, the suspicion certainly came to mind. "I have no wish to cast—"

"I beg your pardon."

Dante's and Willie's attention jerked to the newcomer. Roz smiled pleasantly. He hadn't heard her approach but then he had other things to contend with.

"First," his sister began, "the two of you should know that voices here carry in a remarkable manner. We did not hear every word that passed between you but far more than perhaps we should have." She lowered her voice and leaned toward them. "I do appreciate that your conversation did not include revelations of a more personal nature but I do fear, if you do not remove this discussion to somewhere more private, one or both of you might reveal, oh, details you would prefer to keep to yourselves."

A blush washed up Willie's face. "Yes, of course."

"Excellent idea." He nodded.

"Then we shall retire to the hotel." Roz gestured at the others to join them. "The two of you can discuss the situation in a calm and rational manner." Her gaze shifted between her brother and Willie. "I am willing to act as an arbitrator unless you wish to be alone."

"I would choose to be thrown to the lions in this very arena before I would ever agree to be alone with him again." Willie fairly spat the words.

"I pity the lions," Dante muttered.

"As well you should!" she snapped.

The rest of the group joined them and they made their way back to the hotel. The walk was no more than twenty minutes although it did seem endless. No doubt Roman prisoners doomed to meet their fate in the arena were a jollier band than this company of travelers. Dante had noticed on the first day that the level of noisy chatter of eight women was rarely less than a dull roar. Now they were silent, which was far worse. The Americans walked on either side of Willie, as if protecting or supporting her, the girls—including Harriet—directly behind them. Bertie followed and Roz walked beside her brother, although he was fairly certain she would have preferred to be anywhere else. Apparently, family loyalty counted for something but not much. At least she didn't point out that if he had taken her advice in Paris to tell Willie about the painting none of this would have happened.

"Aren't you going to say anything?" he asked at last.

"Oh, I shall leave that up to Willie," Roz said. "Although I do hate to be ostracized simply because I am connected by blood to an idiot."

"I appreciate your loyalty," he said wryly.

"You shouldn't. I am firmly on Willie's side in this."

"And I also appreciate you not throwing in my face the fact that you warned me."

"I see no need to. You're well aware of your mistakes." The corners of her mouth quirked as if she were holding back a smile. "But 'any number of willing females'? Really, Dante?"

"I was making a point."

"And you do it so well," she said under her breath.

The moment they reached the hotel, the Americans took their leave with Jane and Marian insisting *Harry* and Bertie join them for tea or whatever passed for tea late in the afternoon in Verona. Willie agreed to join Dante and Roz in his sister's suite after she had freshened up. Although he suspected she wished to get her thoughts in order before they continued their discussion. He knew he certainly did.

A half an hour later, he paced the floor in Roz's parlor, a glass of Campari in one hand, the dossier in the other. "What if she doesn't come?"

"She'll come." Roz sat in a chair near the window and paged through a guidebook.

"How can you be so certain?" He wasn't at all sure Willie wasn't even now throwing her things in a bag and preparing to bolt for Venice without him. Nor could he blame her.

"For one thing—" Roz closed the book "—she has nowhere to go. For another, she is the aggrieved party here. She deserves to tell you what a beast you've been. *She* did not lie to *you*."

"I didn't lie. I simply failed to mention anything about the Portinari."

"Or why you and I and Harriet are on her tour in the first place." Roz's brow furrowed. "I do hope she doesn't hold me responsible for any of this."

"Oh, I'm sure she places the blame on my shoulders." Where it belonged.

A knock sounded at the door. Roz glanced at her brother. "Are you ready?"

"No." He had come up with an idea but there was no guarantee Willie would agree to it. Still, it would keep them together and give him the chance to work his way back into her heart. If it succeeded. He tossed back his drink and set the glass aside.

Roz opened the door and Willie swept inside in an air of indignation, her blond hair slightly disheveled as if she had ripped her hat off without thinking and the tiniest glint of sadness in her eyes. He didn't dare to hope that meant he might have a chance.

She looked around and sighed. "Nice room. Before anything else," she said to Roz, "I want to know what your part was in this."

"I assure you, my part was strictly limited," Roz said and shook her head. "I thought it was stupid from the beginning but I did agree to go on this tour so that he could come along. And that is the extent of my involvement. In fact, I told him on more than one occasion he needed to tell you everything." She shot an exasperated look at her brother. "I do wish you would take him off my hands."

Willie's eyes widened. "What?"

"Well, perhaps not." Roz returned to her chair, sat down and picked up her book. "You said you didn't want to be alone, so I'm, oh, chaperoning you. Just pretend I'm not here." She opened the book and pretended to read, as the volume was upside down.

"Very well." Willie turned toward him and crossed her arms over her chest. "What do you have to say?"

"I have a proposal for you."

"Haven't you done this once before?"

"This is more a matter of business."

She narrowed her eyes. "Go on."

"I propose we work together to reclaim the Portinari. A partnership if you will. Once we have the painting, we can then decide its ownership."

"There is nothing to decide," she snapped then paused for a moment to breathe deeply. "The painting is mine. And I see no reason why I need a partner."

"Have you ever met the holder of the painting? This count…" He shook his head. "What was his name?"

"You don't have it in that dossier of yours?"

"Apparently not." He flipped through the folder.

"I find that shockingly incompetent of your detective. I would refuse to pay him if I were you."

"The name, Willie."

"Don't take that efficient business tone with me. I don't believe it for a moment."

"Why not?"

"Because I never would have allowed myself to fall in love with someone so stiff and stodgy."

"Willie—"

"*Lady Bascombe!* Only my friends call me Willie."

"Very well." He could successfully negotiate all day with a shipping company or an import firm but he couldn't seem to make a single point with *Lady Bascombe.* "May I have the name of the count?"

"No." She smirked.

"Why on earth not?"

"Because as soon as I tell you, you can slink off and approach him before I do, offer him a fortune and steal my painting!"

He stared at her. "How could you think I would do such a thing?"

"How could I think otherwise? I have lain in bed at night pondering how to make certain you don't get my painting. And considering all the ways you might try."

He lowered his voice. "That's not what I've been thinking about as I've lain in bed at night."

"Don't, Mr. Montague." Her words rang hard and unrelenting. "As you said, this is a matter of business. I don't intend to warn you again."

"Point noted," he said in a sharper tone than he had intended. But she wasn't the only one who had been hurt. He loved her and she thought he was a cad. It was most distressing. "When are you supposed to meet with this unidentified count?"

"I wrote to him when arrangements for the tour were made, telling him I was traveling with friends to Venice, the dates we anticipated being there and saying I would contact him when I arrived in Venice to arrange a meeting. The day before we left I received his response as well as an invitation to a masked ball given by the conte."

"What fun," Roz murmured from behind her book.

Dante ignored her. "Very well." He thought for a moment. "We arrive in Venice tomorrow. If you arrange to meet him on our second full day in the city—"

"That's the day before the ball," she said.

"All that matters is that I will have enough time to telegraph London and see if I can uncover any pertinent information about the man. It's been my experience that the more one knows of one's opponents in any negotiation, the better off one is."

"I don't know why you think that's necessary. I have the loan agreement between the conte and my late husband. All I have to do is present the document along with the amount borrowed with interest and I receive my painting." She shrugged. "It's as simple as that."

"Is it?"

"I don't see why it wouldn't be."

"You're probably right but what if you aren't? What if he refuses to give you the painting? What if he claims your husband's death is tantamount to defaulting on the loan and the painting remains his?"

"I can't imagine such a thing," she said with a dismissive shrug. "I'm confident he will abide by the terms of the loan."

"His terms or yours?"

"I would think—"

"In addition, he could turn over the wrong painting. Do you remember what the painting looks like?"

"Of course I do." She scoffed. "It's very dark and old. It has people in it I believe. Admittedly, it's been a long time since I've seen it but I will surely recognize it when I do see it."

"Would you?"

"Without question," she said with a confidence he didn't quite believe. Nor, he suspected, did she. "Probably."

"The painting in question was the middle of a series

of three, referred to as a triptych, that together depict a single story or event, something of that nature."

"Go on."

"Galasso Portinari was a student of Titian's who was perhaps the most important painter in Venetian history. Portinari was a member of his workshop and showed great talent. Unfortunately, he died young, apparently a victim of plague." He glanced at her. "Are you still listening?"

"I am still awake."

A groan came from Roz's corner.

"The three paintings told the story of Orpheus and Eurydice. Are you familiar with it?"

"I am not entirely uneducated," she said in a dry manner. "Orpheus was the son of Apollo, a demigod if you will, who lost the love of his life, Eurydice, on their wedding day. She succumbed to snakebite. He went into hell itself to rescue her and made a bargain with the god of the underworld and his wife. Orpheus wasn't to look at Eurydice until they were out of hell but he looked too soon and she was pulled back."

"Oh." He stared in surprise. "That's quite good, Lady Bascombe."

"It's an excellent story. Quite like *Romeo and Juliet* in that neither ends well. Perhaps there's a lesson to be learned here about the perils of love and why one should avoid it."

"There isn't," he said firmly. "It was a common enough theme, as were most myths. Even Titian painted the story of Orpheus and Eurydice. But Portinari's are unusual in that he uses three paintings to tell the story. The first—the death of Eurydice surrounding by wedding guests. The third—Orpheus watching his wife be wrenched away from him. And the middle—the missing Portinari—"

"*My* Portinari."

"—depicts Orpheus pleading for Eurydice in front of the god of the underworld and his wife with Eurydice standing off the one side."

"That does sound familiar."

"Are you confident enough that you could recognize it? I have that knowledge and I am not unskilled in the art of negotiation." He chose his words with care. "Let us join forces."

"You and me? Why should I?"

"I have just pointed out that you need me."

"I have never needed anyone less," she said in a sharp tone then paused. "However, in a strictly business sense, I could use a man of your skills. Which puts me in a bit of a difficult position." She met his gaze. Any hint of sorrow he had thought he'd seen earlier had vanished. "There is no time to find another man with your particular skills. But unfortunately, I will not associate in any way with a man I cannot trust."

He tried not to wince. He had brought it on himself. "I assure you, Lady Bascombe, I will never again do anything that would cause you to distrust me. And once more, you have my most sincere apology."

She studied him for a long moment. "Shall I believe him, Rosalind?"

"Oh, I would. He's unfailingly honest." She turned a page in her book. "At least he was."

"Very well." Willie nodded. "I shall consider it." She turned and headed to the door.

"I need to know as soon as possible." He stepped toward her. "If I am to send a telegram today."

"I said I would consider it."

He stepped around her and opened the door.

"I miss you," he said quietly.

"Good." She nodded and took her leave.

He closed the door and sighed.

"That went well," Roz said brightly.

"Your definition of well and mine are at odds." He shook his head. "She detests me."

"Only for the moment."

"She doesn't trust me." He tossed the file on a table and looked for the Campari decanter.

"And why should she? At least right now. You will have to earn back her trust." She shook her head in a pitying manner. "It's been quite easy for you up to now. You and she have simply fallen in love with hardly any effort at all on your part. Now, dear brother, you're going to have to work for it."

CHAPTER EIGHTEEN

Itinerary.

Venice.

After bidding farewell to the charms of Verona, we head toward the canals and palaces of Venice. La Serenissima was once considered the jewel of the Adriatic and has retained its allure and elegance to this day. Venice's fabled history is part of life in this enchanting city.

Here we shall discover the secrets of the Palace of the Doges and the Bridge of Sighs and walk the streets once trod by Mozart and Balzac and Goethe. We shall relish the magnificence of St. Mark's Cathedral, marvel at the architecture of the grand palazzos and explore the mysterious passageways and narrow canals.

It is not uncommon for visitors to Venice to end their day in the extraordinary Piazza San Marco. Here we may reflect on our journey of adventure and relish the endless pageant of life that is Venice.

"I ASSUME THE NOTE that had been slipped under my door when I returned to my room yesterday means you have agreed to my proposal," Dante said casually.

"Excellent assumption." Willie directed her words to

him but her attention fixed on whatever she was writing in her ever-present notebook.

They had two reserved compartments on the train to Venice, more than enough to suit ten people. But while Willie was busy seeing their luggage was properly loaded, Dante had convinced the rest of their party that they could all make do in one compartment, leaving Willie to share the second compartment with him alone. Although *convinced* probably wasn't the right word. In spite of the blatant curiosity of everyone—with the possible exception of Bertie—no one had any particular desire to be trapped for the next few hours in a small space with the two of them. Jane, Marian and Roz had pointed out that Willie would not be especially pleased by the arrangement. They were of course right. Willie was not happy to find the only available seat was across from his. The journey from Verona to Venice was no more than three hours but they were alone together in a confined space and he intended to make good use of it. Willie had never let him explain the circumstances of his alleged deceit and this was his opportunity. He might not make things better but surely he couldn't make them worse. Hopefully.

"I could certainly have been mistaken as you didn't write anything beyond the name of the gentleman who has the Portinari."

"I believe that was all you needed," she said coolly.

"I have already sent a telegram to my investigator. With any luck, we should have some information on this Conte de Sarafini by tomorrow."

She made a notation in her notebook.

"It's always a good idea to know your adversary before confronting him," he said.

"I don't know that the conte is an adversary."

"But you don't know for certain that he isn't."

"Neither do you."

This was going nowhere. He tried again. "Then we are to be partners in this endeavor?"

"So it would appear." She tucked her pencil in her notebook, closed it and looked at him. "You made some excellent points yesterday, Mr. Montague. I am not used to business dealings and while I am confident my repayment of the loan and subsequent recovery of the painting will be uncomplicated, it does seem to me one can never be too careful." Her tone hardened. "Even if a man presents himself as an honorable, decent sort that is no guarantee that he is not in truth a vile, despicable, lying beast."

He winced.

"And, as you are well versed in the nature of vile, despicable, lying beasts, your assistance will no doubt be quite valuable." She placed her notebook in the traveling valise on the seat beside her, then took out one of her many guidebooks and opened it, effectively dismissing him. Or trying to.

"It's always wise to be prepared."

She turned a page.

Willie could ignore him all the way to Venice if she wished but he had no intention of giving up. "Perhaps we should discuss our plan?"

"I shall send a note to the conte upon our arrival in Venice requesting a meeting for the day after tomorrow." Her gaze stayed firmly on her book. "On the day after tomorrow we will meet with him. I will repay the loan and he will return the painting to me. That, Mr. Montague, is the plan. You may consider it discussed."

"And a fine plan it is too," he said weakly. So much for considering the details of recovering the Portinari.

She was right. It should be a simple enough transaction. Certainly he hoped so and he didn't want anything to go wrong. But it would be rather nice if circumstances were such that he had to come to her rescue. Be her hero as it were.

"Do you speak Italian?"

"Dove è il treno per Roma?"

He frowned. "Where is the train to Rome?"

"I can also ask where the train is for Milan, Florence and very nearly any other city in Italy." She unfolded a map from her book and studied it.

"Is that all?"

Her jaw clenched. "Yes."

"I speak Italian quite well."

"Good for you."

"It might come in handy in meeting with the count."

"Our discussion will be entirely in English." She lowered the map and glared at him. "If you think for a moment you are going to carry on a conversation in Italian and exclude—"

"The thought never crossed my mind."

She considered him closely, obviously debating whether to believe him. "Good," she said at last and promptly returned to her map.

"You've never been to Venice either have you?"

"I thought we had established I am not an experienced traveler."

"Nonetheless, we haven't missed a train, lost any of our luggage—and eight women do have a great deal of luggage—and, aside from that problem with the hotel in Monte Carlo, which was not at all your fault," he added quickly, "you are doing a brilliant job."

She continued to stare at her map then sighed. "That's very nice of you to say."

"Well, I am extraordinarily nice."

"Were, Mr. Montague," she said and folded the map. "You *were* extraordinarily nice."

"Are you saying I can't be a vile, despicable beast and extraordinarily nice, as well?"

"A vile, despicable, *lying* beast." She leveled a look at him that was as much scathing as skeptical. "One usually precludes the other."

"But what if, just as an exercise in semantics mind you, a vile, despicable, lying beast wasn't really vile and despicable, and not exactly lying, but more not revealing a minor fact or two—"

"As opposed to *concealing* a *significant* fact or two?"

"You're quibbling over a word choice." He waved off her comment. "Whether you call it *concealing* or *not revealing*, it's very much the same thing."

"On the contrary, they are entirely different. The very definition of concealing is hiding whereas not revealing could possibly be, I don't know, inadvertent."

"Aha! My point exactly."

She crossed her arms over her chest. "And what point would that be?"

"Well…" This was his chance to explain. He chose his words with care. "Even in the beginning I had planned to tell you about my family's claim to the Portinari."

"*My* Portinari."

"But the closer we became, the more difficult it was to bring up the matter. I knew it might upset you."

She snorted. "Might?"

"And obviously I was right." He smiled in a modest manner.

"Indeed you were."

"Frankly, by the time we reached Monaco, the painting was the furthest thing from my mind. You were far more important to me."

"Oh?" She studied him suspiciously.

He nodded. She was softening, not a lot but enough to listen to him. "All I could think about was you. The way your hair sparkled in the sunlight and how your blue eyes reflected the sea. The way your laugh sounds like pure joy made audible and wraps around my very soul. The feel of your lips against mine—"

"That's quite enough." She drew a deep breath. "I can see how, possibly, your intentions might have changed from the time you joined the tour."

"And I fully intended to tell you everything before we reached Venice but…" His gaze met hers directly. "I didn't want to lose you."

"I see."

"I didn't intend to deceive you, Willie, really I didn't." He moved to her side of the compartment and sat beside her. "I am willing to spend the rest of my life making amends. I would do anything in the world to make it up to you." He took her hand in his.

A slight smile curved the corners of her lips and his hopes soared. "Anything?"

"Anything at all." He was winning her back. It wasn't nearly as hard as he thought it would be. Of course not, she loved him as much as he loved her. An enormous weight that had settled in his stomach yesterday lightened.

"Then give up your claim to my painting." A determined glint shone in her eyes.

"No." He straightened in the seat and released her hand. "That painting is mine."

"I thought you said it was your family's?"

"It is but it might as well be mine. I'm the only one

who gives a damn about that blasted collection. But it was important to my grandfather, so it's important to me."

"How very touching." Her eyes widened in feigned sympathy. "I'm sure your grandfather would be terribly disappointed by your failure to get it back. Now—" her tone hardened "—get off my seat." She shoved him. The train hit a small bump and he flew across the compartment to sprawl across the seats.

She sighed. "Are you all right?"

"Do you care?" He gingerly untangled himself and struggled to his feet. Obviously it was going to take a great deal of effort to appease Willie and earn her forgiveness. Perhaps one step at a time would be best.

"Not at all." She shrugged. "I just think it would be most awkward if I were witness to yet another absurd death."

"You mean your husband's?" He brushed off his jacket.

"I prefer not to talk about it."

"Very well. But the rest of this conversation is far from over."

"I suspected as much. However, right now it's over for me." She took her hat off, set it on the seat beside her guidebook then folded her hands in her lap. "I intend to rest. Please have me awakened when we are approaching Venice." She rested her head against the seat cushions and closed her eyes.

"Dare I ask if you've been having difficulties sleeping? I know I have."

"Good. And I assure you, my slumber has been quite restful."

The slightly drawn look of her face in recent days said otherwise. Dante let a full minute go by. "Perhaps we could talk about something else?"

"I don't wish to talk."

"Of course you do." He paused. "You do talk quite a lot you know."

She bit back a smile.

"You think I'm amusing."

"I think you're an ass." She paused. "I find them funny too."

"Well, if you don't wish to talk, what would you suggest I do to pass the time?"

"I can think of any number of things but I don't think they're anatomically possible."

He tried not to laugh. Good God—he liked her as much when she was angry as when she wasn't. Annoying her was oddly exhilarating. And somewhat exciting. "Other than those?"

"Here." Without opening her eyes, she reached for her guidebook—"Read about Venice"—and tossed it in his direction.

He caught the book and flipped it open. "I've been to Venice."

"Then you should know all the words."

He paged through the book. "As you have never been to Venice, I shall endeavor to assist you by reading aloud."

"Delightful."

"'A glance at the manifold attractions of Venice may be obtained in three to four days with the aid of steamers and gondolas. An occasional walk will also convey an idea of the manner—' This is rather dry."

She sighed. "Is it?"

"Isn't it?" He shook his head. "Do you really want to see 'manifold attractions'?"

"Yes."

"I could do better."

"I don't care."

He thought for a moment. He'd visited Venice twice. The first time he was young and on a grand tour with a group of rowdy comrades and a great deal of alcohol so those memories might not have been accurate. But the next time he set foot in the fabled city, he'd been enchanted. It had been years ago—six or so—and Venice had been magical. He couldn't imagine anything being as extraordinary as sharing it with Willie.

"Before stepping foot in Venice one should know something of the city, in the way in which one anticipates an excellent cuisine. Her buildings rise from the water as Venus rose from the sea. She is La Serenissima, the serene republic."

Willie opened her eyes.

"She is, as well, mysterious and exotic and unexpected. She disdains the ordinary. Her streets are paved with water, canals both grand and barely wide enough for the slimmest of crafts. By day, the light, unexceptional everywhere else, is here so unique, so remarkable, artists have tried again and again through the ages to capture its elusive enchantment. Her houses and palaces adorned with carving and columns and archways sparkle in the sunlight, like treasure boxes concocted to rival the beauty of any gem within them. But by night, beneath the stars, in the moonlight, she becomes a place of secrets and magic and passion."

"I had no idea you were so poetic."

"I can be extremely poetic." He paused. "And charming."

"You needn't waste your time," she said and closed her eyes. "I refuse to allow myself to be charmed by you again."

"Regardless, my intentions are not to give up."

"The road to hell, Mr. Montague. And please remember to have someone awaken me when we arrive."

He stifled a laugh. She was stubborn and determined not to give in to him in the slightest. In that, they were evenly matched.

"When we reach Venice..." He leaned forward and took her hands in his. Her eyes snapped open and she tried to pull her hands away. He held tight and stared into her eyes. "I want a truce. I want to enjoy Venice and I want you to see it as I do. I want to introduce you to La Serenissima." He lifted one hand and brushed his lips across it. "I want to share the city with you." He raised her other hand and kissed it. "If not as lovers then as friends or fellow travelers."

She might not realize it yet but he was seducing her. Minute by minute, hour by hour. Seduction had always been a rather straightforward thing for him. It had never taken any particular effort. But this—with Willie—was a battle, a game of conquest in which it really didn't matter who won. As long as they were unified in the end.

"Lovers, Mr. Montague—" she yanked her hands from his "—is completely out of the question. And friends are not so forward as to kiss another friend's hands while they are asleep."

"First, you were not asleep." He settled back in his seat. "And second, your friend, *your good friend*, Lord Brookings did not hesitate to kiss your hand on any number of occasions."

"Never when I was asleep."

"Again, you were not asleep." He shrugged. "If you had been asleep, I would never have kissed your hand. I would have awakened you with a gentle, teasing—"

"That is quite enough."

He grinned. "Now do you wish to talk?"

"Not particularly but I see no other choice. And you needn't be so smug about it."

He gasped. "I'm not the least bit smug."

Skepticism shone in her eyes.

"Well, perhaps a little." His grin widened.

"Then let's talk about this truce of yours. Exactly what did you have in mind?"

He stared. All sorts of things she did not intend flitted through his head.

"I meant in terms of your truce," she said with a frustrated sigh.

"Yes, that's what I thought." He cleared his throat and shifted in his seat. Good God, what the woman could do to him with no more than an innocent question. "Very well." He drew a deep breath. "I don't want to discuss ownership of the painting until we have it back. I don't even want to think about it. And I want you to stop glaring at me as if I truly were a vile, despicable, lying beast."

"Because you aren't?"

"No, I'm not," he said staunchly. "I am neither vile nor despicable. And I did not actually lie, although I did fail to tell you my original purpose. That was a mistake on my part."

"A mistake?"

"Yes, a mistake, an error in judgment. Admittedly, a dreadful one but—"

"Oh, please." She crossed her arms.

"But I didn't know you in the beginning beyond what was in the dossier. And surely you recall that I did tell you I'd had you investigated."

"You might have mentioned it. In passing."

It was an admission, albeit a reluctant one, but better than nothing. "And even you have to admit, it did not paint you in an especially good light."

She shrugged.

He wasn't at all sure how she would take this but if he was going to be honest—and it did seem the time for anything less than total candor had passed—he was going to have to confess everything.

"Even so, I found you intriguing. Most intriguing. More free in spirit and outrageous than irredeemably improper and scandalous. And then when I met you…"

Her eyes narrowed. "Yes?"

"And you were…" He shook his head helplessly. "More."

She frowned. "More?"

"More than I expected. You were intelligent and amusing and far more interesting than I had imagined. You were, as well, determined to succeed at something you had never attempted before. I found that admirable. And you are perhaps the loveliest woman I have ever met."

"My nose is too narrow. I have an annoying tendency to freckle. My hips are entirely too wide, my bosom too full, my toes are fat and stubby and one of my ears is just a touch higher than the other."

"I didn't say perfect."

She bit her lip and he would have wagered she was trying not to laugh or at least smile.

"I want your forgiveness but I realize that might take a considerable amount of time as well as a great deal of effort on my part."

"Very perceptive of you."

"For now, I would like for us to be, well, friends if you're willing."

"I trust my friends."

He winced.

"However…"

He held his breath.

"In the spirit of comrades on the road together, I shall accept your truce and endeavor to treat you with the cordiality due a fellow traveler and a member of my party."

"It's not what I had hoped for—"

She raised a brow.

"—but better than I deserve," he added quickly.

"Far better."

He had no idea how to earn her trust back but he would do whatever it took. For one thing—he was familiar with the nature of Venice and Venetians. He was confident his knowledge of the city from his previous visits would prove useful. It was entirely possible that Venice would work its magic... And why shouldn't he help it?

"As we are going to be partners—" it was a brilliant idea. He couldn't believe he hadn't thought of it before "—and as you have already acknowledged my familiarity with Venice is impressive—"

"I don't believe I did. *Poetic* is the word I used."

"Regardless—" he shrugged off the comment "—allow me to show my heartfelt intention to make amends by alleviating you of the burden of leading us around Venice. Thereby freeing you to enjoy the city."

Suspicion hung in the air around her.

"Tomorrow," he said with a sweep of his arm, "I shall show you—all of you—Venice." He would make himself indispensable. "You could not have a better tour guide than I."

"Unless, of course, we were to hire some handsome Italian gentleman. My books all say the guides in St. Mark's Square can be quite disreputable. One could scarcely ask for more adventure than a handsome, disreputable Italian."

"Let me show you Venice as I know her." He too had guidebooks.

"I'm certain a handsome, disreputable Italian would know Venice quite well."

He rested his forearms on his knees, clasped his hands together and leaned forward. "The ladies will love it."

"As they would love a handsome, disreputable Italian. Although they do all seem to be fond of you for some odd reason." She considered him thoughtfully. "I'll not pay you."

He gasped. "I would never accept pay."

"We do have a schedule."

"There are no schedules in Venice." She would rely on him. And he could regain her trust.

"Very well."

"You won't regret this."

"Nonsense, Mr. Montague, I already do."

He grinned. This was going well. Oh, certainly she'd said she never wanted to speak to him again. Or be in the same room alone with him again but she'd never said she didn't wish to ever see him again although that was possibly an oversight on her part. But above all else, she didn't say she didn't love him. All he had to do was make her admit it. Or accept it.

"Now then..." She sighed. "Tell me more about Venice."

CHAPTER NINETEEN

"THIS IS A very special day, Mr. Montague." Willie raised her chin and gazed out over the Grand Canal. "This is the day I reclaim my painting and with it my financial independence."

"*My* painting." Dante stepped up beside her and braced his hands on the balustrade. "And you make every day special."

"What utter nonsense." She sniffed.

"Which makes it no less true."

Did he really think complimenting her every five minutes or so would turn her head? Would make her forget his deception? She was not nearly that shallow. Although it was rather nice and he'd been doing it since their arrival in Venice the day before yesterday. The man certainly could be damnably charming when he wanted to be. And clever. He didn't just direct all that charm at her. Oh no. So much smarter to spread it among all the ladies, regardless of age. Lure them to his side perhaps. He was very good. Young Bertie apparently thought so. Willie had noticed him studying Dante for lessons in how to appeal to the fairer sex.

She glanced at him and narrowed her eyes. "Are you trying to charm me again?"

"Is it working?"

"No." She returned her gaze to the busy waterway filled with steamers and gondolas floating like black swans on the water and fishing boats with their brightly colored sails. "Perhaps."

"Then indeed I am trying. With all of my heart."

"I do wish you wouldn't say things like that. What we have at the moment is a truce. Nothing more."

"My apologies." A sincere note rang in his voice. She didn't believe it for a moment. "I can't seem to help myself."

"Then try harder."

Although, to his credit, the man was already trying very hard to make amends. The moment they'd stepped off the train, he took command of their group, arranging for their luggage to be transported to the Grand Hotel via a small steamboat provided by the hotel. Willie vowed to question Miss Granville upon their return as to why nearly every hotel she had arranged for them was called the Grand Hotel. Even though Willie had managed their transportation and luggage quite nicely before now, Venice was an entirely different matter as people and baggage had to be transported by boat. Dante's Italian was more proficient than anyone else's, and it was hard not to be grateful for his assistance. Obviously part of his diabolical plan to work his way back into her good graces.

They proceeded to the hotel in two separate gondolas, black in color as decreed by law some four hundred years ago, and Dante pointed out various sights along the way. Here was the palace where Lord Byron had lived with his monkeys, his dogs, a fox and his Italian lover. There was the palace owned by Robert Browning's son and the famed poet was said to reside there at this very moment. While their gondola did appear quite steady, it rocked in a most alarming manner when Geneva attempted to get a better look. They passed by the Palazzo Vendramin where the famed composer Richard Wagner had died. Dante drew their attention to the Byzantine, Moorish and Gothic influences on the architecture of the city that had flourished for more than a thousand years. And while every fact and figure Dante delivered was surprisingly interesting, and Willie suspected the others agreed with her, Venice needed no explanation. The city was quite simply magical.

Guidebooks did not really prepare one for the reality of La Serenissima. Venice was every bit as remarkable as Dante had claimed. Willie had seen pictures, of course, but nothing could do justice to the manner in which the vibrantly colored, whimsical buildings with their marble steps and ornate carvings seemed to emerge directly from the sea itself. Dante said the posts rising from the waters provided a place to moor the gondolas that served as the main form of transportation and the posts were painted with the colors of the owners of the palaces. He explained how the city was built on a series of islands with wood pilings driven deep into the ground beneath the water to support the structures above.

And was there any better way to travel than to glide silently through the water as a dashing man named for an Italian poet explained everything you might possibly ever want to know? Willie doubted it. For a fleeting moment she tried to summon a measure of guilt for allowing Dante to commandeer the tour but failed. It was scant penance for his crimes. Besides, it was entirely too delightful to leave her hosting duties and the myriad of details that required constant juggling to someone else.

Dante allowed them all time to settle into their rooms—not nearly enough but probably more than Willie would have allocated—before escorting them to the Piazza San Marco and their introduction to Venice. He was clever enough to lead them through narrow winding

streets to reach the plaza and they emerged at the far end,
opposite the great cathedral. It nearly took one's breath
away. The square that Napoleon had called the drawing
room of Europe was far larger than she had expected,
bounded on the far end by the extraordinary St. Mark's
Basilica with its domes and arches and spires that glit-
tered in the late-afternoon sun. The other three sides
were palaces with arcades stretching the length of each
building. Occupied, Dante had reluctantly admitted, by
cafés and shops. To the right, one could see part of the
doge's palace. Slightly in front, was the Campanile, the
square brick bell tower for the cathedral. It rose more
than three hundred feet into the heavens and had been
built nearly a thousand years ago then rebuilt again and
again through the ages. Geneva pointed out that Galileo
had studied the stars here. There was modest interest in
climbing to the top sometime during their stay.

Venetians and visitors filled the massive piazza, although it did not strike Willie as overly crowded. People
were very nearly outnumbered by pigeons, much to the
delight of the younger members of their party. It was apparently the duty of visitors to feed them and indeed the
birds did seem to expect it. Odd that creatures one found
rather repulsive in London were charming and delightful
here but then they were Italian.

Dante held out his arm and a pigeon settled on it. He
said these birds were descendants of pigeons who had
saved Venice six centuries ago during a dispute with
Crete. When it was discovered they were carrying mes-
sages for the enemy, the Venetians used that information
to their advantage. They captured Crete and brought the
carrier pigeons they found there back to Venice. The birds
have been welcomed and venerated ever since. Although
there did seem to be a great many of them.

They were quite done in by the time they had returned to the hotel and Willie questioned the wisdom of allowing Dante free rein in showing them the city. Still, she was entirely too tired to protest, although in hindsight it might have been wise.

Dante set a punishing pace yesterday, the day going by so quickly, the memories in Willie's mind jumbled together in bits and pieces, a series of moments. Willie wasn't sure if it was the haste with which they sped through the city or the barrage of information Dante imparted— good Lord, the man did seem to know a great deal about everything—or simply that there was so very much in Venice to fill the eyes and the senses.

Venice was a place of mystery and whimsy. And something of a blur.

They began yesterday entirely too early but Dante insisted there wasn't a moment to spare. So much for *there are no schedules in Venice.* The man was unrelenting. There were things to see and he was going to make bloody well sure they saw them all. He was worse than she was.

They fairly raced through the doge's palace, which looked very much like a grand wedding cake made of variegated marble and decorated with pinnacles and arches and twisted columns. Dante declared there was no greater symbol of the past glory of Venice than this stone monument to excess and elegance. The structure was massive and they did not do it justice but then one could have spent days within its corridors and council rooms in admiration of architecture and works by grand masters—Veronese and Tintoretto and Titian. They admired the splendor of the interior of St. Mark's, decorated with mosaics and gold and bronze and climbed to the upper gallery to see the amazing bronze Roman horses that looked out over the city. They did indeed ascend to the top of the Campanile and even the least fit among them agreed the view was well worth the climb. But while one could see the lagoon and the city, oddly enough the canals that wound through Venice were not noticeable.

They wandered through narrow streets and over tiny canals. Even in a city of bridges one could not help but be moved by the Bridge of Sighs, the loveliness of the ornate stone conduit at odds with its history of being the passageway and the last glimpse of freedom for those doomed prisoners of Venice.

Like her brother, Rosalind had been to Venice before but for everyone else this was new and unique. No one was more impressed than the Americans. After all, their country was little more than a hundred years old and the enthusiasm and tirelessness of the Americans—mothers and daughters—was impressive. Rosalind took it as an unspoken challenge. And what was Willie to do if not to come to the aid of an another Englishwoman? They summoned their strength, squared their shoulders and refused to fall behind the other ladies.

They were approaching the Rialto Bridge, for centuries the marble structure was the only bridge spanning the Grand Canal, when Harriet drew Willie aside for a private moment. As the others were eager to see not just the bridge itself but the many shops it now housed, Willie waved them on and gratefully sank onto a convenient stone bench.

"Might I ask you a question?" Harriet asked.

"As long as I can sit down for a moment." Willie blew a long breath. "Your uncle is tireless."

"And given his age too." Harriet shook her head in disbelief.

"I think he has a few active years left," Willie said, trying not to laugh.

"I do hope so."

Harriet reminded Willie a great deal of herself at Harriet's age, although Dante's niece was rather spoiled and far more headstrong than Willie had been. Of course, Willie had married George in defiance of her father so her memory might be flawed on that point. "What is it?"

"Have I made a dreadful mistake?" Harriet's gaze strayed to Bertie. He and the twins were listening to Dante expound on some historic note about the bridge's history or original construction or something probably at once interesting and endless.

"Not yet." Willie paused. "You haven't, have you? At least not any kind of irreversible mistake?"

Harriet's cheeks reddened. "Of course not. I would never." She sighed. "Am I an idiot? I thought Bertie was so…so perfect in London. But he's really not at all, well, dependable, is he? He's quite delightful and I do so enjoy his company but he's not the type of man one can count on. He is a dreadful flirt."

"Is he?"

"Oh my, yes." She paused. "And then there is the question of money."

"Oh?"

"He doesn't have any at the moment." She grimaced. "It's rather distressing. Oh, he does have an allowance and he did mention something about a trust."

"Bertie doesn't have a care in the world but then he is barely twenty-one. It's very nearly too early to know what kind of man he will become." Willie chose her words carefully. "However, it has been my experience that men who do not display any sense of responsibility when they're young may not manage it when they are older. When it's important."

Harriet's brow furrowed. "Do you think Bertie will?"

"I don't know. He does seem a decent sort." Willie studied Harriet for a moment. "If you are asking for my advice, I would suggest waiting to see what kind of man Mr. Goodwin becomes in a year or so from now."

Harriet nodded thoughtfully. "I was thinking much the same thing." She leaned closer and lowered her voice. "Actually, I'm fairly certain that Bertie is entirely too young for me. I'm most mature for my age, you know."

"I had noticed that." Willie wasn't sure if she should feel sorry for Bertie or congratulate him.

By the time the day had ended, Willie had no idea how many churches they had visited—although it did seem most were built either in an effort to beg some saint to protect the city from plague or in gratitude to another saint for ending the plague—or how many museums or galleries. Willie wasn't sure if Dante was trying to exhaust the rest of them or himself.

The group returned to the Piazza San Marco after a tasty dinner at a restaurant Dante had patronized on a previous visit. They settled in chairs under the stars and ordered scandalously overpriced coffees and ices. A band played in the piazza and couples danced. One of her guidebooks had mentioned how Venice was fascinating by day but by night became something conjured of fairy dust and magic. The book was right.

Dante and Bertie had made it a point to dance with every female and refusing would have been awkward when Dante asked her to dance. It was a terrible mistake. The feel of his body moving next to hers. The faintest scent of spice on his coat. The magic of the stars overhead. They were in the midst of a sizable group of people and yet it seemed they were all alone. He didn't attempt conversation and she was grateful that he wasn't trying to press his case. And perhaps a bit disappointed. There was nothing quite as rousing as trading barbs with him.

But that was last night and she had other matters to concern herself with today. Still, she couldn't help but wonder if Dante's determination not to pause for breath since their arrival in Venice was intended to keep her mind off their meeting with the conte. The Italian had responded to her note by inviting them to join him late in the morning today at his palazzo. His missive had been quite cordial and she wasn't the least bit nervous. Or at least she hadn't been until she recalled all the possible problems Dante had pointed out in his effort to convince her to join forces. How on earth was she going to do this? She would never admit it to him but she was quite glad that he was coming along.

"I think our truce is working nicely." Dante's tone was matter-of-fact, as if he were commenting on something no more important than the weather.

"I have not forgotten that you lied to me. You would do well to remember it, as well."

"I did not lie," he said smoothly. "I simply failed to mention a few unimportant details."

"Unimportant?" She turned toward him and ticked the points off on her fingers. "One—you joined my tour, and forced your sister and niece to join it, as well, only so that you could lay claim to my painting when I finally retrieved it. And two—you believe my painting—*my salvation*—belongs to your family."

He shrugged. "Relatively insignificant really."

"You deceived me."

"Only in the narrowest definition of the term."

"And then you seduced me."

"Yes, I did." He grinned.

"You needn't look so proud of it."

"I feel many things about that night but pride is not one of them. It was not some sort of accomplishment. Indeed, it took very little effort on my part. If I recall correctly—"

"Which I'm sure you don't," she said in a lofty manner. Admittedly, she had practically fallen into his arms but then—at that particular moment—she had thought she was in love with him. And had thought he was in love with her. But could one truly be in love with someone who had deceived you from the first moment you met? Someone you could no longer trust? A tiny voice in the back of her head whispered *yes*. She ignored it.

"I will continue to apologize and grovel if you wish about everything else but—" he shook his head "—I will not apologize for taking you in my arms and—"

"That's enough."

"—kissing that delectable spot—"

"Stop it right now!"

"You're quite lovely when you're angry," he said. "When your eyes shoot fire and your cheeks are flushed. It's terrifying but extremely exciting."

"Don't be absurd, Mr. Montague. And that sort of amiable banter will not work with me."

He smiled in a knowing manner and she wanted to smack him.

"And would you stop being so blasted nice."

"I'm afraid not." He grinned. "I am, if you recall, extraordinarily nice. Why shouldn't I be nice now?"

"Because I am starting to trust you again!" She huffed and turned her attention back to the view of the canal, dominated by the baroque Santa Maria della Salute. According to Willie's guidebook, this church too had been built in dedication to the Virgin Mary in hopes she would protect the city from plague. "And I fear, Mr. Montague, trusting you again would be a grave mistake."

"Or brilliant. Forgiving being divine and all."

She ignored him and moved off the balcony and back into Rosalind's suite. No doubt Dante's was at least as big. They had told the others there was nothing on the schedule for the day and they would be free to do as they wished. As Jane, Marian and Rosalind had all taken note of the location of shops they had passed yesterday, Willie had no doubt they would find something to pass the time.

Dante had sent her a note requesting she meet him here before they left for the conte's palazzo. Wise on his part. Partner or not, she was not going to be alone with him in her room or his. Not after that dance. She wasn't sure if he was the one she didn't trust or herself. Better to avoid the situation than find out. And while they were indeed alone, Rosalind was expected back at any moment.

"Your note said you had heard back from your investigator."

"Information was remarkably easy to gather once he had a name. The conte is a well-known collector of Renaissance works and quite passionate about those that can be traced back to Venice, although rumor has it that his wife is more knowledgeable. Do you know how your husband met him?"

"No."

"Have you ever met him?"

She shook her head. "Not that I recall."

His brow rose.

"Parties, Mr. Montague, balls, soirees, musicales, hunts—one meets a great number of people and one often indulges in spirits far more than one should."

"According to my information, he's considered quite a ladies' man."

"Really?" She nodded. "That is good to know."

"Why?"

"You're not the only one who can be exceptionally charming when circumstances demand. I too can be quite delightful."

"Exactly how delightful do you intend to be?" he said slowly.

"As delightful as necessary."

"What if he tries to take advantage of you? Say perhaps to kiss you?"

"I daresay that's not going to happen. This is a meeting, not a rendezvous. Good Lord, Mr. Montague, perhaps you've forgotten the plan." She rolled her gaze toward the ornate, painted ceiling. "We meet, I give him the bank draft, he gives me my painting. There is nothing in the plan about kissing."

"Plans change," he said darkly.

"You're being absurd. Besides, don't forget you'll be there, as well. I can't imagine any man attempting a seduction with another man present."

"You have a point." He paused. "But you didn't answer my question. What if he tries to kiss you?"

"It was a stupid question."

"Nonetheless—"

"Very well." She thought for a moment. "I suppose it would depend."

"On what?"

Good Lord, the man was serious. "On whether I have my painting back." This could be fun. "And whether I find him attractive."

"Attractive?"

"Yes, handsome. Dashing. *Italian.* I have met a few Italian noblemen before and they have all been most attractive. And very romantic. I think it has something to do with the climate here." She studied him coolly. "I am willing to do very nearly anything to get my painting back."

His eyes widened in something akin to horror. "Anything?"

She struggled to keep from laughing. "Within reason, of course. Although what I consider within reason and what you consider within reason might be entirely different."

"Willie," he fairly growled her name and took a step toward her.

"*Lady Bascombe.* And it's really none of your concern."

"It most certainly is my concern." He moved closer. "As is your definition of *within reason.* My God, Willie—*Lady Bascombe*—if you think I am going to idly stand by and allow you to—"

She burst out laughing.

He stared for a moment. His eyes narrowed. "Was that supposed to be amusing?"

"It was supposed to be and it was." She choked back a laugh. "Most amusing."

"I'm glad you think so. I, however, did not think it was at all funny."

"Well, it was." Without thinking she reached out and straightened his necktie. He would hate it if he knew it wasn't perfect.

He caught her hand and stared down at her. "In spite of our disagreement—"

"Disagreement?" She scoffed but didn't pull away. Her heart thudded. "We haven't had a disagreement—you deceived me."

"I made a mistake. Admittedly, a big mistake—"

"An enormous mistake."

"That I am trying my best to make amends for." He moved closer. Why, the man was close enough to kiss her if he wished. Not that she would permit such a thing. She could certainly step back and wasn't at all sure why she hadn't or why her hand was still trapped by his.

"Neither my feelings nor my intentions have changed."

"Oh?" Her breath caught at the look in his eyes.

"I love you and I still intend to marry you."

She couldn't tear her gaze from his. She swallowed hard. "Intentions, Mr. Montague, like schedules, change."

"Not mine," he said softly and bent his head to hers.

A knock sounded at the door and it immediately opened slightly. They sprang apart as if one or the other was on fire. Blast it all, he was about to kiss her. And she was about to kiss him back. How could she do such a thing?

Rosalind peered into the room. "As much as I hate to interrupt you, I find myself in a bit of a quandary."

"I'm sure it's nothing you can't manage," Dante said through gritted teeth.

"It involves a confidence that I am unwilling to break." She opened the door wider, stepped inside and waved at the corridor. A moment later Jane appeared in the doorway followed by Marian, Geneva and everyone else.

"They know something is amiss. I, being the admirable sister and exceptional friend that I am, did not feel it was my place to tell them anything."

"We are not the type of friends who are unaware when something is afoot." Jane paused. "We did hear quite a bit of your conversation in Verona, you know."

"We'll disregard the more personal aspects of what you said," Marian began. "Although we all agree you make a lovely couple."

Willie snorted. Dante smirked and everyone else murmured in agreement.

"However, that is not the matter at hand." Marian pinned Willie with a firm look. "As your friends and traveling companions and as clients of the Lady Travelers Society, we want to know exactly what is going on."

"Rosalind refused to tell us anything," Jane added. "And Harry wouldn't confide in the other girls. Which I suppose was admirable of her."

Harriet shrugged as if being admirable was nothing new to her.

"If it's something illegal, which we assume it's not—" Jane glanced at Marian who nodded "—but we do think we should be prepared in order to come to your aid should you be arrested—"

"Arrested?" Willie choked.

"And we want to offer our assistance in whatever nefarious scheme you have planned." Eagerness rang in Emma's voice.

"Whether it requires scaling palace walls in the dead of night—" Tillie's eyes sparkled with excitement "—or swimming through canals lit only by moonlight with an army of archers behind you."

"You might possibly have the wrong century for that." Dante smiled.

"We've discussed this a great deal, Mr. Montague." Geneva cast him a pointed look. "We are prepared for any eventuality."

"Such as leaping from rooftop to rooftop to escape the authorities," Bertie said, apparently caught up in the group enthusiasm.

At once all eyes were on him.

"This is an adventure and I intend to be included in it," he said staunchly. "I know I did not start out as a member of this group but I am now and I want to do my part. Whatever that entails."

"I am touched by your offers." Willie shook her head. "But it's not nearly as exciting as all that."

"Regardless." Geneva's determined gaze met Willie's. "We are willing to do whatever is necessary to help if you need us."

"All of us." Harriet grinned.

"That's very kind but not necessary," Dante said. "Lady Bascombe and I have a simple meeting of a business nature. I assure you, we are not engaged in anything the least bit illegal."

"Of course not." Jane scoffed. "We never really thought you were." Even so, Jane, along with everyone else, looked the tiniest bit disappointed.

"Please, all of you, sit down." He glanced at Willie and she nodded. "And we'll explain everything."

A few moments later, everyone had settled in a chair or sofa with the exception of Bertie, who lounged in the doorway leading to the balcony and Rosalind who lingered by the door to the corridor.

"My grandmother left me a valuable Renaissance painting by Galasso Portinari, a Venetian artist." This was more difficult to admit than she had expected but then she hadn't told anyone but Poppy the entire story. "Unfortunately, my husband used it to secure a loan and then failed to pay it back before he, well, died. The painting is held by a Venetian nobleman. I have the money to repay the loan and reclaim my painting. Mr. Montague, however, believes the painting belongs to him."

"To my family, actually," Dante said. "My grandfather purchased it along with two others that were meant to be displayed together. It was replaced with a copy some time ago. The paintings hang at Montague House, which has been our family's London residence for generations. My grandfather had extensive collections of art and antiquities and he arranged for Montague House to become a museum upon his death. I am currently the director. Return of the Portinari in question will establish the museum's position thus ensuring its future."

"I don't believe we went to Montague House. Did we?" Geneva said quietly to her mother.

"I thought you had dragged me to every museum in London," Marian said, "but it doesn't sound familiar."

"Which explains so much," Rosalind said under her breath.

"In a few hours we are to meet with the gentleman who has the painting. At which time I will repay the loan and receive the painting." Willie glanced at Dante. "We have agreed not to discuss ownership until we have the Portinari in our possession."

"And we have returned to England," he said.

As Willie planned to return to England tomorrow, she could easily agree. She would have to tell Jane and Marian before she left but she had intended to do that. Admittedly, she had originally thought she'd leave a note along with their travel documents but that was before they had become friends. One didn't forsake one's friends in that manner. Besides, anyone willing to help with something that might not be entirely proper deserved more than a brief note. Now that they knew everything they would certainly understand.

Dante pulled out his watch and glanced at it. "We should be on our way."

"We shall leave you to it, then," Rosalind said and the group got to their feet. "I'm confident all will go well." She cast Willie an encouraging smile.

A determined gleam shone in Marian's eyes. "I believe we noticed some extremely interesting shops yesterday."

They bid their farewells and a few moments later Willie and Dante were once again alone.

"I've never had anyone willing to assist me in nefarious schemes before. That was really quite..." She shook her head, the oddest lump in her throat. "Quite touching. I have friends, Mr. Montague. True friends who would do anything for me."

"One can always use a true friend."

"I believe you're right." Willie had friends and was within hours of reclaiming her painting, the means to her financial stability.

The sun was shining. The air shimmered with the magic of La Serenissima. And Lady Wilhelmina Bascombe had friends she could count on.

It was indeed a very special day.

CHAPTER TWENTY

GOODNESS, ONE WOULD THINK Willie had never been in a grand palace before, given it was all she could do to keep from staring like a fool. Conte de Sarafini's residence on the Grand Canal was the sort of place one read about in books of fairy tales with painted, gilded ceilings and ornate, carved moldings. Certainly they had painted, gilded ceilings in England, and she had been in any number of remarkable residences, but they weren't lit by the most extraordinary chandeliers Willie had ever seen made of exquisite blown-glass flowers and leaves and fruits. The grand houses and castles in England seemed much more practical when compared to these fanciful edifices that rose from the sea as if by magic.

As much as Willie was impressed by the grandeur of the building, more important, she was about to get her painting and with it her independence. And no man who was practically a stranger was going to take it from her.

They arrived by gondola and entered the palazzo into a grand, ornate foyer with scenes of Venetian life painted on the walls, framed by gilded moldings. A wide marble stairway led to the first floor. A distinguished-looking gentleman of indeterminate age greeted them.

"Welcome to the Palazzo Sarafini, Lady Bascombe," he said in nearly perfect English, glancing curiously at Dante but too well mannered to question his presence. "I am Giuseppe Montalvado, secretary to the Conte de

Sarafini. He is expecting you in the gallery. I'm afraid he has a tight schedule today so your meeting will be brief. If you will come with me."

"Thank you." Willie smiled politely and followed the secretary, Dante a step behind.

Instead of taking them up the stairs, Signore Montalvado turned to the right and led them through a short corridor.

"The conte's family has owned the palazzo next to this one for decades. While the upper floors remain for storage, a few years ago the conte decided to use the ground floor for the display of his father's—and now his—collection. It is open for public viewing several days a week. This is not one of them." He opened a set of tall carved doors, waving them ahead of him. When they had entered, he stepped back and closed the doors behind him.

If she hadn't been told it was a gallery, Willie would have thought she was in the grandest of ballrooms. Ceilings soared a good two stories above them, every inch painted in a classical style with scantily clad, frolicking figures apparently having a good time of it. Lavish plaster carvings bordered the ceilings and defined the doors and the windows, which were placed high on the wall, no doubt to catch the best light. Marble columns created a sort of arcade around the four sides of the room. A long walnut table with massive carved winged lions—the symbol of Venice—was positioned in the center of the room. Very nearly every inch of wall space was covered with framed paintings. Dante practically quivered with excitement beside her. The man was like a hungry dog who had just spotted a pile of bones.

"Ah, Lady Bascombe." A tall, handsome, dark-haired man perhaps a decade older than she appeared from who knew where, coming toward them with a broad welcoming smile. He took her hand and raised it to his lips. "Welcome to my city and my home. It is a very great pleasure to see you again."

Again? "My apologies, Conte." She stared. "I am dreadfully sorry but have we met?"

"Once only, in London and far too briefly. I do not expect you to remember." His gaze remained locked with hers. She resisted the urge to yank her hand free. "But I would never forget beauty such as yours." He released her hand and straightened. "My condolences on the loss of your husband. He was an engaging, I don't know, spirit I think. He had—what is the phrase? *Gioia di vivere?* The French have a saying. Ah yes, joie de vivre. The enjoyment of life."

"He certainly had that." To the exclusion of everything else. If he hadn't, she wouldn't be here.

The conte glanced at Dante and his eyes narrowed. "Please, do not tell me you have married again. It will devastate my heart."

"What a delightful thing to say." She adopted a teasing manner. "Although I don't believe you for a moment." Willie couldn't recall meeting him before but the look in his eye was certainly familiar. The handsome Italian was one of those men who truly believed he was a gift to all women. And all women were fair game. "Allow me to introduce my—"

"Her brother," Dante said, extending his hand. "Allan Quatermain. Pleasure to meet you."

Brother? And really—*Allan Quatermain?*

"Her brother?" The conte's expression cleared. "And a thoughtful brother he is to escort you to Venice."

"I am nothing if not thoughtful." Dante shrugged modestly. "And I certainly could not have her coming all this way by herself."

"No, indeed. Who knows what misadventures could befall a woman alone on such a journey." The conte nodded. "Come, Lady Bascombe. The Portinari awaits you." He escorted them toward a far wall. "My family has always had a great love of art. There are paintings here that were commissioned by some of my ancestors. It is in our blood, I think. Every generation has added to the works you see in this room. My father was an avid collector, scouring the world for works he wished to have. Alas, I was a great disappointment to him in that I did not share his passion. But perhaps some things come with age." He cast Willie a knowing glance. "Do you not agree, Lady Bascombe?"

"I suppose so." She smiled wryly. "I am certainly far wiser now than I was in my youth. At least I hope I am."

"And candid, as well." The conte grinned. "I do like a woman who says what she thinks."

"Then you'll like my sister," Dante said in an oddly jovial manner. "But then everyone does."

Good Lord. How much more absurd did *Allan* intend to be?

"As I was saying," the Italian continued, "it was not until after my father's death that I began to feel the same desire to surround myself with the most remarkable examples of genius the world has known. I have followed in the path of my father and his father before him with one minor difference. Whereas my father and grandfather pursued art regardless of provenance, I prefer those works that were produced here in my own country, especially those painted during the glory of La Serenissima. Also, I believe, where they did not, that such brilliance should be shared and so we open the doors of the gallery to the people. Three days a week. No more, of course." He waved his hand dismissively. "Three is enough."

"That's very kind of you."

"I can be very kind. I only regret that I do not have time to personally show you everything in my collection today. Perhaps you can return when we are open tomorrow, although I will not be able to join you. My time, alas, is not my own."

"Unfortunately, my time too is limited. And as much as I hate to admit it, particularly here, surrounded by all these magnificent works, I am not the connoisseur of art that you are."

"What a very great shame, Lady Bascombe. And what a pity we are both so busy." An oddly satisfied gleam showed in the conte's eyes. "I would like nothing better than to educate you in the joy to be found in the appreciation of artistic achievement."

"Are these Titians?" Dante interrupted, nodding at two paintings on the wall behind the conte.

"Excellent eye, Mr. Quatermain." The Italian studied the works with a smile. "They are copies of one of Giovanni Bellini's most famous works. Did you know Titian was a student of Bellini's?"

"I had no idea," Dante lied. Willie tried not to stare. What was he up to?

"Several of Bellini's students made copies of his paintings, fortunately for us. Bellini's originals were lost to fire centuries ago. These are Titian's copies of works Bellini painted of the Venetian wars with Rome. The one on the left has been in my family for generations and I was fortunate enough to acquire the second a few years ago."

"Magnificent." Dante stared with obvious appreciation.

"And to the left of the Titians—" the conte gestured at

the paintings "—is the work of Bellini, his teacher. You are a lover of great art, Mr. Quatermain?"

"Who would not be a lover of works like this?" Dante said smoothly. "I recognize a Titian when I see it but I am not well versed in the works of the Renaissance."

"Ah well. Perhaps your stay in Venice will be an enlightening one for you, then."

"No doubt." Dante smiled in a noncommittal manner.

The conte nodded his approval. "And now that you have seen the work of the master Bellini and his student, who became Venice's greatest artist, we shall turn to the work of yet another student." He gestured at the painting to the right of the Titians. "Titian studied with Bellini, Portinari studied with Titian and so the legacy of great art continues through the ages."

There was no need for him to point out the Portinari. Her memory might have been somewhat vague when it came to describing it to Dante but Willie recognized the painting immediately. And why wouldn't she? It had hung on the wall in her grandmother's bedroom for as long as Willie could remember.

There was Orpheus pleading for the life of his beloved before Hades and his wife, with the beautiful Eurydice looking on, her eyes filled with sorrow as if she knew this would not end well. Willie had never before noticed the striking detail of the faces, the emotions conveyed on canvas nor the power of the scene itself. But then, why would she? As a child, she'd paid little attention to the work nor had she been especially interested when she had received it after her grandmother's death nine years ago. She loved it because her grandmother had loved it. It was a keepsake, a memory made precious because it had belonged to someone she loved. Willie had hung it in an unused parlor and really hadn't given it a second thought until she'd assessed her assets and discovered it was missing. The work was brighter than she remembered, the colors more vibrant but then it had been a very long time since she last saw it.

"Well," the conte said lightly, "is it as you remember?"

"No." Willie shook her head.

"No?" His brow furrowed.

"I don't remember it being this...wonderful." She sniffed back an unexpected tear. "Thank you for taking such good care of it. It belonged to my grandmother and I am delighted to be able to reclaim it and return it home."

The conte smiled with satisfaction and turned his attention back to the painting. "It is indeed a great work and one of three depicting the legend of Orpheus and Eurydice. You are familiar with the story?"

Willie nodded.

"Orpheus went to the underworld to try to save his wife, if I recall correctly," Dante said. "And even though success was within reach, he ultimately failed because of an error in judgment. A simple mistake if you will."

"A mistake, Mr. Quatermain?" The conte's brow rose. "A mistake is the wrong wine served with dinner. Orpheus struck a bargain with the gods then failed to do his part. And paid dearly for it."

"But surely it was understandable," Dante continued. "Orpheus never meant to break his word after all. He was distracted by the love of his life and eager to have her in his arms once again. One would think he could be forgiven for that."

"Some things are simply not forgivable, *Allan*." Willie gave him a pointed look.

"The gods do not look kindly upon those who fail," the conte said. "This work is the middle of the story, intended to be displayed between the other two. It is a great pity that the whereabouts of the others are unknown. They could be in a private collection somewhere in the world. Possibly even here in Venice. Or they may no longer exist, lost to us forever. I imagine all three together would be most extraordinary."

"Probably," Dante said. He was very good at acting as if he had no idea what the conte was talking about. The man had all kinds of skills one would never suspect. He met her gaze and nodded slightly.

"Well then," she said in her brightest tone, "to the business at hand." She pulled the bank draft from her bag and handed it to the conte. "You'll see the amount is for the loan plus the accrued interest for these past five years."

The conte studied it for a moment then nodded. "It appears very much in order. However..." He paused. "I would like nothing more in life than to keep the work here in Venice where Portinari created it. Where the painting has taken the place it belongs here beside the artist's great master. While your late husband did not wish to sell the painting, he did indicate it was possible that he would be willing to part with it in the future. Should you wish to do so now—" his gaze met hers directly "—I would give you double the amount of the loan. And the interest," he added.

"What an interesting proposition, my lord," Dante said quickly, "although I suspect my sister—"

"Thank you, Allan, but I am quite capable of managing my own affairs, particularly in this respect. Your offer is exceedingly generous, my lord." Although not even a third of what Mr. Hawkings had mentioned. She cast him a brilliant smile. "But I'm afraid I must turn it down. The painting is of great sentimental value to me and I cannot bear to part with it." Not for that price.

"Of course, but you cannot blame me for the trying. I would offer more but…" He shrugged. "The fortunes of my family are not what they once were." He cast a longing look at the painting then sighed and gestured to someone unseen. "I shall have the painting securely wrapped for you, to protect and keep it safe on your return travel to England."

"That would be most appreciated." Willie beamed. Very soon now, her painting would once again be hers.

Signore Montalvado appeared as if by magic followed by two footmen. The conte handed him the bank draft and spoke to him in Italian. The secretary nodded, took the painting off the wall and carried it to the table. Dante casually wandered over to observe. Goodness, why on earth was the man so suspicious? Everything had gone exactly as Willie had expected. One of the footmen spread out a large piece of oilcloth, removed the canvas from the frame and quickly wrapped the painting. The other footman tied it thoroughly, all under the watchful eye of Montalvado. And Dante.

"And that is that," the conte said with a resigned smile. "As you are taking the beloved Portinari away from its native land, dare I hope that you will at least do me the great honor of attending our ball tomorrow night?"

"As much as I would be delighted, there is still quite a lot we wish to see in your legendary city and, as I said, our time is limited so I am afraid—"

"No, no, my Lady Bascombe, do not say no. How could you be so cruel? You are taking my painting and yet you refuse my hospitality." He shook his head in a mournful manner.

"I do apologize. I don't mean to offend you. But—"

"Let me tell you about the ball. For many, many centuries in Venice there was held a great carnival in the

months leading to the Lenten fasting. There were grand
balls and great festivities and exquisite costumes and
masks—always the mask. Works of art to be worn to enhance or disguise. It was a time of celebration and making
merry and passion. But alas, nearly a century ago, that
bastardo, the French despot Napoleon conquered our city
and proclaimed no more *carnevale*. No more costumes.
No more masks." His shoulders sagged in resignation.

"But you are having a masked ball?"

"Ah, there was no prohibition against parties of a private nature. Still…" He heaved a sorrowful sigh. "It is
a great loss for the spirit of our city." He fell silent for a
moment then brightened. "But we are nothing if not dedicated to the joy of celebration. So we accepted the ty-
rant's decree and my family has hosted a grand ball with
costumes and masks, halfway between one Easter and
the next, ever since. So, my lovely Lady Bascombe—"
he again took her hand and lifted it to his lips "—how
can you possibly say no?"

"You're not making it easy."

"I do not intend to."

Willie had always planned to return to England when
the others headed for Rome in three days. Now that she
had the painting, she would much rather leave immediately. Still, it was only one more day.

She pulled her hand free. "For one thing, we have no
costumes or masks."

He scoffed. "We are a city of many shops."

"And my brother and I are not traveling alone. We
have a number of friends with us. Female friends for the
most part and half of them are American."

"Indeed." His eyes widened. "I very much like Americans. They are so friendly in nature. Much like my own
countrymen. They are all most welcome." He gestured

in a grand manner. "You shall give Giuseppe their names and we shall have invitations delivered by this evening."

She smiled and surrendered. "That's very kind of you. I'm sure everyone will be delighted."

"And you will save a special dance just for me." That look was back in his eyes again. "Promise me, *cara mia.*"

"Of course." A thought occurred to her and she smiled. "You have already been most kind but could I beg a small favor?"

"You have but to ask."

"As I do not remember our meeting, I cannot recall if I have met your wife. I would hate to embarrass myself yet again."

"My wife is no longer with me." He shrugged.

"Oh my. I thought…" Hadn't Dante's investigator said the contessa was more knowledgeable about art than her husband? Good Lord. Dante really did need to find someone who would do a better job as it appeared the woman was dead. "My condolences, my lord. I am so sorry for your loss."

"She is not dead." He scoffed. "We had, how you say, words. She is residing elsewhere for a time." He scowled. "To make me suffer but I will fool her." He grinned. "I am not suffering the tiniest bit. She will see. She will be back tomorrow."

"I look forward to meeting her."

"And I look forward to our dance." Given the wicked look in his eyes, he intended that dance to lead to something far more intimate than a mere turn on a dance floor.

"What dance?" Dante said in a pleasant tone that struck her as not quite right. The painting was wrapped and under his arm.

"The conte has graciously invited us to a masked ball tomorrow night. All of us."

"That is very kind of him," Dante said slowly.

"It is nothing." The conte spoke to his secretary who pulled a small notebook from a hidden pocket.

"Lady Bascombe?" Montalvado waited, a stub of a pencil poised over the now open notebook. "If you would be so kind as to give me the names of your friends."

"Of course." Willie rattled off the names of the others.

"To that I will add your name and—" He glanced at Dante.

"My brother," Willie offered, "Mr. Quatermain."

"Mr. Quatermain. Excellent." Montalvado noted the name. "I shall send, as well, a list of the finer mask and costume shops. Most choose to dress in the manner of the last century when La Serenissima was still in her glory. While costumes and masks are usually made at the request of specific patrons, there are always some available for immediate purchase."

"Now, Lady Bascombe," the conte said, "I shall have one of our boatmen take you to your hotel. And I shall count the hours until you return."

A few minutes later Willie and Dante were once again in a gondola.

"Allan Quatermain?" She scoffed. "Really?"

"It was the first name that came to mind," he said absently, his thoughts obviously on something else.

"I don't understand why—"

"I'll explain later."

"I think you're being silly. It all went quite well." She considered him cautiously. "But then I knew it would."

"And you were right," he said through a tight smile.

"It did go well, didn't it?"

"So it would appear."

She frowned. "Whatever is the matter?"

He looked over his shoulder at the gondolier then

leaned close and spoke softly into her ear. "I don't think it's wise to discuss this until we are back at the hotel."

"Very well," she said slowly.

The moment they entered her room, he strode toward the bed in a determined manner.

"I beg your pardon." Willie stalked after him. Why, the man was practically racing toward the bed. Certainly she was grateful for his assistance but she hadn't forgiven him and she was not about to fling herself into bed with him. She knew coming to her room was probably a mistake as she didn't have a separate parlor, simply a sitting area, but it was far better than going to his. At least the Portinari was now in her possession. "What do you think you're doing? Just because we have agreed to be partners and because I might not possibly be as furious with you as I was and you've really been quite wonderful since we've been in Venice doesn't mean…"

He stared at her then grinned. "Quite wonderful?"

"I misspoke. I meant to say adequately wonderful."

"That will do." His smile faded and he was at once completely serious. He put the package on the bed and started to work at the knots. "This is obviously not meant to be untied until we return to London."

"Then why are you opening it now?" Unease trickled through her. She took off her hat and placed it on the dresser.

"Because I want to see the painting." He huffed. "Do you have a knife?"

"No." She pulled off her gloves. "Why would I have a knife?"

"I don't know," he snapped and continued to try to work the knots free.

"Why didn't you use your own name?"

"Because a serious collector might well be aware of

my grandfather's collection and I am not unknown in the world of collecting." He managed to loosen one knot. "I simply thought it wise not to reveal my connection to Montague House as well as my knowledge of art."

"Not necessary as it turned out but admittedly rather clever."

"It seemed like a good idea. Blast it all." He yanked at the string in a futile effort to break it. "I saw these knots being tied. They did not seem this tight."

She watched him struggle for a moment. "I do have a pair of scissors. Would that help?"

He glared at her. "Yes, that would indeed help."

She retrieved her scissors from a dresser drawer and handed them to him. "One of the Lady Traveler Society pamphlets included scissors in a list of items one should never travel without."

"What a shame they didn't say the scissors should be sharp," he muttered. Even so, within a minute he was able to discard the string and unwrap the oilcloth.

The painting lay on the bed on top of the oilcloth looking exactly as it had on the wall.

"My grandmother loved that painting. It meant a great deal to her. I never really appreciated it before." She smiled. "But now I have heard several lectures on art and I may well have learned something."

"You like it, do you?"

"I do—it's really quite remarkable. The figures and the underworld setting, the expressions on the faces, the colors—"

"That's right, you said it was dark."

"Obviously I was mistaken. I simply wasn't remembering it correctly. Why, look at it." She waved at the work. "The colors are quite vivid." She drew her brows together. "Do you think perhaps it's been cleaned?"

"No."

"Do you think there's something wrong with it?"

"Not really."

"Then as I said, I was mistaken."

"I don't think so," he said slowly.

"Then what do you think?" She huffed. "You've been acting strangely since we left the conte's and I insist on knowing why."

"Do you?"

She resisted the urge to stamp her foot. "Yes, I do. You obviously think there's some problem with my painting and I want to know what it is."

"I don't think there's anything wrong with your painting."

"Thank God." She released a breath she didn't know she held. "Then what is it?"

"I could be wrong."

Her jaw tensed. "Take that risk."

He blew a long breath and met her gaze. "I'm fairly certain this is not your painting."

CHAPTER TWENTY-ONE

"WHAT DO YOU MEAN it's not my painting?" Her voice rose. "Of course it's my painting."

"No, it's not." He picked up the painting and slanted it toward the light. "Your Portinari is nearly four hundred years old. This painting was probably created no more than three years ago."

"Three years? Three years!"

"Possibly two."

"That's impossible. I don't believe you."

"Believe whatever you wish." He tilted the painting one way then another. "But when you try to sell it, it will be exposed as a copy, a forgery, a fraud." He blew a long breath. "A fake."

She struggled against a rising sense of panic. "What makes you think so?"

"A number of things, most of which would not be apparent to anyone who was not well studied in the history of art and the techniques of artists through the ages. First of all, the craquelure is wrong."

"The what?"

"The craquelure—the series of fine cracks in a painting." He held the painting up at eye level, angling it to catch the light from the window. "Oil paints shrink slightly when they dry, creating a pattern of fine cracks. Those cracks fill with dust and dirt through the years and take on a dark appearance. These cracks look painted on."

"Are you sure? Perhaps, Portinari did that himself?" Even as the words left her lips, she knew it was an absurd suggestion.

He ignored her. "Furthermore, it takes years for paint to dry to the hardness of an old work. Look at this." He pressed the tip of his thumbnail into the paint in the corner of the painting leaving a crescent shaped indentation. "That simply couldn't happen if this was centuries old."

The tiny little dimple was hard to argue with.

"In addition—"

"There's more?" she said weakly.

"You noticed this yourself. The colors appear more vivid than you remember and, I might add, far brighter than the other Portinaris. Which makes no sense if they were all painted at the same time. You've also commented on the darkness of the paintings we've seen at the Louvre and elsewhere. That's a result of the aging of the varnish because it's the varnish—meant to protect the paint—that darkens and clouds with age. In addition, you see this blue color..." He pointed to a part of Orpheus's cloak. "I'm fairly certain that's Prussian blue. It was not available until the early eighteenth century. Was your husband knowledgeable about works like this?"

She scoffed. "I am better versed than he was and that only because I've been listening to you."

"This was not produced to fool an expert but then it was not expected to be unwrapped until we returned to London." He lay the painting facedown on the bed and studied it for a minute or two or a lifetime.

What was he looking for? As impatient as she was, it did seem best to allow him to take whatever time he needed to realize he was wrong.

"The canvas itself is dark as it should be. The wood bars used to stabilize the canvas are not original."

She winced. That did not sound good.

"Neither are the ones on the paintings at Montague House. They were replaced when my grandfather bought the paintings to strengthen the works." He glanced at her. "Do you have a buttonhook?"

"Of course." She fetched the implement and handed it to him.

"The Portinaris were among the first works my grandfather bought and he was not as cognizant of the need to preserve works exactly as they were as he was later in his collecting. He placed a small red stamp on the back in the lower right-hand corner. A circle enclosing his initials." He took the hook and worked at the tacks securing the canvas to the wood. Once he had them all removed, he carefully lifted the wood from the canvas. The canvas was far lighter where the wood had been. He shook his head. "As you can see—"

She stared, she moved closer, she squinted her eyes. "There's no stamp, is there?"

"I'm afraid not. And it appears the canvas itself has been treated to give more of an aged appearance."

"I see." She already knew the answer but wasn't ready to give up all hope. She drew a deep breath. "You are completely, totally without question certain this is not my painting?"

"As much as I hate to say it—" he met her gaze directly "—yes, I am."

"Couldn't you be mistaken?"

"I wish I were." He ran his hand through his hair. "I have always been fascinated by my grandfather's collection. I studied the history of art as well as methods of identification, dating and authentication. I considered it my responsibility as the guardian of the collection. And I'm rather good at this."

"Then the value of this painting," she said slowly.

"It is a nice-looking copy."

That was it, then. Her last recourse. The only means she had to regain any semblance of financial solvency. She wanted to throw herself onto the bed and weep. What was she going to do now? She rubbed her temples in an effort to ease an awful throbbing. It didn't help. "Did you know this when we were at the conte's?"

"I suspected it."

"Why didn't you say something?" Despair abruptly gave way to anger. Not really at Dante; it wasn't his fault. He was simply close at hand. "Why didn't you do something?"

"First of all," he said in that annoyingly calm manner men tend to adopt when they think women are being irrational. It was enough to set her teeth on edge. "I couldn't be entirely certain until I examined it more closely. Second, I had no idea how the conte would respond. We are guests in his country after all. I can think of any number of things he might have said."

She crossed her arms over her chest. "Name one."

"One—" his eyes narrowed "—he could claim he had no idea it was a copy."

"Do you think he did know?"

"Everything indicates he not only knew, he probably had the copy made. As I said, I would estimate the copy was only made a few years ago." He paused. "When did the conte give your husband the loan?"

"According to the document I have, five years ago, three years before George died."

Dante nodded. "Given what we know about the conte's passion for works created here in Venice, I would suspect he never intended to return the painting as I imagine he never expected your husband to repay the loan."

"In that he was not alone among George's creditors." Willie wrinkled her nose.

"He could have had the copy made as soon as he had the painting in his hands." Dante thought for a moment. "Or it could have been painted when he heard your husband was dead, on the chance that if anyone came to reclaim it, they would not be knowledgeable enough to recognize it as a fake."

"And I wouldn't have been." She heaved a frustrated sigh. "So you think he intended to keep the real Portinari—my Portinari—all along?"

"I wouldn't be surprised. Collectors are an odd lot. Extremely passionate and insanely possessive. Especially when national pride is involved, when they believe a work belongs in the country of its origin."

A horrible thought struck her. "What if my Portinari really was a fake all along?"

He shook his head. "The conte is a collector from a family of collectors in a country and a city that reveres art far more than we do in England. Art is part of the fabric of life here. I would wager my train ticket home that he is as knowledgeable as I am. He never would have agreed to a loan if he wasn't confident the painting was genuine."

"We need to go back to the conte's at once." She grabbed her hat and gloves. "I repaid the loan. I want my painting." She yanked open the door.

He reached around her and closed it sharply. "You can't simply go over there accusing him of trying to cheat you."

"Then I'll…" *What?* "I'll contact the authorities, that's what I'll do. The British embassy or what passes for police here. I'll tell them—"

"What will you tell them, Willie? That your late husband used a painting that rightfully belonged to you to secure a loan? And that the conte made a copy because he wanted to keep the original? You have no way to prove any of this. As I said, he could claim he had no idea it was a copy."

"But you and I know it wasn't."

"It doesn't matter what we know, it matters what we can prove. Don't forget, we are visitors here. No one here is going to take the word of an English viscountess over a Venetian conte whose family has been a part of Venice for hundreds of years."

"Then what do we do now? How do I get my painting back?" She paced the room. Nothing came to mind. Nothing clever at any rate. Dante was right. They simply couldn't demand the conte return the Portinari. She paused in midstep. "What if he doesn't have it?"

"I doubt he would go to all this trouble if he didn't have it."

"I have to have that painting, Dante." Her voice rose and quivered in a horribly embarrassing way. "I kept up George's end of the bargain. I scraped together enough to repay the loan. I maneuvered nine—now ten—people through all the treacheries of travel without the loss of luggage or life. I prayed with nuns! My future depends on that painting. Without it…" She shook her head. "I don't know what I'll do."

Dante considered her for a long thoughtful moment. "It seems to me there is only one thing to do. Well, two really."

"Very well. What are they?"

"First, we have to determine exactly where the Portinari is. And then…" He set his jaw in a determined manner. "We're going to steal it."

"ARE YOU INSANE?" Willie stared at him.

"Possibly."

The moment the words were out of Dante's mouth he

wondered what on earth he was thinking. He'd never in his life so much as considered larceny. He had always been unfailingly honest. His integrity in business matters was unquestioned. Aside from that one error in judgment of not telling Willie about his claim to the Portinari—and really that could be considered more a simple omission rather than true deceit—he couldn't recall any time he had done anything dishonest and certainly never anything illegal.

She scoffed. "You've never stolen anything in your life."

"No, I haven't," he said sharply. Still, the very idea was oddly exciting. And what better way to prove to the woman he loved that he could be trusted than by stealing a painting for her? The irony of the thought was not lost on him. "Have you?"

"Of course not, but of the two of us I am the one more likely to have done something of this nature."

"Not something to be proud of, Lady Bascombe."

"I not especially proud of it but I'm not particularly ashamed about it either. It's simply a fact." She shrugged in an offhand manner. "And the fact is that my life has better prepared me for an escapade of a criminal nature."

"A what?"

"I was trying to spare your eminently proper sensibilities."

"No, please, go on. I shall brace myself." He wasn't sure if this was amusing or insulting.

"Very well then—a robbery, a theft, an act of larceny." She crossed her arms over her chest. "You may choose at random."

"Does it matter?"

"I suppose not. I was just trying to say that I am better

suited to do something like this—or frankly, even to suggest it. After all, your life has been extraordinarily dull."

"I would more accurately call it *respectable*."

"Whereas mine has been somewhat more adventurous."

"Don't you mean *scandalous*?"

Her eyes narrowed. "I mean exciting."

"Or improper?"

"I would term it *amusing*. Most amusing. And not the least bit boring."

"Boring?" He drew his brows together. "You think my life is boring?"

She smirked.

"My life is not boring. Not at all. I have my work and the museum. I have any number of interests—art, antiquities, literature, opera. My life is…reputable. Responsible. Sensible. Well-ordered." Even to him it did sound, well, boring.

"Stuffy, staid, uninteresting, expected."

"It hasn't been the least bit *expected* since I met you."

She raised her chin. "Since you digressed from your ever-so-proper life of complete and utter honesty to deceive me, you mean."

"No, that's not what I meant but you're right." He grabbed her hands, pulled her close and gazed into her eyes. "I never would have so much as considered larceny in any form or by any name before I met you. You, Wilhelmina Bascombe, have changed my life."

"You're most welcome," she said loftily but made no effort to move away.

"Oh, I am indeed grateful. And I find the idea of larceny with you rather exciting." His gaze dropped to her lips and back to her eyes. "Shockingly so."

Willie stared. "Do you?"

"You have no idea." He wanted to kiss her, to pull her tight against him and ravage her mouth until her knees weakened and she was limp in his arms. He was fairly certain right now she would kiss him back with an enthusiasm and desire matching his own. Even so, that was probably not the way to win Willie back permanently. Besides, one kiss was not—would never be—enough. And this was not the time. Without warning he released her and turned to pace the room. "The first thing we need to do is determine exactly where the painting is."

She stared, disappointment mixed with indignation on her face. "Did I misunderstand?"

"What?"

"Weren't you going to kiss me?"

"Did you want me to kiss you?"

"No." She scoffed. "Of course not. The thought never entered my mind. Indeed, I was prepared to slap your face."

"You might well have slapped me afterward just to prove a point but the thought more than entered your mind. You wanted me to kiss you and you know it as well as I. However, if you wish to pretend you didn't—" he shrugged "—that's probably for the best because at the moment we have other matters to consider."

"You are my partner in this endeavor and this endeavor alone, Mr. Montague, nothing more. You'd do best to remember that. Wanted you to kiss me indeed," she added under her breath.

He stifled a satisfied grin and resumed pacing. "As I see it, there are several possibilities for the location of the Portinari."

"Only several?" Her brow arched upward. "It could be anywhere in Venice."

"It could but Sarafini is a dedicated collector and his

favorites are those works by Venetian artists. There is nothing he likes more than seeing the Bellini, the Titians and the Portinari all displayed together. You could see it on his face."

She frowned. "I thought that was lust."

"It was but not for you." He glanced at her. "The man is a fool."

Her cheeks flushed. He never would have imagined Wilhelmina Bascombe was the type of woman who blushed but she did and each and every time it did something absurd to his heart.

"Very well then." She thought for a moment. "You said collectors are possessive."

He nodded. "As a rule."

"Then, logically, he would have the Portinari nearby. So dare we assume it is in his house or the building that houses the gallery?"

"That makes sense." Dante considered the problem. He had spent much of his life studying art and one couldn't really study art and not stumble across the men who coveted rare works. "He had the painting wrapped for travel and obviously assumed we wouldn't open it until we had returned to London."

"He said as much."

"You also told him we could not return to the gallery. Which would mean he would be safe to put the real painting back in its place."

"Do you think so?"

"I think it's possible. He really has nothing to lose by doing so."

"He did strike me as being exceptionally arrogant."

"And confident. If we accuse him of anything, he could always claim he'd given you the Portinari and kept a copy for himself. Experts would have to decide which painting was which and they would probably be his experts, which might lead to litigation. This could drag on for a long time. And don't forget the conte has a great deal of influence here." He shook his head. "It seems to me we have little choice."

"If it makes you feel better about this bit of larceny—and I must say, I rather like the way that sounds. *Larceny*." She grinned. "It has a nice ring to it."

He snorted.

"As I was saying, you may want to consider this not as *larceny*—" she drew out the word with a distinct show of delight "—but as a repossession. I repaid the debt. That painting is mine."

"You're right." He grimaced. "I feel much, much better."

"Try to remember that. It will sound plausible when we're being led over the Bridge of Sighs to prison." She paused. "I fear we will need help in this."

"I'm afraid so." The last thing he wanted to do was involve his sister or any of the other ladies in this venture that was at best illegal and at worse—possibly dangerous.

"Don't look so distraught. I suspect our group of lady travelers can best an arrogant Italian conte."

"With a guidebook in one hand and a sturdy parasol in the other?" he said wryly. "Although I would like to see that."

She ignored him. "Why, I shall lead them into battle myself."

"We are not going to storm the palazzo with swords and daggers, you know."

"I find that a very great pity. And I do realize I am not leading them into an actual battle. More a figurative one."

"Ah well, as long as you realize that."

"I am invoking the appropriate spirit." She straightened her shoulders. "And I have tried to do my very best whether it is in navigating the treacherous waters of French customs agents or an act of larceny."

He smiled. "I am aware of that."

"You may, however, have Bertie to lead."

"I am a lucky man."

"Yes, Mr. Montague." She met his gaze firmly. "You are."

He wasn't sure exactly what she meant and preferred to consider it in a positive light. But now was probably not the best time to discuss their future. Not until he had her painting. And her trust.

"As are you, Lady Bascombe." He pulled her into his arms and grinned down at her. "The intrepid hero Allan Quatermain is at your service."

"You are not Allan Quatermain." She huffed. "You are not the hero of a novel of adventure."

"I am something much better."

"Are you indeed?"

"I am the man who would do anything for you." He nodded and released her. "And regardless of what it takes, no matter the risk or the danger, I intend to prove it."

And how could she not trust him then?

CHAPTER TWENTY-TWO

"ARE YOU READY?" Dante stood near the top of the marble stairway and gazed over the mass of celebrants in the conte's grand ballroom, grateful for the first time this evening that his mask was annoyingly tight against his skin. It had bothered him since he'd first put it on and he wanted nothing more than to rip it off his face but at least it did not obscure his vision.

If Dante did not know it was 1889, he certainly would have thought he was in another time when Venice ruled the seas and was the center of wealth and elegance, excess and decadence. He had no idea how many people were here but the crowd flowed from the entry up the grand stairway and into an immense ballroom. This ballroom put the gallery they had visited yesterday to shame with soaring ceilings painted with celestial beings—by Tiepolo if he was correct—carved marble columns and ornate gilded plasterwork. All illuminated by huge glass chandeliers. A bit overdone to his taste. It was all Dante could do not to shield his eyes against the splendor and the sparkle. The crowd itself was no less impressive. Not a face was uncovered by a mask—some made simply of fabric covering only the wearer's eyes, others extravagant with jewels and beads and feathers. Rich silks and brocades had been fashioned into the styles of the last century. It was a setting straight from a stage play or an opera or an enchantment. Or the oddest dream he'd ever had.

"I've been ready since we arrived," Willie said on his left.

"Let's get on with it," Jane added on his right.

All in all, it was a relatively simple plan. They'd worked out the details last night. It had taken several hours simply to gather the group in Rosalind's suite as nearly everyone had been out enjoying the sights—or the shops—of Venice.

Dante had long known women were odd and unexpected creatures. Even so, the devious plotting and planning of these lady travelers was a revelation. It was impossible to determine which proposal excited the group more—the prospect of a masked costume ball at a genuine Venetian palazzo or the idea of stealing a Renaissance work of art. Poor Bertie seemed the slightest bit taken aback by it all. Apparently, the young man thought ladies were above such diabolical machinations. Best to shatter that illusion—and the pedestal it sat on—once and for all.

While Willie and Dante began their quest for masks and apparel, Roz and the others had started their day with a discreet stop at the conte's gallery to confirm that the Portinari was indeed back where the copy had hung yesterday. Dante refused to consider what would happen to their plan if the painting was not in the gallery.

It was agreed among the older members of their party that the girls and Bertie would not play a role in the actual retrieval of the painting—a no doubt futile effort to keep them at a distance should tonight not go well. The Portinari's reclamation would be left to Dante and Willie and to Jane to a certain extent. Who would have imagined the seemingly sensible American would have the skills necessary to pick a lock? Jane had taken the opportunity during their visit to the gallery to take a good look at the door separating the public area from the conte's residence and had declared the lock to be insignificant, meant primarily for interiors and easy to force. Jane did not disclose how she had come by this knowledge and had waved off inquiries by saying she had brothers and sons and she read a great deal. The other ladies accepted her explanation without question.

If Dante had ever imagined himself in the midst of a plot to steal a painting from a Venetian palazzo—and he had not—he certainly wouldn't have thought it would be in the company of eight stunning women in the costumes of another era. Casanova would feel right at home but then Venice had been the infamous scoundrel's home. The ladies had all managed to find powdered wigs, exquisite masks, flowing cloaks and perhaps the most voluminous gowns he had ever seen. Indeed, it had taken four separate gondolas to transport the party to the ball. He had never given much thought to the whims of fashion and certainly had never before considered the dress of another century and yet whether or not they were successful tonight was entirely at the mercy of fashion. Willie had secured the carefully rolled up copy beneath the paniers of her gown and had also hidden a few candle stubs somewhere within the yards of fabric, which would be necessary to provide light as it would be dark in the gallery. The plan called for Dante to remove the Portinari from its wooden supports and replace it with the copy.

Once Jane opened the door, she would remain on guard while Willie and Dante traded the copy for the Portinari. The others were to keep an eye on the conte to make certain he didn't follow Willie. In the hour or so they'd been here, she had already danced with him more than once. The man did seem determined to seduce her, although—even if she'd been interested—Dante suspected his efforts would be futile. The conte was well on his way to complete inebriation and was as taken by Marian, Roz and the girls as he was by Willie. Not that any of them were identifiable. There was much to be said for a crowded ballroom and the anonymity of the disguises of another era.

"Jane," Willie said quietly, "as much as I appreciate your willingness to assist us, this will make you complicit in a questionable—"

"Illegal," Dante murmured.

"—endeavor in a foreign country. It is not too late to change your mind."

"Goodness, Willie, I never in my wildest dreams even imagined an adventure like this. Why, it's exactly the type of thing the Wilhelmina Bascombe Miss Granville told us about would do, and I do not intend to miss it. Furthermore, the painting belongs to you. Our retrieval effort may be unorthodox but I do not consider it wrong either morally or legally," Jane said firmly. "It's the sort of thing one does for friends and I would expect my friends to do no less for me."

"You must have very good friends," Dante said under his breath.

"I do." Jane nodded at Willie. "And so does she."

"If you're certain," Willie said. "I would not blame you if you reconsidered and it will not affect our friendship in the least."

"I am certain. Besides—" Jane chuckled "—the literary society will be beside themselves. Imagine, quiet Jane Corby assisting a viscountess to steal a painting from an Italian conte at his palace on the canals of Venice. It's better than most of the books we read."

"Then after you, ladies." Dante turned and gestured toward the stairway.

Jane started down the stairs.

"Lady Bascombe." Dante leaned close and spoke quietly into her ear. "You look exquisite tonight."

"Yes, Mr. Montague, I know." Her eyes twinkled behind her mask.

Willie's gown was a cream-colored satin embroidered with crystals and touched with lace dripping from her sleeves. Every move she made caught the light and cast a glow of magic around her. He had already noticed how that same lace framed the gown's shockingly low bodice in a most enticing manner. It was apparently the nature of this antiquated style of dress that flattened the torso and pushed the bosom upward in a tantalizing display of feminine charms. Dante had warned Bertie that he might try not to stare quite so obviously at the girls in their costumes, although to give the boy his due—they did all look tempting. And each and every one of them knew it. The thought struck him that someday he might be the father of daughters. And while he would hope they were as lovely as their mother, the idea was as terrifying as it was delightful. Stealing Willie's painting was one step closer to winning her heart.

"But I must say, I never suspected a man in a powdered wig, short satin pants and stockings would be quite so… seductive. And romantic."

He grinned. "You think I'm seductive and romantic?"

"I think the *costume* is seductive and romantic, Mr. Montague, as is the setting we find ourselves in. But one can certainly see how such an ensemble would enhance the charms of a man like Casanova."

"And a man like myself?"

"Your charms are still in question," she said in a lofty manner and started after Jane.

He chuckled and followed a scant step behind. The crush of guests on the steps impeded their descent and they made their way down at a frustratingly slow pace. Dante was surprised to note his own impatience. On one hand, he wanted this over with. On the other, it was indeed the most exciting thing he had ever done.

In spite of his annoyance at their sedate progress, he couldn't help but appreciate the view.

The broad width of Willie's skirt swayed with her hips at every step she took in a way that could only be called inviting and he tried to force his thoughts back to the task before them. It wasn't easy. His gaze kept drifting to the nape of her neck and he couldn't dismiss the memory of how she had melted in his arms when he had kissed her there. And how much he enjoyed kissing her there.

She paused at the bottom of the steps and gazed up at him, a vision straight from a Venetian artist's canvas. For a long moment he could do nothing but stare.

"Dante," she said quietly although she needn't have bothered. There seemed to be just as many people on this floor as there had been on the floor above. He could barely hear her over the din of riotous chatter, unrestrained laughter and explicit flirtation, not to mention the music that drifted down the stairway. "What on earth is the matter?"

He shook his head to clear the fog of a past Venice that would never be again and perhaps a ghost or two. "Nothing." He nodded toward the passageway. "Shall we?"

They shouldered their way through the crowd to the corridor leading to the gallery, smiling and laughing as if they had nothing more on their minds than a jolly good time. The ladies stepped into the hall, Dante lingering behind to see if anyone noticed them. No one did, although Dante would have wagered almost anything outrageous could happen here and these partygoers would barely pause for breath.

A conveniently lit sconce glowed softly on the wall, illuminating the door to the gallery. Dante remained positioned where he could keep watch on the entry to the passageway. Jane removed her mask and sank down in front of the door. She studied the lock for a moment then pulled a long, thin tool from her powdered wig.

"What is that?" Dante stared. Good Lord—did the American really have lock-picking tools? Who was she anyway?

Jane and Willie traded amused glances.

"You must forgive him," Willie said. "He's never done anything improper before."

"Neither have I. But I do know a buttonhook when I see one." Jane turned her attention to the door. "Although I am flattered that he thinks I have nefarious tendencies." Jane inserted the buttonhook and bent to the task at hand.

"The literary society will be most impressed." A grin sounded in Willie's voice.

Why weren't these women taking this in the serious manner it deserved? They were breaking into a building owned by a Venetian nobleman while said nobleman and hundreds of his closest friends frolicked well within reach. They acted as if this were some kind of a lark. A picnic in Hyde Park. A stroll along—

"There it is." Satisfaction sounded in Jane's voice and Willie helped her to her feet. "That was far easier than I expected."

Jane stepped back and Willie carefully opened the door. The gallery was dark as expected. She and Dante removed their masks and handed them to Jane.

"A candle if you please, Lady Bascombe." He held out his hand.

She started to reach in her bodice then paused. "Turn around."

"I really don't think it's nec—"

"Turn around!"

"Very well." He turned his back to her. "I daresay this is not the time for needless modesty."

"I would have thought a man of your nature would never think modesty needless."

"As I have told you—" his jaw tightened "—I have changed."

"You may turn around, Mr. Montague," Jane said. "I assume you remembered to bring matches."

"Of course I did." He pulled a match from his waistcoat pocket, struck it and lit the candle Willie held. "Are you sure you're ready for this?"

"Goodness, Mr. Montague, let's just get on with it." Impatience rang in Willie's voice.

"I am as eager to get this over with as you are," he said sharply, even as he realized her tone—and his—was as much a product of apprehension as anything else. In spite of her bravado up to now, she knew as well as he that this was still a potentially hazardous endeavor.

Willie stepped into the darkness and he started after her.

"Mr. Montague." Jane leaned toward him as he passed. He paused. "Yes?"

"To alleviate your concern that you have fallen into a den of American miscreants—" her eyes sparkled "—you should know my grandfather was a locksmith."

"I assure you, Mrs. Corby, I never suspected…" He sighed. "Well, there might have been a moment."

She grinned and stepped aside. He followed Willie, and Jane closed the door quietly behind them.

Aside from the faint starlight from the high windows, the pool of candlelight around Willie was the only illumination. She was a good ten feet in front of him and moving quickly toward the far wall where the Bellini and Titians and—hopefully—the Portinari hung. In spite of the riotous revelry in the other palazzo, the gallery was unnervingly silent. Outside of Willie's circle of light, shadowy fingers reached out for them. If Dante had a more fanciful imagination it would have been most unsettling. Even so, it was disconcerting and he picked up his pace.

"Don't forget there's a table in the middle of the room."

"I know there's a table."

Something unidentified skittered across the floor. Willie squeaked and stopped short, so quickly Dante collided into her. She stumbled forward. The candle flew out of her hands, hit the floor and plunged them into darkness.

"Blast it all, Dante! Look what you've done."

"I didn't do anything," he said sharply. "You're the one who stopped without warning."

"A bloody rat ran over my foot." She shuddered. "I don't like rats."

"No one does. And I doubt it was a rat." Although it probably was. It had sounded rather large. "Where are you?"

She huffed. "On the floor. I tripped over these damnable skirts. I'm trying to find the candle."

"Good idea."

"Then perhaps you could get down here and help me."

"I was just waiting for my eyes to adjust to the light. Or the lack of light." He dropped to his knees and swept his hand along the floor. "Did you see where it fell?"

"If I did, I would have it by now."

He was now able to make out a few dim shapes. Judging from the sound of her voice, the large shadow in front of him to his left was Willie. Something near her glinted in the faint light.

"I think I see it. Don't move." He moved closer, braced his hand by her side and reached over her.

"What are you doing?" Her voice was closer to his ear than he thought it should be but then the dark was disorienting. "Goodness, Dante, this is not the time."

"I'm not trying to seduce you. I'm trying to reach the candle."

"Oh. Couldn't you have gone around me?"

"I didn't want to lose sight of it." He stretched farther but still couldn't reach. "Do you see it?"

"No." She shifted beneath him. Under other circumstances this would indeed be quite exciting. But not here. In the dark. On the floor. In an ancient palace filled with eerie shadows and creaking timbers. At least he thought it was timbers.

She froze. "What is that noise?"

"What noise?"

The creaking sounded again although it did sound more like footsteps—

"Rats!" Willie frantically pushed at him in an effort to get to her feet. He caught hold of her but his feet tangled in her skirts and they both went down, Willie landing on top of him.

The distinct sound of a match being struck rang in the dark and a moment later a gas lamp glowed on the other side of the room.

"My, my, this is not at all what I expected," a female voice said in accented English.

Willie lifted her head and squinted at the light. "Who are you?"

"I would ask you the same thing." The woman came closer; a man in the shadows behind her held the lamp. She turned and murmured something to him. He set the lamp on the table then strode out of sight to light the sconces on the walls. "But I suspect I know the answer."

Dante wrapped his arms around Willie and rolled over then raised his head and stared.

"Ah, Mr. Montague, how lovely to see you again," she said. In the increasing light, he could see her face. She was quite lovely and she too was dressed in the style of the last century. But Dante would wager significant money he'd never met her before. "Or should I say Mr. Quatermain?"

"My apologies, but have we met?" Dante asked.

"No." She shrugged. "But I know who you are."

"Would you please move off me?" Willie huffed.

"Yes, of course. Sorry." Dante scrambled up and grabbed Willie's hand to pull her to her feet then turned back to the newcomer. "I fear you have me at a disadvantage."

She laughed. "You Englishmen are so good at the— what is the word? The understatement? Yes, that's it. I find you on the floor, in the dark, in a room that is locked, with a lovely woman in your arms—"

"I really wasn't in his arms," Willie said and adjusted her wig, which was leaning in a precarious manner. "I tripped and he fell and one thing led to another—"

"One thing often leads to another." The Italian grinned. "It is what makes *one thing* so very enjoyable."

"It really isn't what you think," Willie began. Dante shot her a pointed look. Much better to claim this was an amorous assignation than the truth. Willie's eyes widened in understanding then she heaved an exaggerated sigh. "You're right, of course. This is, well, exactly what it looks like. We thought we were safe here and, well, surely you can understand?"

"I understand many things, Lady Bascombe." She grinned.

"How do you know my name?"

The gentleman who had lit the sconces returned to the lady's side. Dante's stomach twisted.

"A pleasure to see you again, Mr. Quatermain," Signore Montalvado said wryly.

Dante nodded. "Good evening."

"Allan Quatermain, how very clever. The dashing hero. The seeker of lost treasure." She chuckled. "And you are here seeking treasure, are you not?"

"The treasure in question rightfully belongs to me," Willie said staunchly. "And I demand to know who you are and how you know my name."

The lady's eyes narrowed. "You are in no position to demand, Lady Bascombe. And yet—" she grinned "—I like a woman who is not cowed when she is caught with the hands red."

Montalvado leaned toward her. "It's red-handed, contessa."

Contessa?

"Allow me to introduce the Contessa de Sarafini," Montalvado said with a nod of his head.

"Well, you're definitely not dead," Willie said then winced. "My apologies. It's just, the way your husband talked—"

"My husband says many stupid things. But I shall fool him. I shall live at least one day longer than he."

Willie snorted back a laugh.

"You understand stupid husbands, do you not, Lady Bascombe?" The contessa studied her curiously. "You would not be here if your husband was not *idiota*."

"To my eternal regret." Willie shrugged.

"I beg your pardon, contessa, but if we have never met," Dante said, "how did you know who I was?"

"My dear Mr. Montague, while it is most tempting to say I have many ways and allow you to think me most mysterious, the answer is simple and I am not in the mood for games tonight. Well—" her gaze flicked over him in an assessing manner "—not this kind of game."

Willie choked.

"Last year, no..." She thought for a moment. "The year before perhaps? Giuseppe?"

"Not quite two years ago, contessa," Montalvado said smoothly.

"Are you certain?"

He nodded.

"Regardless—" she waved dismissively "—it was then that I traveled to London where, among many other things, I visited a tiny museum, *molto piccolo*, very small. Even so, Giuseppe—" she nodded at Montalvado "—had heard there was an impressive collection of art, including some pieces from Venice. My husband collects but I appreciate. I revere. I cherish. Pietro is noble by birth but has the soul of a peasant. My family was ruling Venice when his was still crawling about in the mud."

Montalvado cleared his throat.

"Which is not of importance at the moment." She shrugged. "You can imagine my surprise to find a room with two original Portinaris as well as a copy of the painting my husband had in his possession." She pinned Dante with a chastising look. "Not well displayed, Mr. Montague, not worthy of the genius of the artist. I saw you at that time but you were engaged in conversation, so I did not think it necessary to introduce myself. You have something of a reputation and who am I to tell a man the painting he displays is not what he thinks it is."

"That would have been around the time I began as director." Dante shook his head. "I had no idea then that the Portinari was a copy."

"How did it come to be in Lord Bascombe's possession?" she asked.

"It didn't, not really," Willie said. "I had no idea he had used it to secure a loan until after he died. It was mine, left to me by my grandmother."

"The true ownership of the painting is still to be determined," Dante said firmly.

Willie's jaw tightened. "The painting is mine."

"Ah, I see." The contessa's gaze shifted between Willie and Dante. "There is much more to this than I suspected."

A thought struck Dante and he stared. "You were expecting us, weren't you?"

"You are very clever, Mr. Montague." She grinned. "But not so clever as I."

"I shall simply have to try harder, then."

The contessa laughed. "And amusing, as well. There is much to be said for a man who makes me laugh."

"I am flattered but somewhat confused," Dante said. "Your husband—"

"My husband is an ass and perhaps you are little better, no? But then all men are asses." She studied him curiously. "Forgive me but I speak only the truth."

"One can't argue with the truth." Willie smiled.

"It is worse," the contessa continued. "Pietro is not always a man of honor, especially when he thinks he will not be caught. But—" she scoffed "—he is not so clever as he believes and he is often caught. I knew when he had the painting copied—"

"When was that?" Dante asked without thinking.

Willie glared. "You just want to know if you were right."

"Of course I do." How could she not understand that?

"Approximately three years ago," Montalvado said.

"I was right." He grinned.

Willie rolled her gaze toward the ceiling.

"I am most impressed, Mr. Montague, but there is more." The contessa thought for a moment. "When my husband had the painting copied, I realized he never intended to return it. He was most confident when he heard Lord Bascombe had died." She cast Willie a sympathetic look. "I hope you did not care for him too much. It is most enjoyable to be a widow. Pietro is my second husband. I look forward to the day I am a widow again."

"If only for a day?" Willie grinned.

The contessa laughed. "It will be a magnificent day and I shall enjoy it immensely."

Dante wasn't at all sure he liked this turn of the conversation. "You were saying?"

"I knew when he received the letter from Lady Bascombe saying she would soon be here to repay the loan and claim her painting, that Pietro would give her the copy and hope she did not discover the deception until she left Venice, if ever. He did not expect her to be accompanied by an expert in art." She favored Dante with an admiring look. "Allan Quatermain, very good, Mr. Montague. I liked *King Solomon's Mines* very much. Very good adventure."

"But how did you know we would be here tonight to take the painting?" Dante said.

"First, you should know the ladies of Venice have never through the centuries had any, oh, official power, yet we have always ruled the city nonetheless. In spite of the men." She cast a disparaging look at Dante.

He was not personally responsible for the treatment

of women in Venice in the past thousand some years and rather resented that look. "See here, contessa—"

She waved him silent. When it came right down to it, they were caught with the red hands as she said. He had no right to be indignant.

"And we still do. The world here is not entirely as it appears. Venice has always been a city of undercurrents and illusions, intrigues and secrets. And the women here are nothing if not determined." She smiled pleasantly. "My eyes and ears are everywhere and Giuseppe has more cousins than I can count." She glanced at the secretary. "How many?"

Montalvado shrugged.

"Many of whom work at the Grand Hotel. And as gondoliers and tourist guides and any number of other positions. A maid might have noted the unwrapped copy in your hotel room. A bellman might have listened at the door to your meeting last night. In Venice, knowledge has always been power."

"I see," Dante said. It was not far-fetched to assume the contessa had had her *eyes* on them from the moment they stepped foot in Venice.

"I knew as soon as you entered the gallery tonight." She grinned. "But it was a very nice plan. I would have had someone else steal it for me but then you are English."

He adopted a modest manner. "And we do like to commit our acts of larceny in person."

"Oh, that does indeed sound like fun." The contessa laughed. "You are a charming man, Mr. Montague, and I would like nothing more than to know you much, much better but, alas, we do have a matter to resolve. It is a great shame."

"Contessa," Willie asked slowly. "Where is the Portinari?"

Dante's gaze shot to the wall with the Titians.

The space was empty.

"I took the opportunity to remove it from the frame for you." She nodded at Montalvado. He stepped to the table, reached under it and straightened with the painting in his hand. The secretary laid the work on the table. "Would you care to examine it?"

"I don't think that's necessary," Dante said.

"Very good, Mr. Montague." The contessa smiled. "No, it is not necessary, this is the true Portinari. But I would prefer you assure yourself as to the painting's authenticity nonetheless."

"As you wish." Dante moved to the table and examined the work. It was pointless. He knew the moment he laid eyes on it that it was genuine. He turned it over, tilted it toward the light from the lamp and noted the faint edge of a red circle peeking from under the wood supports. He set it down and nodded at Willie. "This is indeed the genuine Portinari."

Relief washed across Willie's face. "Excellent." She nodded and addressed the contessa. "I am eternally grateful but I have to wonder why you are doing this."

"I have many reasons. As I said, my family is an old and noble Venetian family but Pietro's family is now mine, as well. I cannot let him sully the name of either of our houses. It is a great pity but his honor shifts with the tides. I would prefer the Portinari stay here as much as he but I could not allow him to cheat you. He has never really understood the sanctity of one's word as I do. But he is a handsome devil." She shrugged. "Besides, women, regardless of where they come from, should help one another. There is no one who can understand the life of a woman better than another woman." She raised a brow at Dante. "I was under the impression you were to substitute the copy for the Portinari."

He nodded.

"If you will give it to Giuseppe he will arrange everything."

"I have it," Willie said and turned away. "One moment…" Her skirts rustled and bunched and then she turned back with the rolled up copy in her hand. She presented it to Montalvado with a flourish.

"Well done, Lady Bascombe." The contessa nodded. "It will be back in place before the night is over."

"As much as I am grateful for your help—" Willie wrinkled her nose "—won't the conte be angry when he discovers the Portinari is gone?"

"Angry?" She scoffed. "He will be livid." She chuckled. "I cannot wait. But it could be days or weeks or even months before he discovers he has been tricked. And then I will tell him exactly what I have done. Oh, he will rant, he will rave and he will fling things about like a little child. But he knows that in certain circles I have influence that he does not. And he knows he was wrong.

"Now, Mr. Montague, Giuseppe will wrap the painting under your watchful eye and it will be placed in a bag made of silk. Much less obvious than a wrapped painting, do you not think so?"

He didn't but he nodded in agreement nonetheless. Montalvado wrapped the painting quickly, placed it in the bag and handed it to Dante.

"Their cloaks, Giuseppe?" The contessa nodded to him and he disappeared. "There is one tiny detail, a bit of advice if you will. From me to you."

"You've done so much already." Willie smiled. "We can never thank you enough."

"It will, unfortunately, all be for nothing if my husband notices the Portinari is missing too soon. He too has eyes everywhere. Not so good as mine but enough. When are you to leave Venice?"

"Our party had planned to stay another few days and then travel on to Rome," Dante said.

The contessa winced. "I do not think that is wise. I would suggest you leave Venice at once."

"Tonight?" Willie asked, a distinct note of unease in her voice.

"No, no, of course not." She gestured dismissively. "Fleeing in the middle of the night is not necessary." She paused. "Tomorrow, early, that will do."

"Tomorrow it is, then." Willie nodded.

Montalvado returned with their cloaks and handed one to Willie and two to Dante. "The second is for the lady in the hall. The painting will be much easier to carry under your cloak as opposed to under her skirts."

"One would think." Dante nodded.

"The rest of your party, including the young man you made to wait outside, has been gathered and they are on their way to your hotel even as we speak. A gondola awaits the two of you and your friend outside the door."

"Then we should be off." Dante took the contessa's hand and raised it to his lips. "Thank you for your assistance. If I can ever be of service, please do not hesitate to call on me."

"You have a reputation in the world of art, Mr. Montague. It is a pity you choose to devote yourself more to business than to art." She smiled wryly. "But then, even when Portinari walked the streets of Venice, business and art have always gone hand in hand."

"The nature of the world, contessa."

"So it is." She shrugged. "Might I have a private word with you, Lady Bascombe?"

"Of course." Willie nodded and indicated the door they'd entered through. "Why don't you give Jane her cloak, Dante? I'll join you in a minute."

"Very well." He nodded and accompanied Montalvado to the door. What on earth would the contessa want to tell Willie? He didn't like the idea of that one bit.

"You are worried," Montalvado said quietly.

"No." Dante waved off the question. "Not at all. It's probably some matter that would only be of interest to women."

"Venetian women, Mr. Montague, especially those from the old families, are unique and fascinating creatures." He chuckled. "They rarely discuss matters only of interest to women."

Willie joined him not more than a minute or two later. They bid their farewells then joined Jane in the passageway. It couldn't have been more than another ten minutes—the longest ten minutes of his life—before they were safely in the gondola and on their way back to the hotel. No one said a word on their return—probably for the best. He was entirely too tense to say anything remotely rational as he was certain there would be a hue and cry behind them at any minute. Bertie's comment about leaping from rooftop to rooftop to escape the authorities was no longer as far-fetched as it had originally sounded.

Under other circumstances, sliding through the canals of Venice under the starlight would have been enchanting. As it was he didn't take a decent breath until they finally reached the hotel. And was there any slower mode of transportation than a gondola? Not in this century.

"What did she say to you before we left?" he said to Willie as they waited for the others in Rosalind's suite.

"I'm not sure you want to hear." She stood in the open doorway to the balcony, staring into the night and the stars reflecting on the Grand Canal.

"I'm not sure I've ever wanted to hear anything more."

"She didn't tell me anything I didn't already know."

"You're evading my question."

"Because it's really none of your concern."

He knew even as he said the words they were wrong. "Everything from this point on is my concern."

"You're confident of that, are you?" She glanced at him, a slight smile on her lips.

"Not overly confident but..." They had committed—or attempted to commit—larceny together. It was perhaps the most exciting thing he'd ever done. And he'd done it for her. "Yes, I believe I am. We are partners after all."

"In larceny only, Mr. Montague." She turned back to the night. "In larceny only."

CHAPTER TWENTY-THREE

"...AND MR. MONTAGUE AGREES, that given the circumstances and the advice of the contessa, you should all depart for Rome the first thing in the morning." Willie drew a deep breath. This was so much more difficult than she had anticipated. And a bit unreal, as well, given that everyone was still in their eighteenth-century grab. "And I do hope that when you look back on this journey of adventure we have shared with one another, as you each continue along your own journey of life, you remember this trip fondly." The oddest lump formed in her throat. "I know I will cherish these days we have spent together always."

Silence greeted her statement. Surely someone would say something?

"That sounded dreadfully rehearsed," Harriet said.

"Like something from a guidebook," Emma added.

Tillie sniffed. "A bad guidebook."

Geneva crossed her arms over her chest. "Are you saying that you're not coming with us?"

"First of all," Willie said firmly. "It was indeed rehearsed. I have been trying to find the best way to say this. This is not something I do lightly, even if I had always intended to do it. But it certainly isn't easy. And I do cherish the days we have spent together as well as the bonds of friendship we have forged. Second—" she pinned Tillie with a hard look "—I do not employ *bad* guidebooks."

"But you were never planning to accompany us to Rome," Marian said slowly.

Jane frowned. "You intended to abandon us once you had your painting all along."

"I was going to tell you before I left. I would never simply sneak off in the middle of the night."

"That makes it so much better." Tillie glared.

"The situation is…awkward." Willie struggled for the right words then sighed. "What I haven't told you is that my finances are, well, precarious. My husband left a great deal of debt. I have managed to pay it all off but there is little left. The sale of the painting will enable me to live adequately for several years. I have an agent who has arranged a private auction for next week. Obviously I need to have the painting back by then."

Dante stared.

"Your financial state is not a complete surprise," Marian said with a casual shrug. "You ordered nothing at the House of Worth and you haven't purchased so much as a single souvenir anywhere."

"You've been on a quest." Admiration shone in Geneva's eyes. "How very independent of you. We're simply disappointed that the object of your quest is ultimately quite practical as opposed to something more exciting—a matter of the heart or something of that nature."

"You're still going to sell it?" Disbelief sounded in Dante's voice. "After everything we've been through?"

"Yes, I am. How can you possibly think otherwise?" She glared at him. Certainly he'd been incredibly charming and most endearing and he had helped her reclaim the painting. But why wouldn't he? He wanted the Portinari as much as she did. "I have not forgiven you, nor have I forgotten how you deceived me. Nothing has changed."

"Everything has changed!"

It was pointless to argue. Not here and now. She drew a calming breath and looked at Geneva. "It was not a matter of the heart but my grandmother did love that painting. I daresay I would have tried to recover it even if my finances were excellent. I hate to sell it. But—" she paused for a moment then braced herself and continued "—I have few other assets. I really have no choice."

"You do have a choice," Dante said in a hard tone. "I have offered you a choice."

She raised her chin. "Will you give up your claim to the Portinari?"

He hesitated then blew a long breath. "No."

"And I will not marry anyone to alleviate my financial difficulties." Willie narrowed her eyes. "I will not be forced into marriage because I have no other choice."

"There is no forcing about it. I love you and you love me. That is an excellent basis for marriage."

"There is that," someone murmured.

"Do you really think this is the time and place to be discussing this?" Willie gestured at the others. "In front of everyone?"

"Why not?" he said sharply. "We've discussed nearly everything else in front of them and they'd probably find out everything eventually anyway. They are aware of the situation and they are your friends."

A murmur of assent washed through the room.

"And mine," he added.

The wave of agreement was not quite as pronounced. It was most satisfying.

"Marry me, Wilhelmina."

As much as her heart yearned to say yes, her head

pointed out she had married too quickly once before. But she was young and perhaps that was a legitimate excuse. She was no longer a girl. And there was no longer any excuse for making the wrong decision. The truth of the matter was she had only known Dante for a few weeks and he had spent much of that time deceiving her as to his true purpose. Yes, he made her heart flutter and her toes curl and warmed her soul. Once again her head battled with her heart. And how was she to trust her heart? She'd been wrong before. "I will not marry a man I cannot trust."

"Haven't I proved how trustworthy I am? I stole a painting for you!"

"Not in the strictest sense of the word, given the contessa's help," one of the girls said.

"It was as much in your best interest as it was mine to steal that painting."

"What more can I do?"

She raised a brow.

His jaw tightened. "I will not relinquish my claim to *my* painting."

"Then there is nothing more to discuss." Her heart twisted. For a moment she had thought, perhaps, for her...

"There's a great deal more to discuss!" He drew a deep breath.

"You could offer to buy it from her," Rosalind suggested.

"No!" Willie and Dante said in unison.

Willie shook her head. "I'll not give up my painting to him and I will not take his money."

"I refuse to pay for something that rightfully belongs to us." Dante huffed.

"Then you both deserve to be dreadfully unhappy for the rest of your days," Rosalind snapped.

"So much for sisterly support!"

"Might I make a suggestion?" Geneva said cautiously.

"Geneva dear." Panic shone in Marian's eyes and she grabbed Geneva's arm. "Perhaps it might be best to keep our thoughts to ourselves."

"On the contrary, Marian." Willie clasped her hands in front of her. "Geneva is both clever and observant. I would very much like to hear what she has to say."

"As would I," Dante added.

Marian's gaze shifted between Willie and Dante then she sighed and nodded at her daughter.

Geneva rose to her feet, the others leaning out of the way of her skirts. "If one looks at this logically and rationally, here are the salient points." She ticked them off on her fingers. "One, Lady Bascombe received the painting from her grandmother and intends to sell it to provide income necessary to live. Which is quite admirable of her and one should give her credit for that.

"Two, Mr. Montague wants the painting to save his museum and, more important, his grandfather's legacy. He, furthermore, believes it rightfully belongs to his family. Regardless of who the painting truly belongs to, his intentions too are commendable.

"Three, Mr. Montague wants to marry Lady Bascombe for reasons of affection but the fact remains that by marrying her, he will acquire the painting anyway. Which does put his desire to marry her as well as his declarations of affection into question." Geneva glanced at Dante. "Sorry."

Dante shrugged.

"Four, she does not wish to marry simply because she has to do so for financial reasons. We all understand that." Geneva glanced around the room. The younger women nodded. "And regardless of questions of affection, the fact remains that she would enter into marriage with nothing, except the painting, of course. She has few assets and I assume no dowry, given her age?" She glanced at Willie who saw no reason to deny it, although she did think the reference to her age was unnecessary. "And while I am certain all of the mothers here would prefer their daughters marry wealth, I am just as sure that none of them want those daughters to bring nothing whatsoever to marriage. In this day and age, it does not seem a good way to begin."

"I had a substantial inheritance of my own," Marian said under her breath.

"I didn't." Jane paused. "But then my husband had nothing to speak of either."

"And five, there is the question of trust. Mr. Montague joined this tour under false pretenses because he suspected Lady Bascombe intended to reclaim the painting while in Venice."

"We never said anything about that." Suspicion furrowed Dante's brow.

"I might have mentioned it." Harriet winced.

"Much like you didn't tell us you intended to leave after you had your painting," Jane said pointedly.

"It's not the same thing at all." Willie squared her shoulders. "Yes, I agreed to host this tour as a way to travel to Venice but I have not shirked my responsibilities in any way. Indeed, I think I've done a rather brilliant job and I am seriously considering escorting more tours for the Lady Travelers Society."

"I'd join your tour." Bertie grinned. Willie had almost forgotten he was there.

"It does seem to me the two of you need to decide what you want more." Geneva looked at Willie. "The painting and with it the means to your independence. Or Mr.

Montague." She turned to Dante. "Your choice is just as simple. The painting and its worth to your grandfather's legacy. Or Lady Bascombe."

"Well put, Geneva." Rosalind nodded. "I would suggest that the two of you consider Geneva's summation. You both need to decide what you really want and what you are willing to give up to get it. Fortunately, you have time. It will take us—" she thought for a moment "—four days, I believe, to return to London. And your auction, Willie, is two days after that?"

"Three," Willie said.

"More than enough time for the both of you to stop being so stubborn." Rosalind pinned Willie with a firm look. "Remember you cooperated quite nicely to acquire the Portinari." She turned to her brother. "Don't be an idiot."

Dante's eyes narrowed.

"Now then, if we are to leave for London the first thing in the morning," Rosalind continued, "we should probably retire for the night."

"Wait." Willie stared. "You're not going to Rome?"

"Of course not." Rosalind shrugged. "Neither, I assume, is my brother."

"Absolutely not," Dante said with a short laugh. "I intend to accompany Lady Bascombe back to London."

Marian and Jane traded glances.

"We're coming too," Jane said.

"I thought you wished to see Rome?" Willie looked around the room. "All of you."

"Rome is the eternal city. I suspect it will always be there." Jane glanced at the twins and they nodded. "We would much rather see what happens in London."

"We have been together for this entire quest," Marian began, "not that we knew it was a quest at the time. But not seeing it through with you to the end would be like reading an entire book and discovering the last chapter was ripped out." Her jaw set. "We are going with you to London and there will be no more discussion about it."

Willie's gaze shifted from Jane to Marian and Geneva and the other girls. Her spirits inched upward a fraction. These were her friends and would stand beside her. It did indeed feel as if, once again, she were marching into battle.

"You didn't answer my question," Dante said.

Her gaze locked with his. She wasn't at all sure why she was fighting him. Why she refused to give up. She could marry him and share the painting. But it did seem like giving up. To going back to being the type of woman who had no sense of responsibility and assumed others would take care of her. A woman no one assumed could be counted on. A woman who slid through life like a gondola on a canal. No, if she was going to be the woman she wanted to be, the woman these girls seemed to think she already was, she needed to do it on her own terms. She shook her head. "I don't have an answer right now."

"Why not?"

"Because I can't be wrong about this, Dante. I made a mistake once and I will not make the same mistake again."

"It's the second time I've asked." His tone hardened. "One would think you'd have an answer by now."

"A great deal has happened since the first time you asked," she snapped.

"Very well then, I withdraw the question." He turned and started for the door.

"Can he do that?" Shock rang in Emma's voice.

"Apparently," Tillie said.

"I shall see everyone in the morning. Good evening."

Dante was out the door before Willie could say another word, snapping it closed sharply behind him.

Willie's jaw clenched. Yes, she would become the woman she wanted to be.

No matter how high the price.

THEY WERE RETURNING very nearly the way they'd come. Venice to the western Italian coast then along the coast to France, north to Paris and across the channel to London. The journey was at once endless and yet not nearly as long as Willie needed. The more she pondered the question of what to do about Dante, the more confused she grew.

There was no doubt in her mind that she did indeed love him. That he was a good man and that more than likely she could trust him. Geneva had laid out the various considerations quite well. But how could Willie put her faith in a man who was unwilling to put her above the possession of a painting? As much as he claimed to love her, it was impossible to move past the thought that the Portinari was more important to him than she was.

One might say she was in the same position but one would be wrong. For Willie, in spite of its sentimental value, the painting was nothing more than the means to an end. The only way she had to keep her head above the swirling waters of financial ruin. If another means of survival were to present itself, she'd grab it at once.

It would be so very easy to give in. To exchange the painting for a life married to the man she loved. But what kind of future could they have together? She would always wonder if she was no more than second in his life. And wouldn't he question if they were together because she had no choice? She had been married once to a man who—while claiming to love her—never put her above all else. And really, wasn't that the very definition of love?

"It's not at all fun, you know," Willie said in a sharper manner than she intended.

Beside her, on the train to Genoa, Rosalind looked up from her magazine. "What is not at all fun?"

"Trying to live up to principles you didn't know you had."

"Congratulations, my dear." Rosalind turned her attention back to her magazine. "You are learning two lessons most of us learned when we became adults. First—it is far easier to talk about one's principles than to live up to them."

"And the second?"

"Life, for the most part, is not fun. Oh, it might be most amusing but fun is secondary, a bonus if you will. You and your husband spent your lives having a great deal of fun without regard to responsibility or rules or, for that matter, principles in general." She turned a page. "Now you are discovering the difficulty of doing what you think is right. *Right* is not the least bit easy. Or fun."

Willie rubbed her forehead. Her head had throbbed on and off since they left Venice. "What should I do?"

Rosalind sighed and met Willie's gaze. "I do so love to give advice, and it's usually quite good, but I have no idea what you should do. However, I do wish you and my brother would at least speak to each other."

"We agreed not to deal with the matter of ownership of the painting until we were back in London. Beyond that—" Willie shook her head and tried to ignore the lump in her throat "—we have nothing to talk about."

"Are you still in love with him?"

"Apparently."

Rosalind studied her. "Men rule the world, Willie.

There's nothing to be done about it, it's simply the way things are. It is only in these little matters of dignity that we have any say at all."

Willie stared. "I have no idea what you're trying to say."

"It's simple, my dear." Rosalind smiled, opened her magazine and turned her attention to it. "Do nothing."

CHAPTER TWENTY-FOUR

"WE SERVED NOTICE on Mr. Montague this morning regarding the Portinari," Mr. Hawkings said in a brisk manner. "He has until three o'clock the day after tomorrow to provide proof of ownership of the painting. If proof is not received before then, we shall open the bids for purchase of the painting precisely at 3:01."

"Very well." Willie had contacted Mr. Hawkings as soon as they had arrived in London yesterday afternoon. He had collected the painting from her yesterday evening for perusal by experts representing various potential purchasers. Necessary given there were already at least two known copies in existence.

Willie had called on Aunt Poppy the first thing today. Her godmother had suggested Willie meet with the solicitor here at Poppy's house, saying she would be more comfortable in familiar surroundings rather than at an impersonal office. Although Willie suspected the older woman knew Willie's residence looked a bit sparse at the moment as she had also mentioned how it was always better to avoid appearing as if one needed money. Especially if one did.

"I do wish you had mentioned this might be a problem before we offered the painting for bids," Mr. Hawkings said in a chastising manner.

Willie was in no mood to be chastised. She narrowed

VICTORIA ALEXANDER . 389

her eyes. "If I had known there was a problem, you may rest assured I would have said something."

"Yes, of course," he said quickly, distinctly paler than a moment ago but then he should be. She had no patience for masculine superiority today. She wanted—needed— this to go smoothly and quickly. "My apologies, Lady Bascombe, I did not mean to imply that you were trying to hide something."

"My grandmother did not steal that painting."

"No, no, I would never think such a thing. Nor do I expect Mr. Montague to claim that." He paused. "However, if he could provide proof that the painting was indeed stolen, he could say she was innocently duped into accepting or purchasing a stolen item through no fault of her own. No blame would fall on her but the painting would probably be returned to Mr. Montague."

She glanced at her godmother. Poppy offered her an encouraging nod. As much as Willie hated to cast aspersions on her grandmother's reputation, Mr. Hawkings did need to know everything. "It was given to her by a gentleman friend. I assume now by Mr. Montague's grandfather."

"I see," the solicitor said. "I don't suppose you have any proof of this liaison?"

"Grandmother was very discreet."

Poppy smiled in an overly innocent manner.

"Well, I am confident this will prove to be nothing of consequence and we can proceed with the sale as planned."

"Excellent, Mr. Hawkings." Willie rose to her feet in a manner befitting a viscountess, a manner she had been trained in at Miss Bicklesham's, a manner she had only used once before, with a desk clerk in Monte Carlo. It did seem to work better today. "Then I shall see you at your office the day after tomorrow shortly before three."

Hawkings stood at once. "Yes, my lady."

"I assume if there is word from Mr. Montague before then, you will contact me at once."

"Most definitely." He nodded. "Without question, the moment I hear anything, you shall be the first to know."

"Very well." She offered him a curt nod. "Mrs. Fitzhew-Wellmore's butler will see you to the door. Good day."

"Good day." Mr. Hawkings nodded a bow and practically scurried toward the door.

"I don't believe I have ever heard you sound quite so imposing before." Poppy's eyes twinkled. "It's amazing what the adventure of travel can do for a woman."

"Yes, I'm sure that's what did it." Willie sank back onto the sofa. "It has nothing whatsoever to do with the fact that in providing for my own financial future I may very well be throwing away my only chance for—" *love* "—a good marriage."

"Nonsense. There are any number of men in the world you have yet to meet. Why, I was older than you when I met my dear Malcolm." Poppy poured a cup of tea and handed it to Willie. "Besides, you said Mr. Montague was a vile, despicable beast."

"And he is. Without question." Willie scoffed. "But he is…extraordinarily nice."

"He lied to you."

"A lie of omission." She stared at the tea in her cup. "Not acceptable, of course, but somewhat understandable."

Poppy sipped her tea. "And he deceived you."

"He did indeed." Willie set her cup down, stood and paced the room. She was entirely too restless to sit still.

The day after tomorrow could not come soon enough. Until then, it was as if she were constantly on edge, waiting for something to happen. Some kind of resolution, good or bad, would be better than this interminable limbo she found herself in.

She was doing exactly as Rosalind suggested and it was exceptionally difficult. But Willie could see the wisdom in Rosalind's advice. There was nothing more pathetic than a woman giving up everything she wanted and throwing herself on the mercies of a man. How could a man possibly respect a woman who thought so little of herself? And Willie would never be able to respect herself.

She and Dante had barely exchanged more than a handful of words on the entire trip back to London. Nor were they as pleasant to their fellow travelers as perhaps they should have been. She had avoided looking in his direction or walking too closely to him or being caught alone with him. She needn't have tried so hard as it did seem he was making the same effort. Tension hovered ever present between them, and their fellow travelers were not immune. The return to London was awkward and uncomfortable for all concerned. Willie did hear Tillie mutter something about a strongly worded letter to the Lady Travelers Society.

"Although he didn't know me when he began his deception. He had no idea what kind of person I was."

"He knew everything that his investigator could supply. I think you're being far too kind to him."

"Indeed I am." Willie paused. "He was always quite kind to the girls, you know, and he certainly didn't have to be. He escorted them when necessary and danced with them and never made Emma feel embarrassed when she

blatantly flirted with him. And he was very nice to young
Bertie."

Poppy's brow rose. "The miscreant who followed you
around Europe? Two of a kind I'd say."

"Bertie really is just a boy, Aunt Poppy. You can't fault
him for the mistakes of youth."

"And yet you fault yourself for your own."

"Nonsense." Willie waved off the comment. "I don't
fault myself for my mistakes." Although Poppy might
have a valid point. "I have acknowledged my past errors in judgment and I have moved ahead with my life."

"And what of your Mr. Montague's mistakes? He is
not a boy."

"No, he is responsible and respectable and quite, quite
wonderful. I wish I could simply give him his painting
and be done with it. But…" She shook her head.

"We all wish to make sacrifices for the ones we love."

Willie glanced at her sharply. "I said he asked me to
marry him—"

"And rescinded the offer."

"But I never said I loved him."

"You didn't have to." Poppy smiled. "You wouldn't be
nearly this distraught if you didn't care for him."

"Perhaps but regardless of my feelings, he is the most
annoying man I've ever met." She crossed her arms over
her chest. "Did I tell you he believes Grandmother stole
the painting?"

Poppy gasped. "He doesn't!"

"He didn't actually say it but it was obvious that's what
he was thinking." She thought for a moment. "What I
need is some kind of definitive proof that his grandfather
gave my grandmother that painting."

"No, you don't," Poppy said firmly. "He is the one

who needs proof. Mr. Hawkings just said the burden of proof in this case falls on him, not you."

"He has a very powerful family."

"So do you." Poppy straightened in her chair. "You have me and Gwen and Effie as well as the entire Lady Travelers Society. We will never desert you."

Willie's heart warmed. "I do so love you, Poppy."

"And I love you too, dear."

"But I'm afraid even your indomitable friends and all the lady travelers in the world won't be of help if he comes up with some way to claim my painting."

"Don't be absurd, Wilhelmina. We can be a great deal of help." Poppy smiled in a somewhat wicked manner. "Especially as we have absolutely no difficulty in not playing fair."

"YOU LOOK AWFUL." Roz settled in the chair in front of Dante's desk in his office in his spacious quarters on the top floors of Montague House.

"Do I?"

"Yes, rather frightening really. I never see you less than perfectly dressed and you're positively disheveled." She pulled off her gloves. "When was the last time you combed your hair?"

He ran his hands absently through his hair. "My appearance is the least of my problems."

"It's not like you, it's not like you at all."

"I'm so sorry I have failed to live up to your standards."

"They're not my standards, they're yours." She peered at him closely. "Have you been sleeping?"

"More or less."

"I see."

"What?" He narrowed his eyes.

"Nothing." She shook her head. "Nothing at all."

"Good," he said sharply.

"Now, see here, Dante Augustus Montague." She glared at her brother. "I will not put up with your foul mood. Remember you are the one who sent for me. If you did so simply to have someone to growl at—"

"No, of course not, my apologies." He blew a long breath. "You're right, I have not been sleeping well." Or at all. "Take a look at this." He passed her a handwritten page.

"What is it?" Roz scanned the paper.

"It's a claim against some sort of private insurance policy in which Grandfather says the Portinari was stolen. It was discovered by the firm I hired to examine all of Grandfather's papers." He heaved a frustrated sigh. "Unfortunately, I don't believe it."

"Which part?"

"All of it. Oh, I believe Grandfather claimed the painting was stolen but I would wager he actually gave it to a Lady Grantson." His gaze met his sister's. "Willie's grandmother."

"Oh?"

"I've been going through his private journals, back more than forty years ago, and there are a great number of affectionate references to Lady Grantson."

"We all know Grandfather was quite the devil in his younger days. No doubt, there are any number of women mentioned in his journals."

Dante snorted. "You'd be surprised. But this was different." He paused. "He believed himself in love with her. But he was married and, while she was a widow, nothing could come of it. He compared their circumstances to those of Orpheus and Eurydice, a great love but ultimately doomed."

Roz's eyes widened. "How very poetic of him."

"The center painting, the one depicting Orpheus begging for his wife's return, is the only one of the three that has a suggestion of hope."

"And he gave it to the woman he loved." Roz shook her head. "I would imagine Grandmother was livid."

Their grandmother died long before either he or Roz were born. According to family gossip she was eminently proper, unyielding when it came to correct behavior and not especially pleasant in nature. She was also not overly fond of Grandfather.

"I suspect he had the copy made so she wouldn't know he had given it to another woman."

"Then grandfather lied about it being stolen?"

"I think so."

"Regardless—" she handed the paper back to him "—doesn't this give you the proof you need regarding ownership of the painting?"

"With this, I can claim the Portinari."

"And destroy Willie's future," Roz said slowly.

He stared at the paper in his hand.

Roz studied him for a long moment. "You're not going to do it, are you?"

"No." He stood, strode to the fireplace and tossed the paper into the fire, watching it curl then burst into flames. In less than a minute it had turned to ash. "I am giving up any claim to the painting."

Roz stared.

"You needn't look so shocked." He chuckled.

"There's no other way to look." Roz continued to stare as if he had just grown two heads. "You do realize this might mean the end of the museum."

"I do."

She narrowed her eyes. "You're willing to give up Grandfather's legacy for her?"

"Apparently." He returned to his seat.

"Good Lord, Dante." She grinned. "You really are in love."

"I'm glad you're pleased," he said wryly. "I, however, have never felt quite so miserable in my life."

"That's entirely your fault. You have mucked this up from the beginning. I told you—never mind. It really doesn't matter now." Roz stood and waved her brother to his feet. "You need to tell her, right this very instant, that you've given up all claim to the painting and she may do with it as she pleases. And then you need to rescind your withdrawal of your proposal of marriage." She shook her head. "That was not your brightest idea."

"No." He settled back in his chair.

"What do you mean no?" Roz sank back down. "Why on earth not?"

"I don't know exactly." He had given this a great deal of thought. Indeed, he'd thought about nothing else since he learned of his grandfather's fraudulent claim. "I think, if I told her this now, she would question my motives. I probably would if I were her."

"As would I but—"

"I did everything I could to regain her trust."

"Except what you're doing now—giving up the painting."

"I don't think she can question my trustworthiness in any area except when it comes to the Portinari."

"This is no doubt the best way to prove your love, as well," Roz pointed out.

"Possibly." He met his sister's gaze directly. "But until that painting is out of our lives, Roz, I don't think we have a chance together."

Roz stared. "Then what are you going to do?"

"Nothing, about the painting at least." He shook his head. "If I do not present proof of prior ownership the day after tomorrow by three o'clock, she intends to sell the painting to the highest bidder. I intend to let her."

"But you're not going to tell her about this rather impressive sacrifice you're making for her?"

"No, I'm not." He blew a long breath. "After everything that's happened, I have no idea how she feels about me. If she still cares about me. I might have destroyed everything."

"You committed larceny for her," she said indignantly. "I know I've never had a man steal for me before."

"I don't want her to feel obligated to me."

"That's absurd." She frowned. "And it sounds very much like you are giving up. Are you?"

"Only the painting, Roz." These past few days without Willie had made clear what he had already known in his heart. Nothing—not the Portinari, not the museum, not his grandfather's legacy—was more important to him than she was. Now he had to take the advice he had given Bertie. If there was ever a time that called for a grand romantic gesture, this was it. He had until the day after tomorrow to come up with something grand and romantic and brilliant. Pity he had no idea what that might be. "Only the painting."

CHAPTER TWENTY-FIVE

SIX MINUTES UNTIL THREE—a scant two minutes later than the last time Willie had looked at the clock on the wall.

Willie sat alone in a private conference room at Mr. Hawkings's office, the very picture of unruffled serenity. Exactly the image she wished to portray. Precisely how she wanted to appear to the world. But with every tick of the clock, every move of the hour hand closer to twelve, her stomach clenched.

She fully expected Dante to charge in at any minute with some way to prove ownership. Or his admission that he couldn't live without her and would give up his claim. Something that would prove he cared more about her than the blasted painting. It did seem that three o'clock was the appointed time not only for his proof but for the rest of their lives. It was probably silly but she couldn't shake the firm conviction that if he didn't do something by three o'clock, any chance of a future together would be gone forever.

Five minutes until three.

The Portinari sat on the table, the image of Orpheus begging for his wife a constant reminder of eternal love. And what one man was willing to do for it.

She hadn't heard from Dante since their return to London. Surely a man who said he loved her, who'd asked her to marry him, wouldn't give up this easily? Unless, of course, it had all been part and parcel of his ploy to acquire the painting.

Four minutes until three.

She didn't want to believe that of him. But really, how well could you know a man you'd met only a few weeks ago? A man who had spent much of that time lying about his real purpose. Why, she'd known George longer when they had wed and look at the mistake that had been.

Three minutes until three.

Still, Dante was nothing like George. He was extraordinarily nice and quite, quite wonderful. Poppy had taken it upon herself to ask some of her acquaintances about Dante and, aside from that business with Juliet Pauling, there was no untoward gossip about the man. His reputation was spotless. He was not at all the kind of man to lie to a woman to get what he wanted. But he had, even though he had, as well, tried to make amends for it. He was rational and sensible and yet he couldn't understand her need not to depend on anyone but herself.

Two minutes until three.

Poppy had also learned he was quite passionate about Montague House, although really Willie had assumed as much. Fine. Willie did hope he and his museum were very happy together.

One minute to three.

Surely he would not let this hour pass? Surely he would storm in at the last possible minute? Her heart thudded. *This was the last possible minute.* Where was he? Was he really going to let her go without so much as a word?

The clock struck three.

For a moment, the world stopped. Her breath caught against an ache in her throat. And her heart shattered.

The door opened and Mr. Hawkings stepped into the room, a bundle of envelopes in his hand. "The time has come, Lady Bascombe. I have the bids and they may now be opened." He studied her cautiously. "Are you all right?"

"I have rarely been better, Mr. Hawkings." She mustered her brightest smile. "This is simply quite exciting."

"It is indeed, Lady Bascombe." The gentleman chuckled and took a seat at the table. "We gave all interested parties a minimum acceptable amount and we have here a total of eleven bids. Most of them were received before your return to London but several came this week and the last only this morning. Frankly, having never dealt with a Portinari before, I didn't know what to expect. If you're ready, I can begin."

"Please do, Mr. Hawkings." Under other circumstances, she would be quite proud that she managed to adopt a composed smile—calm, steady, pleasant tempered with aloof. Exactly the kind of smile a woman who was not in serious financial straits would wear. The smile of a woman whose heart had not just broken.

"I'm not sure if you are aware of the importance of Portinari," Mr. Hawking said as he slit the first envelope with a pearl-handled letter opener, "but he has only recently been recognized as the genius…"

Willie hadn't imagined she would ever be pleased by any man droning on and on about art but at least it was easy to pay no attention whatsoever and simply nod on occasion. She needed all her strength not to dissolve into a small quivering puddle of despair.

She had no idea how long the entire process took— it did seem endless. Mr. Hawkings had any number of papers that needed her signature and he was constantly being called from the room for one thing or another. But at last she was in a cab pulling up to her house.

What on earth was she doing?

The thought struck her like a bolt through her battered

heart. She had been waiting for Dante to prove his love for her. She hadn't given the tiniest thought to proving that she loved him. Her mind raced. If she sold her house, she and Majors and Patsy could find something smaller and less expensive to run.

Willie called to the driver to return to the solicitor's office. She would cancel the sale, retrieve the painting and donate it to Montague House. Anonymously. Yes, that would be perfect. There was no need for him to know this. She would not have him taking pity in any way on her. Even if he had never loved her, she had loved him. And that was enough. She was not about to start a new life funded by the very thing that brought them together only to tear them apart and leave her in shreds.

A practical, rational voice in the back of her head noted that she had given up this sort of impulsive behavior when George had died. That she would regret this. She ignored it.

"Mr. Hawkings." She swept into his office. "I am sorry to inform you of this, but I have changed my mind."

He stared. "I beg your pardon?"

"I have reconsidered, Mr. Hawkings," she said in her best Lady Bascombe tone. "I assume you have not yet deposited the payment into my accounts."

"Well, no, but—"

"Excellent." She nodded. "Then we may consider the sale canceled. If you would be so good as to fetch my painting, I shall be on my way."

"I'm afraid I can't."

"Of course you can."

"The painting is gone, Lady Bascombe. It's already on its way to its new owner." He shook his head. "There is nothing that can be done about it. I am sorry, but it's too late."

APPARENTLY, THERE REALLY WASN'T anything that could be done. The highest bid had been submitted through a solicitor, the buyer wishing to remain anonymous. That was that then.

As much as she hated the idea of funding her life with the proceeds of the Portinari there was nothing to be done about it now.

A scant twenty minutes later she was once again in a cab pulling up in front of her house.

The only consoling thought was that as Dante hadn't made any effort to contact her, their affection was obviously one-sided. Best to learn that now before he had a series of lovers and mistresses that she would pretend not to know about. With George it had been annoying. With Dante it would have been devastating. She would not live the rest of her life that way.

"Lady Bascombe." Majors greeted her at the door. "There have been some, well, deliveries and you have callers."

"I wasn't expecting anything or anyone. I'm certain you can see to the deliveries and I am in no mood for visitors." She heaved a weary sigh. All she really wanted to do was to curl up in a small ball and weep. "Could you please inform them I'm not feeling well and ask them to leave?"

"There are quite a few of them, my lady," he said and opened the parlor door.

Willie stepped into the room and pulled up short. There were indeed quite a few. All her new friends as well as Aunt Poppy and her cohorts were milling about her parlor. A parlor now filled to overflowing. Flowers in urns and vases were everywhere. Several tall, classical statues were scattered throughout the room. Venetian masks dangled from the chandelier and the draperies and, somewhere, a violin was playing.

"What on earth?" Willie stared but there was entirely too much to take in.

"We have no idea what this is about although it certainly is intriguing," Jane said, stepping forward and skirting around—good Lord, was that a gondola? In her parlor? "We went to your solicitor's office but you had already left."

"You didn't think we'd let you do this alone." Marian smiled.

"And we did want to know what happened with the painting." Geneva glanced around. "Although this is interesting too."

"Did you sell it?" Tillie asked.

"Or did Mr. Montague sweep in to rescue you and the painting?" Emma's eyes sparkled. "Did he make a grand, romantic gesture at the last minute? He does seem the type."

"My uncle?" Harriet scoffed. "I don't think he has a romantic bone in his entire body. Or at least he never has before."

"Go on, dear." Poppy waved. She, Lady Blodgett and Mrs. Higginbotham sat in the gondola. "We are all dying to know what happened."

"I must say, this is quite unique," Lady Blodgett said, looking around. "A few too many flowers perhaps but I might have to get a gondola for my own parlor."

"What happened?" Willie shook her head in an attempt to clear it. What was going on here? "Nothing unexpected." She shrugged. "I sold the painting to the highest bidder. The proceeds will enable me to live quite nicely for a number of years. But..." This was remarkably difficult to say even to these women who were on her side and truly her friends. "I changed my mind. I realized I didn't want anything to do with the painting or the income it would provide. I didn't want to live my life dependent on the very thing that might have destroyed my chances for…well, happiness, I suppose. Even if that might have been nothing more than a delusion on my part. I decided to give it to Montague House, anonymously. And sell this house to make ends meet." She glanced at Rosalind. "You were right. Principles are difficult to live up to."

"I am usually right," Rosalind said.

"Unfortunately, I was too late." Willie shook her head. "The painting was already on the way to its new owner and there is nothing I can do."

"Oh good Lord." Rosalind heaved a resigned sigh. "Dante didn't want you to know—which I thought was ridiculous, mind you. But he found documentation that would have allowed him to claim the painting." Rosalind met Willie's gaze firmly. "He destroyed it."

"What?" Willie stared.

Emma nudged her sister. "Grand romantic gesture. I knew it."

"It doesn't seem to have made much difference," Tillie murmured.

"Why would he do such a thing?" Willie asked slowly but the oddest flicker of hope flamed inside her.

"Come now, Willie. Don't be as much of an idiot as my brother." Rosalind rolled her gaze toward the ceiling. "He gave up the painting for you, you tried to give it up for him. The reasons why are obvious."

Rosalind's words were not making a great deal of sense. Willie shook her head. "I don't under—"

"Because I love you." Dante's voice sounded behind her and she swiveled to face him. He was dressed as he had been for the conte's ball, complete with powdered wig and satin pants. He looked completely absurd and absolutely wonderful. "Because I may have loved you from the moment I opened that damnable dossier." He stepped toward her. "Because nothing is more important to me than you."

"Oh?" Willie tried to maintain a measure of calm.

"My grandfather gave that painting to the woman he loved." He moved closer. "How could I not give it up for the woman I love?"

She swallowed past the lump in her throat. "How much did you hear?"

"Enough." He chuckled. "I had planned on being here when you arrived back from your solicitor's but I had a slight delay." He cast an annoyed look at his sister. "What I did not expect was an audience."

"You did all this?" Willie waved at the room. "For me?"

"I would do anything for you."

"Grand romantic gesture," someone murmured.

"You gave up the painting for me."

"And you tried to give it up for me." He grinned. "It seems we are a perfect match."

"But we scarcely know each other." It was not what she wanted to say but it was true.

"We know enough." He took her hands in his. "I know how you look when you're deep in thought gazing over the city of Paris from the top of a cathedral. I know how your eyes shine with awe and newfound understanding when you study a fresco on a church ceiling and how they flash with all the anger of an avenging goddess when you're challenged by, well, an idiot in a Roman arena. And I know how you inspire me to do things I never would have thought I could do."

"Larceny?"

"Larceny is just the beginning." His tone sobered. "I

think you will inspire me every day for the rest of our lives."

"I say, Mr. Montague, you should kiss her now." Bertie's voice rang from somewhere in the room. Willie hadn't even noticed him. "I would."

Somebody giggled.

"Not quite yet, Bertie." Dante's gaze locked with hers. "You said you wanted a proper, romantic proposal. Here it is." He paused. "Wilhelmina Bascombe, you now have the income to live an independent life. You have proved you can manage your own life. You have no need to marry anyone for reasons other than those of affection." He drew a deep breath. "I have made one serious mistake in my life—"

"Just one?"

"Perhaps two. I should have told you about the Portinari from the very beginning."

"And the second?"

"Not realizing sooner that the most important thing in the world to me is you." He paused. "All I am asking is that you continue to let me prove you can trust me. Let me love you and try to make you happy for the rest of my life. Willie, would you do me the very great honor of becoming my wife?"

She stared up at him and adopted a lighthearted tone. "Even if I don't intend to be the least bit convenient or easy?"

"I would have it no other way."

She considered him for a long moment.

"Was that not proper or romantic enough?" He frowned. "I tried to get pigeons but the blasted birds were not the least bit cooperative and I thought possibly—"

"I think perhaps the best thing to do, Mr. Montague—"

she raised her chin and smiled into his dark eyes "—would be to take Mr. Goodwin's advice."

"Gladly, Lady Bascombe." He grinned and pulled her into his arms. His lips met hers and Willie sent a silent prayer of gratitude to dear, departed George, wherever he might be.

Oh, not for dying of course, but for setting her on a journey. Not merely to Paris and Monte Carlo and Venice and all those places she had never been but to the person she needed to become. A woman who could depend on herself. A woman she could be proud of.

And to the dashing stranger who would be by her side and hold her hand in his for the rest of their days.

Larceny was indeed only the beginning.

Six months later...

ON THE DAY Wilhelmina Montague and her husband were to set sail for America to visit very dear friends, she received a notice from her father's solicitors informing her an amount equal to that of her dowry would be deposited into an account of her choice as her father now approved of her marriage. Willie promptly donated it to a society for the education and betterment of young women. Father would hate that.

Later that same day, a well-wrapped parcel arrived at Montague House with a note of donation.

The parcel contained the Portinari.

The note was anonymous.

* * * * *

THE RISE AND FALL
OF REGINALD EVERHEART

a Lady Travelers Society novella

CHAPTER ONE

London, 1868

AT THE TENDER AGE of twenty-three, Miss Dulcie Middle-worth, the youngest daughter of Viscount Middleworth, had just been declared a social failure.

Dulcie stared at the nearly blank sheet of laid paper affixed to the board in front of her and tried to concentrate on her preliminary pencil drawing of a fragment of ancient pottery. The barely started work was part of her continuing commission to document in pen and paint the endless collection of the Explorers Club. Her efforts at the moment were pointless really. She simply couldn't focus on her work. As much as she didn't care for the most part about her standing in society, it was rather bothersome to be considered a failure. Mother was certainly upset.

Oh, there hadn't been a notice in the *Times* or any sort of official announcement in *Notes for Ladies*, the London ladies' magazine her mother and sisters devoured for the latest news on society's approved activities as well as scandalous escapades. The latter were discreetly detailed and rarely mentioned anyone by name, although determining who was the subject of the latest bit of gossip usually took no more effort than an afternoon of calls and a few cups of tea. No, in the world of London society, there were no official announcements as to who had done what, but the end result was the same.

For the first time since Dulcie had come out in society, she had not been invited to Lady Scarsdale's grand ball, the acknowledged start of the social season ever since Lady Scarsdale's daughter had been a debutante some twenty or so years ago. Mother had long said the ball was intended to ensure Lady Scarsdale's daughter a position of some power in society as well as guaranteeing she would not be overlooked. According to Mother the girl was not one of that season's great beauties but she did have a certain wit and cleverness about her that was not apparent simply by looking at her. By the time the Scarsdale offspring had indeed married well—her fourth season, Mother said—Lady Scarsdale's ball had become *the* place to be and be seen for any young woman looking for entry to society and to make a good match. While the new season's crop of debutantes in its entirety was routinely invited to the ball, those who were in their subsequent seasons were given the prized invitation based on any number of mysterious factors known only to Lady Scarsdale and her cohorts.

This year—Dulcie's fifth in society—the invitation to Lady Scarsdale's ball had not been forthcoming. Mother was livid and blamed Father. Her three older sisters were nearly as distraught over the slight and vowed to redouble their efforts to find Dulcie an appropriate match.

It wasn't as if Dulcie didn't wish to be married. She did but she wanted to marry for reasons of affection. Dulcie Middleworth wanted love and rather feared she had found it. Pity it appeared to be one-sided.

She casually glanced across the large library in the impressive Bloomsbury mansion that housed the Explorers Club to the only other person currently in the room and tried not to sigh. Not that he would have noticed.

Michael Shepard's gaze shifted back and forth between the book opened to his left and the notebook in front of him. His dark hair was slightly disheveled as if he had just run his hand through it as, no doubt, he had. His pen flew across the notebook page with a life of its own. Any minute now, he'd stop to push his spectacles—which had an endearing tendency to slide down his perfectly straight nose—back into place. He didn't look up but she knew his eyes were the deepest shade of gray, like the sky on a stormy day. His shoulders were broad, which bespoke some sort of physical exercise, and he stood a good head taller than she. Not that she had ever been close enough to measure.

Dulcie and Michael—she couldn't possibly think of him as Mr. Shepard—had each separately occupied one of the six tables in the library on very nearly a daily basis for the last three months and yet had scarcely exchanged more than a handful of polite greetings. Their conversation rarely varied.

"Good day, Mr. Shepard," she would say when he had arrived before her. "Pleasant day" or "dreadful weather we're having," she would add, depending on whether or not the day was pleasant or dreadful.

"Indeed, Miss Middleworth," he would respond with a polite smile.

Or, if she was in the library when he arrived, he would acknowledge her presence with a courteous, "Good day, Miss Middleworth."

To which she would inevitably reply, "Good day, Mr. Shepard," and then comment on the weather when what she really wanted to say was, "Goodness, Michael, don't you think it's past time you took me in your arms and kissed me senseless or threw me onto a table and had your way with me?" She would never say such a thing but she did consider what might happen if she did. He would no doubt be horribly shocked, which would at least be something.

Dulcie had never had the tiniest problem talking, even flirting, with gentlemen before. But there was something about Michael Shepard that turned her from a self-assured young woman into the worst sort of shy, retiring creature. But then most gentlemen were far more eager to talk to her than she was to talk to them whereas Michael barely acknowledged her existence.

He was not substantially older than she, four or five years perhaps, and was acknowledged to be brilliant in matters of history and botany and any number of other disciplines encouraged by the Explorers Club among those promising young men who showed a legitimate interest in exploration and discovery. In spite of his scholarly bent, there was an air of anticipation about Michael. A promise of adventure and excitement just waiting to come to fruition. It permeated the library when he was present and was both intriguing and most intoxicating. Indeed, Michael was set to join an expedition in another month. Which was rather awkward as it did limit the time Dulcie had to earn his affections. If that was what she wished to do.

She already knew a great deal about him. Information was not at all hard to come by in the rarified atmosphere of the Explorers Club. While ladies were not allowed to be members—God forbid one should even think of such a thing—wives of members had banded together years ago to form the Ladies Committee. They were graciously permitted to plan social activities, dinners honoring outstanding members—even if they were not always allowed to attend—as well as assist in the management of the club's library and extensive collection of artifacts and memorabilia from its supported expeditions. Dulcie had become acquainted with several ladies who were frequently in the library. Many of whom had a great deal of free time as their husbands were off in some barely accessible part of the world, hacking their way through tropical jungles or digging for evidence of ancient civilizations.

The ladies were an interesting lot with the sort of freedom usually allowed widows and an independent spirit that was most admirable. But then they had little choice. Their husbands had decided to explore the unknown and their wives were left behind to make certain home was ready and waiting for those rare moments when they chanced to be in England. It didn't seem at all fair but it was the way of things. Dulcie had become quite good friends with one of the ladies. Mrs. Persephone Fitzhew-Wellmore was here somewhere today although she did have the oddest tendency to vanish and then reappear at the most unexpected moments. She had taken an interest in Dulcie's work as she had confided she was something of an artist herself and was most impressed that Dulcie was actually being paid for her labor. She insisted Dulcie call her Poppy as Mrs. Fitzhew-Wellmore was a bit of a mouthful.

The fact that Dulcie had the opportunity to work at her art at all was thanks to Father. Dulcie was twelve years younger than the sister nearest to her in age and, after three daughters, Father had hoped his last, unexpected child would be male. When yet another daughter had appeared, Father was resigned but determined. His youngest daughter would be the son he never had. He encouraged her to become an excellent horsewoman and a superb shot. While Mother tried to instill in her all those attributes needed to run a household and be an accomplished hostess, Father taught her the details of managing an estate and had passed on his interest in all things ancient and all parts unknown. And indeed, while her sisters were everything her mother could wish for in dutiful daughters, Dulcie was her father's child. When she wanted to study art after she had completed a level of education above that of her sisters, Mother was appalled. But Father declared even females should be encouraged to pursue higher learning should they be blessed with natural abilities. Dulcie would never forget the shocked look on Mother's face as Father was not known for his progressive attitudes. Even so, he not only allowed her to attend the South Kensington School of Art but used his influence at the Explorers Club to secure her current position. Father had been a member of the Explorers Club nearly forever even though he had never explored anything beyond a good brandy and a fine cigar.

Perhaps Father was tolerant of her dreams because he had once had far-fetched dreams of his own. While there were a handful of female illustrators making their way in the world, there were even fewer English lords abandoning responsibility for the excitement of following poor Dr. Livingstone into the jungles of Africa. Still, there was nothing Father liked better than inviting those gentlemen who pursued such adventures into his home for a fine meal, excellent brandy and even better conversation. Dinner was often host, as well, to interesting young men who were hoping to follow in the footsteps of Mr. Burton or other explorers, although Father hadn't started inviting them until after her sisters were married. They were indeed quite exciting and usually somewhat flirtatious, at least when Mother wasn't glaring at them. Mother did not consider them suitable marriage material. Dulcie knew full well she was somewhere in the middle in terms of appearance with her older sisters but they were, all in all, a pretty lot. Dark hair in varying shades, blue eyes and fetching figures. Although her forthright demeanor and obvious intelligence soon dampened the ardor of most gentlemen visitors. Still, there had been one or two...

That Michael Shepard had not shown even a modicum of interest in her might well be one of the reasons why he was so undeniably appealing. It couldn't possibly be anything more significant than that. She certainly couldn't claim to know him although it was shocking how much information Poppy and her friends had about the man. Surely she couldn't be so shallow as to be swept away by the fact that he had no interest in her. No, if that were the case, she would have been able to say something to him by now because it would not have seemed so frightfully important. And her heart wouldn't flutter in her chest whenever he was in the room.

Dulcie Middleworth, who had never been afraid of anything in her life, apparently was now.

Making life even more awkward at the moment was the fact that her sisters and mother had increased their efforts to find her a match. It would only get worse thanks to Lady Scarsdale. But they seemed to have high hopes for the latest sacrificial lamb they had thrown at her.

Preston Drummond was the youngest son of an earl and a decent enough sort, if more arrogant than either his nature, his prospects or his appearance would justify. He too hoped to explore the world at some point or at least he said he did. Dulcie suspected his membership in the Explorers Club was more for appearances than any true desire for adventure. Dulcie had made it clear to Preston that he could continue to call on her if he so wished but she had no feelings of affection for him save that of friendship. He wasn't the least bit discouraged, apparently thinking this was her manner of flirtation—how could any woman not want him? It was far easier at the moment to allow Preston's attentions then to incur Mother's wrath at her throwing away a perfectly good prospect. Preston had the unwavering support of her mother and all of her sisters with the possible exception of Livy, the youngest of the three, who had always been more inclined toward Dulcie's way of thinking. He was, as well, one of those rare men who wasn't completely disapproving of Dulcie's straightforward manner and obvious intelligence. Or at least so it appeared. Which was a point in his favor but not an overly significant one. She simply had no interest in the man.

No, in spite of their minimal conversation, her hesitance to approach him and his usual lack of awareness as to her very existence, it was Michael who pulled at her heart. She knew from Poppy that, while not titled, his family had a significant fortune as his grandfather had founded Shepard's department store, an establishment nearly as large and prestigious as Harrods. He had attended Oxford, he spoke three languages fluently and several others passably and he was well versed in ancient Greek, Roman and Coptic texts. Every now and then he would look up from his work to catch her staring at him and she would pretend to be staring into the distance, contemplating whatever it was she was working on and not thinking about the way his lips would feel on hers. Now and again she would look up to find him studying her and she would smile politely in response and immediately look away.

But regardless of their lack of conversation, Dulcie knew the sound of his laughter and the cadence of his speech. She had overheard any number of discussions between Michael and gentlemen who wandered into the library with the express purpose of engaging him in conversation. None of whom ever seemed to realize—or care—that Michael was not alone in the room. Under the strictest definition of the term, one might consider her attention eavesdropping but she made no effort to hide her presence and any idiot could see she was there.

It was fascinating to be privy to these chats even if she was not included. Just as it was impossible to overhear those discussions that were quiet and discreet—she was on the far side of the room after all—it was equally impossible not to listen to the more raucous debates on the most fascinating topics. Was Mr. Calvert really correct in his theories of where the legendary city of Troy might be located? Would Dr. Livingstone ever be found or had he perished in the jungles of Africa? Had all the tombs of the kings and queens of Egypt been discovered or were there still untold historic treasures and riches waiting just under the sands? In even the most amicable of these conversations voices would rise, words would fly and passion would fill the air.

The first time Michael's gaze had met hers with any significance had been in the midst of a debate on the relative merits of Lake Victoria versus Lake Albert as the source of the Nile. He'd appeared quite startled but hadn't paused in his discussion and had acted as if his gaze hadn't meshed with hers for one glorious moment of unique and perfect communication. It then happened again and again. Sometimes she would nod in agreement with something he had just said or frown when she thought he was wrong. His eyes would narrow slightly but he didn't seem to mind.

Even if they never spoke directly, there was something between them. Something fraught with potential and possibility. Something that might well be quite wonderful.

Obviously Michael's courage—and there was no question as to the bravery of any man preparing to head into the unknown—did not extend to furthering their connection.

Unfortunately, neither did hers.

CHAPTER TWO

THE BLASTED WOMAN was staring at him again. Michael didn't need to look up from his notes on the indigenous species of the upper Amazon to know Dulcie was studying him. He had long ago stopped thinking of her as Miss Middleworth. Quite improper but how could he think of her as Miss Middleworth when he could feel her gaze on him as if it were a physical touch. As if she were laying her hand on the side of his cheek. Not that such a thing would ever happen.

As much as he would like to further his acquaintance with the lovely Dulcie Middleworth, it was pointless. He was to join an expedition—his first—into the jungles of South America on a venture to settle the question of the true headwaters of the Amazon in a little over a month. It didn't seem right, and certainly not fair, to engage any woman's affections if he intended to go off without knowing with any certainty that he would return. He'd observed firsthand what happened to such women and he had vowed never to marry. Of course, it wasn't fair either that this particular woman with her blue eyes and her engaging laugh had not only taken up permanent residence in the sanctuary of the Explorers Club library but had invaded his dreams, as well.

He had thought he would discourage any attraction between them by keeping to himself. Aside from a cordial daily greeting and insipid agreement on both their parts as to the state of London's weather, they scarcely ever spoke. Nonetheless, he was continually acutely aware of her. How could he not be? She was so annoyingly *there*.

She left the faintest scent behind whenever she walked through the room, something vaguely floral and slightly spicy, like an exotic jungle blossom. When any of the women from the Ladies Committee were present doing whatever it was they did—it seemed suspiciously like puttering, but they did go about it in a determined manner—they routinely chatted with Dulcie or stopped to admire her work. Or shared surprisingly astute observations on the events of the day. Inevitably someone would say something amusing and Dulcie's laughter would drift through the air and wrap around his heart. He wasn't sure there was any sound quite so delightful and enchanting as that of Dulcie Middleworth's laugh.

She was as talented as she was lovely. Whenever she left the library for whatever reason, he would find it necessary to stretch his legs or he would require a book on the far side of the room and would inevitably pass by her table where her work would be spread out for all to see. He knew nothing about artistic endeavors but anyone could see her work was good. Very good. With pen and ink and paint she made the bits of ancient pottery or rare Roman coins or artifacts from long dead civilizations come alive.

Keeping his distance from her was perhaps the hardest thing he had ever done. He had known it would be difficult from the moment he had first walked into this room three months ago. She had been sitting where she was now but the time of year and time of day had conspired to bathe her in a ray of sunlight, gilding her dark hair and casting a glow around her. As if she were an ethereal being composed entirely of light and beauty. Or a goddess sent to tempt unsuspecting mortals. A man of less practical sensibilities would have thought it a sign of divine intervention and not simply the angle of the sun and the placement of the windows. Michael's plans for the foreseeable future did not include falling head over heels for anyone, let alone the daughter of a viscount and an influential member of the Explorers Club.

Dulcie Middleworth was not making his resolve any easier.

For one thing, she might well be every bit as attracted to him as he was to her, although he was grateful she had never said or done anything to confirm his suspicions. It was far easier to ignore any foolish feelings he might have if he pretended there was nothing between them. But aside from the fact that she stared at him rather frequently, just as he stared at her, there had been any number of times their gazes had met for longer than a fleeting instant. Understandable really. When he was in the midst of a heated discussion with other club members about a past discovery or some as yet unknown find, he forgot his determination to avoid any connection with her. The first time his gaze had caught hers in the midst of an impassioned debate about something he couldn't even remember now, he was stunned to note she was not only listening but appeared to be quite interested. But then why wouldn't she be? After all, her father was an ardent supporter of the club and known for inviting promising younger members, as well as those well-known experienced explorers, to his home for dinner and stimulating conversation. Michael had never been fortunate enough to receive such an invitation and wasn't entirely sure he would be comfortable accepting as Dulcie would surely be in attendance.

Her obvious intelligence only made her more intriguing. It was his understanding that women were not, as a rule, particularly interested in matters of this sort. The next time he had been engaged in a rousing discussion, he couldn't help but glance her way, only to find her nodding in agreement with him. His heart—which apparently had a mind of its own—had clenched at her approval. Utter nonsense of course and yet he found himself catching her gaze more and more when he was in the midst of a discourse. On occasion, it was obvious she did not agree with whatever point he had made, and while her disagreement was annoying it was also rather amusing and it was all he could do to ignore the desire to continue the debate with her alone after his companions had gone. But who knew where that might lead? He suspected a talk of an intellectual nature would never suffice.

Aside from the fact that his plans did not include a female, there was the very practical matter of their respective stations in life. Regardless of his family's impressive wealth, his was a family of merchants and she was the offspring of a viscount. His father and two older brothers ran the small empire his grandfather had built. A union between a daughter of society and a man of ambition would be awkward at best. Michael was a man of principle but he was not blind. He was well aware that position and favor in the Explorers Club was based as much on social standing as abilities. He did not want any attention he might direct toward Dulcie to be construed as trying to curry favor with her father.

The door to the library opened and Preston Drummond strode into the room. Michael's jaw clenched.

"Shepard." Drummond nodded as he passed Michael on his way to Dulcie's table.

Beyond everything else, Dulcie was apparently about to be married. To an idiot no less. Perhaps she was not as intelligent as he thought. Preston Drummond was universally considered an ass and a pretender. It was widely suspected that Drummond's desire lay more toward the ultimate directorship of the organization rather than any exploration of his own. There was serious money currently in a pool as to whether or not he would ever actually venture beyond the safety of London for the deserts of Asia Minor or anywhere else for that matter. Drummond was one of those men who liked the idea of adventure, if only it wasn't quite so inconvenient and dangerous. Unfortunately, his father too was a patron of the Explorers Club.

According to rumor, put out by Drummond no doubt, he was looked favorably upon by Viscount Middleworth and was about to ask for Dulcie's hand in marriage. Drummond had no particular qualms about currying favor with her father. Michael was not one to put credence in unsubstantiated gossip, but on several occasions Drummond had appeared in the library to chat with her or escort her home, apparently at the request of her parents. Which did seem to indicate some sort of understanding between them. Although how any parents could allow a young woman to accompany a man without an appropriate chaperone was beyond him.

"Good day, Dulcie," Drummond said with his usual smirk. "Might I say how lovely you're looking today."

"How very kind of you to say." Even from across the room Dulcie's smile seemed no more than polite. "I'm not quite finished yet, so if you don't mind I would like to get back to it. Was there something you needed?"

Their conversation was low but, in the cavernous room where sound carried surprisingly well, impossible to ignore completely.

"I've been invited to join your family for dinner."

Drummond's smirk widened with satisfaction. "Your mother suggested I stop here and offer you a ride to your house."

Dulcie sat back in her chair, her smile a shade less polite than before. "Again?"

"She likes me," Drummond said in an immodest manner.

And why not? A mother eager for a good match for a daughter somewhat past her prime marriageable years would no doubt see Drummond as a prize. The man was of good family and sound fortune. Even if he was a prig.

"Your offer is most gracious, and I do thank you, but as I said my work is not quite done. I would very much like to complete this before I leave for the day. Besides, my carriage is expected in an hour or so. Please be so good as to tell my mother I shall return home then." She nodded and returned her attention to the paper in front of her.

"Don't be absurd, Dulcie," Drummond said firmly. "Surely that nonsense can wait until tomorrow."

"Nonsense?" Her brow rose.

Michael almost felt sorry for the man. Certainly Dulcie's employment was unusual, but female artists and illustrators were not unheard of, although it was his understanding that their work was typically more in the fields of botany and horticulture rather than ancient artifacts.

"Perhaps *nonsense* was the wrong word and this a conversation for another time," Drummond said smoothly.

Michael stifled a disdainful snort.

"I should hate to arrive without you." Drummond chuckled. "And your mother would be most annoyed."

"Yes, I suppose she would." Dulcie sighed.

"Besides, there is a matter I wish to discuss with you."

"Oh?" She considered him for a moment then nodded. "Very well." She stood and gathered her things, putting them on a shelf on the wall behind her. She turned and her gaze caught Michael's. He immediately shifted his attention back to his notebook.

"Good Day, Mr. Shepard," she murmured as she passed him on her way to the door. What might well have been a note of resignation sounded in her voice.

"Miss Middleworth." Michael glanced at her and, without thinking, cast her an encouraging smile.

Her eyes widened in surprise. Admittedly, he rarely offered her anything more than a polite, disinterested sort of smile—part of his ongoing effort to avoid entanglement as well as the odd way his heart thudded when her smile lit her blue eyes. She returned a grateful smile and continued on, Drummond a scant step behind. She certainly didn't look like a woman about to tie herself to a man for the rest of her life. Perhaps she was already aware of what an utter fool Drummond was. If not, someone should say something to her before she committed herself to the pretentious ass for the rest of her days.

Not that it mattered. Who she married or whether she married at all was none of Michael's concern. Their fates were not even remotely connected. His was to seek knowledge and adventure in the unknown and follow in the footsteps of his uncle Henry. Hers was to marry well and be a credit to her family.

"Do you ride, Mr. Shepard?"

Michael jerked his attention to the unexpected female voice. "Mrs. Fitzhew-Wellmore." He stood at once. "I beg your pardon. I didn't realize you were here today."

"I've been here for hours, Mr. Shepard. You were entirely too absorbed in your work to notice and I do try not to disturb anyone." She smiled pleasantly. "I was just about to leave myself."

"It is growing late," he said cautiously. "Why did you want to know if I rode?"

"Oh, I was just curious." She studied him for a moment. "You look like the kind of man who rides."

"Do I?"

"Indeed." She nodded. "I was just saying to Miss Middleworth what excellent physical exercise it is. Keeps a person fit and in top form, don't you agree?"

"Yes, I suppose it does."

"Did you know Miss Middleworth rides in the park every morning? I am thinking of joining her some morning but—" she sighed "—I find when one is past one's prime, with every passing year simply mounting a horse becomes a more awkward endeavor."

"Nonsense, Mrs. Fitzhew-Wellmore," he said with a smile. "You don't look anywhere near past your prime."

"How terribly gallant of you to say, Mr. Shepard. You shall quite turn my head with such compliments." The older lady dimpled. "Well, I shall leave you to your work. Good day." She nodded, turned and swept from the room.

Michael retook his seat, the smile still on his face. Mrs. Fitzhew-Wellmore nearly always made a point of stopping for a word or two with him. She reminded him very much of his beloved aunt Grace. The older lady was quite kind, even if she struck him as a bit flighty, and she frequently mentioned Dulcie in passing. She also on occasion chatted about her husband, usually the latest news from his dispatches. Malcolm Fitzhew-Wellmore had a stellar reputation among members of the Explorers Club and frequently ventured into the unknown with the newly knighted Sir Charles Blodgett. Lady Blodgett was often in the library with Mrs. Fitzhew-Wellmore and Mrs. Higginbotham, the wife of a military officer. Michael had the impression the three were quite good friends. They certainly seemed to cope well without the presence of their husbands. In that, in Michael's experience, they were exceptionally rare.

How would Dulcie fare in their place?

He ignored the question. He would soon head toward adventure and she would probably wed Drummond, who would no doubt put an end to her work. Rather a shame given her talent, but that was the way of things. She would no longer be present in the library, indeed, in his world. His heart twisted at the thought of not seeing her every day, bent over her work, her eyes narrowed in concentration. Not hearing her laugh. Not savoring the faintest hint of her scent in the air. Never knowing the feel of her lips on his, save in his dreams late in the night. Although he feared that might well continue.

In spite of the impracticality, pointlessness and sheer absurdity of it, it did appear Dulcie Middleworth had worked her way firmly into his affections.

And even the jungles of the Amazon might not be far enough away to banish her from his heart.

CHAPTER THREE

"I BELIEVE DULCIE MIDDLEWORTH has feelings for Mr. Shepard," Mrs. Persephone Fitzhew-Wellmore—Poppy to her friends—said and played a card. She hadn't particularly liked whist, or card games of any type really, when she and her dear friends Mrs.—now Lady—Guinevere Blodgett and Mrs. Ophelia Higginbotham had begun playing together some twenty years ago. Nor had she been very good at it. Now, she had moments where she was quite a wicked sort of player, much to Gwen and Effie's mixed dismay and amusement. "And I am fairly certain Mr. Shepard shares those feelings."

"I suppose that's entirely possible." Gwen studied her cards. "They're together for hours every day in that library and quite frequently alone."

"Oh, I don't think anything untoward has gone on," Poppy said quickly. "Not any sort of impropriety that is."

"The parties involved usually don't announce their improper activities." Effie played a card. "People tend to be discreet when having a liaison in a library."

"I doubt there's anything even approaching a liaison. Why, they scarcely even talk. At least not to each other." Poppy thought for a moment. "It's extremely odd given they have been in that room nearly every day since he began frequenting the library some months ago but they do *look* at one another all the time."

"Well, if they *look* at one another there must be something going on." Gwen played her card with a flourish, grinned and took the trick. "Three more tricks and I win this hand."

Poppy ignored her. "I know you think I'm being silly but I'm quite observant when it comes to this sort of thing." She set her jaw firmly. "And I know what I've seen."

"You did say they look at each other," Effie murmured, her attention more on the cards Gwen was dealing than on Poppy's comments, as if she could somehow influence them by mere force of thought alone.

"It's not merely *looking*. That would indeed be silly." Poppy drew her brows together. There was nothing more frustrating than trying to explain, even to her dearest friends, how something that had started as nothing more than a feeling had—through ardent observation and a very keen eye—become a conviction. "I first noticed when I would stop to chat with her and admire her work—she's very good you know. I do think she could become quite successful. And there are a fair number of lady illustrators these days—"

"All painting overly sweet pictures of children or flowers," Effie pointed out.

"There's nothing wrong with children or flowers." Gwen leveled Effie a chastising look. Effie did tend to be rather curt when she played cards. Gwen nodded at Poppy. "Do go on, dear. You were telling us about why you think Miss Middleworth has feelings for Mr. Shepard."

"Although I daresay I wouldn't blame her." Effie chuckled. "Nor would I mind spending my days alone in a library with him."

Gwen grinned. "He is quite dashing, isn't he?"

"And entirely too young for any of us even if we

weren't already married." Goodness, it could be difficult at times to keep her friends attending to the matter at hand. Poppy wasn't the only one who tended to digress. She tried again. "As I was saying, quite often, when she and I are chatting about her work or art in general or any number of things, if I chance to look in his direction, I catch him gazing at her as if she were the moon and the stars."

"I heard Miss Middleworth is soon to be engaged to Mr. Drummond," Effie said absently, her attention back on her cards.

"Mr. Drummond probably thinks so judging by the manner in which he smirks at her." Poppy paused. "But she has no intention of marrying him."

"Wise of her," Gwen murmured and set down a card.

"Dulcie is too busy gazing longingly at Mr. Shepard to give Mr. Drummond a second thought. Beyond that there's, well, an odd sort of tension in the air when they're together. Like the taut string on a violin that could snap at any moment."

Effie looked up from her hand. "Goodness, Poppy, if they both have feelings for one another, what on earth is the problem?"

"The problem is neither of them have made their feelings known. Dulcie is a spirited young woman yet the thought of approaching Mr. Shepard seems to sap her courage." Poppy shook her head. "And I suspect he thinks an entanglement would be difficult as he is soon to join a new expedition."

"The one to the Amazon?" Gwen asked.

Poppy nodded and played a card, biting back a smile. Depending on the next card played, she might well win this hand. "I believe so."

"I'm not sure I would encourage anything between them," Effie muttered.

"Why not?"

"Oh, for goodness sakes." Effie smacked down her card and glared at Poppy. "Would you really want any young woman to enter into the life we've had?"

Gwen stared. "I don't see why not."

Poppy quietly collected the trick and tried not to look smug. Three more tricks and Gwen would win? Not bloody likely.

"Because we have spent most of our married years with our husbands off risking their lives in the most dangerous places on earth in the name of military duty or scientific advancement. Why, we are worse than widows. We have husbands—they simply aren't in evidence." Effie huffed. "I, for one, am quite tired of it."

It wasn't the first time Effie had expressed dismay at the state of their existence. All three ladies were married to men of daring and adventure who were far more likely to be found in some remote area of the world than in London. Gwen's husband, Sir Charles, was currently leading an expedition in the jungles of Africa. Poppy wasn't entirely sure what the purpose of it was other than Sir Charles did hope to locate the missing Dr. Livingstone, although most people assumed he was dead as he had not been heard from for several years. Poppy's dear Malcolm was somewhere in Turkey on a quest to find the lost city of Troy. Effie's husband was a military man. Colonel William Higginbotham was even now part of a mission to rescue British citizens and government officials in Abyssinia. From what they'd read in the papers and the infrequent letters Effie received, it did seem that he was safe and all had gone well.

Poppy dealt the cards. It was pointless to argue with

Effie when she was in this mood and one really couldn't blame her if on occasion the state of their existence annoyed her. Of the three friends, Effie's husband was usually the one in the most obvious danger—the lot of a military man of course. Still, one couldn't discount the threat of malaria or other tropical diseases, accidental injury in some uncivilized and probably uncharted location, native uprising or any number of other possibilities that could claim the life of any explorer. Poppy would never disparage Effie's fears for her husband aloud but Poppy did think of the three friends, Effie's lot was a tiny bit better than Poppy or Gwen's. At least if something happened to the Colonel, Effie would be informed of his demise. Sir Charles and Malcolm could bid their wives farewell one day and head off into the unknown never to be heard from again. Not knowing what fate had befallen the man you loved was surely a unique kind of hell on earth.

"We do have each other." Gwen picked up her cards.

"Thank God." Effie blew a frustrated breath then mustered a reluctant smile. "I don't know what I would do without you."

"There is much to be said for family." Poppy nodded and played a card.

Effie and Gwen were indeed her family. While they were originally connected only by circumstance, they were now bound together as tightly as if by blood. They had met some twenty years ago at a meeting of the Ladies Committee of the Explorers Club and had found they had absolutely nothing in common save the lack of a husband within sight. Still—and not one of them today could say exactly how it had happened—from mere acquaintances they had become friends and now were as close as sisters. None of them had much in the way of family and none had been blessed with children. At this point, in their mid to late fifties, they had shared much of their lives together through good times and bad, tears and laughter. They counted on each other for companionship and comfort and support. And would until they day they breathed their last.

"Let me ask you this, Effie." Gwen set her cards on the table and folded her hands on top of them. "When you met William, all those years ago, and someone older and wiser had warned against marrying him as you would probably spend much of your life with him off somewhere in the service of Her Majesty, would you have listened?"

Effie stared at her cards. "William has always looked exceptionally dashing in his uniform."

"Excellent answer," Poppy murmured.

Gwen ignored her. "Would you have given up the handsome officer on the advice of another wife of a military man?"

Effie frowned. "I don't think that question is at all fair. I fell in love with William very nearly the first moment we met." She paused. "I did, however, give due consideration to his life and the future we might have together."

"And you married him anyway," Gwen said pointedly.

"How could I do otherwise?" Effie shrugged. "The man laid claim to my heart."

"And even now, after all these years spent more alone than with him, you would marry him again. As I would marry Charles, and Poppy would marry Malcolm."

"Yes, I suppose I would." Effie heaved a resigned sigh. "Blast it all, of course I would."

"My point exactly," Poppy said firmly. "Dulcie and Mr. Shepard were meant for each other. We just need to make them see what is so obvious to anyone who looks at them."

Gwen narrowed her eyes. "What do you mean *we*?"

"I haven't figured that out yet." Poppy chose her words with care. "But I thought the three of us together might come up with something. We can be quite clever when we join forces."

Effie groaned.

"Your claim that they belong together is based on nothing more than an odd lack of conversation, the fact that they occasionally gaze at each other, something in the air and your own assessment of the situation," Gwen said in that mildly patronizing way she employed when she thought Poppy's ideas absurd. "I really don't think—"

"See for yourself." Poppy's gaze shifted from one friend to the other. "Come to the library tomorrow. If you don't see what I see, then I shall drop this matter altogether."

"Will Mrs. Lithgow be there?" Effie asked.

Mrs. Lithgow was the head of the Ladies Committee, on her third husband, superior, sanctimonious and one of those people who thinks she knows everything. While she was not universally loved, she did manage to accomplish quite a lot that no one else wanted to do, so she was tolerated. In moderation.

Poppy grimaced. "I do hope not."

"And if we see what you see?" Caution sounded in Effie's voice.

"*When* you see what I see—" Poppy beamed "—you will help me come up with a brilliant way to make the two of them accept their, well, fate."

Effie and Gwen traded glances.

"Oh, that does sound like fun," Effie said drily. "Not to mention a great deal of effort."

"Goodness, Effie, you know as well as I—" Poppy played her card and collected the trick "—love is always worth the effort."

CHAPTER FOUR

"Do TELL US more about your plans, Mr. Drummond," Mother said, gazing at Preston as if he was the answer to her prayers. Which no doubt he was. "I'm certain we would all find them most fascinating."

In truth, no one at the table except Mother seemed to find anything Preston said even remotely fascinating, even if her three older daughters—Cora, Rose and Livy—had adopted rapt expressions of interest. Although it did seem there was a fine line between rapt and glazed. Good. Dulcie would need all the support she could gather once she told Preston, and then Mother, she would prefer he not call on her again.

"Are you certain, Lady Middleworth?" Preston said in a mildly flirtatious, teasing manner. The sort of manner one might employ if trying to convince a woman you were the right man for her daughter. "I should hate to be a bore."

Judging by the impassive expression Father usually adopted when he was bored and the total concentration on the food in front of them by her three brothers-in-law, that possibility was no longer in question.

"Don't be absurd, Mr. Drummond." Mother waved off his objection. "I can't imagine anything more interesting than your plans for the future." Mother shot a pointed look at Dulcie. "Don't you agree, dear?"

Any number of answers flashed through Dulcie's

head, none of which even remotely approximated what her mother expected to hear. Nonetheless, Dulcie affixed her brightest smile. "I do indeed, Mother."

Still, there must have been something in her tone. Mother's eyes narrowed slightly, Father choked and Rose's husband coughed, although it sounded suspiciously like a stifled laugh, earning him a stern look from his wife.

"As you wish then." Preston smiled at her in a satisfied and rather possessive manner, as if he were already her husband. Regardless of what Mother or her sisters thought, even if it meant Dulcie would never wed, she had to put an end to this.

Dinner did seem to drag on endlessly but at last came to a merciful close. The ladies stood to take their leave and allow the gentlemen to their brandy.

"Dulcie." Preston cleared his throat. "Might I have a word with you? Privately?"

Mother beamed. Father looked resigned.

His intentions were obvious. Damnation. Dulcie thought she had forestalled a proposal tonight by deflecting any hint of the subject during their ride home. Preston must have spoken to Father while she was changing for dinner. Well, it couldn't be helped and it was probably for the best simply to get it over with.

"Of course, Preston." She cast him a brilliant smile. "Shall we adjourn to the parlor?"

"Excellent." He smiled with complete and utter confidence. One might almost feel sorry for him.

A few minutes later, Dulcie perched on the edge of the sofa in the main parlor, hands folded demurely in her lap, a pleasant smile on her lips although she suspected this was going to be anything but pleasant. Preston stood by the mantel, the very picture of unquestioned self-assurance.

One would think a man about to propose marriage would be at least a little nervous.

"Dulcie, I—" Preston began.

"Preston." She held out her hand to stop him. It wasn't at all fair to let him go on. "I really would prefer—"

"I think we should marry," Preston said in a firm tone.

She stared at him. "Is that a proposal?"

He frowned. "Yes, of course it is."

"It sounded more like a declaration." As if there were no need to actually ask. As if he simply assumed the answer. Preston was making this so much easier for her than she had expected.

"Yes, I suppose it does." He chuckled. "Well, Dulcie, what do you say?"

"I say if you wish me to marry you, the proper thing to do would be to actually ask rather than assume."

"Very well then." He sighed in the manner one does when dealing with a petulant child. "Dulcie, would you do me the very great honor—"

"No."

"No?" His brows drew together. "What do you mean no? I haven't asked you anything yet."

"I thought I would save you any embarrassment you might feel at being turned down by saying no before you actually asked the question."

He stared at her in confusion. "I don't understand."

"Of course you do, Preston." She resisted the urge to roll her eyes toward the ceiling. "It's really quite simple. You wish to marry me but I do not wish to marry you."

"Come now." He scoffed. "Of course you do. I am eminently eligible. My family is well respected, my fortune is more than adequate and any number of women find me most attractive. I am considered quite a catch."

"And indeed you are. Why, anyone can see that. However—" she shrugged "—you are not the catch for me."

"Why on earth not?" His frown deepened with indignation. "We are quite suitably matched. Your mother likes me."

Not a point in his favor.

"*And* your father has given me his permission."

She would have to have a word with Father about that.

"I should think you'd be grateful."

She narrowed her eyes. "Grateful?"

"Without question. While you're quite pretty, you do have a shocking tendency to say whatever is on your mind without regard to how it might sound." He shook his head. "I know your mother finds it distressing, as do I. However, I am certain, once you are wed to a husband who will not tolerate such nonsense, you can overcome that particular flaw in your character. In addition, you have an unbecoming bent toward independence. Proper ladies paint only for their own edification and not for commercial purposes. I cannot believe your father allows such a thing. I would not."

Was Preston really this much of an idiot? Did he truly not realize he was not helping his case?

"Aside from everything else, there is the matter of your age."

Apparently not. "My age?"

"You have past your twenty-third year and are no longer in the first blush of youth." He shook his head in a chastising manner. "Potential matches at your age are few and far between. Coupled with your other flaws, I might very well be your last opportunity."

She widened your eyes in feigned dismay. "Do you really think so?"

He shrugged.

"Goodness, Preston, with all my flaws, I don't understand why you are willing to marry *me*."

"I think you have a great deal of potential, Dulcie," he said firmly. "Indeed I believe with a bit of effort on your part you will make an excellent wife."

"How kind of you to think so." It was all she could do to keep her expression serene given she wasn't sure if she wished to slap his face or laugh in it.

"Besides, your family is socially prominent and your father is an influential voice at the Explorers Club. It would be most beneficial for my future to be related to him."

"In terms of support for an expedition you mean?" Although she would wager all of Father's fortune that Preston would never venture far from civilization.

Preston paused. "Or whatever else might arise."

"I see."

"Furthermore, I am under a great deal of pressure from my family to wed." Preston's brow furrowed. "My father believes it will be of benefit to my nature. Settle me down as it were."

"Really?" She arched a brow. "I can't imagine anyone more settled than you."

"My sentiments exactly." He shook his head in disbelief. "But Father does hold the financial purse strings and he wants me to marry. And I can think of no one I would rather marry than you."

"In spite of my flaws?"

He cast her a condescending smile. "We shall take care of those soon enough. So, what's it to be, Dulcie? Will you marry me?"

"No, Preston, I'm afraid not."

"This is becoming bothersome." He heaved an annoyed sigh. "Did you wish for something more romantic? I could kneel if you want."

"Please, do us both the great favor of not kneeling." She studied him. "Obviously, you are not in love with me."

"I am quite fond of you," he said staunchly. "But I am a practical man and marriage is a practical matter."

"Not to me."

"You need this marriage every bit as much as I do." He paused in a meaningful manner. "I hesitate to mention this."

"Oh no, Preston, please continue."

"It is becoming common knowledge that you did not receive an invitation to Lady Scarsdale's ball. You know as well as I that that omission signals to society that you are no longer considered as marriageable as you once were."

"And less than a month ago I was quite marriageable," she murmured.

He ignored her. "I am willing to overlook that significant social condemnation. Most men won't. This marriage will be of benefit to us both."

"And yet my answer is still no."

"If you are trying to be coy—"

"I am trying to be honest."

"I warn you, Dulcie, I have asked three times already. I will not ask again."

"Excellent." She smiled. "Then we are in agreement."

"If I walk out that door—" he gestured at the door in a grand manner "—I shall not return."

"Oh dear. That is something to consider." She paused for a moment then nodded. "And I have duly considered it." She stood, moved to the door, pulled it open and stepped aside. "I wish you all the best in your future endeavors, Preston."

He stared at her as if she had lost her mind.

"Good evening, Preston," she said with a polite smile.

"You'll regret this, Dulcie." He stalked through the doorway. "You'll never find another man like me."

"One can only hope, Preston," she said under her breath. "One can only hope."

CHAPTER FIVE

THERE WAS NOTHING quite as beneficial for clearing one's head than a brisk early morning ride. Certainly Hyde Park was not as conducive to profound thought as Middleworth Park given that in the country Dulcie could ride by herself. Even though it was barely past dawn and there was hardly anyone about, she was not allowed to ride unaccompanied as Father thought anything could happen to a woman alone in London. Fortunately, her sisters liked to ride every bit as much as she did, but between husbands and children and various obligations, they rarely had the opportunity. Several years ago, they began taking turns accompanying her on her early morning rides. Between Rose, Cora, Livy and Father, Dulcie was able to ride most mornings. Mother did not ride unless it was absolutely necessary. She claimed horses were not overly fond of her. The feeling was mutual.

Today was Livy's turn. They'd had a lovely ride thus far and Dulcie was grateful her sister had not brought up her refusal of Preston's proposal last night. With any luck, that subject would not rear its head.

"We think you did the right thing," Livy said abruptly.

But it was really too much to hope for.

Dulcie glanced at Livy. "We?"

"Rose, Cora and I."

"Really?" Dulcie stared at her sister in surprise. She couldn't recall her sisters ever taking her side in a dispute with Mother. "I thought you were all in support of this match."

"I suppose we were initially. Mr. Drummond did seem to be quite suitable. But the more we were around him…"

"Go on."

"Goodness, Dulcie, he's a dreadful bore and horribly arrogant and well…" Livy wrinkled her nose. "We are all glad you turned him down."

"Mother obviously disagrees." Mother had had a great deal to say after Preston had taken his leave and Dulcie suspected that would not be the end of it.

"Mother thinks no woman can be happy unless she is married and settled into a life of domesticity." Livy shook her head. "Rose, Cora and I believe it's better not to be married at all rather than married to the wrong man. And we are convinced Mr. Drummond was wrong in so many ways."

Dulcie grinned. "I had come to same conclusion myself."

"Which is not to say that we don't think you should be married. We do. It simply means finding the right man."

It was on the tip of Dulcie's tongue to say she might well have found the right man, even if he didn't seem to feel the same.

"And we are going to do all that we can to find him for you. Not that you make it easy."

Dulcie laughed. "Where would be the challenge in that?"

"This isn't amusing," Livy said, but the corners of her lips quirked upward.

"Come now, you think it's a little amusing."

"Admittedly the indignant look on Mr. Drummond's face as he left last night was rather comical. Good Lord, the man has an exaggerated sense of his own worth."

Livy chuckled then sighed. "And while I do think you had a narrow escape, none of us want you to become a spinster aunt living—"

"Good day, Miss Middleworth." A horse pulled up beside her.

Michael? "Good day, Mr. Shepard." He was the last person Dulcie expected to see. "What a lovely surprise. I didn't know you rode."

"There's nothing like a good brisk ride to start the day." He glanced at Livy. "My apologies. I did not mean to interrupt."

"Not at all." Livy waved off his comment. "We weren't discussing anything of particular significance."

"Allow me to introduce my sister, Lady Carswell. Livy, this is Mr. Shepard."

"A pleasure to meet you, Lady Carswell."

"Lovely weather we're having," Livy said with a pleasant smile.

Dulcie might have been mistaken, but it did look like a hint of amusement flashed through his eyes. Good Lord. He must think she came from a family of blithering idiots who could think of nothing clever to say and could only discuss the weather. "It does look an excellent day ahead."

Dulcie bit back a groan.

"How are you acquainted with my sister, Mr. Shepard?" Livy asked lightly but there was a speculative gleam in her eye.

"We frequently find ourselves sharing the Explorers Club library. I'm sure you're aware of Miss Middleworth's work documenting with pen and paint the club's various collections."

"Indeed I am," Livy said with pride. "She's quite good, don't you think?"

Dulcie stared. Here was yet another surprise in a morning that seemed to be filled with them. Her sisters had never given any indication that they considered her work more than a frivolous pastime.

"I do." He nodded. "I have rarely seen illustrations that are both accurate and yet seem to capture the essence, the soul if you will, of whatever artifact the artist is attempting to portray." He cast her an admiring smile. "It really is most impressive."

"Thank you," Dulcie said weakly. She had no idea he had ever looked at her work. She cleared her throat. "Mr. Shepard is preparing for an expedition he hopes to join next month."

"Oh?" Livy's brow rose.

"Reacquainting myself with the native flora and fauna to be found in the upper Amazon." He adopted a vaguely professorial manner. It was most endearing. "I do feel if one is going to venture into an area that is very much unknown, one should learn as much as possible about what is known. It only makes sense to thoroughly prepare."

"Yes, well, that does make sense." Livy nodded and changed the subject. "I don't believe I've noticed you here before, Mr. Shepard. Do you ride often?"

"I try to ride whenever I can but it's often difficult to find the opportunity and I'm not overly fond of crowds." He glanced around. "Now, however, does seem to be the perfect time of day."

"Perhaps we will see you again then." Livy smiled pleasantly. "One of my other sisters or myself usually joins Dulcie nearly every day."

"I shall keep that in mind." He turned to Dulcie. "Miss Middleworth, might I have a private word?" The tiniest furrow appeared between his brows. "I have a matter of some importance I wish to discuss with you."

What on earth was this about? Given the man had never spoken more than a handful of words to her, he was already well over his limit.

"Yes, of course." She glanced at Livy.

Her sister nodded. "Why don't you both ride ahead and I'll follow along behind you."

Dulcie smiled in gratitude.

Livy held her horse back until Dulcie and Michael were a few yards in front of her. Dear Lord. Here was her opportunity to finally talk to him—at his request no less—and she could think of nothing to say. But then he'd had that effect on her from nearly the first moment they'd met. She drew a bracing breath and plunged ahead.

"A matter of some importance, Mr. Shepard?"

"I feel in the last few months, we have become, well, not exactly friends but companions in a manner of speaking."

"We do share the library."

"Exactly." He nodded. "And I have come to respect your, well, your mind."

"My mind?" She wasn't sure a man had ever complimented her mind before although several had said her eyes were quite lovely.

"Yes, well, do forgive me, but on occasion I can't help overhearing your conversations with some of the other ladies. Much of what you discuss is mindless frivolity—"

So much for his admiration of her mind.

"But you frequently talk about matters I had no idea women ever spoke of." He shook his head in obvious disbelief. "I've heard you and some of the Ladies Committee members discuss politics, the state of the world, various explorations and any number of other topics. I must say, it's been quite a revelation."

Dulcie wasn't sure if she should be offended or

amused. She chose amused. "You're not used to being around women are you, Mr. Shepard?"

"Not really." He shrugged. "My aunt Grace lived with us for much of her life but my mother died when I was quite young and I have no sisters."

"My condolences. About your mother. And your aunt." She smiled. "Although it is a shame not to have sisters, as well. I have three and they are as dear as they are annoying."

"It might have better prepared me," he said under his breath.

"To speak about this matter of some importance? My advice would be simply to boldly forge ahead." Goodness, the man was willing to brave the unknown recesses of the Amazon jungle yet he couldn't seem to say what he wanted to say in the relative civilization of Hyde Park. One would think this *matter of some importance*...

The answer struck her and her heart skipped a beat. Was it possible that Michael had the same sort of feelings for her that she did for him? Was that what this was all about? Was he going to declare himself even though they'd scarcely ever spoken? Was their unspoken bond as significant to him as it was to her?

"This is rather awkward."

Awkward? How very charming. She mustered an encouraging smile. "Do go on, Mr. Shepard."

"I'm not sure how to begin."

She leaned toward him. "I have always found a deep, bracing breath to be an excellent way to start any awkward discussion."

"Very well." He drew a deep breath. "For good or ill, you have not escaped my notice these past few months."

"Nor have you escaped mine." Her pulse raced.

"And while I realize we rarely speak of anything beyond the weather, I do feel we have forged a quiet sort of bond between us."

"Go on." Delightful anticipation shivered up her spine.

"An unspoken friendship if you will."

She nodded.

"Which is the only reason why I feel it necessary to say something."

Necessary? An odd choice of words.

"This is really not none of my concern."

Her smile slipped a bit.

"But I would be remiss if I did not urge you to thoroughly consider any decision you might make regarding Mr. Drummond."

She stared. Surely he wasn't suggesting she reconsider rejecting Preston's proposal? And how could he possibly know about last night? "I beg your pardon."

"My apologies." He shook his head. "I'm not saying this well."

"Exactly what are you trying to say, Mr. Shepard?" she said slowly.

"Miss Middleworth." He drew another breath then met her gaze firmly. Behind his spectacle his eyes blazed with sincerity. "I think it would be a very great error on your part to marry Mr. Drummond."

"You do?"

"Without question." Michael nodded firmly. "A marriage to Mr. Drummond would not serve you well. From my observations the man is unprincipled, lacking in honor and concerned with nothing beyond his own well-being. Nor, I might add, does he hold his alcohol well. A man who cannot be trusted to hold his tongue after a few drinks of a good Scottish whiskey, is not a man one can trust with one's future."

Dulcie had no idea what to say.

"He has said on any number of inebriated occasions that he intends to marry you and, by doing so, elevate his position in society. He has mentioned, as well, your considerable dowry." He paused. "Apparently Mr. Drummond's finances are not as sound as they might appear. Furthermore, the man's arrogance knows no bounds. He has also said that a marriage with you would allow him to become close to your father. Which would be of benefit to him in his ambitions regarding the Explorers Club, none of which, I might add, even remotely involve venturing beyond the boundaries of England. He has further declared his intention to one day serve as director of the club. I personally consider his membership in the Explorers Club to be a travesty."

She stared.

"As I said, I am well aware that this is none of my concern but I did feel I would be derelict in my responsibility as a, well, a friend of sorts, if I did not make you aware of Mr. Drummond's reprehensible nature. Although, on further consideration, as I do feel you are an intelligent woman, you are probably already cognizant of Mr. Drummond's less than stellar character. However, that was not a chance I was willing to take." He squared his shoulders. "You cannot marry Mr. Drummond, Miss Middleworth. It would be a grave mistake that would ruin your life and destroy any chance you might have for happiness. And I would hate to see that happen." He nodded. "I shall leave you to your ride. Good day." He reined his horse to the side and trotted toward the nearest gate.

Dulcie stared after him.

Livy pulled up beside her. "My, that was certainly interesting."

"Did you hear what he said?"

"Most of it. Sound carries surprisingly well at this

time of day." She paused. "Why didn't you tell him you have already turned down Mr. Drummond's proposal?"

"I don't know."

"In fact." Livy's brows drew together. "You really didn't say much of anything to him."

"I never do." Dulcie sighed. "When I'm anywhere near him I can't seem to say a word. My mouth becomes dry and my tongue seems to swell. Words stick in my throat and I can't manage a coherent sentence that doesn't involve the weather."

"That explains it then."

"Explains what?"

"Why you didn't put him in his place. I've never seen you let any man get the better of you in a conversation. And I never imagined you allowing a man, any man, to dictate to you in that manner. Why, he had the unmitigated nerve to tell you who you should or shouldn't marry."

"It was rather high-handed of him," she said slowly.

"It was a lecture—that's what it was. And he certainly had no right to say anything whatsoever. Did he?"

"No, he did not." She glared at the retreating figure on horseback, indignation rising within her. Why, he was very nearly as presumptuous as Preston. "No right at all."

"Although he did say you were friends."

Dulcie scoffed. "We are barely more than acquaintances."

"And he called Preston arrogant."

"Preston's arrogance pales in comparison." Outrage swept through Dulcie, sweeping aside her initial shock at Michael's unsolicited advice. "The audacity of the man to tell me what I should do with my life when he's never done anything but comment on the blasted weather. And he has had every opportunity."

"Perhaps he has the same sort of difficulty talking to you as you seem to have talking to him?" Livy suggested.

"He certainly had no particular problem speaking his mind today," Dulcie said sharply.

"Well…" Livy stared thoughtfully in Michael's direction. "Perhaps you should do something about it."

"I assure you, Livy—" Dulcie narrowed her eyes and watched Michael fade from sight "—I intend to."

CHAPTER SIX

WHAT IN THE name of all that was holy had he been thinking?

Oh, certainly his motives were noble enough, but in fact Michael had absolutely no right to give unsolicited advice of such a personal nature to a woman with whom he had barely ever spoken. It was presumptuous of him and arrogant and, without question, he would do it all again.

Dulcie Middleworth deserved better than Preston Drummond.

Michael had tried to bury himself in his research books and notations since his arrival at the library an hour or so ago but the effort was pointless. He could not get the possible consequences of his rash behavior out of his head.

It had only been a few hours since their early morning encounter and she had yet to make an appearance in the library. Highly unusual as she was frequently here before him or shortly thereafter. On one hand he was relieved, even if it only delayed the inevitable. On the other he couldn't quite dismiss an overriding sense of curiosity. He had no idea what to expect. She had said nothing in the park in response to his comment but then he had quite cowardly taken his leave before she had the chance. And really he wasn't sure she'd ever said anything to him at all that wasn't about the weather but then he'd never really spoken to her either. Even so, there was some kind of *something* between them. He'd said they shared a sort of friendship, which was as good a way to describe it as any.

Still, regardless of what you called whatever this was, he had overstepped the bounds of acceptable behavior. Perhaps she'd decided not to come today. Perhaps she'd never return at all. A chilling sense of loss squeezed his heart at the thought.

"Good morning, Mr. Shepard." Mrs. Fitzhew-Wellmore's voice rang out behind him and he rose to his feet and turned to greet her. "How are you on this beautiful spring day? Deep in the jungles of Brazil no doubt."

"Good day, Mrs. Fitzhew-Wellmore. Indeed, I am," he lied. It was impossible to concentrate on tropical flora when his thoughts kept drifting back to an English park.

"I believe you've met my friends, haven't you?"

"I have." He nodded. "Good day, Lady Blodgett, Mrs. Higginbotham. How lovely to see you all again."

All three ladies were somewhere in their fifties and one could well imagine, in their youth, they each must have been quite striking.

"How very kind of you to say, Mr. Shepard." Lady Blodgett smiled.

"Quite nice to see you again, Mr. Shepard," Mrs. Higginbotham said. "Well, we hate to disturb you. Do carry on." She nodded and started toward the far side of the room, near Dulcie's work area.

"Mr. Shepard," Lady Blodgett began. "My husband has quite an extensive collection of books and reference materials on the Amazon. Should you ever need something you cannot find here, you are welcome to peruse them."

"Thank you, Lady Blodgett. That's very kind of you to offer."

"Not at all." She smiled and followed her friend.

"We shall be in the stacks and the storage room beyond if you have need of us," Mrs. Fitzhew-Wellmore said.

The shelf behind the table Dulcie usually occupied was not affixed to a wall and served to cut off a quarter of the library from the rest of the room. While all four walls were lined with shelves, at some point it was decided it was simply not enough. Now, the area behind the far shelf was filled with metal book stacks and beyond that was a former parlor, now used as a combination office, storage room and workroom. Nearly as large as the library, the room housed most of the club's collections of antiquities as well as files, desks and worktables.

"But then you have never called on us for assistance before. Although you may if you so desire. We are overflowing with sage advice. And it never hurts to have another point of view, don't you agree?"

He smiled. "You're very wise, Mrs. Fitzhew-Wellmore."

"You have no idea, Mr. Shepard." She waved at his books. "Now, back to work. I would hate for you to miss something that might prove useful." She nodded and started after the other ladies.

"Actually, Mrs. Fitzhew-Wellmore..." he began without thinking.

She turned. "Yes, Mr. Shepard?"

"I might..." He searched for the right words, the words that wouldn't make him look like a complete idiot. "I might seek out your advice later today. On a, well, a personal matter."

"I see." She studied him curiously. "We are exceptionally good with personal matters, Mr. Shepard. And we are always willing to help. Do keep that in mind."

"I will do so."

She smiled and headed after the others. Michael sat back down and stared at his notes.

Confiding in Mrs. Fitzhew-Wellmore might not be a bad idea. But confiding what? That he had feelings of affection for Dulcie Middleworth even though anything of significance between them was foolish? That he had quite inexplicably violated every rule of propriety and privacy and stuck his nose in where it had no right to be? That he was totally and completely lost as to what— if anything—he should do now? And worse—what he wanted to do now.

A heavy book slammed onto the table in front of him, the sharp, shocking noise echoing through the room and probably the entire building. He jumped to his feet. "Bloody hell, what on earth—"

"Mr. Shepard." Dulcie stood in front of the table, arms crossed over her chest. He hadn't even heard her come in. Judging by the look on her face, a grave mistake on his part.

"Was that necessary?" He ran a shaky hand through his hair. "Good God, I thought the building had collapsed."

"I wanted to get your attention."

"You could have simply said, 'Good day. How are you?'"

"Lovely weather we're having?" She shook her head. "I think this morning we progressed beyond weather, don't you agree?"

"About this morning," he said slowly.

"You had no right, Mr. Shepard. No right at all!"

"Perhaps, if you will allow me to explain—"

"Explain?" Her brow rose. "There are no words that could possibly explain your behavior."

"I simply thought—"

"No, Mr. Shepard," she snapped. "You had your say this morning. It is now my turn."

He stared. He had not seen this Dulcie before. Her blue eyes blazed and her cheeks flushed. She looked like an ancient goddess come to life. A goddess of death and destruction but a goddess nonetheless. "Very well."

"For the past three months we have seen each other nearly every day right here in this room. And you've said nothing to me beyond your observation of the weather."

"Might I point out, you've never before mentioned anything other than the weather either."

"No, you may not!" She huffed. "A man who has never shown even the vaguest interest in my life cannot out of the blue tell me who I may or may not marry!"

"I don't think I *told* you. I believe it was more in the way of a *suggestion* on my part."

"A suggestion? Hah! You told me I could not marry Mr. Drummond. You said it would be a dreadful mistake and destroy the rest of my life."

"I'm not sure that's how I phrased it—"

"Believe me, Mr. Shepard, your words are burned into my memory."

"As well they should be," he said without thinking. "If they make you consider, just for a moment, the dire consequences of marrying Mr. Drummond."

"Who I marry is none of your concern!"

"I believe I stated that this morning."

"And we are not friends! *Friends*, Mr. Shepard, talk about more than the blasted weather!"

"I realize that, however—"

"Furthermore, I am not an idiot."

"I did not say you were." Indignation rang in his voice. "You implied it!"

"On the contrary, Miss Middleworth, I think you're one of the most intelligent women I have ever met."

"And yet you think I would be so stupid as to marry Preston Drummond?"

She did have a point. "Well, he says—"

"I don't care what he says." She dismissed his comment with a sharp wave of her hand. "I have no intention of marrying him. I never have. I told him so last night."

"You did?"

"Indeed I did."

He stared. "Why?"

"Aside from all the reasons you listed?"

He ignored her. "Even so, in many ways he is perfect for you."

"You said he was an ass."

"Oh, I never said that. Not to you."

"Again, it was implied."

"But his father is an earl and—"

"I am not so shallow as to marry a man for his position in society. If that was my prerequisite for a husband, I could have married long ago." Outrage burned in her blue eyes in a most magnificent manner. "However, you would not know that as you do not know anything about me as you have made no effort to find out!" She gestured at the table. "You sit here day after day and never once think to cross the room and share an observation with me. Why, I wouldn't know anything about you at all if not for the frequent discussions you have here with colleagues."

"Why did you turn him down?"

"Because, Mr. Shepard." Her gaze met his directly. "I fear my affections lie elsewhere."

"Oh." His stomach plummeted. "I see." Of course. He should have expected as much. A woman like Dulcie Middleworth no doubt had any number of suitors beyond

Drummond. Why, there was probably no need to try to save her from Drummond at all. What a fool he was.

"If you'll excuse me." He quickly gathered up his things. "I have an important appointment and I shall be late if I do not leave at once." He nodded and fairly sprinted toward the door.

"You're leaving? Now?"

"My apologies. I don't wish to be late."

"You're the worst sort of coward, Mr. Shepard!" she called after him.

He pretended not to hear. It was better this way. But she was right and he knew it.

Somewhere between noticing how the sun this morning in the park had turned her hair to stands of burnished gold and the look in her eyes this moment when she told him she had feelings for someone else, the truth had struck him with the force of a bolt from above. It didn't matter if she cared for another man, nor did it matter that he was soon going to leave for grand adventures and for an undetermined amount of time.

He was in love with Dulcie Middleworth and there was nothing he could do about it.

CHAPTER SEVEN

DULCIE STOOD STARING after Mr. Shepard as if rooted to the floor. As if she couldn't believe he had just walked out. Poor dear girl. Poppy, Gwen and Effie stood in the opening between the shelves leading to the book stacks. Dulcie's encounter with Mr. Shepard had happened so quickly they'd had no time to retreat from view. Not that they probably would have anyway.

At last Dulcie shook her head, heaved a great sigh and turned toward her usual table. Her gaze met Poppy's. Poppy fluttered her fingers in a weak wave.

"I do so hate to be caught eavesdropping," Gwen said quietly then paused. "Do you think we heard everything?"

"I've always been quite impressed with how sound carries here. But just to be certain…" Effie raised her chin and sailed to Dulcie's side. "My dear girl." She took the younger woman's hands in hers. "What was that all about?"

"We do apologize," Poppy said quickly. "We didn't mean to overhear."

"But now that we have," Gwen added, "perhaps it would be beneficial if you told us everything."

"Oh, I don't know," Dulcie began.

"Do sit down, dear." Poppy pulled out a chair and Effie gently shoved Dulcie into it.

They all three took seats, Effie settling in a chair beside Dulcie. "One always feels much better after unburdening oneself."

"There's really not very much to say. I suspect you heard a great deal of it."

"But we were trying very hard not to listen." Poppy smiled apologetically and sent a silent request heavenward for forgiveness for the lie.

"This morning, when I was riding in the park, I ran into Mr. Shepard who took it upon himself to tell me I cannot marry Mr. Drummond."

Effie gasped. "The nerve of the man."

Dulcie nodded. "That's what I thought."

"But it was my understanding that you have no intention of marrying Mr. Drummond," Poppy said.

"No, and I told Mr. Drummond so last night."

"And today Mr. Shepard tells you that you can't marry him?" Gwen asked. "Which apparently you did not take well."

Dulcie's gaze snapped to Gwen. "Would you?"

"Not for a moment." Gwen patted her hand.

"I daresay I wouldn't be nearly as angry if he... I thought perhaps... One would think a man who didn't want you to marry someone else had, well, feelings for you, but apparently I was wrong. And I as much as told him..." Dulcie straightened her shoulders. "Never mind. It doesn't really matter now I suppose. Thank you for being so very kind." She stood. "But I think I would prefer to work at home today."

They chatted for a few more minutes and Dulcie took her leave.

"I told you," Poppy said the moment the door closed behind the young woman.

"Might I point out there was not a declaration of affection," Effie said. "On either side."

"No, but there was certainly something of significance." Gwen shook her head. "It's obvious to me that Dulcie cares for him. And no man takes it upon himself to tell a woman who she may not marry unless he is related by blood or has feelings of affection for her himself. Besides, did you see the stricken look on his face when he left?"

Effie scoffed. "When he fled like a frightened bunny you mean."

"Because he's in love." Poppy smirked. "That tends to make even the strongest man flee like a frightened bunny."

"I have to agree with Poppy," Gwen said. "There is definitely something between them."

"Well then." Poppy beamed. "What are we going to do about it?"

Effie grimaced. "And we are going to have to do something, aren't we?"

"You did give me your word."

Gwen looked at Effie. "We did promise."

"Very well." Effie threw up her hands in surrender. "The question is how to get two people together who don't wish to admit they belong together."

"Oh, I think Dulcie is willing to admit it." Poppy nodded. "She did tell him her affections were not with Mr. Drummond."

"But she didn't say those affections were for Mr. Shepard. So being a man, he obviously assumed the worst," Gwen said. "That there is someone aside from Mr. Drummond that she cares for."

"Oh dear." Poppy sighed. "This is awkward."

"Nonsense." Effie scoffed. "That's the easiest part of this to straighten out. A casual word to him from one of us will clear up that misunderstanding."

Poppy tried not to grin. Once Effie was engaged in any sort of scheme Poppy or Gwen had proposed, she was not halfhearted about it.

"Still, for whatever reason, Mr. Shepard is reluctant to make his feelings known." Gwen frowned. "And I suspect Dulcie is too proud to pursue a man who she thinks is not interested in her."

"So all we have to do is encourage him to show interest in her?" Effie shook her head. "No difficulty there."

"We'll find a way." Gwen drew her brows together. "We all have husbands. We've never found it all that challenging to encourage them to do what we want them to do. Usually by convincing them it's something they want, as well."

Effie's eyes narrowed thoughtfully. "Men do always seem to want what they can't have."

Poppy straightened. "That's it, Effie. I should have thought of it myself. That's exactly what we should do."

Effie and Gwen exchanged cautious looks.

"What exactly should we do?" Effie asked.

"It's quite clear to me." Poppy thought for a moment. "Mr. Shepard acted when he thought Dulcie was going to marry Mr. Drummond. It was an excellent beginning on his part but, as Mr. Shepard has absolutely no respect for Mr. Drummond, it didn't, oh, push him far enough to declare his own feelings. I can't imagine he truly thought Dulcie would be foolish enough to marry the annoying man, so really Mr. Drummond was no actual threat."

"Then why did he say anything to her at all?"

"That's the point," Poppy said. "There was no real need, was there? But he went out of his way to do so. It seems to me if Dulcie was to be pursued by someone Mr. Shepard admired, an extraordinary explorer and a true hero, it might be just the thing to make him acknowledge his feelings and declare himself." Poppy beamed. "It's brilliant."

"And where do you suggest we find such a hero?" Effie asked wryly.

"Oh, I already have."

Gwen stared. "Dare we ask who?"

"Why, the very man who made my Malcolm come up to snuff when he was dragging his feet and made him realize I was the true love of his life and the best thing to ever happen to him. The elusive, extremely humble, extraordinary explorer, adventurer and lecturer." Poppy grinned. "The legendary, unparalleled, incomparable Reginald Everheart."

CHAPTER EIGHT

IT HAD BEEN a very long two days and an even longer two nights.

Not only was Dulcie's head filled with questions and any number of possible reasons behind Michael's outrageous admonition, but Mother was not letting Dulcie's refusal of Preston's proposal go without further reproach. She had gone on and on about it until Dulcie had seriously considered taking up permanent residence in the Explorers Club library. Impossible of course although she had stayed as late as possible every day. Partially in an effort to avoid her mother and partly because Michael had not returned to the library since they had last spoken. Perhaps he really was a coward, at least when it came to matters of—of what? The heart? Or simple male arrogance?

Dulcie had returned home yesterday in time for tea only because she'd received a note at the library from Cora saying her sisters intended to speak to Mother and Dulcie really should be present. It had been a shocking—and most gratifying—display of sisterly support as they tried to convince Mother Dulcie's rejection of Preston was for the best. While Mother's tirade barely lessoned, it did warm Dulcie's heart that, for what might be the first time in her life, her sisters were on her side.

While Cora and Rose tried to reassure Mother that Dulcie had not thrown away her life, Livy pulled her younger sister aside for a private word, wanting to know what had transpired with Michael. Dulcie related their conversation, omitting her final comment, but mentioning his abrupt departure. Livy thought that most significant and wondered aloud why a man would presume to tell a woman who she shouldn't marry unless he harbored certain feelings for her himself. Dulcie had had the same intriguing idea herself. Still, one would think a man who had *certain feelings* for a woman would do something about them. Although one could also argue that by pointing out all the reasons why she shouldn't marry Preston, he had done just that. And beyond anything else that had happened, the possibility of *certain feelings* is what lingered in Dulcie's head.

She'd made it a point to arrive at the library far earlier than usual in the past two days in hopes of already being well into her work should Michael deign to make an appearance. It would be much easier to ignore him that way. Not that she was sure she wished to ignore him, at least not altogether, but she'd had her say. It did seem it was his turn. An apology—*his* apology—might well be a beginning for the two of them. But it would have to be contrite in tone, utterly sincere—she had waited two days for it after all—and accompanied by an explanation. Something along the lines of "I care for you deeply, Dulcie, and I couldn't bear the thought of losing you to another man," followed immediately by the kind of passionate embrace and unreserved kiss one read about in novels disapproved of by Mother. And who knew where that might lead? Dulcie shivered at the deliciously wicked thought of what kind of delightfully immoral pleasures might be found in the arms of the handsome and brilliant Michael Shepard. Dulcie had certainly been kissed before but she had never, of course, experienced delightfully immoral pleasures. Her sisters, however, whispered of such things on occasion and Dulcie did read quite a lot.

The door creaked and she glanced up from her work for no more than the time it took to ascertain the new arrival was indeed Michael—she had no intention of allowing her gaze to meet his—then firmly turned her attention back to the barely progressing pottery drawing. If he wished to say good day and comment on the weather, he would have to make an effort to do so. She heard his footsteps—rather cautious, she thought—pause at his table, then somewhat more determinedly start toward her. Her fingers tightened around her pencil but she would not give him the satisfaction of looking up. His footsteps stopped and his shadow fell across her paper.

He cleared his throat. "Good morning, Miss Middleworth."

"Good morning, Mr. Shepard," she said coolly, refusing to look up at him. "You're blocking my light."

"Sorry." He stepped aside but did not leave.

"Is there something else?"

"Well, yes, actually, there is but… I say, Miss Middleworth." Exasperation sounded in his voice. "This is not easy under the best of circumstances but would you please do me the courtesy of looking at me when I speak to you? It's most disconcerting to be talking to the top of your head."

"Very well, Mr. Shepard." She set down her pencil, folded her hands together on the table and looked at him. He appeared at once repentant and determined, charming and irresistible. It was all she could do not to leap to her feet and fling herself into his arms. But that would surely be a mistake and probably horribly humiliating and embarrassing, not to mention improper. Still, it was tempting. "What did you wish to say?"

"I have been giving our recent discussions a great deal of thought."

"As have I."

"And I believe an apology might well be in order."

And then you can toss me on the table and have your way with me. She tried to ignore the thought but he was so endearingly sincere. "I cannot disagree with that."

"I have considered exactly what to say in such an apology over and over since we last spoke. Indeed, I have thought of little else."

"Then perhaps you should just say it and be done with it." *And then you might wish to kiss my hand, and that sensitive spot on the inside of my wrist and then pull me into your arms...* She drew a calming breath. "It's not that difficult is it?"

"It's far harder that I had imagined." He thought for a moment then squared his broad shoulders and met her gaze directly. "Miss Middleworth, I do feel I overstepped the bounds of our, well, our friendship. I had no right to express my opinion on any man you might consider marrying, even one I feel is unworthy of you. And I do regret any upset I might have caused you."

"Thank you, Mr. Shepard."

"My father believes an apology that is not sincere is worse than no apology at all, therefore—" he shook his head "—I cannot—I will not—apologize for my words although I am sorry I cannot do so."

She stared. "What?"

"I think I was perfectly clear," he said in a lofty manner.

She rose to her feet. "Did you just say you were sorry for not apologizing to me?"

"I believe that's exactly what I said."

She crossed her arms over her chest. "And even though

you admit you had no right to do so, that you overstepped, you are not apologizing for that?"

"Apparently not. I had planned to, however..." His jaw tightened. "It would be wrong of me to do so."

"Because you are not sincere?"

"Exactly."

"I thought we agreed that an apology was in order?"

"I have reconsidered. Upon further consideration, I cannot apologize for something—" he braced his hands on the table and leaned toward her "—that I would do again."

"Would you indeed?" She set her own hands on the table, leaned forward and glared.

"Oh, I would, Miss Middleworth, I absolutely would." Resolve gleamed in his gray eyes.

"That's extremely presumptuous of you."

"Perhaps."

"There's no perhaps about it." She narrowed her eyes. "Why, Mr. Shepard?"

"Why would I do it again?"

"Or in the first place." She shrugged. "Your choice."

"Someone needed to. If I were to see a total stranger about to step off a cliff, I would consider it my duty to try to stop him."

"I see. Then I was nothing more than a moral obligation."

"No." His brows drew together. "That's not at all what I meant."

"What did you mean?"

"As I said, someone needed to say something as apparently no one else was."

"And you took it upon yourself."

"I did."

She studied him. "Surely you have a better reason than that."

"I believe you deserve better than Mr. Drummond."

"Do I?"

"You deserve someone who would cherish you for the brilliant, talented woman that you are. Someone who would see you as more than a…a means to an end. A stepping stone as it were."

"And do you have someone in mind, Mr. Shepard?" She leaned closer and stared into his eyes. "Because if you do, I would very much like his name."

"Come now, Miss Middleworth. I am well aware there is someone with whom your affections already lie."

She frowned. "What on earth are you talking about?"

"You said it yourself. That you refused Mr. Drummond because you feared your affections lay elsewhere."

Dulcie stared. Obviously the silly man didn't realize she was talking about him. And why would he? She had done no more to show her interest in him than he had in her. If indeed he had any interest in her. But it did seem if he didn't, he would have no particular problem apologizing. Still, it was up to him to do something, although it certainly wouldn't hurt to let him know he was mistaken about some unknown man engaging her affections.

This was her opportunity to confess her feelings. If she was wrong this would be dreadfully humiliating. But if she was right…if she were right, it was worth the risk of dire embarrassment. She drew a deep breath. "Mr. Shepard, about that   "

"No." He shook his head. "It's really none of my concern and I should probably not intrude any further into your personal affairs."

"Oh?" Her brows shot upward. "You were willing to intrude when it involved a man you did not think worthy of me but when you don't know who the man might be, you are more than willing to let me walk off that cliff?"

"I thought we agreed I had already been presumptuous and—"

"What I think you are, Mr. Shepard, is a coward."

His mouth dropped opened and he straightened. "I was willing to overlook your calling me a coward given that you were upset but I will not—"

"Good day, Dulcie." Poppy's voice rang out over the library and at once Michael took a step back. "And Mr. Shepard. I'm so glad you're here. Could you carry something in for us?" Poppy beamed from the doorway, flanked by Mrs. Higginbotham and Lady Blodgett.

"Of course." He leaned toward Dulcie and lowered his voice. "And now I believe, Miss Middleworth, *you* owe *me* an apology."

"Why, Mr. Shepard?" She cast him her most charming smile. "As I would most certainly say it again."

He shot her an annoyed glare then headed for Poppy and the other ladies.

The man was completely infuriating. He not only intruded into areas he had no right to be but then he refused to apologize for his actions. It would be one thing, and quite forgivable, if he did indeed have feelings for her and something else entirely if he was just an arrogant ass who thought he knew what was best for everyone. No, in spite of her own feelings for him, she'd had quite enough. Why, even if he were to turn around right now, yank her into his arms and kiss her quite thoroughly until she melted into a puddle of unimagined bliss and the older ladies had to fan themselves with the heat of it, she would still not wish to have anything further to do with him. Probably.

Michael disappeared into the corridor with the ladies and a few minutes later reappeared carrying a crate, perhaps two feet square. In spite of its size it did appear heavy.

Poppy skirted around him and indicated the table next to Dulcie's. "Set it right here if you will."

"It was mistakenly delivered to my house rather than here," Lady Blodgett added. "Careful, please, it is fragile."

Nonetheless, there was a bit of a thunk when Michael set the crate on the table.

"Now then, Mr. Shepard." Mrs. Higginbotham handed him a short iron pry bar. One did wonder how she came by it. "If you would be so kind as to remove the top."

"Very well." Caution sounded in his voice. He took the tool and began prying off top of the crate.

The wood screamed and Lady Blodgett winced. "Do be careful, Mr. Shepard." She cast the oddest look at Mrs. Higginbotham, almost accusatory in nature. "We didn't realize it was secured quite so well."

"One would hate for anything to happen to it," Mrs. Higginbotham murmured then paused. "Whatever it might be, that is."

"What it is is a delightful surprise," Poppy said firmly.

"What kind of surprise?" Dulcie studied Poppy cautiously. She had the distinct impression these ladies were up to something.

"You'll see." The older lady's eyes twinkled.

Michael finally removed the top. The crate was filled with wood shavings.

"Do go on, Mr. Shepard." Lady Blodgett waved at the box then glanced at Dulcie. "Isn't this exciting?"

"You don't know what it is?" Dulcie asked.

"Not specifically but we do know who it's from." Poppy beamed.

"Do you plan to share that with us?" Michael dug into

the crate, pulling out fistful after fistful of shavings. Dust caught the light and danced in the air around him.

"Certainly." Poppy glanced at her friends who nodded in encouragement. "It's an artifact being loaned to the club for a special exhibit to accompany a lecture being given by a man who is very nearly a legend." She paused in an overly dramatic manner. "The extraordinary explorer and adventurer Mr. Reginald Everheart."

Michael paused, shavings in either hand. "Who?"

Lady Blodgett gasped in horror. "Surely you have heard of Reginald Everheart? Why Reginald Everheart has ventured beyond the boundaries of civilization in all corners of the world."

"And you call yourself an explorer," Mrs. Higginbotham said disdainfully.

"Why, even I have heard of Reginald Everheart," Dulcie added with a superior smirk. Admittedly, it was something of a lie although the name did sound vaguely familiar. At least it was an excellent name for an explorer.

Michael's brow furrowed. "No, I don't think—"

"Well, he is American," Poppy said in a blithe manner. "Which unfortunately means he cannot be a full member here but I believe he is an honorary member."

"And quite fond of the Explorers Club," Lady Blodgett added. "Brothers-in-arms and all. And his mother was English."

"As is his wife," Mrs. Higginbotham said.

"But she's dead," Poppy blurted.

"I forgot." Mrs. Higginbotham winced. "It was a very long time ago. Lost in a jungle I believe…"

Dulcie stared. "Really?"

"One would think someone so extraordinary would not be so careless as to misplace a wife in a jungle," Michael said under his breath.

"We don't know him as well as our husbands do. They hold him in the highest regard," Lady Blodgett said in a confidential manner.

"Although we have each met him on occasion." Poppy heaved an adoring sigh. "He is the very picture of a heroic adventurer."

"Tall." Lady Blodgett nodded. "With the most extraordinary blue eyes and blond hair."

"Exceptionally handsome." Mrs. Higginbotham smiled. "Really a fine figure of a man."

"And so dashing. Why, there's an air of excitement about him that is very nearly irresistible." Poppy shivered with ill-concealed delight. "Perhaps the most charming gentleman I have ever met."

Michael paused and glanced at Dulcie. "And have you met this explorer of legendary proportions?"

"No, but I would certainly like to meet him. He sounds quite remarkable." She thought for a moment. "I wonder if Father knows him?"

"He's not in England often," Lady Blodgett said quickly. "This is a rare visit for him."

Michael hesitated. "As you mentioned your father, Miss Middleworth, I should perhaps—"

"I think I see something." Poppy leaned around Michael and peered into the crate. "Do pull it out, Mr. Shepard."

"Very well." Michael plunged his hands into the shaving-filled crate and slowly drew out a wool-wrapped object. He placed it carefully on the table then pulled off the wrapping to reveal a dark granite figure.

It appeared to be a seated baboon, his hands resting on knees spread apart to reveal… Heat washed up Dulcie's face yet she couldn't seem to tear her gaze away. It was really quite…impressive.

Michael cleared his throat. "Ladies, I don't think—"

"Poppy." Lady Blodgett glared at her friend. "This was not the—"

"It's an ancient artifact, for goodness' sake." Effie huffed in exasperation, stepped forward and stuffed a large, lace trimmed handkerchief between the baboon's legs, which tended to emphasize rather than detract. "There." She nodded. "That should take care of that."

"Hardly." Michael frowned. "What are we to do with it?"

"*We* are not going to do anything with it," Lady Blodgett said. "Miss Middleworth is."

Dulcie started. "What am I to do with it?"

"The exhibit isn't for several months but it was thought an excellent idea to produce a program as quickly as possible illustrating some of the artifacts to be displayed." Poppy cast Dulcie a brilliant smile. "And you will be the illustrator. Mr. Everheart requested you himself."

Michael's frown deepened. "Why would he ask for her?"

Dulcie glared. "Thank you, Mr. Shepard."

"She comes highly recommended." Lady Blodgett smiled at Dulcie.

"She's very good, Mr. Shepard," Mrs. Higginbotham said in a chastising manner. "You sit in the same room with her day after day. I'm surprised you don't know that."

"I am well aware of Miss Middleworth's talents," he said staunchly and promptly changed the subject. "Do you know what that is?" He waved at the statue.

"I would say it's a rather enthusiastic baboon." Mrs. Higginbotham's eyes widened with innocence.

Lady Blodgett sighed. "Some sort of Egyptian god, I believe."

"That, ladies, is Babi," Michael began. "He was not

a particularly pleasant sort, called Master of Darkness, among other names. He devoured the souls of the unrighteous and was worshipped for a number of things including—" he paused, unease on his face "—virility."

"Oh, that explains it then," Poppy murmured.

"And while the ancient Egyptians may have revered this creature and his excesses, it's highly improper for Miss Middleworth to draw it." Michael huffed. "She absolutely cannot do this."

"I can, Mr. Shepard." Dulcie glared. "And I intend to. I am a professional illustrator and I assure you I am not so delicate as to faint away at the sight of something carved thousands of years ago regardless of how realistic it may appear."

"Nonetheless, Miss Middleworth, you can see this is not something a respectable woman should do." He squared his shoulders. "It's scandalous, Miss Middleworth, that's what it is. Scandalous."

"I did not expect him to be quite so narrow-minded," Mrs. Higginbotham said under her breath.

"Are you telling me what I can and cannot do?" Dulcie narrowed her eyes. "Again?"

"Someone has to if you are too stubborn to see having anything to do with a statue like this would be detrimental to your reputation and your future." He crossed his arms over his chest. "The cliff, Miss Middleworth, is perilously close to your toes."

"Neither my reputation nor my future nor my toes are any of your concern," she said sharply.

"Come now, Mr. Shepard," Mrs. Higginbotham said firmly. "It's an ancient deity. What we consider improper now was simply part of the world then. Surely this sort of thing is to be expected and tolerated given the historic nature of the artifact. And here." She grabbed the statue and swiveled it to the right. "If she draws him from an angle, or the side perhaps, one won't see the more indiscreet portions of the sculpture."

"I can't imagine any proper gentleman suggesting a young woman do such a thing," he said staunchly. "Which makes me question the wisdom of this Mr. Everheart."

"Oh, he's quite brilliant," Lady Blodgett said.

Mrs. Higginbotham nodded. "And unquestionably courageous."

"And extremely handsome," Poppy added. Then, as one, all three woman heaved heartfelt sighs and adopted the most absurd expressions of adoration.

"Apparently, my opinion counts for nothing," Michael muttered.

"Should it count for something, Mr. Shepard?" Lady Blodgett asked. "It seems to me, you are simply an observer here. Unless of course, you and Miss Middleworth—"

"Absolutely not!" he said.

"Never," she snapped, which was more a reaction to his *absolutely not* than any true feeling on her part. Although, at the moment, with him once again telling her what she could and could not do, she did rather mean it.

"Besides, her affections lie with someone else."

"Actually, they don't." Dulcie smirked.

"They don't?" Suspicion sounded in his voice.

"No."

"But you said…" Confusion drew his brows together. "Never mind. Ladies, if you will excuse me, I have work to resume." He nodded, turned on his heel and marched back to his desk, the very picture of righteous British manhood.

Was the man really incensed about a woman drawing a likeness of an explicit and highly improper ancient statue or was he annoyed that Dulcie was the woman doing that drawing? Regardless, as much as she wasn't sure if she wished to have anything whatsoever to do with Michael ever again, it was an interesting and extremely satisfying idea.

And one well worth considering.

CHAPTER NINE

"OF ALL THE ancient clutter in Charles's storage room, I cannot believe you picked that baboon creature." Gwen glared at Poppy. The ladies had adjourned to the library workroom, making it a point to close and latch the door. It would not do to be overheard or interrupted.

Dulcie had set aside her other work and had already begun preliminary sketches of the immoral baboon. Whether because it was more interesting than the shard of pottery or to annoy Mr. Shepard, Poppy wasn't sure, although she suspected a bit of both. Mr. Shepard had retreated back to his usual table. Both of them were doing their best not to glance for so much as an instant at the other.

"Why, even I can see the impropriety of that," Gwen continued. "Dulcie is obviously an innocent. This will be most embarrassing for her."

"Nonsense, Gwen." Effie scoffed. "The girl is well past twenty and even if she hasn't seen something like that—"

"Oh, I don't believe anyone has seen anything like that," Poppy murmured.

"She can't be totally unaware of male anatomy. This cannot be the first artifact she's seen with exaggerated features. One can stroll any of the ancient galleries at the British Museum and see things far more objectionable. Some of the paintings on Greek pottery are quite explicit. Regardless—" Effie shrugged "—it certainly did not seem to upset her."

"No, she was entirely too busy being annoyed at Mr. Shepard's presumptuous attitude." Poppy turned a firm eye toward Gwen. "Which means my choice was perfect. Something less outrageous might not have produced the same response."

Poppy would prefer not to explain it to her friends but she really hadn't noticed the baboon god's extreme appendage. The light was not good in the storage room and her eyes weren't quite as sharp as they once were—something else she hated to admit. Besides, she'd only seen the sculpture from the back and had wrapped it in the wool immediately to avoid getting dust on her skirt, although it did now strike her that she had wondered why the thing seemed to have a handle. But it was a good size for their purposes and behind other artifacts so probably would not be missed from among the vast array of items Sir Charles had dragged home from his various travels.

Those mementos Gwen deemed acceptable were displayed throughout their house. Those she thought especially odd or ugly, or for which there was simply no space, were relegated to a private storage room off Sir Charles's library. Gwen and Effie had charged Poppy with selecting something appropriate to come from the legendary Reginald Everheart while they wrote a brief biography and a few assorted informational documents that might be found in any member's file to be surreptitiously slipped into the Explorers Club records. Should Mr. Shepard become overly curious in his expected jealousy, there would be a stellar—if brief—account of some of the more intrepid exploits of Reginald Everheart. It really was a shame that the dashing, romantic hero did not exist beyond the fertile realm of Poppy's—and now Gwen's and Effie's—imagination.

Reginald—Poppy always thought of him by his given

name—had sprung into glorious existence more than twenty years ago when Malcolm was reluctant to accept his feelings about Poppy. It was obvious to her that the blasted man just needed a gentle shove or perhaps a firm kick in his posterior region. She was right of course. It really hadn't taken much attention from her imaginary suitor for Malcolm to step up and declare his undying affection. For her part, Poppy promised to give up Reginald as indeed she did. And if, through the years, Malcolm never heard anyone in the Explorers Club mention the name of the incomparable adventurer and if he ever learned of the extraordinary explorer's less than solid existence, he had never felt it necessary to say anything to his wife. The man was far wiser than he appeared and Poppy loved him with her whole heart and soul.

They had already managed to slip Reginald's documentation into the Explorers Club files. It wasn't at all difficult as Mr. Fennell, the club director's secretary, was easily distracted by the latest gossip, a freshly brewed cup of tea and some of Gwen's cook's remarkable biscuits. They also took the opportunity to bring up Reginald's name, feigning shock that Mr. Fennell—who prided himself on knowing everything there was to know about, well, everything—had not heard of Reginald Everheart. They did go on and on in praise of the imaginary hero and by the end of the conversation, Mr. Fennell realized he was indeed familiar with the American explorer but only by reputation as he was so rarely in London. Poppy was fairly certain a few more minutes of conversation with Gwen alone and Mr. Fennell would have been declaring what good friends he and Reginald were.

Poppy didn't think all this was necessary. They were simply trying to make Mr. Shepard realize his feelings for Dulcie. But Effie pointed out, if Mr. Shepard thought for even an instant that Reginald did not exist, it would ruin everything. Why, he would probably think Dulcie herself had a role in this scheme and that would be disastrous. And once Effie agreed to take part in any sort of plot, she did so with the single-minded determination of a general leading troops into battle. The influence of her husband no doubt.

"Still." Gwen's lips pressed together in a chastising line. "You could have chosen something more appropriate and less offensive."

"Well, then you should have paid more attention when Effie secured it in the crate," Poppy said sharply.

Gwen glared. "You had already wrapped it."

"I wanted to protect it." Poppy sniffed. "I would imagine it's extremely valuable. Why, I suspect Sir Charles would be quite upset if any of it was to be chipped or snapped off entirely."

"It will be back in Charles's storage room long before he returns home," Gwen muttered. "Although I daresay he'll never notice it's missing. Still, he does have a strong attachment to all of his souvenirs."

"Regardless, what's done is done," Effie said firmly. "And you're right—as soon as the artifact has served its purpose, and Dulcie and Mr. Shepard have acknowledged their feelings and are walking hand in hand down the path to a happy future, Reginald Everheart will unfortunately be forced to cancel the lecture and exhibit. His baboon will be returned and that will be that."

"I do hope so." Gwen sighed. "And we have at least a month until Mr. Shepard joins his expedition."

"I think it's an excellent plan, brilliant in its simplicity." Poppy thought for a minute. It did seem rather perfect. "I can't imagine it won't be most successful. Indeed, my dear friends, what could possibly go wrong?"

CHAPTER TEN

"THERE YOU ARE." Livy stepped out of the parlor, directly in front of Dulcie. "I was just coming up to speak with you."

"It will have to wait. I'm afraid I lost track of time and you know how Mother is about punctuality, especially when we have guests. Of course, I didn't know you were the guests."

"We were an unexpected, spur-of-the-moment addition."

"Mother hates the unexpected." Dulcie studied her sister curiously. "Why are you here?"

"Why?" Livy's eyes widened.

"You were just here a few nights ago."

Dulcie's sisters and their husbands had already been here once this week for the obligatory weekly family dinner and rarely, if ever, came more often. Their husbands' doing no doubt. Dinner with Mother was frequently something to be survived rather than enjoyed. Mother had an appalling tendency toward letting her daughters and their spouses know when she thought they were not living their lives precisely as she thought they should. Father was a moderating influence although he usually simply muttered and nodded, rarely interceding unless Mother was being particularly outrageous.

"Why?" Livy said again then her expression brightened. "My cook is sick. Yes, that's it. So Thomas and I thought we would join you tonight. Besides, there is nothing I like better than spending time with my parents and beloved younger sister."

Dulcie stared. "Yes, that's what I thought." This was not at all like Livy. "Very well, then we should…" A male voice caught her attention and she peered around her sister to see into the parlor.

Preston sat near the fireplace chatting with someone still out of sight.

"Good Lord." Dulcie groaned. "Mother invited Preston?"

"So it would appear." Livy winced. "I did want to warn you. But I should also tell you—"

Another familiar voice sounded and Dulcie's breath caught. "And is that Michael?"

Livy's brow rose. "You mean Mr. Shepard?"

"Yes." Dulcie leaned farther to the side and spotted Michael in conversation with Father and Livy's husband. The most annoying sense of panic swept through her and she struggled against an irrational need to escape back to her room. It was absurd of course. She had no reason to run. He was the one who had meddled in her business. If anything, he should flee the moment she stepped into the parlor. "What is he doing here?"

"You called him Michael."

"That's his name," Dulcie snapped. "Why is he here?"

"I believe Father invited him for dinner. You know how Father enjoys having those promising young members of the Explorers Club for dinner." Livy smiled in an overly innocent manner. "Does he call you Dulcie, as well?"

"He most certainly does not." Dulcie huffed. "And he doesn't know I think of him as Michael, so I would be grateful if you would keep that to yourself."

"I won't say a word." Livy took her sister's arm and chuckled. "It's going to be an interesting evening."

"I'm glad one of us thinks so." Dulcie drew a calming breath and let her sister escort her into the room.

"There you are at last." Mother's welcoming smile belied the gleam of triumph in her eyes. "Mr. Drummond has agreed to join us tonight."

"And I understand you already know Mr. Shepard," Father said. "He tells me the two of you have encountered each other at the Explorers Club."

Dulcie nodded weakly. She wasn't sure what to say. What could she say? Here was one man she wanted nothing whatsoever to do with and another she, well, wanted.

Preston and Michael both started toward her but Livy took a quick step to effectively block Preston's approach. Dulcie could have kissed her.

Michael reached her, took her hand and gazed into her eyes. "You're looking lovely this evening, Miss Middleworth."

The oddest shiver of heat ran from his hand up her arm and wrapped around her heart. They had never so much as inadvertently brushed each other's hands before. A tiny voice in the back of her head noted how perfectly her hand fit in his.

"Thank you," she said faintly.

Mother's brow arched upward. Dulcie never said anything faintly. Mother cleared her throat and Michael reluctantly—or at least it seemed reluctant to Dulcie—released her hand.

"You arrived just in time. Dinner was announced a moment ago." Mother glanced pointedly at Preston. "Mr. Drummond if you would be so good as to escort—"

"Me," Livy said brightly. "Why, Mr. Drummond and I never have a chance to talk."

Thomas frowned in confusion. "We're only going into the dining room."

"And you should escort Mother." Livy aimed a hard look at her husband.

Thomas hesitated then mustered a convincing smile. "It would be my pleasure." He offered his arm. "Shall we, Mother?"

Mother did not look happy even if she managed to keep a smile on her face. "How delightful, Thomas."

"Which leaves my youngest daughter to you, Mr. Shepard." Father had obviously taken an instant liking to Michael, or perhaps he'd rather see her on the arm of anyone but Preston. Or he might just enjoy annoying Mother. Father chuckled and followed the others.

Michael offered Dulcie his arm. "Miss Middleworth?"

She took his arm and tried not to swoon at the feel of his hard muscles beneath the fabric of his coat. This was ridiculous. She had never swooned in her life.

"What are you doing here?" she said under her breath.

"I was invited."

"Why didn't you tell me?"

"I tried," he said smoothly.

"Not hard enough."

"I could leave if you'd prefer." He paused. "After all, Mr. Drummond is here."

"Don't be absurd."

He chuckled and she had an almost irresistible urge to smack him.

The evening was not nearly as awkward as she had expected. Certainly Mother was annoyed that her obvious plan to push Preston's suit was not going as she had intended, given there were three more people at dinner than she had expected, but Mother was nothing if not the consummate hostess. She was at all times gracious and charming, chatting as much with Michael as she did with Preston although she missed no opportunity to point out what an exceptional man Preston was. Michael, as well as everyone else at the table with the possible exception of Preston himself, realized Mother's intentions when they were still on the first course. Every now and then his gaze would catch Dulcie's and his wonderful, stormy eyes would twinkle with amusement behind his spectacles.

Dinner was something of a revelation. The conversation around the table ranged from scientific discoveries to Trollope's latest work to keen and often amusing observations about various members of parliament and the government itself. Certainly, she knew Michael had a fine mind from the discussions she'd witnessed in the library but she had no idea he was witty and amusing, as well. He'd always seemed so very serious. It was obvious that Father, as well as Thomas and Livy, were taken with him. Even Mother and Preston appeared to enjoy the evening. This was a Michael she'd never met before, relaxed and friendly and utterly charming.

Mother did her best to steer the conversation to subjects of mutual interest—as she insisted any good hostess would—and they had nearly finished dinner when talk inevitably turned to the Explorers Club.

"I understand you'll be joining the new Amazon expedition next month," Father said to Michael.

"The details are not entirely set as to a departure date but I do hope so, sir," Michael said. "I am quite looking forward to it."

"I can't imagine why anyone would want to wander around a hot, nasty jungle filed with all sorts of vile creatures." Mother shuddered. "Why do you?"

"Curiosity, the lure of the unknown, that sort of thing." Michael chuckled but his eyes gleamed with sincerity.

"There is much man has not yet discovered about the Amazon and the world around it."

"But surely a man doesn't just wake up one day and say, 'I'm off to explore the jungle'?" Genuine interest sounded in Mother's voice.

"I've wanted to do this since I was a boy. I've never wanted to do anything else." Michael paused. "My uncle Henry was an explorer. He taught me to navigate by the stars, to find true north and filled my head with stories of adventure and excitement. He vanished on an expedition to the Amazon when I was ten years of age. My family never knew his fate. After all this time, the possibility of finding any trace of him is futile, but one never knows. I could be lucky." Michael smiled and took a sip of wine.

"How very thoughtful of you, Mr. Shepard," Mother said softly, something that sounded suspiciously like admiration in her voice.

"As we are now apparently on the topic of explorers—" Michael turned to Father "—I was wondering, Lord Middleworth, if you are familiar with a Mr. Reginald Everheart? I understand he's quite accomplished in global exploration."

"He's American," Dulcie said.

"Everheart?" Father drew his brows together and thought for a moment. "It does sound familiar."

"It certainly is a perfect name for a heroic explorer. Reginald Everheart." Livy said the name slowly as if savoring the sound of it. "Why, it fairly screams of daring adventure and dashing exploits. I daresay, a man with that name would probably be quite handsome, as well."

Dulcie nodded. "He is reputed to be a fine figure of a man."

"I knew it." Livy grinned.

"Perhaps I should change my name to something more

adventurous and exciting," Thomas said wryly, staring at his wife.

"Nonsense. I can't think of anything more exciting or adventurous than Thomas, Lord Carswell." Livy flashed him a smile that struck Dulcie as a bit more than merely affectionate. But then they did have three children.

Dulcie glanced at Michael and for no more than the briefest moment, his gaze met hers with a look of utter longing and desire so intense her heart stuttered in her chest. It was over nearly as quickly as it had begun but was long enough. Dulcie knew as surely as she had ever known anything in her life, knew as if he'd said the words aloud, without question, without doubt.

The man did indeed have *certain feelings* for her.

Then why on earth didn't he do something about it?

"Lady Blodgett was talking about him today," Michael said, as if the world had not just shifted off its axis and was now spinning wildly out of control. "Apparently, he's rarely in London but is to give a lecture here sometime in the future. They were rather vague about the details. Lady Blodgett, Mrs. Higginbotham and Mrs. Fitzhew-Wellmore said Mr. Everheart is quite well-known although I confess I have never heard of him."

"I have never paid the least bit of attention to such things," Mother said, "but the name sounds familiar to me, as well. Perhaps he's joined us for dinner?"

"It's that sort of name, Mother." Livy shrugged. "Why, you couldn't have invented a better name for an explorer."

"Still." Father shook his head. "I find it most annoying that I cannot place the man. I didn't think there was an accomplished explorer alive who was unknown to me."

"According to Lady Blodgett, Sir Charles thinks quite highly of him." Michael frowned. "I must confess, I too am bothered that I cannot recollect—"

"I know him," Preston blurted.

At once all eyes turned toward Preston.

"Or rather I've met him. At a lecture, I believe. It was a long time ago," he added in an offhand manner.

Preston had an annoying tendency to proclaim himself acquainted with every well-known personage whose name might crop up. Dulcie would have wagered her favorite gown that Preston had never so much as been in the illustrious explorer's presence.

"Have you indeed, Mr. Drummond?" Thomas said with a cool curiosity. Apparently, now that Dulcie had made it clear Preston would not be joining the family, Thomas no longer felt it necessary to be anything more than polite. "Do tell us about him. What is he like?"

"Modest," Preston said without hesitation. "And quite humble. He never speaks of his accomplishments."

"Unless he's lecturing, of course." Dulcie cast Preston an overly innocent smile. "What was his lecture on?"

"Oh, you know. The usual topics well-known explorers expound upon. The unexpected pitfalls one can encounter. The need to be thoroughly prepared, that sort of thing." He shook his head in regret. "It was a long time ago and I'm afraid I really can't remember specific details. But I do recall he was most impressive."

"Is he married?" Mother asked. A man's marital status was always the most important point to Mother.

"The ladies said he was a widower, Mother." Dulcie thought for a moment. "They mentioned something about his wife being lost in a jungle."

Mother's brow furrowed. "How very inconsiderate of her."

"And precisely the reason why men pursuing the great unknown do not bring wives with them on such excursions," Preston said in that all-knowing manner he had.

"It's dangerous enough for a man but for a fragile, delicate creature…" He shuddered at the mere thought of it.

"Come now, Mr. Drummond." Dulcie adopted a casual tone. "Not all of us are fragile, delicate flowers. I know any number of women who would do quite well on an expedition to a jungle or a desert."

"Nonsense." He scoffed. "Women do not fare well in primitive conditions. Why, when Mrs. Livingstone went to Africa simply to meet her husband, it cost her her life."

"I believe she died of malaria," Father said.

"I daresay we are all exposed to equally deadly diseases every day when we walk the streets of London," Dulcie noted. She wasn't at all sure why she was pursuing this—she had never really considered women going on expeditions but the idea was surprisingly appealing. "I scarcely think the threat of illness is a good reason to keep women from accompanying their husbands if they so wish."

"I fear I must agree with Mr. Drummond on this point." Michael nodded. "Ladies have no place on journeys that take them beyond the reach of the civilized world."

"Then you would never bring a wife along on any kind of exciting venture?" Livy asked.

"Absolutely not," Michael said firmly.

Livy nodded. "You would leave your wife safely at home?"

"Without question but it's rather a moot point, Lady Carswell," Michael said slowly, "as I have no intention of ever marrying."

"Ever?" Mother looked as if she had just been slapped. Hard.

"No."

Dulcie's stomach lurched.

Mother's eyes widened. "Why on earth not?"

"A number of reasons." He paused and studied his plate for a moment then looked at Mother, steadfastly avoiding Dulcie's gaze. "My aunt Grace lived with us after my mother died because my uncle was so rarely at home. I still distinctly remember how hard it was for her to say goodbye to him, never knowing when or if he would return. And then, of course, he didn't. Until the day she died, she never gave up hoping that he would come back to her. That hope sustained her but ultimately hastened her death."

"Oh my," Livy murmured.

He shook his head. "I could not do that to a woman I cared for. The life I have chosen, one of exploration and discovery, requires commitment as well as personal sacrifice. I expect to be gone from England more than I am here. It seems neither right nor fair to pledge my life to someone and then go off and leave her to fend for herself."

"Excellent reasoning, Mr. Shepard," Father said thoughtfully. "I think that's wise of you."

"I think it's stupid," Dulcie said before she could stop herself. Michael's gaze shot to hers. "And somewhat cowardly."

Michael's brows drew together.

"Come now, Miss Middleworth," Preston said in a chastising manner that set her teeth on edge. "That's a bit harsh, don't you think?"

Dulcie's gaze remained locked with Michael's. "The truth is often harsh, Mr. Drummond. Don't you think so, Mr. Shepard?"

Michael nodded. "And exceptionally difficult to accept."

"Perhaps if one had more than just the courage of one's convictions—"

Mother gasped.

"If one had faith in, well, in love, the truth might be entirely different." Dulcie shrugged. "If, of course, one had the courage to follow one's heart."

"Or perhaps—" Michael's words were measured "—if one was selfish enough to think only of oneself. I have always thought the very definition of love was caring more for someone else than you do for yourself. Being willing to sacrifice your own happiness for the sake of someone else."

"It has been my observation that unyielding adherence to any particular position, no matter how noble the intentions, Mr. Shepard," she said in a hard tone, "rarely results in happiness. Mr. Dickens's Sydney Carton had the noblest of intentions and yet the saddest of lives."

"Do you think Mr. Everheart is in London now?" Livy said without warning, abruptly changing the subject.

Dulcie's gaze shot to her sister's and a warning shone in Livy's eyes. Dulcie drew a deep breath and managed a pleasant smile. "Do forgive me, Mr. Shepard. I'm afraid I am overly fond of a good debate. Even if the topic is not one I have a particular interest in."

He stared at her for a moment and smiled slowly. "It was my pleasure, Miss Middleworth."

A minute later Mother declared dinner at an end and the ladies took their leave. Preston hurried into the gallery after them. "Dulcie."

She turned toward him. "Yes."

He moved close and spoke low into her ear. "I think we should talk."

"If you'd like a moment," Mother said hopefully, "you can join us in the parlor when you're finished."

"I'll wait for her," Livy said with a pleasant smile. "I'll

just sit over here." She moved to a bench along the wall a few feet away and sat down. "You go on ahead, Mother."

A distinct look of defeat crossed Mother's face and she sighed. "No, I'll wait, as well." She joined Livy and the two of them pretended not to listen.

"We have nothing to talk about, Preston," Dulcie said quietly.

"Of course we do." He frowned. "I realized after I left the other night that you couldn't possibly have meant what you said, and your mother agreed."

"On the contrary, Preston, I meant every word of it." The man was nothing if not persistent. She braced herself. "However, you apparently did not."

"I said nothing I do not stand behind," he said staunchly.

"I believe you said if you walked out the door you would not return. And yet—" she shrugged "—here you are."

"I was invited."

"Not by me."

His eyes narrowed. "Your mother knows what a mistake you are making."

"And yet, it is my mistake to make."

"Very well then." He sniffed. "I regret to inform you, Miss Middleworth, that any further involvement between the two of us is at an end."

"I shall try to bravely carry on."

He huffed, turned on his heel and strode down the gallery to the entry where a well-trained footman showed him the door.

She stared after him and released a long breath. "How much of that did you hear?"

"You were speaking exceptionally low," Livy said, "but I think we managed to hear most of it."

She turned toward her Mother. "Mother—"

"Don't say a word." Mother held out her hand in a long suffering manner. "I cannot believe—" she shook her head "—what an ass that man is."

Dulcie and Livy stared.

"Are you all right?" Livy asked cautiously.

"Quite, thank you dear." She met Dulcie's gaze. "You have my utter and sincere apology. The man seemed so, well, perfect for you." She heaved a disbelieving sigh. "But he's an ass."

"Mother!" Dulcie bit back a gasp. Mother did not use words like *ass*.

"I just don't want you to be alone. I can't imagine your being alone for the rest of your life." She paused. "Your father and I drive each other quite mad nearly every day but I could not bear my life without him."

"I understand and I do appreciate the thought but—"

A familiar light lit in Mother's eyes. "Perhaps Mr. Shepard…"

"Mother!"

"I saw the way you looked at one another. I thought nothing of it at the time." She glanced at Livy. "I attributed it to something in the cream sauce, but in hindsight…" She narrowed her eyes thoughtfully.

"I would appreciate it if you would not continue to throw me in the path of every man who wanders by." Dulcie glared.

"Nonsense." Mother waved off the comment. "Not every man. That would be absurd." She paused. "Every suitable man perhaps."

Dulcie's jaw tightened.

"It's a pity Mr. Shepard's family is not titled." Mother sighed. "I did so want titles for all of my girls. But I suppose your choices are getting limited."

"Mother!"

"His family is rich," Livy pointed out.

Mother brightened. "There is that."

"Stop it! Both of you!" Dulcie huffed and glanced into the dining room. The gentlemen were paying them no attention. Good. She really didn't want either Michael or Father to hear this.

She crossed her arms over her chest and addressed her mother in her best no-nonsense manner. "You will not set your sights on Mr. Shepard—"

Livy nudged her mother wither her elbow. "She already calls him Michael."

"Neither of you." Her jaw tightened. While she was hopeful that he did indeed share her feelings, she had no wish to share that particular fact. "As for you." She pinned her sister with a hard look. "Why was Mr. Shepard of all people invited to dinner here? Tonight?"

"I suppose it's because Father likes to invite young men who are following in the footsteps of men he admires." Livy adopted an overly innocent manner.

"Why Mr. Shepard?"

"I would imagine Father received some sort of recommendation."

Dulcie narrowed her eyes. "From you?"

"Me?" Livy scoffed. Dulcie didn't believe her for a moment. "I don't belong to Father's club."

"I'm quite serious about this." Dulcie's gaze shifted between her mother and her sister. "I don't want either of you interfering. Mr. Shepard and I are friends of a sort, nothing more. And you heard him—he does not intend to marry."

Mother sniffed. "Utter nonsense."

"Men change their minds all the time." Livy shrugged. "They're worse than we are."

Mother looked past her then rose to her feet. "I believe the gentlemen are about to join us."

Father stepped into the gallery, followed by Thomas and Michael.

"We decided to have our brandy in the parlor with the ladies," Father said. "Unfortunately, Mr. Shepard has to be on his way."

"I'm afraid so." He nodded a bow to Mother. "Lady Middleworth, thank you for your gracious hospitably." He turned to Father. "It was a most engaging evening, my lord. Thank you for the invitation."

"You should plan on joining us again." Father smiled and directed the group toward the parlor then paused. "Dulcie, please see our guest to the door." He nodded and proceeded to the parlor.

"Of course," Dulcie murmured.

Mother cast an anxious look at her youngest daughter then followed Father, Livy and Thomas in her wake.

Dulcie walked Michael to the entry then turned to him. "I'll not apologize for what I said."

He chuckled. "I did not expect you to. Although you did call me a coward. Again."

"And indeed, while one can be terribly brave when it comes to facing physical peril, matters of, well, the heart are something else entirely." She gazed up at him. In spite of the discreet presence of a well-trained footman in the shadows near the door, with very little effort Michael could pull her into his arms and kiss her. It would be highly improper and yet… Her pulse quickened. Would he?

"Matters of the heart?" His gaze met hers and the longing she'd seen at dinner was back, no doubt matching her own. "I suspect, Miss Middleworth, those are far more dangerous than anything one might encounter in even the most treacherous of environments."

"Do you have that sort of courage, Mr. Shepard?" Her voice had the oddest breathless quality to it.

"Excellent question, Miss Middleworth." His gaze slipped to her lips then back to her eyes. "Unfortunately, when it comes to matters of the heart, one cannot think only of one's own desires. Therefore, one must maintain the courage of one's convictions."

"Michael." She moved closer. There was no more than a breath of air between them. "I would—"

The clock in the hall chimed and the moment shattered.

Michael cleared his throat. "Once again, allow me to thank you and your family for a most enjoyable evening." He nodded and moved toward the door. The footman immediately sprang into view, handed Michael his hat, then opened the door.

"Mr. Shepard?"

He paused and glanced at her. "Yes?"

"Will you be in the library tomorrow?"

"I'm not sure it isn't wiser for me to continue my studies elsewhere." He blew a resigned breath. "But yes, I will be there."

She smiled slowly. "Good evening, Mr. Shepard."

"Miss Middleworth." He nodded and took his leave.

Her smile lingered long after the door had closed.

The footman bit back a grin.

She raised a brow. "Something to say, Miles?"

"The staff was not at all fond of Mr. Drummond, miss."

"And you like Mr. Shepard?"

"He is not Mr. Drummond, miss."

"Something to be grateful for indeed, Miles." She

smiled and slowly headed toward the parlor. She had a great deal to think about.

The man cared for her. There wasn't a doubt in her mind. The only thing holding him back was his principles, his belief that his ambitions in life were unfair to her.

If she truly loved this man, and she had no doubt about that either, why should she wait for him to do something? She was a capable, competent woman who could surely make him see he was entirely wrong not to acknowledge his feelings. Why, the best thing in the world for any man would be to have a wife. Whether or not that wife accompanied him, even in part, to the far recesses of the world was another question altogether and one that did not have to be considered at the moment. Now, she simply had to convince Michael to follow his heart rather than his handsome, bespectacled head. She wasn't entirely certain how to do that but something would come to mind.

It was hard to fault a man for wanting to save a woman from the sorrow his aunt knew. For being too noble and gallant.

And very hard not to love him.

CHAPTER ELEVEN

DULCIE WAS ALREADY in the library, sketching the indecent baboon, when Michael arrived. She was spending entirely more time with this illustration than one would think necessary. He could have been here much earlier, it wasn't as if he had slept, but it was impossible to get their exchange last night out of his head.

Was he really a coward when it came to matters of affection? Was his adherence to his principles nothing more than a way to avoid entanglement and possible heartbreak? Didn't she realize keeping his distance from her was the hardest thing he had ever done?

Of course not. How could she possibly know how he felt about her? He'd been extremely vigilant in keeping his feelings to himself. Aside from a moment last night when her gaze had caught his unexpectedly and then another where he had come very close to kissing her, he'd managed to avoid letting his feelings show in any way. It wasn't easy but kissing her would have been a dreadful mistake. One kiss with Dulcie Middleworth would surely lead to another and then he would be lost. Better not to know exactly what he was missing.

And, when it came right down to it, he had no idea how she might feel about him. Did she really think his determination to avoid involvement with a woman was stupid and lacking in courage? Were her comments prompted only by her enjoyment of a good debate or was there more to it? She did call him Michael after all. Was it a mere slip of the tongue or something much more significant?

He stopped at his usual table and she glanced at him with a smile one could only call radiant. His heart sped up. The least he could do was say good morning. Good morning was not a commitment. He was halfway across the room before he realized he was grinning like an idiot. He sobered immediately. Perhaps he was indeed a coward but he still believed avoiding romantic entanglement to be best for all concerned. Now, he simply had to make that clear to Dulcie. And apparently to his rebellious heart, as well.

"Good day, Mr. Shepard," she said brightly, rising to her feet, the faint, delightful scent of exotic flowers and spice drifting past him. Her blue eyes twinkled with welcome.

"Good day, Miss Middleworth." Good God. He had no idea what to say now. It wasn't as if he hadn't practiced any number of things in the long, sleepless hours of the night but at the moment absolutely nothing came to mind. All he could do was stare like an idiot. "Fine weather we're having."

Amusement flashed in her eyes. "Indeed we are."

"Miss Middleworth." He drew a deep breath. "About last night…"

"Lovely evening don't you think?"

He nodded. "Yes, it was but—"

"You should join us again sometime."

"Perhaps but…"

"Yes?" She smiled up at him.

"I think we should talk about last night. About, well, you and me."

Her brow rose. "You and me?"

"I thought perhaps you might have gotten the impression…that is, that I…" He studied her with a growing sense of horror. "But you didn't, did you?"

She stared at him as if he were daft. "Apparently not as I have no idea what you are talking about."

Hot humiliation washed through him. Just because he felt the way he did did not mean she shared his feelings. "My apologies then, Miss Middleworth." He nodded and started toward his table.

How could he have been so stupid? Certainly, he didn't have a vast amount of experience with women although he was not completely inexperienced either. But then he had never before known anyone who made his head spin and his blood pound. And as much as it was for the best, he couldn't help regretting that he did not kiss her last night. The way she had looked at him… He pulled up short, swiveled and strode back to her.

"I nearly kissed you last night." He glared at her.

Dulcie frowned thoughtfully. "Did you?"

"I did and you well know it."

Dulcie shook her head slowly. "I really don't recall."

"Of course you recall." He refused to believe something that had kept him up all night was not worth remembering.

"Perhaps…"

"And I am fairly certain, Miss Middleworth—" he rested his hands on the table and leaned forward "—you would have kissed me back."

"Goodness, Michael." She shook her head and sighed. "Indeed I would have."

He frowned. "You would have?"

"And with a great deal of enthusiasm I suspect."

"Then I must tell you—" he straightened and squared his shoulders "—that it would have been a dreadful mistake."

"I know."

"What?" He stared. Dulcie Middleworth might well be the most confusing creature he had ever met.

"While last night I would have indeed kissed you back and no doubt thoroughly enjoyed every moment, fortunately for us both, I have given this a great deal of thought since then." She clasped her hands together in front of her in a manner entirely too prim for this type of discussion. "And I agree with you."

"About what?" Caution edged his voice.

"About your resolve not to marry." She smiled. "The more one thinks about it, the more it makes a great deal of sense."

"It does?" He cleared his throat. "Of course it does."

"Well, I began thinking about poor Mrs. Livingstone and then of course the roses—" Dulcie waved at a vase behind her filled to overflowing with roses "—reminded me of Mrs. Everheart's unfortunate demise."

"Why would an extravagant display of roses remind you of Mrs. Everheart?" He wasn't sure he wanted to hear the answer.

"Because they're from Mr. Everheart of course." She gazed at the roses with admiration. "They were here when I arrived along with a lovely note."

"Why would he send you flowers?"

"In appreciation for my work." Her gaze remained on the flowers and she sighed. "Wasn't that thoughtful of him?"

Michael wasn't sure what he'd call it but he was fairly sure it wouldn't be *thoughtful*. "He hasn't seen your work. How could he appreciate it?"

"I don't know nor do I care." She plucked a rose from the vase, held it to her nose and inhaled deeply. "The note that accompanied the flowers was extremely flattering and rather romantic."

"Romantic?" His brow rose in disbelief. "How can a note from a man you've never met be romantic?"

"I have no idea. And yet…" She sighed. Again. "It was."

"Utter rubbish." He snorted. "And would you please stop sighing like a lovesick schoolgirl. It's most unbecoming."

"Goodness, Michael." Her eyes widened innocently. "One would think you were jealous."

"Hardly," he muttered. "Enjoy your flowers, Miss Middleworth." He nodded, turned and strode to his table.

Jealous? Ha! Why on earth would he be jealous? Yes, he was in love with the blasted woman, but that was even more reason why he should do all that he could to make sure her life was happy.

But Reginald Everheart? She had never met the man. Certainly Mrs. Fitzhew-Wellmore spoke well of him, but for any woman to have the look in her eyes that Dulcie did from nothing more than a charming note and a pretentious array of posies was utterly absurd.

He sank into his chair a moment before Mrs. Fitzhew-Wellmore, Lady Blodgett and Mrs. Higginbotham sailed into the library. Good. He got to his feet. Who better to ask about the character of this Everheart than people who actually knew him.

"Good morning, Mr. Shepard." Lady Blodgett nodded as she and her friends breezed past him. "My goodness, what lovely roses!"

The other ladies responded with exclamations of out-of-proportion delight and headed toward the flowers with the single-mindedness of bees to, well, flowers. Until this very moment, Michael had never realized how very different women were from men, from normal people.

He followed after the ladies. "Mrs. Fitzhew-Wellmore?"

She stopped and turned. "Yes, Mr. Shepard?"

He lowered his voice. "I was curious about Mr. Everheart. He's never even met Miss Middleworth and yet he has been so presumptuous as to send her—"

"The roses are from Mr. Everheart?" The older woman's eyes widened in delight. "How exciting."

"Exciting?"

"Yes, of course. When a man sends a woman roses, it is a clear indication of his intentions." She leaned close in a confidential manner. "Mr. Everheart is an eminently eligible bachelor—handsome with fame and fortune. Why, a woman could scarcely do better. And younger women marry older men all the time."

"How much older?"

"It scarcely matters when love is involved."

"Love?" He choked. "How can love possibly be involved when he's never met her?"

"And you never talk to her." She smiled pleasantly, moved to greet Dulcie and join her friends in excessive admiration of the ostentatious floral arrangement.

Being older and hopefully wiser, one would think Mrs. Fitzhew-Wellmore and the other ladies would be less taken in by such an unoriginal ploy on Everheart's part to work his way into Dulcie's affections. But apparently women, regardless of age, disregarded rationality when it came to flamboyant gestures.

"Lady Blodgett." A voice rang over the room from the doorway. "And Mrs. Fitzhew-Wellmore and Mrs. Higginbotham, as well." Mrs. Lithgow, the head of the Ladies Committee, swept into the room like a force of nature. "Just the people I wished to see."

Mrs. Higginbotham wisely threw her shawl over the baboon and moved to block it from sight. Michael discreetly stepped out of the way of Mrs. Lithgow's approach, as was the universal advice from the majority of club members regarding Mrs. Lithgow.

"Mr. Shepard," she said in passing, her gaze focused on the ladies in front of her. "I need to speak with you on a matter of some importance."

"Really, Margaret?" Lady Blodgett's brow arched. "A matter of some importance."

"Yes, I understand—" Mrs. Lithgow paused. "Roses, Miss Middleworth? For you?"

Dulcie nodded.

"From Reginald Everheart," Mrs. Fitzhew-Wellmore said, and the three older ladies sighed in unison.

"Most impressive." Lithgow studied the flowers with a calculating eye. "Three dozen if I'm not mistaken."

"Five would have been too many." Mrs. Higginbotham shrugged.

"And one not nearly enough." Lady Blodgett studied the arrangement with the oddest look of satisfaction. "Three is perfect."

"Do you know him well, Miss Middleworth?" A thoughtful note sounded in Mrs. Lithgow's voice.

"In truth, Mrs. Lithgow, we have never met." Dulcie gazed at the roses—apparently it was her turn to sigh. "But I am looking forward to meeting him in person."

"Pity. That you haven't met that is." Mrs. Lithgow turned to the other ladies. "But I understand you are well acquainted with the eminent American."

"Indeed we are," Mrs. Fitzhew-Wellmore said proudly.

"Excellent." Mrs. Lithgow smiled with satisfaction. The ladies traded cautious glances.

"Once I learned that Mr. Everheart was making one of his rare appearances in London, it seemed to me the Explorers Club would be remiss if we did not seize the opportunity to pay tribute to such an illustrious honorary member. He is exceptionally accomplished," Mrs. Lithgow said in an aside to Michael. "His member file is quite extraordinary."

"Thank you," Mrs. Higginbotham said faintly.

Mrs. Lithgow continued. "I'm fairly certain he was quite good friends with my first husband although I don't remember ever meeting him myself." Her brow furrowed in a puzzled frown. "Indeed, I can't recall hearing much about him at all even if his name is quite familiar."

"These things happen with age, Margaret," Lady Blodgett said in an overly patronizing manner given she and Mrs. Lithgow did appear to be contemporaries. "Did Mr. Fennell say anything else?"

"Fennell," Mrs. Fitzhew-Wellmore said under her breath. "Of course."

"Only that he had heard Mr. Everheart is to give a lecture here in a few months. Unfortunately, we could not find it noted on the club calendar." Mrs. Lithgow's lips pursed in disapproval. Michael didn't know the woman but the consensus among the membership was that she was not to be crossed. Woe be it to whomever had left Everheart's lecture off the sacred calendar. "That will be rectified soon enough." She smiled. "If you will be so good as to give me the name of his hotel—"

"No!" Mrs. Fitzhew-Wellmore eyes widened. "Absolutely not. We can't. We simply can't."

"What Poppy is trying to say," Lady Blodgett said smoothly, "is that Mr. Everheart guards his privacy fiercely. He would quite frankly never forgive any of us for giving away his residence in London. Even to you. We are sorry."

"But I must reach him." Mrs. Lithgow huffed and glanced at Dulcie. "Was there a note on the roses? Perhaps there was the name of a flower shop that we might inquire at?"

"There wasn't." Mrs. Higginbotham smirked in an oddly satisfied way.

"There was a note but nothing to indicate what shop the roses came from." Dulcie hesitated. "It does seem to me, Mrs. Lithgow, if Mr. Everheart prefers his privacy we should respect his wishes."

"Yes, I suppose." Mrs. Lithgow tapped her foot impatiently. "Regardless, I must get word to him. I'm sure you are all aware of the quarterly membership banquet next week."

The ladies nodded.

"We thought that would be the perfect opportunity to honor Mr. Everheart. Why, everyone in the entire club is already talking about his presence in London. As you well know, he's quite famous." Mrs. Lithgow fairly glowed with triumph. "It shall be an unforgettable evening. An unqualified success."

Mrs. Higginbotham choked.

"You and Mr. Fennell decided this?" Lady Blodgett asked.

"And the director agreed." Mrs. Lithgow shook her head. "Although he too had a difficult time placing Mr. Everheart."

"I often find it hard to remember Americans," Mrs. Fitzhew-Wellmore said helpfully. "They are all so interchangeable."

"Yes, well, in the director's case I would indeed attribute it to age." She thought for a moment. "At the very least, I do need to have a note delivered to him."

"We can deliver it for you." Mrs. Higginbotham smiled. "He is joining us for dinner tonight."

"Oh?" A calculating look shone in Mrs. Lithgow's eyes. "Perhaps I should pay a call—"

"Or rather *we* are joining *him*," Lady Blodgett said.

"I see." Mrs. Lithgow heaved a sigh of surrender. "Then if you would deliver the note?"

"It would be our pleasure." Mrs. Fitzhew-Wellmore beamed.

A minute later Mrs. Lithgow took her leave and Michael was finally able to escape back to his usual table. It struck him as exceptionally odd that, while Reginald Everheart's name was familiar to nearly everyone, no one—with the exception of Mrs. Fitzhew-Wellmore and her friends—could recall actually meeting the man. Oh, Drummond claimed to have met him but Drummond claimed at least a passing acquaintance with every notable personage in existence.

There was something extremely odd about a man with an outstanding reputation that no one could remember. Perhaps there was something in his file that would shed light on the mysterious American. Explorers Club files were not freely available to members but they were not especially guarded either.

In spite of Dulcie's claim, this wasn't jealously. Far from it. If he truly cared for her, the least he could do was make certain this man was not some sort of aging charlatan who was no doubt determined to lead her down a path to ruin. No, indeed. Even if Michael could not claim Dulcie's heart, he was not about to let a man obviously unworthy of her work his way into her affections. This was yet another cliff he would not let her step off. She deserved better. It was up to him to make certain she had a chance at better.

Even if it killed him.

CHAPTER TWELVE

"I DO HOPE someone has a good idea." Poppy paced the floor of Gwen's parlor. After Mrs. Lithgow's announcement yesterday about honoring Reginald, they had agreed to ponder their predicament separately then meet after church today to decide their next step. Poppy wasn't sure about her friends but she did request a bit of divine intervention during the interminably long sermon. Indeed, she and the Almighty had had a lengthy one-sided chat. Poppy assumed he had bigger things on his mind and was not simply ignoring her as she left St. Anne's without being struck by any kind of answer. "No, good is not enough. It will have to be brilliant."

Gwen and Effie traded serene looks.

Poppy narrowed her eyes. "You already have a plan, don't you?"

"Not exactly a plan," Effie said. "But we do have an idea. Which is the start of any good plan."

"And we do have a little bit of time," Gwen added. "Admittedly, far less than we thought we'd have."

"I believe things are going quite well with Dulcie and Mr. Shepard," Effie said thoughtfully.

Poppy nodded. "He did seem to find the flowers most annoying."

"I think another artifact or two for her to draw would further incite him." Effie shot Poppy a firm look. "Gwen and I will select them."

Poppy shrugged.

"Another heartfelt note, perhaps more." Gwen paused. "Even better—an invitation."

"To the banquet." Poppy brightened. "What an excellent idea. But..." She winced. "He won't actually be attending the banquet because, well, you know..."

"Because he's not real, you mean?" Gwen asked.

"There is that..."

"Therein lies our problem." Gwen sighed. "The original plan was, once Dulcie and Mr. Shepard had accepted their feelings, to send Everheart off to the ends of the earth—"

"If not farther," Effie murmured.

"Cancel his lecture and that would be that. Now, however, we have only a few days to bring them together." Gwen grimaced. "And do something about Everheart."

Effie glanced at Gwen. "We do think we have come up with a solution."

"Excellent." Poppy perched on one of Gwen's overstuffed arm chairs. "Go on then, what is it?"

"Well..." Gwen's brow furrowed as if the words were somehow painful. "You see, we were thinking... And it does seem...well..."

"Oh for goodness' sake, Gwen." Effie huffed. "Just spit it out." She turned to Poppy. "We're going to have to kill him."

"What!" Poppy leaped from her chair. "You can't!"

"Don't be absurd." Effie scoffed. "We most certainly can."

"No," Poppy wailed. "We can't!"

"Do sit down, Poppy." Gwen sighed. "Why can't we kill him?"

"Because he's mine."

"Nonsense." Effie studied her curiously. "You do understand he doesn't exist, don't you?"

"Yes, I know that." Poppy sank back into the chair. "But he holds a special place in my life, in my heart. I don't want to see him go."

"It's for the best, dear." Gwen leaned over and patted Poppy's hand. "There really isn't another way to get out of this. You heard Margaret—everyone is already talking about Everheart."

"Can't we just send him away?" Poppy said hopefully. "To a remote jungle or a far distant desert or, I know. On a quest for the North Pole."

"I'm afraid it would be entirely too suspicious if he were to up and leave on some sort of heretofore unmentioned exploration." Gwen shook her head.

"Far too many people know about him now," Effie pointed out. "As long as he exists there exists, as well, the possibility he—*we*—will be found out. That's not the sort of gossip that easily goes away. And when your husband next goes to the club..."

A chill ran up Poppy's spine. She would prefer Malcolm never know of Reginald's imaginary state.

"No, he needs to go permanently," Gwen added. "And we need to make his demise as plausible as possible."

"We promise to give him a hero's death," Effie said, the most inappropriate note of eagerness in her voice. "Something fearless and noble."

"No!" It scarcely mattered what Poppy said. They had already made up their minds and there was little she could do to stop them.

"Don't you think he'd rather leave this world in a daring display of courage and valor than simply fade away?" Effie shook her head in a mournful manner. "That would be dreadfully sad for a legendary hero like Reginald Everheart."

"Regardless." Poppy squared her shoulders and glared. "I don't want him killed."

Gwen and Effie traded glances.

"Fine." Gwen sighed. "If you come up with something better, we're willing to listen to it. But there is not much time. Today is Sunday and the banquet is on Friday."

"Which means Everheart has to die by Wednesday," Effie said firmly. "Thursday morning at the latest."

"I'll think of something not requiring death no later than Thursday morning then." Her friends were right, there wasn't much time. But Reginald had come to her aid when she'd needed him. The least she could do was be there for him now.

Regardless of whether he was real or not.

CHAPTER THIRTEEN

WHEN SHE FINALLY did meet Reginald Everheart, it would take every bit of resolve Dulcie had to keep from throwing her arms around him and kissing him quite soundly on the cheek. Without his knowledge, he was proving a huge assistance in her campaign to make Michael realize he could not live without her.

She'd taken inspiration from the outrageous arrangement of roses Mr. Everheart had sent the day after Michael had joined her family for dinner. It was entirely too extravagant. But one look at the expression on Michael's face when he had seen the flowers and she immediately knew the way to this man's heart was a bit of competition coupled with her absolute agreement that he was right.

Not jealous indeed.

On Monday, a jolly little sculpture of an Aztec god had arrived along with several ancient coins depicting frolicking satyrs and nymphs all to be drawn for the program to accompany Mr. Everheart's lecture. Michael was most disapproving. Indeed, his disposition had grown increasingly dour with every passing minute. Dulcie took it as an excellent sign. She had feared at the end of the day yesterday he might choose not to return today. But he did and that too was an excellent sign.

This morning when she arrived, there was an envelope on the table addressed to her. She recognized Mr. Everheart's excellent penmanship immediately. Whatever this was, she was confident Michael wouldn't like it. In spite of her curiosity, she waited until Michael opened the door to the library then casually slit open the envelope, pulled free a note and kept her gaze firmly fixed on it.

"Good day, Miss Middleworth," he said from across the room.

She pretended not to hear.

He approached her table and cleared his throat. "Miss Middleworth?"

Dulcie looked up in feigned surprise. "Hmm? Oh, Mr. Shepard. My apologies. I did not hear you come in."

"You were otherwise occupied." He hesitated as if he wasn't sure whether to say anything else or retreat. Or perhaps he was trying to recall the exact state of today's weather. "Something important?"

"Important?" She rose to her feet and glanced at the note in her hand. "Why, yes, I suppose it is. Mr. Everheart has asked to accompany me to the banquet."

"Without a chaperone?" Disapproval rang in his voice.

"Goodness, Mr. Shepard, I wouldn't have thought you were so stuffy about such things."

"Such things are for the protection of the reputation of the woman involved."

"I'm certain my reputation is quite safe with Mr. Everheart. Especially as we will be attending with my parents."

"Regardless, Miss Middleworth. Dulcie." He huffed. "The man is not to be trusted."

He'd called her Dulcie. She tried not to smile. "Nonsense."

"I don't think he's who or what he claims to be."

"Why on earth would you say something like that? He has a sterling reputation."

Michael paused. "I have serious doubts as to his credentials."

"I've never heard anything more ridiculous in my life." She widened her eyes and stared. "Why, you really are jealous."

"Hardly." He scoffed. "I'm simply concerned about you. As I would be any friend."

"Are we friends?" She considered him thoughtfully.

"Well, yes, I think so." He looked decidedly uncomfortable. "Something of that nature."

"What do you mean?" She circled the table to stand in front of him. "Something of that nature?"

"I simply mean…" The most amusing expression of unease washed across his face. "Blast it all, Dulcie, I'm not sure what I mean."

She gazed up at him. "You're not?"

"Apparently not but that's not the matter at hand at the moment." He huffed. "We were discussing Everheart and my concern about you and him."

"Are you concerned?"

"Of course I am," he said staunchly.

"Why?"

"Because I… Because we…"

"Yes?"

"Because…" A look of sheer panic shone in his eyes like a trapped animal or a lost soul. "I looked in his membership file," he blurted.

That was certainly not what she expected. "Did you?"

He nodded. "I thought it necessary."

She crossed her arms over her chest. "That's a bit beneath you, don't you think? It strikes me as somewhat devious. Even, oh, I don't know, dishonorable."

"In this case—" he straightened his shoulders "—the ends completely justify the means."

"The ends being my toes on the edge of yet another cliff?"

"Exactly."

"So what did you find that has you so concerned?"

"What didn't I find? Good Lord, Dulcie." He shook his head. "According to his file, the man has discovered ancient tombs, fought his way out of the clutches of cannibals, survived for months alone on an island in the South Seas. He's explored the jungles of the Amazon, traveled with nomads in the Sahara and climbed some of the tallest mountains in the alps. Why, I'm surprised he isn't credited with discovering the Americas."

"My, he is accomplished."

"No, he's not." Michael glared. "What he is—" He glanced around the library. "Are we alone?"

"And you were worried about the impropriety of my being with Mr. Everheart."

"This is not a joke, Dulcie, nor is it amusing." He stepped closer and lowered his voice. "I very much fear Mr. Everheart is a fraud."

Her mouth dropped open and she stared.

"I debated whether or not to tell you but I did think you should know."

She wasn't sure how to respond.

"Well, say something."

She grinned. "You are jealous."

"I am not," he said sharply then paused. "Well, perhaps I am, I suppose."

"Because we are friends or *something of that nature*?"

"Yes," he said firmly.

"No." She shook her head. "That simply isn't good enough. I'm afraid I find *something of that nature* to be rather confusing. You'll have to do better."

"Better?" His brow furrowed. "What do you mean

better? I admit *something of that nature* is perhaps confusing. But only because…" He ran his hand through his hair. "Damnation, Dulcie, I am confused."

Her breath caught. "Oh?"

"I had my life entirely planned. I would spend it searching out the undiscovered wonders of the world never before seen. Follow my uncle's path and succeed where he did not. I would walk in the footsteps of long dead civilizations and bring the past to life. I would discover places man never imagined existed. What I didn't plan was…"

"Something of that nature?"

"Exactly." His gaze met hers. "What I didn't plan was you."

"I see." She chose her words with care. "It seems to me, even when we have the best of plans, life itself does not always cooperate."

"Nonetheless—"

"Do you have feelings of affection for me?"

"Dulcie…" Longing mixed with regret in his gray eyes.

"Come now, Michael." Impatience sounded in her voice. Past time for the man to step up and admit his feelings. "This is not a difficult question. Do you or do you not care for me?"

"Yes," he snapped. "Bloody hell, Dulcie, I love you. There now—are you happy?"

"I don't think—"

"And it's because I love you that I will not subject you to a life alone. A life of not knowing when or if I would return to you. It's not right. It's not the kind of thing—"

"Oh, for God's sake, Michael." Without thinking, Dulcie grabbed the lapels of his coat with both hands, pulled him close and pressed her lips hard against his. Exactly what she'd wanted to do for the last three months. Shock froze him in place for an endless moment. Or forever. Had she just made a horrible mistake? Then his arms wrapped around her and he pulled her tight against him.

Her chest flattened against his and she could feel the pounding of his heart echoing her own. She clung to him with a hunger that took her breath away. His arms tightened around her, embraced her. Enfolded her. A sense of complete and utter surrender swept through her. Powerful and terrifying and quite, quite wonderful.

This man had claimed her heart and she lost herself in the heat of him, the spicy clean scent of him, the feel of his hard body against hers. Her knees weakened with desire and her head spun with the sure and certain knowledge that he was her fate, her destiny. For now and forever.

Without warning the most awful sense of realization swept through her. Her soul twisted. She stilled then released her grip on his coat and stepped back unsteadily.

Michael had the dazed appearance of a man who had just been struck by lightning or worse. He adjusted his spectacles. "That was…"

"A mistake," she said quickly. "Yes, I know." Before he'd taken her in his arms and her lips had met his, before she had reveled in the scent and the feel and nearness of him, she'd thought his resolve not to marry was ridiculous. Now, it made all the sense in the world. "That's what you were going to say isn't it?"

"Um, well, yes. Something like that, I suppose." He shook his head as if to clear it. "I should apologize for taking such liberties."

"Nonsense, Michael, it was entirely my fault." She summoned a pleasant smile and hoped her face wouldn't crack from the effort.

His gaze locked with hers. "But I can't."

Because he would do it again. As would I. Her chest tightened.

"Even so, we shall pretend it never happened." Her throat burned with an ache so intense it threatened to rip her apart.

He blew a long breath. "Very well."

"Didn't you mention an appointment?" It was all she could do not to turn and flee but she wasn't entirely sure she could move. "You would hate to be late."

He stared at her for a long moment then nodded slowly. "Yes, perhaps I do need to be on my way."

Dulcie couldn't seem to do anything more than nod, afraid of what might happen if she tried to speak.

"Good day, Miss Middleworth." He turned and strode across the room, grabbing his hat off his table as he passed.

"Farewell, Mr. Shepard," she whispered.

The moment the door closed behind him, her resolve failed. She sagged against the table and slowly sank to the floor, her wide skirts collapsing around her. Tears fogged her eyes and the most horrible feeling of loss and despair curled within her. She had just sent the love of her life away probably forever because she knew with a blinding clarity he was right. And there was no other choice.

It struck with the force of an undeniable truth. Now she understood how very hard it would be to watch him go off to places unknown. Not knowing if he would ever return. If he would perish somewhere far away from her and she would never know where or how. How could she ever bear to let him go? But how could she ask him to stay? To give up his dreams, give up the life he had planned, the life he wanted. He would grow to hate her for the opportunity he had lost. That would be worse than losing him to the world he was so eager to explore.

She had no illusions about herself. It would take someone with a great deal of strength to live that way. Someone with far more courage than she. She'd accused Michael of being a coward when it came to matters of the heart. At least he had the courage to accept the truth.

And the true coward here was Dulcie Middleworth.

CHAPTER FOURTEEN

"MY GOODNESS, MR. SHEPARD." Poppy gasped. Mr. Shepard had come out of the library as if the hounds of hell were at his heels. "Is something amiss? You nearly ran me over."

Mr. Shepard stared at her for a moment as if he couldn't quite place her, then shook his head. "My apologies, Mrs. Fitzhew-Wellmore. I had something on my mind."

"I can see that." She studied him closely. He had the look of a man who had just lost something dear to him. Or had his heart shattered. "Is it something you wish to talk about? I can be a very good listener."

"Thank you but no." He managed a weak smile. "I should be on my way. Good day." He turned to go.

Poppy started toward the library. If Mr. Shepard looked like this, she was very much afraid what Dulcie might look like. She was to receive Reginald's invitation today but jealousy made a man appear angry not forlorn. Poppy did hope—

"Mrs. Fitzhew-Wellmore?"

She turned. "Yes, Mr. Shepard?"

"Miss Middleworth received a note from Mr. Everheart today asking if he could escort her to Friday's banquet. It's not at all improper," he added quickly. "Her parents will be present."

"How wonderful." Poppy beamed. She wasn't at all sure this was wise but poor Mr. Shepard was so very upset and no doubt susceptible to suggestion. And there wasn't much time left if they were to do Reginald in no later than the day after tomorrow. In the morning. "It's always a good sign when a man wants to meet a girl's parents."

Mr. Shepard stared. "Surely you don't mean…"

"I mean there's every possibility he wants to ask for her hand." Poppy paused. She usually wasn't at all good at deception but this was rather fun. "He could have already spoken to her father by now."

"But he doesn't even know her." Disbelief sounded in Mr. Shepard's voice. "They haven't met. He hasn't even seen her."

"Not as far as we know."

"But—"

"Come now, Mr. Shepard, I know any number of people who had barely met each other before they were wed. And most of them have managed quite nicely."

"I've met Lord Middleworth and he does not strike me as the kind of man to blithely hand over his daughter to a virtual stranger. I thought he was quite level-headed and sensible."

"Oh dear, Mr. Shepard." She cast him a pitying look. "You really have no idea how these things work." She glanced from side to side as if making certain no one could hear them, then leaned closer in a confidential manner. "Dulcie was not invited to Lady Scarsdale's grand ball."

It was obvious from the blank look on Mr. Shepard's face that he had absolutely no idea of the significance of Dulcie's snub.

"The Scarsdale ball is the unofficial start of the season. An invitation is crucial for any young lady who is hoping for a good match. That Dulcie was not invited signals to society that she is now firmly on the shelf and doomed to a life of spinsterhood."

"That's ridiculous."

"I agree but that's the way things are." It was time for the final thrust of the sword. "And as Lord Middleworth is a sensible man, I can't imagine he would refuse Mr. Everheart permission to marry his daughter."

"But—" Horror shone in Mr. Shepard eyes. "The man's a fraud."

Poppy stared. "A what?"

"He's not what he says he is." Mr. Shepard lowered his voice. "I know you and your friends are acquainted with him and I hate to be the one to tell you about this, but I looked in his membership files. The man couldn't possibly have accomplished half of what it says he's done."

"Oh, those silly files." Poppy waved off his comment and ignored a distinct sense of panic. Good Lord, what did Gwen and Effie put in that file? "They are more often than not extremely overblown. Why, you should see my husband's files. I daresay they are every bit as exaggerated."

"Regardless." Mr. Shepard set his jaw in a stubborn manner. "I think the board should launch a thorough investigation."

"Excellent idea, Mr. Shepard." Poppy hooked her hand through his elbow and steered him toward the door. "However, I would suggest waiting until after the banquet to make the board aware of your concerns."

"Why?" He frowned. "Shouldn't it be done at once, before we honor the man?"

"My dear Mr. Shepard." She shook her head in a mournful manner. "If you bring this to the board now, the banquet will be canceled and there will be a dreadful scandal. It would besmirch the reputation of the Explorers Club if it was discovered that one of the honorary members was not what he claimed to be."

"Even so—"

"No, better to bring this up after the banquet in a quiet and circumspect manner." She paused. "I suspect the board would look far more kindly upon anyone who brought something like this to their attention discreetly. For the sake of the club, you understand."

He paused then nodded thoughtfully. "I see your point."

"Now, I would suggest you retire to your home to consider everything we've discussed." She released his elbow and gave him a gentle shove toward the door.

"Yes, of course," he murmured and left the building.

This was certainly a mess. Poppy hurried toward the library. Hopefully, Mr. Shepard would realize he couldn't possibly let Dulcie marry a fraud and accept his own feelings about her, as well.

Poppy pushed open the door to the library and at once spotted Dulcie sitting in a heap on the floor. What on earth had happened to the girl?

"Dulcie?" Poppy hurried to her.

Dulcie looked up with a sort of vague, shocked expression.

"My dear child." Poppy bent down beside her. Dulcie didn't look injured in any way, just rather stunned. "Are you all right?"

Dulcie swallowed hard. "Yes. Quite fine, really."

"You don't look quite fine." Poppy sank down on the floor next to her. Not something she would usually do but it did seem appropriate at the moment. "You've been crying."

Dulcie reached up and felt the wetness on her cheeks. Her eyes widened. "I didn't realize..."

"Oh dear. That's never good." Poppy pulled a handkerchief out of her bag and handed it to the girl. "I passed Mr. Shepard outside. He appeared rather grim. Did you have a disagreement?"

"No, just the opposite." Dulcie dabbed at her eyes. "Mr. Shepard long ago decided, given his plans for his life, never to marry. I simply realized he was right. It was all quite civil."

Poppy stared. "Why on earth would he be right about that?"

"You of all people should understand."

"Should I?"

"Mr. Shepard's uncle was an explorer who disappeared on an expedition when Mr. Shepard was a boy." Dulcie paused to draw a calming breath. "Not knowing what had happened to her husband devastated his aunt and ultimately led to her death."

"I see," Poppy said thoughtfully. "Wouldn't she have been similarly devastated if her husband had stepped into the street and been run over by a carriage?"

Dulcie nodded. "I would think so."

"Or if he had drowned during a holiday to the shore?"

"Yes, of course."

"Or choked on a bite of overcooked beef at a banquet?"

"Certainly but…" Dulcie shook her head in confusion. "That's not the point. The point is she never knew what happened to him."

"It's the price one sometimes pays for marrying a dashing, handsome adventurer."

"Mr. Shepard never mentioned that he was handsome or dashing," Dulcie said slowly.

"It was an assumption, dear." Poppy waved off the comment. "There is something about those men who choose to venture into the unknown. They are universally daring and courageous, which makes them very nearly irresistible. Curiosity is in their hearts and the stars of far off skies twinkle in their eyes. And we love them for it." She smiled at the memory of the first time she'd met Malcolm. "Mr. Fitzhew-Wellmore and I have been married for almost a quarter of a century and I will admit, even now I hate to see him leave."

"What if he never came back?" Dulcie's voice quavered. "What if you never knew his fate?"

Poppy chose her words carefully. "My friends and I know that is an ever present possibility. Our husbands are smart and always well prepared but one cannot plan for every eventuality. If Malcolm never returned I too would be devastated." She raised her chin. "But life would go on as would I. He would be very disappointed if I were to curl up in a little ball and weep for the rest of my days. No, he would say, in a delightfully stern voice that neither of us would believe, 'Poppy, dear girl, you are an Englishwoman. You are made of sterner stuff. Now carry on and make me proud.' And so I would."

"But not knowing what happened to him." Dulcie shook her head. "Isn't that too high a price to pay?"

"For love?" Poppy scoffed. "Not everyone in this world finds love, Dulcie. It is as elusive as a lost city or a forgotten tomb. And more precious than the richest treasure. And worth whatever price."

"Even so—"

"Dulcie." Poppy met her gaze firmly. "There are times when my friends and I envy those women who know exactly where their husbands are at all times. That they will be home for dinner. Where they will be tomorrow. Their lives are safe and comfortable and expected. And they are probably quite content. But we have an independence few women do. We can live our lives as we wish without having to ask permission for every little thing. There is much to be said for that.

"And if perhaps half of my married life has been spent without my husband, it has still been a good life. No, not merely good." She drew her brows together and thought for a moment. "It has been an adventure. Different than the adventures my husband has had but an adventure nonetheless. And every time Malcolm returns home, it is as exciting as when we first met. I still see the charming, intrepid rogue who captured my heart all those years ago. And he still sees the girl of his dreams. I would rather spend one moment with him than a long lifetime without him and he feels the same." Poppy smiled. "One cannot ask for more than that."

Dulcie shook her head. "You have far more courage than I."

"Nonsense." Poppy scoffed. "Courage isn't something most people are born with. It comes from determination and resolve and faith."

"Nonetheless." Dulcie smiled weakly. "I am a coward, Poppy. I cannot bear the idea of losing him to an unknown end."

"Well, then you are much better off to let him go on his way now," Poppy said briskly and rose to her feet. "Better to avoid love altogether really."

Dulcie stared. "I'm not sure I wish to avoid it altogether."

"Of course you do." She extended a hand to help the girl up. "Because whether the man you love never goes farther away from you than down the road or travels to the ends of the earth, life is full of risk as is love.

"Life, Dulcie, is entirely too short to waste. There are no promises, no guarantees. But love, my dear girl." She took Dulcie's hands and gazed into her eyes. "Love is always worth the effort."

"YOU'RE ABSOLUTELY RIGHT," Poppy said when she had joined Effie and Gwen for tea after a long day spent in the library. She squared her shoulders and adopted a determined expression. "Reginald Everheart must die."

CHAPTER FIFTEEN

How COULD HE have been such a fool?

Michael had known one kiss with Dulcie would never be enough. In that, at least, he was right. He should have stopped it, should never have responded, but the moment her body pressed against his, the moment he breathed in the heady scent of her, the moment his lips tasted hers, he was lost.

Michael's cab drew up in front of the Explorers Club and he practically bounded from his seat. He had stayed away yesterday. It would have been entirely too hard to be in the same room with her as he had fully intended to abide by her suggestion that they pretend nothing had happened between then. In that too he was a fool. There wasn't so much as a single instant since he'd walked out of the library that she had not been on his mind. He had done a great deal of thinking between then and now and had come to some awkward realizations.

First—he was wrong. Utterly and completely wrong. To think for even a moment that he could live his life without Dulcie was to deny everything he had felt from the first day he'd stepped into the library and seen her immersed in an ethereal sea of light. If he was nearly as intelligent as he'd always thought he was, he would have walked out that very day and never come back.

Second—how could he even think of leaving her? Regardless of his long-held desire to seek out the unknown, how he could possibly do anything of worth in this world without her in his life? He'd never believed in foolish nonsense like soul mates, but he knew as surely as he knew how to use the stars to find true north, Dulcie was his fate, his destiny.

He had only one choice. He would forgo travel to the remote corners of the world and stay right here in London. His father would be pleased even if Michael had no intention of joining his family in the running of the Shepard empire. Perhaps he would devote himself to scholarly pursuits. He had quite enjoyed his studies and research for the Amazon venture although, in truth, Michael had been preparing for most of his life. He firmly ignored a sharp stab of what might well have been regret. It was entirely natural to feel a bit of disappointment at abandoning one's dream. No, he corrected himself. He wasn't abandoning anything. He was trading one dream for another. There wasn't a doubt in his mind she was worth it.

Michael waited impatiently for the club door to open, nodded at the attendant, then hurried down the corridor to the library. Urgency probably wasn't necessary but now that he had realized what he truly wanted, he didn't want to waste another second before telling her. Before finding out if indeed she shared his feelings. She hadn't said the words but she had kissed him like a woman in love.

Besides, who knew what Everheart had in mind? If he had already asked for her hand, or worse, if she had already accepted, this would not go well. Dulcie was not the kind of woman to renege on a promise. One would hope everything he had said about Everheart would dissuade her from accepting him. Still one never knew. Regardless, determination hastened his step—Michael would not give her up without a fight.

He pushed open the library door and saw her immediately, standing by her usual table, speaking with Mrs. Fitzhew-Wellmore and her friends. Well, it couldn't be helped. Nor did he care.

"Dulcie!" He strode across the room toward her.

Her gaze snapped to his, her tone was cautious. "Good day, Michael."

"Mr. Shepard," Lady Blodgett said faintly, the other two ladies echoed her greetings.

"Ladies." He nodded, his attention on Dulcie. "We need to talk," he said firmly. "I have spent the hours since we parted giving our...*situation* a great deal of consideration."

"My, they have a situation," Mrs. Higginbotham murmured.

Dulcie stared. "Have you?"

"Indeed, I have thought of nothing else."

"Oh, that is a good sign," Mrs. Fitzhew-Wellmore said quietly.

"Perhaps," Dulcie said slowly, "this might best be discussed at another time."

"Absolutely not. I don't wish to, nor can I, wait another minute." He glanced at the older women. "Forgive me, ladies, if you consider this inappropriate."

Mrs. Fitzhew-Wellmore waved dismissively. "Don't mind us, Mr. Shepard. Just pretend we aren't here."

"Dulcie." He stepped close and took her hands in his. "When I said I loved you, I meant it."

"Did you?"

"With all my heart." He paused. "But I didn't realize exactly what that meant, if that makes any sense."

"Not really." She shook her head. "But now is not the best time—"

"Loving you means I want you in my life forever." He

gazed into her eyes. "It means you are the most important thing in the world to me. It means I want you to marry me. I cannot leave you, Dulcie. And I cannot, I will not, lose you to another man."

She frowned in obvious confusion. "What other man?"

"Mr. Everheart of course." He drew a deep breath. "In spite of my suspicions about him—"

Dulcie winced. "Unfortunately, you needn't worry about Mr. Everheart."

"I know he is considered eminently eligible and I am not the catch he is. He's famous and accomplished and, while I am not without financial resources, he can offer you far more than I can but—"

"Mr. Shepard." Lady Blodgett's sharp tone echoed in the room. "That's enough."

He had almost forgotten the ladies were still here. "What?"

"Miss Middleworth has been trying to tell you something you really should know." Lady Blodgett exchanged looks with her friends. "It's rather difficult to—"

"Mr. Everheart is dead," Mrs. Fitzhew-Wellmore announced with a sob. "We received word last night."

"Dead?" Michael stared.

"I'm afraid so." Mrs. Higginbotham heaved a heavy sigh. "He was attempting to save a kitten—"

"It was a puppy," Lady Blodgett corrected.

"It was a child!" Mrs. Fitzhew-Wellmore snapped.

"Yes, of course." Lady Blodgett nodded. "He was trying to save a child from falling into a hole."

Mrs. Higginbotham frowned. "I thought it was a ditch."

Mrs. Fitzhew-Wellmore's jaw clenched. "It was a cliff."

"Well, then you tell it." Lady Blodgett huffed.

"Very well." Mrs. Fitzhew-Wellmore paused to gather her words. "Mr. Everheart was visiting friends in Sussex.

Yesterday, during a successful attempt to save a child from falling off a cliff, Mr. Everheart unfortunately lost his balance and fell onto the rocks below."

The older ladies shuddered in unison.

"Unfortunately, before anyone could reach his broken and battered body..." Mrs. Fitzhew-Wellmore began.

"The tide came in..." Lady Blodgett added darkly.

"And swept him right out to sea," Mrs. Higginbotham said with a wide, sweeping gesture. "Never to be seen again."

"How terrible." Michael wasn't quite sure what else to say. "My condolences, ladies. I know you were all fond of him."

They did indeed look quite forlorn and heaved heartfelt sighs almost in tandem.

"Mr. Shepard." Mrs. Fitzhew-Wellmore moved closer to him and lowered her voice. "Under these tragic circumstances and given he died in a most heroic manner, I do hope you will refrain from sullying his name with your suspicions. It really is rather pointless now, don't you agree? Speaking ill of the dead and all."

"Yes, of course." Regardless of whether Everheart's claims were true or not, it scarcely mattered now.

"Excellent." Mrs. Fitzhew-Wellmore beamed. "Now then, as you and Miss Middleworth obviously have a great deal to discuss, we shall be on our way and leave you to it." She nodded at the other ladies. They murmured *good day*s and took their leave.

"Dulcie." He turned to her. "I—"

"Michael, I too have been giving this, us, a great deal of thought." She paused and he didn't like the look on her face. "And I've been talking to Mrs. Fitzhew-Wellmore. She disagrees with you, about not marrying that is."

"It's no longer—"

She held out a hand to stop him. "Please allow me to finish." Michael held his breath. "She and her friends are remarkable examples of women whose husbands seek to discover the world. These ladies are kind and clever and frankly have the kind of fortitude and courage I fear I do not."

His heart caught. "Dulcie, I—"

"I'm not finished." She paused. "Mrs. Fitzhew-Wellmore said courage came from resolve and faith. Even so, I didn't think I could manage that. But when I heard about Mr. Everheart…" She shook her head. "Life is short, Michael, and unexpected. If indeed I love you—" her gaze met his "—and I do, I would be a fool to let fear destroy what we might have together. Make no mistake, Michael." She raised her chin. "I am afraid, but in the words of a very wise woman, I would rather have a single moment with you than a lifetime without you."

"And a wonderful lifetime it will be." He pulled her into his arms. "But I've decided not to go."

"Not to go where?" Hers eyes widened with realization. "Not to go to the Amazon?"

"I would rather be with you," he said simply.

She stared. "That's the stupidest thing I've ever heard. Of course you'll go."

He drew his brows together. "I don't want to spend my life without you and I don't want to see what happened to my aunt happen to you."

"Then you shall have to make certain you return." She shook her head. "Admittedly, it will be difficult but I have friends and family and I am made of sterner stuff." She rested her hands on his shoulders. "My dear wonderful man, I would never allow you to give up your dreams for me and I never want you to be unhappy."

"I wouldn't be unhappy."

"Not now perhaps but someday." She smiled. "And I couldn't bear that."

"Do you really mean it?" His gaze searched hers.

"I do." She nodded. "And perhaps, in the future, I shall accompany you on your explorations."

"Absolutely not." He shook his head. "My opinion on that sort of thing is not subject to debate."

"Goodness, Michael, you vowed never to marry either." She wrapped her arms around his neck and pulled his lips to hers. "And look at how that turned out."

Her lips pressed against his and he surrendered. And suspected this was just the first of an endless number of surrenders that would continue for the rest of their days. He couldn't wait.

Michael pulled Dulcie closer against him and tried to ignore an annoying voice in the back of his head that pointed out having this woman by his side wherever in the world he might roam wouldn't be altogether terrible. After all, she was his fate, his destiny and for now and forever, his true north.

EPILOGUE

SOME WEEKS LATER, a small brass plaque engraved with
the name of Reginald Everheart joined those of Explorers Club members who had perished through the years.
Mrs. Lithgow had wanted a formal ceremony but, as no
one could actually remember the American, even if all
agreed he was a man of extraordinary accomplishments,
it was decided the plaque alone would suffice.

Mr. Everheart's file, once easily located amid all the
other files of intrepid men of daring and courage, oddly
enough, could not be found.

* * * * *

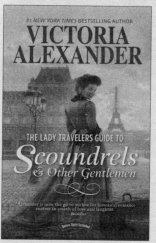

Get 2 Free Books,
Plus 2 Free Gifts -
just for trying the Reader Service!

STRS17R

Get 2 Free Books,
Plus 2 Free Gifts—
just for trying the Reader Service!

⊕ HARLEQUIN

HISTORICAL

HH17R2

Get 2 Free Books,
Plus 2 Free Gifts—
just for trying the Reader Service!

Get 2 Free Books,
Plus 2 Free Gifts—
just for trying the Reader Service!

HP17R2

Get 2 Free Books,

Plus 2 Free Gifts—

just for trying the Reader Service!

YES! Please send me 2 FREE Harlequin® Special Edition novels and my 2 FREE gifts (gifts are worth about $10 retail). After receiving them, if I don't wish to receive any more books, I can return the shipping statement marked "cancel." If I don't cancel, I will receive 6 brand-new novels every month and be billed just $4.99 per book in the U.S. or $5.74 per book in Canada. That's a savings of at least 12% off the cover price! It's quite a bargain! Shipping and handling is just 50¢ per book in the U.S. and 75¢ per book in Canada.* I understand that accepting the 2 free books and gifts places me under no obligation to buy anything. I can always return a shipment and cancel at any time. The free books and gifts are mine to keep no matter what I decide.

235/335 HDN GLWR

Name _____ (PLEASE PRINT)

Address _____ Apt. #

City _____ State/Province _____ Zip/Postal Code

Signature (if under 18, a parent or guardian must sign)

Mail to the Reader Service:
IN U.S.A.: P.O. Box 1341, Buffalo, NY 14240-8531
IN CANADA: P.O. Box 603, Fort Erie, Ontario L2A 5X3

Want to try two free books from another line?
Call 1-800-873-8635 or visit www.ReaderService.com.

*Terms and prices subject to change without notice. Prices do not include applicable taxes. Sales tax applicable in N.Y. Canadian residents will be charged applicable taxes. Offer not valid in Quebec. This offer is limited to one order per household. Books received may not be as shown. Not valid for current subscribers to Harlequin Special Edition books. All orders subject to approval. Credit or debit balances in a customer's account(s) may be offset by any other outstanding balance owed by or to the customer. Please allow 4 to 6 weeks for delivery. Offer available while quantities last.

Your Privacy—The Reader Service is committed to protecting your privacy. Our Privacy Policy is available online at www.ReaderService.com or upon request from the Reader Service.

We make a portion of our mailing list available to reputable third parties that offer products we believe may interest you. If you prefer that we not exchange your name with third parties, or if you wish to clarify or modify your communication preferences, please visit us at www.ReaderService.com/consumerchoice or write to us at Reader Service Preference Service, P.O. Box 9062, Buffalo, NY 14240-9062. Include your complete name and address.

HSE17R2